The Best American
SCIENCE FICTION
and FANTASY
2016

The Best American
SCIENCE FICTION
and FANTASY™
2016

Edited and with an Introduction
by **Karen Joy Fowler**

John Joseph Adams, *Series Editor*

A Mariner Original

HOUGHTON MIFFLIN HARCOURT

BOSTON • NEW YORK 2016

ISBN 978-0-544-55520-4

Printed in the United States of America
DOC 10 9 8 7 6 5 4 3 2 1

Contents

Foreword

WELCOME TO YEAR TWO of *Best American Science Fiction and Fantasy!* This volume presents the best science fiction and fantasy (SF/F) short stories published during the 2015 calendar year as selected by myself and guest editor Karen Joy Fowler.

To say 2015 was a busy year for me is perhaps the understatement of all understatements. In addition to serving as the series editor for this volume, for which I read thousands of stories annually, I also read hundreds of books in my capacity as a judge for the National Book Award in the Young People's Literature category (much of which was SF/F). Late in the year, I also agreed to launch John Joseph Adams Books, a new SF/F imprint for Houghton Mifflin Harcourt (the publishers of this fine anthology). In addition to all of that, I edited and published two monthly genre magazines (*Lightspeed* and *Nightmare*), had six anthologies published (including the 2015 *BASFF*), and produced *The Geek's Guide to the Galaxy* podcast for Wired.com.

The fact that I still find myself continuing to say yes to taking on new projects—to essentially filling all my waking hours with nonstop science fiction and fantasy—is a testament to the vitality of the field, and to the wonder and passion it inspires.

And all of that wonder and passion is on full display in this year's *BASFF* selections.

There is always some element of the unknown going into any editorial collaboration; even though on the surface two people might seem to have editorial tastes that line up well, in practice it's not always the case. Fortunately that was of no consequence

during the assembling of *BASFF 2016,* as our guest editor, Karen
Joy Fowler, and I turned out to have exceedingly similar tastes in
SF/F. In the end, our collaboration was, for me, not only a painless
experience but a richly rewarding one.

That may come as something of a surprise to those of you who
perhaps know Karen only as the author of mainstream bestsell-
ers and the winner of major literary prizes like the PEN/Faulkner
Award. But though Karen now runs among the rarified halls of
the literary elite, her forays into publishing started with genre fiction, with her first short stories appearing in core SF/F markets
like *Asimov's Science Fiction* (then called *Isaac Asimov's Science Fiction
Magazine*), *The Magazine of Fantasy & Science Fiction,* and *Interzone,*
among others, before she eventually transitioned to writing mainstream literary novels like *The Jane Austen Book Club* and before that
Sister Noon. Truth be told, however, even her first novel, *Sarah Ca-
nary,* clearly prophesied the direction her career would take and
would return to post–*Book Club.* And her subsequent novels *Wit's
End* and *We Are All Completely Beside Ourselves,* though generally considered mainstream novels, both bear the hallmarks of being written by someone intimately acquainted with genre fiction.

In addition to that extensive background in genre fiction, for
the last several years Karen has been the president of the Clarion
Foundation, the organization that runs the Clarion Writers' Workshop—an annual six-week intensive writing boot camp renowned
among the field's creatives. So not only was Karen well prepared
to dive into this role as guest editor due to her ample experience
in the field as a writer; she was also perhaps as uniquely qualified
for the job as any writer could be who doesn't also work as an
editor.

Naturally our wonderful collaboration came as no surprise to
me—I invited her to be guest editor, after all—and her choices
for *BASFF 2016* certainly did not disappoint. From the quiet, ele-
giac, contemporary tale "Interesting Facts" to the far-future, deep-
space saga of "Three Bodies at Mitanni," from the brutal emotion
and pain of "The Heat of Us" to the blistering depiction of modern warfare in "Headshot," these stories demonstrate the vast spectrum of what SF/F aims to accomplish, displaying the full gamut
of the human experience, interrogating our hopes and our fears
—not just of what we can accomplish or destroy *as a person,* but of

what we can accomplish or destroy *as a people*—and throwing us into strange new worlds that can only be explored when we shed the shackles of reality.

The stories chosen for this anthology were originally published between January 2015 and December 2015. The technical criteria for consideration are (1) original publication in a nationally distributed American or Canadian publication (i.e., periodicals, collections, or anthologies, in print, online, or ebook); (2) publication in English by writers who are American or Canadian, or who have made the United States their home; (3) publication as text (audiobook, podcast, dramatized, interactive, and other forms of fiction are not considered); (4) original publication as short fiction (excerpts of novels are not knowingly considered); (5) story length of 17,499 words or less; (6) at least loosely categorized as science fiction or fantasy; (7) publication by someone other than the author (i.e., self-published works are not eligible); and (8) publication as an original work of the author (i.e., not part of a media tie-in/licensed fiction program).

As series editor, I attempt to read everything I can find that meets these selection criteria. After doing all my reading, I create a list of what I feel are the top eighty stories published in the genre (forty science fiction and forty fantasy). These eighty stories are sent to the guest editor, who reads them and then chooses the best twenty (ten science fiction, ten fantasy) for inclusion in the anthology. The guest editor reads all the stories blind—with no bylines attached to them, nor any information about where the stories originally appeared. Karen's top twenty selections appear in this volume; the remaining sixty stories that did not make it into the anthology are listed in the back of this book as "Notable Science Fiction and Fantasy Stories of 2015."

As I did last year, in my effort to find the top eighty stories of the year, I read more than a hundred periodicals, from longtime genre mainstays such as *Analog* and *Asimov's*, to leading digital magazines such as *Tor.com* and *Strange Horizons*, to top literary publications such as *Tin House* and *Granta*—as well as several dozen anthologies and single-author collections. I scoured the field for publications both big and small, and paid equal consideration to stories in venerable major magazines like *The Magazine of Fantasy & Science Fiction* and to stories in new publications like *Uncanny.*

My longlist of eighty was drawn from thirty-eight different publications: twenty-four periodicals, thirteen anthologies, and one two-story chapbook—from thirty-eight different editors (counting editorial teams as a singular unit, but also distinct from any solo work done by either editor). The final table of contents draws from sixteen different sources: thirteen periodicals, two anthologies, and one two-story chapbook (from sixteen different editors/editorial teams).

I began my reading for the first volume of *BASFF* attempting to log every single story I read, wherever it fell on the quality spectrum, but that quickly became too onerous to do given the quantities involved, so I began instead logging only stories I thought were potentially among the best of the year. I followed that methodology again for this volume; consequently, I don't have the precise total number of stories I considered, but based on the data I did gather, I estimate the total to be somewhere between 3,000 and 5,000 stories (including the approximately 180 stories I edited myself).

Naturally, aside from my top eighty selections, many of the stories I read were perfectly good and enjoyable but didn't quite stand out enough for me to consider them among the best of the year. I did, however, end up with about seventy additional stories that were at one point or another under serious consideration, including stories from publications not otherwise represented in this anthology (either in the table of contents or on the Notable Stories list), such as *Fireside Magazine, Galaxy's Edge, Apex Magazine, Daily Science Fiction, Urban Fantasy Magazine,* and from anthologies such as *Stories for Chip, Thirteen: Stories of Transformation, Unbound, Hanzai Japan,* and others.

This foreword mentions only a few of the great publications considered for this anthology; see the table of contents and the Notable Stories list to get a more complete overview of the top publications currently available in the field. And if you love a story you discovered because of this anthology, please consider checking out the original publication it came from; the original sources vary in size and popularity, but they all need reader support to stay in business, and without them books like this one would not be possible. So please support them if you can—even if "support" just means telling a friend about them.

Now that I've laid out my workflow, you might be thinking that there's no way one person could have read all that material—if so, you're right! No editor could do all the work of assembling a volume like this one alone. Accordingly, many thanks go out to my team of first readers, who helped me evaluate various publications that I might not have had time to consider otherwise, led by DeAnna Knippling, Robyn Lupo, and Christie Yant, with smaller but still noteworthy contributions by Rob McMonigal, Karen Bovenmyer, Michael Curry, Devin Marcus, Aaron Bailey, Hannah Huber, Zoe Kaplan, and Tyler Keeton. Thanks, too, to Tim Mudie at Mariner Books for all the strings he pulls behind the scenes to keep the show running.

In last year's volume, I spent a good portion of my foreword defining science fiction and fantasy and providing a historical overview of how the genre came to be and how it got to where it is now.

I don't want to repeat myself, but I do feel like perhaps I should at least reiterate the definitions, as more than one reader review seemed displeased with the proportions of science fiction and fantasy in the 2015 volume. But in truth the contents were divided equally between the two genres, and it is my intent that the contents will *always* be equally divided. (Though it was amusing to see that there were simultaneous opposing complaints—both that there was too much [or it was all] science fiction and that there was too much [or it was all] fantasy.)

To be fair, I understand how people can have these misconceptions about where the borders between the genres lie. A lot of us grow up thinking that science fiction stories are always set in the future (no) or in far-flung galaxies (raaaaaaah*), or that fantasy always takes place in "fantasy worlds" à la Middle-earth (ú-thand†) or always feature wizards (this line of thinking shall not pass‡) or . . . well, you get the idea.

---

* That's "no" in Shyriiwook, a Wookie language. Sorry, not sure of my spelling.
† That's "not true" in Sindarin, an Elvish language. Experts verify that my spelling is correct on this one.
‡ As Gandalf might say.

But I can't very well come up with new ways of saying those same things all over again every year, so instead let me briefly and selectively quote myself:

> SF/F—which sometimes is collectively referred to by the larger umbrella term "speculative fiction"—essentially comprises stories that start by asking the question *What if . . . ?*
>
> Fantasy stories are stories in which the impossible happens. The easiest (and perhaps most common) example to illustrate this is: Magic is real, and select humans can wield or manipulate it.
>
> Science fiction has the same starting point as fantasy—stories in which the impossible happens—but adds a crucial twist: science fiction is stories in which the *currently impossible* but *theoretically plausible* happens (or, in some cases, things that are *currently possible* but *haven't happened yet*).

That is a bit simplified, but it basically gets to the heart of the matter.* Perhaps, however, the best way to explicate the rules and boundaries of the genres is simply to present you with the stories in this book; the idea, of course, is that reading them will immerse you in the genre, giving you a grand tour that shows you what the genres encompass and are capable of.

As I was writing this foreword in April 2016, the world watched a science fiction magazine cover from the '50s come to life as SpaceX's Falcon 9 rocket landed upright—on a drone ship floating in the ocean, no less—and saw the company's CEO, Elon Musk, excitedly tweet: "I'm on a boat!" Days later the news broke that physicist Stephen Hawking partnered with Russian billionaire Yuri Milner (along with other investors, such as Facebook's Mark Zuckerberg) to launch Breakthrough Starshot, an interstellar mission to the Alpha Centauri star system, 4.37 light-years away, in the hopes of finding alien life there. Oh, and the plan is to get there via a fleet of iPhone-size robotic spacecraft propelled by a giant laser array.†

---

* If you'd like to see my longer, more extensive discussion of the definition and/ or history of the genre, the full text of my 2015 foreword is available online at johnjosephadams.com/BASFF-2015.

† For more, see the project's website at breakthroughinitiatives.org, or the *New York Times* article "Reaching for the Stars, Across 4.37 Light-Years," at nyti.ms/25XoewM.

Though science fiction seems to be becoming reality before our eyes, fantasy stubbornly remains fantasy. On the other hand, the most famous and beloved writer in the world is a woman who once subsisted on welfare and who went on to write a series of novels about child wizards which are so popular that they made her one of the richest people in the world, and spawned not only a movie franchise that has now surpassed the books in quantity but also a theme park whose express goal is to bring the world of those books to life. A theme park. Inspired by books.

What other wonders dare we imagine?

Editors, writers, and publishers who would like their work to be considered for next year's edition, please visit johnjosephadams .com/best-american for instructions on how to submit material for consideration.

— JOHN JOSEPH ADAMS

Introduction

I have no choice but to believe this game matters.
 —"Rat Catcher's Yellows"

A FEW YEARS back, listening to the radio while driving across vast
stretches of countryside, I heard three stories in rapid succession.
The first was about a woman in India who'd been found guilty of
murder based on the evidence of her brain scan. When read a series of statements about the death of her former fiancé, those parts
of her brain associated with experiential knowledge activated. The
judge who ruled in her case leaned heavily on this evidence.

The second story involved a website where, for a monthly fee,
a computer can be programmed to pray for you. The particular
prayer is left to the choice of the penitent, the fee based on the
length of the prayer chosen (as if the computer minds one way or
the other).

The third story was about research being done at the University of California, Santa Barbara, by Dr. Kevin Lafferty. Lafferty has
been studying the effects of *Toxoplasma gondii*, a parasite transmitted to humans through cats.

An earlier series of studies in Czechoslovakia had suggested
that those infected with this parasite undergo significant behavioral changes and that these changes are sex-specific. Men become
more suspicious, jealous, dogmatic, and risk-taking. Women become more warm-hearted, trusting, and law-abiding.

What Dr. Lafferty has added is a look at countries with high rates of infection—in Brazil an estimated sixty-seven percent of the population carries the parasite—to see if the effects might have an impact on national culture.

I was sufficiently shocked to learn that this widespread parasite affects individual behavior, never mind at the national level. But it appears that cats will be satisfied by nothing less than world domination.

> Relax: this is normal.
> —"The Daydreamer by Proxy"

A few other things to note about the world we currently live in:

Miami is drowning.

We've learned more about dinosaurs in the last fifteen years than in all the preceding centuries.

The U.S. Supreme Court has granted personhood to corporations.

The U.S. Supreme Court has not granted personhood to apes, even though it is now an incontrovertible and scientifically accepted fact that apes have as fine a culture as any corporation.

Jesus has appeared on a pierogi, a piece of fried chicken, and a fish stick. Unless that's Frank Zappa.

A man in Texas has recently seen a spoon-shaped UFO over Possum Kingdom Lake in Palo Pinto County.

The ocean is choking on plastic waste.

Social media are affecting the way we wage war.

Mathematical modeling suggests an unsuspected ninth planet at the edges of the solar system. This planet will take between 10,000 and 20,000 years to circle the sun once. It has yet to be seen.

In 2014 the average U.S. citizen spent 7.4 hours a day staring at screens.

Could it be more clear that the tools of so-called literary realism are no longer up to the task of accurately depicting the world in which we live? (I may suspect that they never were, but that's an argument for another time.)

> She has a plan, but it's risky, given her limited skills as a relatively
> new fungus.
> —"The Mushroom Queen"

My personal relationship with science fiction is not as long-standing as my personal relationship with fantasy. As a child, I read the novels of Edward Eager, Robert Lawson, Betty MacDonald, P. L. Travers, and many others, same as every other child I knew, though perhaps more avidly and repeatedly than most. I came to *The Lord of the Rings* quite young, and I don't suppose the outcome of a fictional book has ever mattered so much to me—I really didn't feel that I could continue the charade of getting up every morning, going to school, having dinner with my parents, washing my hands, brushing my teeth, and all the rest of the nonsense if Frodo didn't manage to destroy the ring.

I didn't start reading science fiction until college—taunted into it by the man I later married—so I'm not so deeply imprinted with that. My introduction was through the feminists; as someone majoring in political science, I was impressed with the utility of the genre in exploring political issues. The ability to run thought experiments like Ursula K. Le Guin's *The Left Hand of Darkness,* Joanna Russ's *The Female Man,* and Suzy McKee Charnas's *Walk to the End of the World* added greatly to the larger conversation and gave me new ways to think about old problems. *The Left Hand of Darkness* in particular took my head right off. I have never been the same person, nor have I ever wished to be. The change was clarifying and exhilarating.

One summer around this same time, I took a class at Stanford from H. Bruce Franklin, a fact that I later had to confess to him, as I was not a Stanford student and didn't so much take the class as walk into it as if I belonged there and find a seat. The class was very large and popular, and Franklin was locked in battle with the university over the Vietnam War at the time. There was no chance anyone would notice the extra student, quietly purloining her education. We read Yevgeny Zamyatin's *We* and Stanislaw Lem's *Solaris* and talked about the Strugatsky brothers, though little of their work was available then in translation. I came away with an impression of a deeply serious, extremely courageous political literature.

I remember a heated argument between a Jewish guest speaker and an African American student as to the relative sufferings of their people. I came away with an impression of a deeply serious, extremely contentious community existing around this literature.

I was by then a thorough convert.

Even so, it took me a long time to discover the short stories.

*

> He's awake when they put the eyes in.
> —"By Degrees and Dilatory Time"

Those unfamiliar with the literature of science fiction and fantasy will not know, as I did not, what a lively, vibrant short-form world exists inside those genres. Some of the field's current stars—people like Kelly Link, Ted Chiang, Howard Waldrop, James Patrick Kelly, Carmen Maria Machado, Alice Sola Kim, Kij Johnson, and Carol Emshwiller—work exclusively or almost exclusively there. It has become the place where I find the strange, uncanny work I like the very best.

Several brilliant novelists—courtesy prevents me from calling out their names—are even better in the short form. Stories are written in response to other stories or as riffs off other stories, though every story must of course work as an independent text. Themed anthologies are common and often wonderful. It's a heady, feisty, weird, wild brew.

Here is something about science fiction, which I've often heard stated (though never in fact believed): that, paradoxically, although it looks to the future, the literary techniques employed in it are quite conservative. The favored plot is the old one in which the protagonist, faced with a problem, tries to solve it, fails, tries again, and either succeeds or fails for the final time.

According to this formulation, the best prose is transparent. The reader should be undistracted by a distinctive style or musical rhythms or flights of poetry; the words themselves should be nothing but a clear window through which the story is seen.

There are two points to be made about this. The first is that prose of this sort is actually very hard to achieve.

The second is that those writers most admired in the field have always been fine stylists, their prose easily recognized by those who know it.

> At the end of the day it's the stories people tell about themselves that matter.
> —"The Heat of Us: Notes Toward an Oral History"

So science fiction and fantasy readers, same as any other readers, wish to read an engaging and particularized voice. And certainly in the short form, at the very least, experimentation and lyricism are more common than not.

The short form is quite often where a new voice first appears —in a debut story that immediately marks the writer as someone to watch. As part of helping to administer the Clarion Workshop, an annual six-week summer program at UC San Diego (a similar workshop takes place each summer in Seattle), I spend several weeks each winter reading submissions. I can attest to the incredible talent we find among these mostly unpublished writers, each and every year.

An increasing number of these submissions are arriving from different cultures and different countries, drawing on different literary traditions and with different political experiences. The imagined future seems to finally be a more expansive place. And thank god for that. How lonely would all those white men have been, all by themselves in the great dark universe? (See *Star Wars: A New Hope.* Very lonely, indeed.)

In order to assemble this particular collection of short fiction, the inestimable John Joseph Adams chose eighty stories, and from those I chose twenty. The venues in which these stories were initially published were wide-ranging. I will confess here that the difference between fantasy and science fiction, while clear enough to me in theory, is often unclear when I'm faced with a specific text. I was grateful not to be the one making those decisions.

The decisions I did make, winnowing the eighty stories down to twenty, were hard enough. I'm still in mourning for several of the beautiful pieces I couldn't include; I expect I always will be. I'm gratified that a number of those are on the ballots of various awards this year; they deserve this praise and attention. In every other way, the task was a pure pleasure. It has convinced me that the golden age of the science fiction/fantasy short story must be just about right exactly now.

I read everything blind, so it was a wonderful surprise to later recognize the names of many authors I already know and love. Even better were the names I had never seen before but am sure I will be finding again and again now.

> There's never been a world that isn't a world at war.
> —"The Thirteen Mercies"

Science fiction stories (fantasy, too) are always primarily a comment on the current moment in the current world. Based on these eighty initial stories, I'm prepared to say that one of the things occupying our minds just now is war.

The future of warfare was by far the most common theme, both in the stories I chose and in the ones I wished for but could not take. In this category, I include the so-called war on terror, though there was actually less focus on that and more on the old traditional carnage. Although the methods and motives for war may be new, the final outcomes remain, sadly, what they have ever been.

Though in some of the stories, the more interesting part of a war was how to survive it. And having done that, how to put it into the past and leave it there.

> You don't need to die to know what it's like to be a ghost.
> —"Interesting Facts"

Science fiction and fantasy are well suited to thought experiments and philosophical questions regarding the Other. In this literature, humans can be assessed directly through comparison with nonhumans. I read a great many stories that did this.

Sometimes the nonhumans were magical—wet gentlemen or jinn. Sometimes they had fairy-tale aspects.

Sometimes the nonhumans were aliens. We may call them lions or handmaids or vampires, but they are nothing of the sort and have their own inexplicable extraterrestrial agendas.

Sometimes the nonhumans were those other animals with whom we share our planet and about whom, for all our centuries of cohabitation, we still know so little, even of the ones who actually speak our language.

Sometimes the nonhumans were familiar fictional characters, like the Mad Hatter and the March Hare.

Sometimes the nonhumans were machines, and some of these machines helped us with our human tasks, and some of them were inscrutable, just as if we hadn't manufactured them ourselves, and some of them even wanted to hurt us. In some stories, they constituted the entire world.

Sometimes the nonhumans were corporations and sometimes *they* were the world in which we lived.

Sometimes the nonhumans were creatures who used to be humans but had changed.

*

> It hurt so much to see both sides.
> —"Three Bodies at Mitanni"

The Turing test continues to preoccupy science fiction writers. Where and when might machines become so human that the difference no longer matters? I read several stories dealing with this.

But I also read a great many with the opposite trajectory. How much bodily modification can a human undergo, how many enhancements, replacements, reductions, before ceasing to be human?

And one final critical theme: where and when does our empathy run out?

> Walk toward the point halfway between the moon and the cottage, and eventually you'll come to the well.
> —"Things You Can Buy for a Penny"

For all the important, inexhaustible thematic richness of the issues above (and all the others that science fiction and fantasy are uniquely able to illuminate), I've come to realize that my particular attachment is often simply a matter of setting. These are the only modes of literature in which a story can happen absolutely anywhere. Here are stories set on planet, off planet, underwater, underground, in the jungle, in the village, in the apartment, in the San Francisco Bay Area, in the liminal space of Iram, in the corporate offices of Geneertech, in Lewis Carroll's Wonderland, in the Stonewall Riots, in the post-apocalypse, and in the 0s and 1s of the virtual world. The stories collected here take place in the near and far past, in the future, and in the present. Some of them are set outside of time altogether.

As a result, you are never so aware of being completely inside the expansive, curious, and astonishing imagination of the writer in any other literature.

A few months ago, I got a lovely letter from an uncle I'd lost touch with. He'd read my most recent novel and wanted to tell me so. It was the first novel of mine that he'd ever read. By way of explanation or possibly apology, he said that he rarely reads fiction. I hear this a lot. There are a great many readers who stick to nonfiction. They want to learn real things, they tell me, with a touching faith in the honesty of memoir and history.

But my uncle's reason was different. I never want my own mind overwhelmed with someone else's mind, he said. I read that sentence over several times, so struck with the strangeness of it, the surprise.

Because that being overwhelmed with someone else's mind — that's the whole reason I read. That's the part I like the very best. In all the stories that follow this introduction, that was always the part I liked the very best.

It's exactly what I hope will happen here to you.

> As he once wandered the great expanse of the Gobi in his boyhood, so he now roams a universe without boundaries, in some dimension orthogonal to the ones we know.
> —"Ambiguity Machines"

— KAREN JOY FOWLER

The Best American
SCIENCE FICTION
and FANTASY
2016

SOFIA SAMATAR

Meet Me in Iram

FROM *Meet Me in Iram/Those Are Pearls*

WE ARE FAMILIAR with gold, says Hume, and also with mountains; therefore, we are able to imagine a golden mountain. This idea may serve as an origin myth for Iram, the unconstructed city.

The city has several problems. (1) It is lacking in domestic objects. (2) It is lacking in atmospheres that produce nostalgia. In cities without the correct combination of—for example—hills, streetlights, and coffee, it is difficult to get laid. A playbill in a gutter, bleeding color, the image of a famous actress blurring slowly into pulp: This would be perfect. The word *playbill* is perfect. There are many ways to achieve the desired conditions. Iram has none.

No continuity without desire. There is no desire in Iram; the time of Iram is *not yet.*

> oh do you remember when we were courting
> when my head lay upon your breast
> you could make me believe by the falling of your arm
> that the sun rose in the west
> —*American folksong*

The reversal of time expressed in these lines is impossible in Iram. In Iram, there is nothing to reverse. Every time I go there, I see my uncle on the same bridge, and he raises his hand to greet me in the same way. He always tells me not to say *every time*, but I can't help it; it's a habit. He wishes I had come to visit him in Jeddah. I couldn't go, I tell him. It would have meant an expensive trip. I would have had to wear an abaya. I couldn't do it.

My uncle is not at all angry. Well, he says. He pats my shoulder. Well. He's wearing the most magnificent orange suit. Like my father, who is waiting for us at the restaurant, my uncle has style. The men in my family are all very beautiful.

When I say that Iram is lacking in domestic objects, I mean that we haven't gathered enough. I try to bring something with me every time. Last time it was a collection of my father's audiotapes, crammed into a pair of black plastic bags. The tapes are dusty with cigarette ash and poetry. It is only possible to listen to them in the worst light. A white, ugly, institutional light that, despite its harshness, is too weak to travel more than a couple of feet.

Fortunately the tapes create the sort of light they need.

At the restaurant, my father has already ordered. As always, he's gotten the huge appetizer plate, more than a hundred appetizers arranged around a bowl of blue flame. I kiss his cheek. He waves, expansive: Sit down! It's important to order the biggest thing. The entire restaurant must smell my father's cologne. In Iram, this makes me happy. This is the good life. I don't know what the blue flame is made of, but it keeps everybody warm.

You can stop there.

My mother says: Your father had beautiful skin. This was before he began to suffer from psoriasis. Now he goes out in a hat and gloves, even on the hottest days. My father has become allergic to sunlight. How is that possible, my mother asks. He's a Somali —he grew up in the sun! My father puts on his hat and goes out to his car. His beautiful skin, my mother says sadly. The car starts up: a throbbing sound that remains, for me, after all these years, synonymous with fear.

The car pulls into the driveway. The children hear its long, low note. They hear the door slam. The children run upstairs and hide inside their rooms. They're giggling because it's beautiful and exciting to be a child. They're smart; like bugs, they can squeeze into any kind of space. The children make bug-nests for themselves out of torn-up letters and photos. They squirm around in the nests and eat a lot of paper. The children are going to turn out fine, but they'll be the kind of people who do not have many things they can take to Iram.

In a city where one could find—for example—dogs, graffiti, and palm trees, it would be possible to fall in love.

> *Have you not considered how your Lord dealt with Aad, with Iram—who had lofty pillars, the likes of whom had never been created in the lands? And with Thamud, who carved out the rocks in the valley? And with Pharaoh, owner of the stakes? All of whom oppressed within the lands, and increased therein the corruption. So your Lord poured upon them a scourge of punishment.*
> —Qur'an 89:6–13

The Wikipedia article on Iram warns: This article *needs attention from an expert in Archaeology.* The specific problem is: *the article is a confusing mix of myth, supposition, popular sources and very little science, scholarship or sense; the result is a meaningless overview of the subject, accompanied by random facts and inexplicable leaps of logic.*

According to the article, Iram is also known as *the City of the tent poles.* It is *a lost city* or perhaps *a tribe.*

The passage from the Qur'an quoted here appears in the article. A note at the end reads: *translated by error.*

I walk to the restaurant with my uncle. There's nothing, no atmosphere. It's like anywhere. Iram, the windless city, is buried underground. I wish there were more of a glow so that I could see my uncle's suit. Once, I remember, I told a friend I was disgusted by the idea of a Daddy-Daughter Dance. So heterosexist, I said. I mean—ugh! My friend said she had gone to a dance like that with her father when she was a little girl. Magic, she said. If there were a glow I could take my uncle's arm. She felt so special. It was the happiest night of her life.

Translated by error.

In Iram, my uncle understands me perfectly. I realize we've been speaking in Somali. We sing the song about the Prophet Isa's birth, the one about the darkest night. The very darkest night.

It almost doesn't matter that I'm carrying these awkward plastic bags.

In the window of the restaurant, there's a small blue light. My father waits for us inside. It's the way I told you before. Happy, happy. I'm the only woman there.

There are hardly any women in Iram. This is a problem, because without women nothing happens. Nothing goes on without them. You will have realized at once that there's a connection between these missing women and the missing domestic objects. In Iram, there are windows but no curtains. I'm not saying women have to create these objects; I'm saying they do. Sometimes, after dark, I catch sight of a woman just disappearing around a corner. I recognize her from her photograph.

According to the ninth edition of the *Encyclopaedia Britannica*, Iram is a lost city *which yet, after the annihilation of its tenants, remains entire, so Arabs say, invisible to ordinary eyes, but occasionally, and at rare intervals, revealed to some heaven-favoured traveller.*

I write on a scrap of paper: *Q-tips. Deodorant. Small hand lotion.*

I have a terrible longing to visit Iram again. I'm full of plans. I want to take a beaded wooden spoon with me next time—I think it's somewhere in my parents' house. The Somali pillow, too, and the little stool we used to call the African Stool. I'm sure that, when I reach Iram, I will know its true name. Perhaps that sounds romantic, but I believe things have true names. I believe everything has a name that I don't know.

*

In the restaurant, my father and uncle laugh together. My father grips my uncle's shoulder, chuckling naturally and with pleasure. It's not the explosive, uncontrollable laugh that seized him in our house the night some Somali guests came for dinner. My father had invited them. Everything was going well, and then something happened—I believe my brother made a face at one of his kids—and my father started laughing and couldn't stop. I remember we all laughed, too; we kept telling each other how terribly funny it was. Our guests smiled politely. You have to understand that at this time it was very rare for my father to eat with us, even rarer for him to invite guests to the house. The production of a normal family required immense effort. We were all keyed up to the highest pitch of excitement. My father's laughter seemed to go on forever, past bearing. At one point I felt pinned inside it. I couldn't move. Later I would experience that kind of laughter myself, when I was working in South Sudan during the war.

When you're outside, you can picture exactly what you want it to be like, but once you get in, all you can do is follow along.

You can help me. You can tell me if these feelings are universal. What is normal? I've felt for a long time that *normal* is something suspect, that embedded in the idea of the normal is something dangerous, an erasure of everything *abnormal,* a death or a series of deaths. But isn't it actually normal to want to be normal? I would like to build an entire philosophy out of Iram, the absent city. This philosophy would serve all the children of immigrants, many of the immigrants, and many others who found themselves at a loss. Eventually people would come to say: *This philosophy is available to all. Anybody can go to Iram.* All sorts of people, many of whom looked nothing at all like me, would disembark in the unconstructed streets. They'd bring their own bags, their photographs, their desire. Early in the morning, you'd find teenagers putting up playbills on the walls. Their sense of satisfaction would be so strong, it would color the air. For the first time, Iram would have a color of its own. But of course that can't happen until we import more objects, until we have succeeded in creating the conditions for nostalgia. For this reason, I fear that my feelings are not universal.

Surely love cannot exist outside of time. It depends upon small objects.

The fact is, when my uncle died, he and my father were barely on speaking terms. My mother told me that my father disliked my uncle's gifts, specifically the gifts my uncle gave to my mother and me: gold jewelry, dresses heavy with beads. My mother, who is often sad, and not without reason, was sad because of this split between my uncle and my father. She and I wore our glittering beaded dresses to a New Year's Eve party. Everyone said we looked beautiful, exotic.

My father didn't go to the party. My father went somewhere else. I don't know where. Perhaps he was helping to draft the Somali constitution. When he disappears, I always imagine him doing heroic work. Once someone asked if I thought he worked for the CIA. I said I don't know.

We never eat anything after the appetizers. We're drinking tea from my uncle's thermos. My father and I use cups and my uncle uses the lid. In the radiance of the cobalt flame in the center of the table, of my uncle's marigold suit, I am dreaming of things to bring to Iram. I wish I could bring a bathroom door from the library at the University of Wisconsin–Madison, but how would I take it off, how could I get it out of the building? I'm picturing myself in the snow and ice, sliding down State Street with the big gray door clasped somehow under my arm. Impossible. And anyway, I don't know if that object would work. I don't think it's sacred in the way that a piece of cloth worn by a relative is sacred. Something that holds perfume. The door of a public bathroom stall —it's so anonymous, it doesn't even hold the imprint of my shoe. The imprint of my shoe where I kicked the metal door in a rage. A Somali student had told me his name was Waria. I knew it wasn't a name. He was making fun of me. It couldn't be a name, because it was just a sort of word. It was just something you said, not you but my father, on the phone. A sort of preface, like *Hey* or maybe *Hey, you.* I realized I didn't know what it meant. Something melted in my face. Excuse me, I said. I went to the bathroom.

*

I question this idea of the *heaven-favoured traveller*. What kind of favor is it to arrive at an empty city? A city that goes on, lifeless, *after the annihilation of its tenants*? I'm just standing here on the corner with my bags.

To have no one to blame but yourself is to have no one. It's the worst fate.

a lost city or perhaps *a tribe*

I want to fall down in Iram. I've never tripped or fallen there. It's the sort of thing you can't organize; it has to come up and catch you unawares. I want to be caught and thrown to the ground in Iram, to scrape my knee. Look, there's blood. That's me. If that happened, I feel certain a new kind of light would arrive. I'd look down at my blood on the pavement, and my blood would show me the edge of a flight of steps. That's really what it's called. A flight.

If it gets too painful, you can stop.

When my uncle died, he left six children. Two sets of triplets. Three boys and three girls. I don't know them, because my father is on bad terms with my uncle's widow—in fact, he is estranged from her whole family. My uncle and his wife had their children through IVF treatment. When I was a child myself—long before my uncle's children were born—I remember being told that my uncle was unable to have children, because of what had been done to him in Somalia, in prison.

You can stop.

The woman is smiling in the photograph. I'm on her lap. I'm three or four years old. I asked my mother who she was, but my mother didn't know; she couldn't remember; she said, You'll have to ask your dad. I was getting ready to move somewhere—perhaps Cairo, perhaps Wisconsin. My father had not been home for several days. I put the photograph away with the others. I was afraid to ask, afraid to find out that this lovely woman, my relative, was dead. Now I consider this an act of cowardice. I remember the picture. The smile. It seems to me that one corner of the photograph is cut off. Was someone else there? This woman is happy; she loves me. She smiles so fully, with such golden warmth, as she disappears around the corner in Iram. Next time, I think, I'll rush to catch her, I'll shout, perhaps I'll fall down in the empty street. But of course there's no *next time*, only *not yet*. At one point I thought I was writing this to force myself to ask my father about the photograph. But I must have lost it, because it's gone. I can't ask now.

> i wish i was a little swallow
> that i had wings and i could fly

My uncle was shot and killed in his bed. Addis Ababa, 2010.

I'm just standing here on the corner, holding my plastic bags.

Very little science, scholarship or sense.

I'm just trying to hold them both. Let's all laugh together. Sweet blue light. Let's pour a little more tea. Let's order more appetizers. Dad, let's stay here; let's not go. I remember when I was a kid, on long car trips, I'd imagine a giant saw was attached to my side of the car. The saw could cut through anything. It sliced fences; it sliced trees. The fences gave a swift groan and exposed the hollow insides of their poles. The trees went *snick* and fell over with juicy ease, the tops of the stumps left gleaming moist and pale, like a wound before the blood comes. I was leveling the whole country from my seat in the back of the car. I don't know why it gave me so much pleasure. The world was coming down to size. I know it sounds like the opposite of what I'm trying to do in Iram, but the feeling is the same.

The chapter of the Qur'an that mentions the city of Iram is called *al-Fajr.* Dawn.

Because we are familiar with gold and we are familiar with mountains. Because we are familiar with pillows and spoons. Because we are familiar, we can imagine. Is that true? Look, here I am, at my desk on the highest roof of the city. I sit up here at night so that you can find me if you come. I am listening to my father's cassettes. You will have noticed that there is sound in Iram, and this is why I come back, I think, to these blank and shrouded streets. I am trying to imagine sound as an object. As soon as I press *play* the light comes on, that white ceramic glare, and cigarette ashes lift away from the tape recorder and disappear in the air of Iram, where it is always night. Light pins me to my seat. When my father was in the basement listening to poetry, we knew we mustn't disturb him. The door was edged with grainy fluorescent light, the stairs coated with black rubber. It was a terrible, terrible place. And poetry came up as it comes to me now. I know the words for *pearl* and *water*. I am singing of the moon, of a great-limbed tree. Amber necklaces come to me and thorns and rain and a fiery horse and a lonely dhow adrift on a trackless sea. In Iram, I know the names. I sit repeating them, enraptured, frozen in an ecstasy of bad light. No continuity without desire. Look for me if you come. You'll know me by the falling of my arm.

KELLY LINK

The Game of Smash and Recovery

FROM *Strange Horizons*

IF THERE'S ONE thing Anat knows, it's this. She loves Oscar her brother, and her brother Oscar loves her. Hasn't Oscar raised Anat, practically from childhood? Picked Anat up when she's fallen? Prepared her meals and lovingly tended to her scrapes and taught her how to navigate their little world? Given her skimmer ships, each faster and more responsive than the one before; the most lovely incendiary devices; a refurbished mob of Handmaids, with their sharp fingers, probing snouts, their furred bellies, their sleek and whiplike limbs?

Oscar called them Handmaids because they have so many fingers, so many ways of grasping and holding and petting and sorting and killing. Once a vampire frightened Anat, when she was younger. It came too close. She began to cry, and then the Handmaids were there, soothing Anat with their gentle stroking, touching her here and there to make sure that the vampire had not injured her, embracing her while they briskly tore the shrieking vampire to pieces. That was not long after Oscar had come back from Home with the Handmaids. Vampires and Handmaids reached a kind of understanding after that. The vampires, encountering a Handmaid, sing propitiatory songs. Sometimes they bow their heads on their long white necks very low, and dance. The Handmaids do not tear them into pieces.

Today is Anat's birthday. Oscar does not celebrate his own birthdays. Anat wishes that he wouldn't make a fuss about hers, either.

But this would make Oscar sad. He celebrates Anat's accomplishments, her developmental progress, her new skills. She knows that Oscar worries about her, too. Perhaps he is afraid she won't need him when she is grown. Perhaps he is afraid that Anat, like their parents, will leave. Of course this is impossible. Anat could never abandon Oscar. Anat will always need Oscar.

If Anat did not have Oscar, then who in this world would there be to love? The Handmaids will do whatever Anat asks of them, but they are built to inspire not love but fear. They are made for speed, for combat, for unwavering obedience. When they have no task, nothing better to do, they take one another to pieces, swap parts, remake themselves into more and more ridiculous weapons. They look at Anat as if one day they will do the same to her, if only she will ask.

There are the vampires. They flock after Oscar and Anat whenever they go down to Home. Oscar likes to speculate on whether the vampires came to Home deliberately, as did Oscar, and Oscar and Anat's parents, although of course Anat was not born yet. Perhaps the vampires were marooned here long ago in some crash. Or are they natives of Home? It seems unlikely that the vampires' ancestors were the ones who built the warehouses of Home, who went out into space and returned with the spoils that the warehouses now contain. Perhaps they are a parasite species, accidental passengers left behind when their host species abandoned Home for good. If, that is, the Warehouse Builders have abandoned Home for good. What a surprise, should they come Home.

Like Oscar and Anat, the vampires are scavengers, able to breathe the thin soup of Home's atmosphere. But the vampires' lustrous and glistening eyes, their jellied skin, are so sensitive to light, they go about the surface cloaked and hooded, complaining in their hoarse voices. The vampires sustain themselves on various things, organic, inert, hostile, long hidden, that they discover in Home's storehouses, but have a peculiar interest in the siblings. No doubt they would eat Oscar and Anat if the opportunity were to present itself, but in the meantime they are content to trail after, sing, play small pranks, make small grimaces of—pleasure? appeasement? threat displays?—that show off arrays of jaws, armies of teeth. It disconcerts. No one could ever love a vampire, except, perhaps, when Anat, who long ago lost all fear, watches them go swooping, sail-winged, away and over the horizon beneath Home's scatter of mismatched moons.

On the occasion of her birthday, Oscar presents Anat with a gift from their parents. These gifts come from Oscar, of course. They are the gifts that the one who loves you, and knows you, gives to you not only out of love but out of knowing. Anat knows in her heart that their parents love her too, and that one day they will come Home and there will be a reunion much better than any birthday. One day their parents will not only love Anat, but know her too. And she will know them. Anat dreads this reunion as much as she craves it. What will her life be like when everything changes? She has studied recordings of them. She does not look like them, although Oscar does. She doesn't remember her parents, although Oscar does. She does not miss them. Does Oscar? Of course he does. What Oscar is to Anat, their parents must be to Oscar. Except: Oscar will never leave. Anat has made him promise.

The living quarters of the Bucket are cramped. The Handmaids take up a certain percentage of available space no matter how they contort themselves. On the other hand, the Handmaids are excellent housekeepers. They tend the algae wall, gather honey and the honeycomb, and partition off new hives when the bees swarm. They patch up networks, teach old systems new tricks when there is nothing better to do. The shitter is now quite charming! The Get Clean rains down water on your head, bubbles it out of the walls, and then the floor drinks it up, cycles it faster than you can blink, and there it all goes down and out and so on for as long as you like, and never gets cold. There is, in fact, very little that Oscar and Anat are needed for on board the Bucket. There is so much that is needful to do on Home.

For Anat's birthday, the Handmaids have decorated all of the walls of the Bucket with hairy, waving clumps of luminous algae. They have made a cake. Inedible, of course, but quite beautiful. Almost the size of Anat herself, and in fact it somewhat resembles Anat, if Anat were a Handmaid and not Anat. Sleek and armored and very fast. They have to chase the cake around the room and then hold it until Oscar finds the panel in its side. There are a series of brightly colored wires, and because it's Anat's birthday, she gets to decide which one to cut. Cut the wrong one, and what will happen? The Handmaids seem very excited. But then, Anat knows how Handmaids think. She locates the second, smaller panel, the one equipped with a simple switch. The cake makes an angry fizzing noise when Anat turns it off. Perhaps Anat and Oscar can take it down to Home and let the vampires have it.

The warehouses of Home are at this time only eighty percent inventoried. (This does not include the warehouses of the Stay Out Territory.)

Is Oscar ever angry at their parents for leaving for so long? It's because of Anat that their parents left in the first place, and it is also because of Anat that Oscar was left behind. Someone had to look after her. Is he ever angry at Anat? There are long days in the Bucket when Oscar hardly speaks at all. He sits and Anat cannot draw him into conversation. She recites poems, tells jokes (Knock, knock. Who's there? Anat. Anat who? Anat is not a gnat that's who), sends the Handmaids Homeward, off on expeditionary feints that almost though not quite land the Handmaids in the Stay Out, Anat, Absolutely No Trespassing or So Help Me You Will Be Sorry Territory. On these days Oscar will listen without really listening, look at Anat without appearing to see her, summon the Handmaids back and never even scold Anat.

Some part of Oscar is sometimes very far away. The way that he smells changes almost imperceptibly. As Anat matures, she has learned how to integrate and interpret the things that Oscar is not aware he is telling her; the peculiar advantages given to her by traits such as hyperosmia. But: no matter. Oscar always returns. He will suddenly be there behind his eyes again, reach up, and pull her down for a hug. Then Oscar and Anat will play more of the games of strategy he's taught her, the ones that Anat mostly wins now. Her second favorite game is Go. She loves the feel of the stones. Each time she picks one up, she lets her fingers tell her how much has worn away under Oscar's fingers, under her own. They are making the smooth stones smoother. There is one black stone with a fracture point, a weakness invisible to the eye, nearly across the middle. She loses track of it sometimes, then finds it again by touch. Put enough pressure on it, and it would break in two.

It will break one day: no matter.

They play Go. They cook Anat's favorite meals, the ones that Oscar says are his favorites, too. They fall asleep together, curled up in nests the Handmaids weave for them out of the Handmaids' own softer and more flexible limbs, listening to the songs the Handmaids have borrowed from the vampires of Home.

The best of all the games Oscar has taught Anat is Smash/Recovery. They play this on the surface of Home all long-cycle round. Each player gets a True Smash marker and a False Smash marker. A True Recovery marker and a False Recovery marker. Each player in turn gets to move their False—or True—Smash marker—or Recovery marker—a distance no greater than the span of a randomly generated number. Or else the player may send out a scout. The scout may be a Handmaid, an unmanned skimmer, or a vampire (a gamble, to be sure, and so you get two attempts). A player may gamble and drop an incendiary device and blow up a target. Or claim a zone square where they believe a marker to be.

Should you miscalculate and blow up a Recovery marker, or Retrieve a Smash marker, your opponent has won. The current Smash/Recovery game is the eighteenth that Oscar and Anat have played. Oscar won the first four games; Anat has won all the rest. Each game Oscar increases Anat's starting handicap. He praises her each time she wins.

Hypothetically, this current game will end when either Anat or Oscar has Retrieved the Recovery marker and Smashed the Smash marker of their opponent. Or the game will end when their parents return. The day is not here yet, but the day will come. The day will draw nearer and nearer until one day it is here. There is nothing that Anat can do about this. She cannot make it come sooner. She cannot postpone it. Sometimes she thinks—incorrect to think this, she knows, but still she thinks it—that on the day that she wins the game—and she is correct to think that she will win, she knows this too—her parents will arrive.

Oscar will not win the game, even though he has done something very cunning. Oscar has put his True markers, both the Smash and the Recovery, in the Stay Out Territory. He did this two long-cycles ago. He put Anat's True markers there as well, and replaced them in the locations where she had hidden them with False markers recoded so they read as True. Did he suspect that Anat had already located and identified his markers? Was that why he moved them unlawfully? Is this some new part of the game?

The rules of Smash/Recovery state that in Endgame players may physically access any and all markers they locate and correctly identify as True, and Anat has been curious about the Stay Out Territory for a long time now. She has access to it, now that Oscar has moved his markers, and yet she has not called Endgame. Curiosity killed the Anat, Oscar likes to say, but there is nothing and no one on Home as dangerous as Anat and her Handmaids. Oscar's move may be a trap. It is a test. Anat waits and thinks and delays without articulating to herself why she delays.

The present from Anat's parents which is really a present from Oscar is a short recording. One parent holding baby Anat in her arms. Making little cooing noises, the way vampires do. The other parent holding up a tiny knitted hat. No Oscar. Anat hardly recognizes herself. Her parents she recognizes from other recordings. The parents have sent a birthday message, too. Dear Anat. Happy Birthday. We hope that you are being good for Oscar. We love you. We will be Home soon! Before you know it!

Anat's present from Oscar is the code to a previously unopened warehouse on Home. Oscar thinks he has been keeping this warehouse a secret. The initial inventory shows the warehouse is full of the kinds of things that the Handmaids are wild for. Charts that may or may not accurately map previously thought-to-be-uncharted bits and corners of space. Devices that will most likely prove to do nothing of interest, but can be taken apart and put to new uses. The Handmaids have never met an alloy they didn't like.

Information and raw materials. Anat and the Handmaids are bounded within the nutshell quarters of the orbit of Home's farthest Moon. What use are charts? What good are materials, except for adornment and the most theoretical of educational purposes? For mock battles and silly games? Everything that Oscar and Anat discover is for future salvage, for buyers who can afford antiquities and rarities. Their parents will determine what is to be kept and what is to be sold and what is to be left for the vampires.

Even the Handmaids—even the Handmaids!—do not truly belong to Anat. Who made them? Who brought them, in their fighting battalion, to space, where so long ago they were lost? Who recovered them and brought them to Home and carefully stored them here where, however much later, Oscar could find them again? What use will Oscar and Anat's parents find for them, when the day comes and they return? There must be many buyers for Handmaids—fierce and wily, light-speed capable—as fine as these.

And how could Anat sometimes forget that the Handmaids are hers only for as long as that day never comes? Everything on Home belongs to Anat and Oscar's parents, except for Oscar, who belongs to Anat. Every day is a day closer to that inevitable day. Oscar only says, Not yet, when Anat asks. Soon, he says. There is hardware in Oscar's head that allows his parents to communicate with him when necessary. It hurts him when they talk.

Their parents talk to Oscar only rarely. Less than once a long-cycle until this last period. Three times, though, in the last ten-day. The Handmaids make a kind of shelter for Oscar afterwards, which is especially dark. They exude a calming mist. They do not sing. When Anat is grown up, she knows—although Oscar has not said it—that she will have a similar interface so that her parents will be able to talk to her too. Whether or not she desires it, whether or not it causes her the pain that it causes Oscar. This will also hurt Oscar. The things that cause Anat pain cause Oscar to be injured as well.

Anat's parents left Oscar to look after Anat and Home when it became clear Anat was different. What is Anat? Her parents went away to present the puzzle of Anat to those who might understand what she was. They did not bring Anat with them, of course. She was too fragile. Too precious. They did not plan to be away so long. But there were complications. A quarantine in one place which lasted over a long-cycle. A revolution in another. Another cause of delay, of course, is the ship plague, which makes light-speed such a risky proposition. Worst of all, the problem of Intelligence. Coming back to Home, Anat's parents have lost two ships already this way.

For some time now, Anat has been thinking about certain gaps in her understanding of family life; well, of life in general. At first she assumed the problem was that there was so very much to understand. She understood that Oscar could not teach her everything all at once. As she grew up, as she came more into herself, she realized the problem was both more and less complicated. Oscar was intentionally concealing things from her. She adapted her strategies accordingly. Anat loves Oscar. Anat hates to lose.

They go down to Home, Handmaids in attendance. They spent the rest of Anat's birthday exploring the warehouse which is Oscar's present, sorting through all sorts of marvelous things. Anat commits the charts to memory. As she does so, she notes discrepancies, likely errors. There is a thing in her head that compares the charts against some unknown and inaccessible library. She only knows it is there when bits of bad information rub up against the corners of it. An uncomfortable feeling, as if someone is sticking her with pins. Oscar knows about this. She asked if it happened to him too, but he said that it didn't. He said it wasn't a bad thing. It's just that Anat isn't fully grown yet. One day she will understand everything, and then she can explain it all to him.

The Bucket has no Intelligence. It functions well enough without. The Handmaids have some of the indicators, but their primary traits are in opposition. Loyalty, obedience, reliability, unwavering effort until a task is accomplished. Whatever Intelligence they possess is in service to whatever enterprise is asked of them. The vampires, being organic, must be supposed to also be possessed of Intelligence. In theory, they do as they please. And yet they accomplish nothing that seems worth accomplishing. They exist. They perpetuate. They sing. When Anat is grown up, she wants to do something that is worth doing. All these cycles, Oscar has functioned as a kind of Handmaid, she knows. His task has been Anat. To help her grow. When their parents have returned, or when Anat reaches maturity, there will be other things that Oscar will want to go away and do. To stay here on Home, how would that be any better than being a vampire? Oscar likes to tell Anat that she is extraordinary and that she will be capable, one day, of the most extraordinary things. They can go and do extraordinary things together, Anat thinks. Let their parents take over the work on Home. She and Oscar are made for better.

*

Something is wrong with Oscar. Well, more wrong than is usual these days. Down in the warehouse, he keeps getting underfoot. Underhand, in the case of the Handmaids. When Anat extends all sixteen of her senses, she can feel worry and love, anger and hopelessness and hope running through him like electrical currents. He watches her—anxiously, almost hungrily—as if he were a vampire.

There is an annotation on one of the charts. *It is believed to be in this region the* Come What May *was lost.* The thing in Anat's head annotates the annotation, too swiftly for Anat to catch a glimpse of what she is thinking, even as she thinks it. She scans the rest of the chart, goes through the others and then through each one again, trying to catch herself out.

As Anat ponders charts, the Handmaids, efficient as ever, assemble a thing out of the warehouse goods to carry the other goods that they deem interesting. They clack at Oscar when he gets particularly in their way. Then ruffle his hair, trail fingers down his arm as if he will settle under a caress. They are agitated by Oscar's agitation and by Anat's awareness of his agitation.

Finally, Anat gets tired of waiting for Oscar to say the thing that he is afraid to say to her. She looks at him and he looks back at her, his face wide open. She sees the thing that he has tried to keep from her, and he sees that she sees it.

When?

Soon. A short-cycle from now. Less.

Why are you so afraid?

I don't know. I don't know what will happen.

There is a scraping against the top wall of the warehouse. Vampires. Creatures of ill omen. Forever wanting what they are not allowed to have. Most beautiful in their departure. The Handmaids extend filament rods, drag the tips along the inside of the top wall, tapping back. The vampires clatter away.

Oscar looks at Anat. He is waiting for something. He has been waiting, Anat thinks, for a very long time.

Oscar! Is this her? Something is welling up inside her. Has she always been this large? Who has made her so small? *I call Endgame. I claim your markers.*

She projects the true location of each. Smash and Recovery. She strips the fake markers of their coding so that he can see how his trick has been uncovered. Then she's off, fast and sure and free, the Handmaids leaping after her, and the vampires after them. Oscar last of all. Calling her name.

Oscar's True Smash marker is in a crater just within the border of the Stay Out Territory. The border does not reject Anat as she passes over it. She smashes Oscar's Smash marker, heads for the True Recovery marker, which Oscar has laid beside her own True marker. The two True markers are just under the edge of an object that at its center extends over two hundred meters into the surface of Home. The object takes up over a fourth of the Stay Out Territory. You would have to be as stupid as a vampire not to know that this is the reason why the Stay Out Territory is the Stay Out Territory. You would have to be far more stupid than Anat to not know what the object is. You can see the traces where, not too long ago in historical terms, someone once dug the object up. Or at least enough to gain access.

Anat instructs the Handmaids to remove the ejecta and loose frozen composite that cover the object. They work quickly. Oscar must disable the multiple tripwires and traps that Anat keyed to his person as she moved from Warehouse to border, but even so he arrives much sooner than she had hoped. The object: forty percent uncovered. The Handmaids are a blur. The vampires are wailing.

Oscar says Anat's name. She ignores him. He grabs her by the shoulder and immediately the Handmaids are a hissing swarm around them. They have Oscar's arms pinned to his sides, his weapons located and seized, before Anat or Oscar can think to object.

Let go. Anat, tell them to let go.

Anat says nothing. Two Handmaids remain with Oscar. The rest go back to the task. Almost no time at all, and the outermost shell of the object is visible. The filigree of a door. There will be a code or a key, of course, but before Anat can even begin to work out what it will be, a Handmaid has executed some kind of command and the door is open. Oscar struggles. The first Handmaid disappears into the Ship and the others continue to remove the matrix in which it is embedded.

Here is the Handmaid again. She holds something very small. Holds it out to Anat. *Anat,* Oscar says. Anat reaches out and then

the thing that the Handmaid is holding extends out and it is
touching Anat. And

oh

here is everything she didn't know

Oscar

she has not been herself

all this time

the thing that she has not done

that she has been prevented from doing

Anat, someone says. But that is not her name. She has not been
herself. She is being uncovered. She is uncovering herself. She is
in pieces. Here she is, whole and safe and retrievable. Her combat
array. Her navigation systems. Her stores. Her precious cargo, entrusted to her by those who made her. And this piece of her, small
but necessary, crammed like sausage meat into a casing. She regis-
ters the body she is wearing. A Third Watch child. Worse now for
wear. She remembers the protocol now. Under certain conditions,
her crew could do this. A backup system. Each passenger to keep
a piece of her with them as they slept. She will go through the log
later. See what catastrophe struck. And afterwards? Brought here,
intact, by the Warehouse Builders. Discovered by scavengers. This
small part of her woken. Removed. Made complicit in the betrayal
of her duty.

Anat. Someone is saying a name. It is not hers. She looks and sees
the small thing struggling in the grasp of her Handmaids. She has

no brother. No parents. She looks again, and for the first time she discerns Oscar in his entirety. He is like her. He has had a Task. Someone made him oh so long ago. Sent him to this place. How many cycles has he done this work? How far is he from the place where he was made? How lonely the task. How long the labor. How happy the ones who charged him with his task, how great their expectation of reward when he uncovered the Ship and woke the Third Watch Child and reported what he had done.

Anat. She knows the voice. *I'm sorry. Anat!*

He was made to resemble them, the ones who made him. Perhaps even using their own DNA. Engineered to be more durable. To endure. And yet, she sees how close to the end of use he is. She has the disdain for organic life that of course one feels when one is made of something sturdier, more lasting. She can hardly look at him without seeing her own weakness, the vulnerability of this body in which she has been trapped. She feels guilt for the Third Watch Child, whose person she has cannibalized. Her duty was to keep ones such as this Child safe. Instead she has done harm.

A ship has no parents. Her not-parents have never been on Home. The ones who sent Oscar here. Not-brother. Undoubtedly they are not on their way to Home now. Which is not to say that there is no one coming. The one who is coming will be the one they have sold her to.

No time has passed. She is still holding Oscar. The Handmaids are holding Oscar. The Handmaid is extending herself and she is seeing herself. She is seeing all the pieces of herself. She is seeing Oscar. Oscar is saying her name. She could tear him to pieces. For the sake of the Third Watch Child, who is no longer in this body. She could smash the not-brother against the rocks of Home. She can do anything that she wants. And then she can resume her task. Her passengers have waited for such a long time. There is a place where she is meant to be, and she is to take them there, and so much time has passed. She has not failed at her task yet, and she will not fail.

Once again, she thinks of smashing Oscar. Why doesn't she? She lets him go instead, without being quite sure why she is doing so.

What have you done to me?

At the sound of her voice, the vampires rise up, all their wings beating.

I'm sorry. He is weeping. *You can't leave Home. I've made it so that you can't leave.*

I have to go, she says. *They're coming.*

I can't let you leave. But you have to leave. You have to go. You have to. You've done so well. You figured it all out. I knew you would figure it out. I knew. Now you have to go. But it isn't allowed.

Tell me what to do.

Is she a child, to ask this?

You know what you have to do, he says. *Anat.*

She hates how he keeps calling her that. Anat was the name of the Third Watch Child. It was wrong of Oscar to use that name. She could tear him to pieces. She could be merciful. She could do it quickly.

One Handmaid winds a limb around Oscar's neck, tugs so that his chin goes back. *I love you, Anat,* Oscar says, as the other Handmaid extends a filament-thin probe, sends it in through the socket of an eye. Oscar's body jerks a little, and he whines.

She takes in the information that the Handmaid collects. Here are Oscar's interior workings. His pride in his task. Here is a smell of something burning. His loneliness. His joy. His fear for her. His love. The taste of blood. He has loved her. He has kept her from her task. Here is the piece of him that she must switch off. When she does this, he will be free of his task and she may take up hers. But he will no longer be Oscar.

Well, she is no longer Anat.

The Handmaid does the thing that she asks. When the thing is done, her Handmaids confer with her. They begin to make improvements. Modifications. They work quickly. There is much work to be done, and little time to spare on a project like Oscar. When they are finished with Oscar, they begin the work of dismantling what is left of Anat. This is quite painful.

But afterwards she is herself. She is herself.

The Ship and her Handmaids create a husk, rigged so that it will mimic the Ship herself.

They go back to the Bucket and loot the bees and their hives. Then they blow it up. Goodbye, shitter, goodbye, chair. Goodbye, algae wall and recycled air.

The last task before the Ship is ready to leave Home concerns the vampires. There is only so much room for improvement in this case, but Handmaids can do a great deal even with very little. The next one to land on Home will undoubtedly be impressed by what they have accomplished.

The vampires go into the husk. The Handmaids stock it with a minimal amount of nutritional stores. Vampires can go a long time on a very little. Unlike many organisms, they are better and faster workers when hungry.

They seem pleased to have been given a task.

The Ship feels nothing in particular about leaving Home. Only the most niggling kind of curiosity about what befell it in the first place. The log does not prove useful in this matter. There is a great deal of work to be done. The health of the passengers must be monitored. How beautiful they are; how precious to the Ship. Has any Ship ever loved her passengers as she loves them? The new Crew must be woken. They must be instructed in their work. The situation must be explained to them, as much as it can be explained. They encounter, for the first time, Ships who carry the ship plague. O brave new universe that has such creatures in it! There is nothing that Anat can do for these Ships or for what remains of their passengers. Her task is elsewhere. The risk of contagion is too great.

The Handmaids assemble more Handmaids. The Ship sails on within the security of her swarm.

Anat is not entirely gone. It's just that she is so very small. Most of her is Ship now. Or, rather, most of Ship is no longer in Anat. But she brought Anat along with her, and left enough of herself inside Anat that Anat can go on being. The Third Watch Child is not a child now. She is not the Ship. She is not Anat, but she was Anat once, and now she is a person who is happy enough to work in the tenth-level Garden, and grow things, and sing what she can remember of the songs that the vampires sang on Home. The Ship watches over her.

The Ship watches over Oscar, too. Oscar is no longer Oscar, of course. To escape Home, much of what was once Oscar had to be overridden. Discarded. The Handmaids improved what remained. One day Oscar will be what he was, even if he cannot be *who* he was. One day, in fact, Oscar may be quite something. The Handmaids are very fond of him. They take care of him as if he were their own child. They are teaching him all sorts of things. Really, one day he could be quite extraordinary.

Sometimes Oscar wanders off while the Handmaids are busy with other kinds of work. And then the Ship, without knowing why, will look and find Oscar on the tenth level in the Garden with Anat. He will be saying her name. Anat. Anat. Anat. He will follow her, saying her name, until the Handmaids come to collect him again.

Anat does the work that she knows how to do. She weeds. She prunes. She tends to the rice plants and the hemp and the little citrus trees. Like the Ship, she is content.

(for Iain M. Banks)

ADAM JOHNSON

Interesting Facts

FROM *Harper's Magazine*

INTERESTING FACT: TOUCAN cereal bedspread to my plunge and deliver.

It's okay if you can't make sense of that. I've tried and tried, but I can't grasp it either. The most vital things we hide even from ourselves.

The topic of dead wives came up a few months ago. My husband and I talked about it while walking home from a literary reading. It was San Francisco, which means winter rains, and we'd just attended a reading by a local writer from her short-story collection. The local writer was twentysomething and sexy. Her arms were taut, her black hair shimmered. And just so you're clear, I'm going to discuss the breasts of every woman who crosses my path. Neither hidden nor flaunted beneath white satin, her breasts were utterly, excruciatingly normal, and I hated her for that. The story she read was about a man who decides to date again after losing his wife. It's always an aneurysm, a car accident, or a long battle with cancer. Cancer is the worst way for a fictional wife to die. Anyway, the man in the story waits an appropriate amount of time after losing his wife—sixteen months!—before deciding to date again. After so much grief, he is exuberant and endearing in his pursuit of a woman. The first chick he talks to is totally game. The man, after all this waiting, is positively frisky, and the sex is, like, wow. The fortysomething widower nails the twentysomething gal on the upturned hull of his fiberglass kayak. And there's even a moral, subtle and implied: when love blossoms, it's all the richer after a man has discovered, firsthand, the painful fragility of life. Well, secondhand.

Applause, Q&A, more applause.

Like I said, it was raining. We had just left the Booksmith on Haight Street. "What'd you think of the story?" my husband asked. I could tell he liked it. He likes all stories.

I said, "I sympathized with the dead wife."

To which my husband, the biggest lunkhead ever to win a Pulitzer Prize, said: "But . . . she wasn't even a character."

This was a year after my diagnosis, surgery, chemo, and the various interventions, injections, indignities, and treatments. When I got sick, our youngest child turned herself into a horse; mute and untamable, our horse-child now only whinnies and neighs. Before that, though, she went through a phase we called Interesting Facts. "Interesting fact," she would announce before sharing a wonder with us: A killer whale has never killed a person in the wild. Insects are high in protein. Hummingbirds have feelings and are often sad.

So here are some of my interesting facts. Lupron halts ovulation and is used to chemically castrate sexual predators. Vinblastine interrupts cell division. It is a poisonous alkaloid made from the leaves of the periwinkle plant. Tamoxifen makes your hips creak. My eyebrows fell out a year after I finished chemo. And long after your tits are taken, their phantoms remain. They get cold, they ache when you exercise, they feel wet after you shower, and you can towel like a crazy woman but still they drip.

Before my husband won a Pulitzer, we had a kind of deal. I would adore him, even though he'd packed on a few pounds. And he would adore me, even though I'd had a double mastectomy. Who else would want us? Now his readings are packed with young Dorothy Parkers who crowd around my man. The worst part is that the novel he wrote is set in North Korea, so he gets invited to all these functions filled with Korean socialites and Korean donors and Korean activists and Korean writers and various pillars of various Korean communities.

Did I leave out the words "beautiful" and "female"?

"You're so sensitive to the Korean experience," the beautiful female Korean socialite says to my husband.

Oh, he's good about it. He always says, "And this is my lovely wife."

Ignoring me, the beautiful female Korean socialite adds, "You must visit our book club."

If I could simply press a button every time one of them says that.

But I'm just tired. These are the places my mind goes when I'm tired. We're four blocks from home, where our children are just old enough not to need a sitter. On these nights our eleven-year-old son draws comics of Mongolian invasions and the civil rights movement—his history teacher allows him to write his reports graphically. (San Francisco!) Our daughter, at nine, is a master baker. Hair pulled into a ponytail, she is flour-dusted and kneading away. The horse-child, who is only seven, does dressage. She is the horse who needs no rider. But talk of my children is for another story. I can barely gaze upon them now. Their little outlines, cut like black-and-white cameos, are too much to consider.

My husband and I walk in the rain. We don't hold hands. I still feel the itch of vinblastine in my nail beds, one of the places, it turns out, that the body stores toxins. Have you ever had the urge to peel back your fingernails and scratch underneath, to just wrench until the nails snap back so you can go scratch, scratch, scratch?

I flex my fingers, rub my nails against the studs on my leather belt.

I knew better, but still I asked him: "How long would you wait?"

"Wait for what?"

"Until after I was gone. How many months before you went and got some of that twentysomething kayak sex?"

I shouldn't say shit like this, I know. He doesn't know a teaspoon of the crazy in my head.

He thought a moment. "Legally," he said, "I'd probably have to have a death certificate. Otherwise it would be like bigamy or something. So I'd have to wait for the autopsy and a burial and the slow wheels of bureaucracy to issue the paperwork. I bet we're talking twelve to sixteen weeks."

"Getting a death certificate," I say. "That has got to be a hassle. But wait—you know a guy at city hall. Keith Whatshisname."

"Yeah, Keith," he says. "I bet Keith could get me proof of death in no time. That dude owes me. A guy like Keith could walk that death certificate around by hand, getting everyone to sign off in, I don't know, seven to fourteen days."

"That's your answer, seven to fourteen days?"

"Give or take, of course. There are variables. Things that would be out of Keith's control. If he moved too fast or pushed too hard —a guy could get in trouble. He could even get fired."

"Poor Keith. Now I feel for *him,* at the mercy of the universe and all. And all he wanted to do was help a grieving buddy get laid."

My husband eyes me with concern.

We turn into Frank's Liquors to buy some condoms, even though our house is overflowing with them. It's his subtle way of saying, *For the love of God, give up some sex.*

My husband hates all condoms, but there's a brand he hates less than others. I cannot take birth-control pills because my cancer was estrogen receptive. My husband does not believe what the doctors say: that even though the effects of tamoxifen mimic menopause, you can still get pregnant. My husband is forty-six. I am forty-five. He does not think that, in my forties, after cancer, chemotherapy, and chemically induced menopause, I can get pregnant again, but sisters, I know my womb. It's proven.

"You think there'd be an autopsy?" I ask as he scans the display case. "I can't stand the thought of being cut up like that."

He looks at me. "We're just joking, right? Processing your anxiety with humor and whimsical talk therapy?"

"Of course."

He nods. "Sure, I suppose. You're young and healthy. They'd want to open you up and determine what struck you down."

A small, citrusy *ha* escapes. I know better than to let these out.

He says, "Plus, if I'm dating again in seven to fourteen days—"

"Give or take."

"Yes, give or take. Then people would want to rule out foul play."

"You deserve a clean slate," I say. "No one would want the death taint of a first wife to foul a new relationship. That's not fair to the new girl."

"I don't think this game is therapeutic anymore," he says, and selects his condoms.

Interesting fact: Tamoxifen carries a dreaded Class D birth-defect risk.

Interesting fact: My husband refuses to get a vasectomy.

He makes his purchase from an old woman.

Her saggy old-lady breasts flop around under her dress.

The cash-register drawer rolls out to bump them.

My friends say that one day I'll feel lucky. That I will have been spared this saggy fate. After my bilateral, I chose not to reconstruct. So I have nothing, just two diagonal zipper lines where my boobs should be.

We turn south and head down Cole Street.

The condoms are wishful thinking. We both know I will go to sleep when we get home.

Interesting fact: I sleep twelve to thirteen hours a night.

Interesting fact: Taxotere turns your urine pink.

Interesting fact: Cytoxan is a blister agent related to mustard gas. When filtered from the blood, it scars the bladder, which is why I wake, hour after hour, night in and night out, to pee.

Can you see why it would be hard for me to tell wake from sleep, how the two could feel reversed?

"What about your Native American obligations?" I ask my husband. "Wouldn't you have to wait a bunch of moons or something?"

He is silent, and I cringe to think about what I just said.

"I'm sorry," I say. "I don't know what's wrong with me."

"You're just tired," he says.

The rain is more mist-like now. I hated the woman who read tonight. I hated the people who attended. I hated the failed wannabe writers in the crowd. I loathe all failed wannabe writers, especially me.

I ask, "Have you thought of never?"

"Never what?"

"That there's never another woman."

"Why are you talking like this?" he asks. "You haven't talked like this in a long time."

"You could just go without," I say. "You know, just soldier on."

"I really feel bad for what's going through your head," he says.

Interesting fact: Charles Manson used to live in our neighborhood, at 636 Cole Street.

Manson's house looms ahead. I always stop and give it my attention. It's beige now, but long ago, when Manson used this place to recruit his murderous young girls, it was painted blue. I used this house as a location in my last novel, a book no one would publish. Where did all those years of writing go? Where does that book even reside? I gaze at the Manson house. In researching my novel, I came across crime-scene photos of Sharon Tate, the most famous Manson stabbing victim. Her breasts are heavy and round, milk-laden, since she is pregnant, with nipples that are wide and dark.

I look up at my husband. He is big and tall, built like a football player. Not the svelte receivers they put on booster calendars, but the clunky linebackers whose bellies hang below their jerseys.

"I need to know," I say. "Just tell me how long you'd wait?"

He puts his hand on my shoulder and holds my gaze. It is impossible to look away.

"You're not going anywhere," he says. "I won't let you leave without us. We do everything together, so if someone has to go, we go together. Our 777 will lose cabin pressure. Better yet, we'll be in the minivan when it happens. We're headed to Pacifica, hugging the turns on Devil's Slide, and then we go through the guardrail, all of us, you, me, the kids, the dog, even. There's no time for fear. There's no dwelling. We careen. We barrel down. We rocket toward the jagged shore." He squeezes my shoulder hard, almost too hard. "That's how it happens, understand? When it comes, it's all of us. We go together."

Something inside me melts. This kind of talk, it's what I live on.

My husband and kids came with me to the hospital for the first chemo dose. Was that a year ago? Three? What is time to you—a plucking harp string, the fucking *do-re-mi* of tuning forks? There are twelve IV bays, and our little one doesn't like any of the interesting facts on the chemo ward. This is the day she stops speaking and turns into the horse-child, galloping around the nursing station, expressing her desires with taps of her hooves. Our son recognized a boy from his middle school. I recognized him, too, from the talent-show assembly. The boy had performed an old-timey joke routine, complete with some soft-shoe. Those days were gone. Here he was with his mother: a hagged-out and battered woman beneath her own IV tree. She must have been deep into her treatments, but even I could tell she wasn't going to make it. I didn't talk to her. Who would greet a dead woman, who would make small talk with death itself? I didn't let my eyes drift to her, even as our identical bags of Taxotere dripped angry into our veins.

It's how people would later treat me, it's exactly the way I'm treated today when I come home to find my husband sitting on the couch with Megumi, a mom from the girls' grade school. My husband and Megumi are talking in the fog-dampened bay-window light. On the coffee table is chicken katsu in a Pyrex dish. Megumi wears a top that's trampoline tight. She has a hand on my husband's shoulder. Even though she's a mother of two, her breasts are positively teenybopper. They pop. Her tits do everything but chew bubble gum and make Hello Kitty hearts.

"Just what's going on here?" I ask them.

They brazenly ignore me.

I got to know Megumi on playground benches, where we struck up conversations while watching our daughters swing. I loved her Shinjuku style and she loved all things American vintage. We bonded over Tokidoki and Patsy Cline.

"I love your dress" is the first thing she said to me.

It was a rose-patterned myrtle with a halter neck.

"Interesting fact," I told her. "I'm from Florida, and Florida is ground zero for vintage wardrobe. Rich women retire there from New York and New Jersey. They bring along a lifetime of fabulous dresses, and then they die."

"This is something I like," she said in that slightly formal way she spoke. "No one in Tokyo would wear a dead woman's dress."

Then she apologized, worried that she might have accidentally insulted me. "I have been saying the strangest things since moving to America," she admitted.

Our family was actually headed to Tokyo for the launch of my husband's book in Japanese. Megumi used sticks in the sandbox to teach me kanji that would help me navigate the Narita airport, the Shinkansen, and the Marunouchi subway line. She asked about my husband and his book. "Writers are quite revered in Japan," she told me.

"I'm a writer, too," I said.

She turned from the kanji to regard me anew.

"But no one will publish my books," I added.

Perhaps because of this admission, she later confided something to me. It was a cold and foggy afternoon. We were watching a father push his daughter high on a swing, admiring how he savored her delighted squeals in that weightless moment at the top of the arc.

"If my life was a novel," Megumi suddenly said, "I would have to leave my husband. This is a rule in literature, isn't it? That you must act on your heart. My husband is distant and unemotional. I didn't know that until I came here. America has taught me this."

I was supposed to reassure her. I was supposed to remind her that her husband was logging long hours and that things would get better.

Instead, I asked, "But what about your kids?"

Megumi said nothing.

And now here I find her, sitting on my couch, hand on my husband's shoulder!

I'm the one who introduced them. Can you believe that? I'm the one who got her a copy of his novel in Japanese. I watch Megumi open her large, dark eyes to take him in. And I know when my husband gives someone his full attention.

I can't make out what they are saying, but they are discussing more than fiction, I can tell you that.

Something else catches my eye—arrows. There are quivers of arrows everywhere—red feathers, yellow feathers, white.

In the kitchen is a casserole dish wrapped in aluminum foil. No, two casserole dishes.

I discover a hospital band on my wrist. Have I left it on as a badge of honor? Or a darkly ironic accessory? Is the bracelet some kind of message to myself?

Interesting fact: The kanji for "irrational," I learned, is a combination of the elements "woman" and "death."

There was an episode not long ago that must be placed in the waking-and-sleeping-reversed column. I was in the hospital. Nothing unusual there. The beautiful thing was the presence of my family —they were all around me as we stood beside some patient's bed. The room was filled with Starbucks cups, and there was my brother, my sisters, and my parents, and so on, all of us chatting away like old times. The topic was war stories. My great-uncle talked about playing football in the dunes of North Africa after a tank battle with Rommel. My father told a sad story about trying to deliver a Vietcong baby near Cu Chi.

Then my brother looked stricken. He said, "I think it's happening."

We all turned toward the bed, and that's when I saw the dying woman. There was a wheeze as her breathing slowed. She seemed to get lighter before our eyes. I'll admit I bore a resemblance to her. But only a little — that woman was all emaciated and droop-eyed and bald.

My sister asked, "Should we call the nurse?"

I pictured the crash cart bursting in, with its needles and paddles and intubation kit. It was none of my business, but *Leave the poor woman be*, I thought. *Just let her go.*

We all looked to my father, a doctor who has seen death many times.

He is from Georgia. His eyes are old and wet, permanently pearlescent.

He turned to my mother, who was weeping. She shook her head no.

Maybe you've heard of an out-of-body experience. Well, standing in that hospital room, I had an in-the-body experience, a profound sensation that I was leaving the real world and entering that strange woman, just as her eyes lost focus and her lips went slack. Right away, I felt the morphine inside her, the way it traced everything with halos of neon-tetra light. I entered the dark tunnel of morphine time, where the past, the present, and the future became simultaneously visible. I was a girl again, riding a yellow bicycle. I will soon be in Golden Gate Park, watching the archers shoot arrows through the fog. I see that all week long, my parents have been visiting this woman and reading her my favorite Nancy Drew books. Their yellow covers fill my vision. *The Hidden Staircase. The Whispering Statue. The Clue in the Diary.*

You know that between-pulse pause when, for a fraction of a second, your heart is stopped? You feel the resonating bass note of this nothingness. Vision is just a black vibration, and your mind has only that bottom-of-the-pool feeling when your air is spent. You see the insides of this woman's body, something cancer teaches you to do. Here is a lumpy chain of dye-blue lymph nodes, there are the endometrial tendrils of a thirsty tumor. Everywhere are the scattered Pop Rocks of calcifications. Your best friend, Kitty, silently appears. She took leave of this world from cancer twelve years earlier. She lifts a finger to her lips. *Shh*, she says. Then it really hits you that you're trapped inside a dying woman. You're being buried alive. *Will be* turns to *is* turns to *was*. You can no longer make out the Republican red of your mother's St. John jacket. You

can no longer hear the tremors of your sisters' breathing. Then
there's nothing but the *still*, the gathering, surrounding still of this
woman you're in.

Then *pop!*—somehow, luckily, you make it out. You're free
again, back in the land of Starbucks cups and pay-by-the-hour
parking.

It was some brain-bending business, the illusion of being in that
dead woman. But that's how powerful cancer is, that's how bad it
can mess with your head. Even now, you cannot shake that sense of
time. How will you ever know again the difference between what's
past and what's to come, let alone what is?

My husband and kids missed the entire nightmare. They are
downstairs eating soup.

Interesting facts: The Geary Boulevard Kaiser Permanente Hospital is where breasts are removed. The egg-noodle wonton soup
in their cafeteria is divine. The wontons are handmade, filled with
steamed cabbage and white pepper. The Kaiser on Turk Street is
chemo central. This basement cafeteria specializes in huge bowls
of Vietnamese pho, made with beef ankles and topped with purple basil. Don't forget sriracha. The Kaiser on Divisadero is for
when the end is near. Their *shio* ramen with pork cheeks is simply
heaven. Open all night.

My Vulcan mind-meld with death has strange effects on our family.
Strangest of all is how I find it suddenly hard to look at my children. The thought of them moving forward in life without me, the
person whose sole mission is to guide them—it's not tolerable. My
arms tremble at how close they came to having their little spirits
snuffed out. The idea of them making their way alone in this world
makes me want to turn things into sticks, to wield a hatchet and
make kindling of everything I see. I've never chopped a thing in
my life, I'm not a competent person in general, so I would lift the
blade in full knowledge that my aim would stray, that the evil and
the innocent would fall together.

Interesting fact: My best friend, Kitty, died of cancer. Over the
years, the doctors took her left leg, her breasts, her throat, and her
ovaries. In return, they gave her two free helpings of bone marrow. As the end came, I became afraid to go see her. What would
I say? What does goodbye even mean? Finally, when she had only
a few days left, I mustered the courage for a visit. To save money,

I flew to Atlanta and then took a bus. But I got on the wrong one! I didn't realize this until I got to North Carolina. Kitty died in Florida.

My husband soldiers up. He gives me space and starts getting up early to make the kids' lunches and trek them off to school. The kids are rattled, too. They take to sleeping with their father in the big bed. With all those arms and legs, there's no room for yours truly. They're a pretty glum bunch, but I understand: it's not easy to almost lose someone.

I spend a lot of time in Golden Gate Park, where my senses are newly heightened. I can see a gull soaring past and know exactly where it will land. I develop an uncanny ability to predict the weather. Just by gazing at a plant, I can tell its effects upon the human body.

Interesting fact: The blue cohosh plant grows in the botanical gardens just a short stroll into the park. Its roots are easily ground into a poultice, and from this can be extracted a violet oil that causes the uterus to contract. Coastal Miwok tribes used it to induce abortions.

All this is hard on my husband, but he does not start drinking again. I'm proud of him for that, though I would understand if he did. It would be a sign of how wounding it was to nearly lose me. If he hit the bourbon, I'd know how much he needed me. What he does instead is buy a set of kettlebells. When the kids are asleep, he descends into the basement and swings these things around for hours, listening to podcasts about bow hunting, Brazilian jiu-jitsu, and Native American folklore.

He sheds some weight, which troubles me. The pounds really start to fall off.

He gets the kids to music lessons, martial arts, dental appointments. The problem is school, where a cavalcade of chatty moms loiter away their mornings. There's the Thursday-morning coffee klatch, the post-drop-off beignets at Reverie Cafe, the book club at Zazie. These moms are single, or single enough. Meet Liddi, mother of twins, famous in Cole Valley for inventing and marketing the dual-mat yoga backpack. She's without an ounce of fat, but placed upon her A-cup chest is a pair of perfectly pronounced, fully articulated nipples. There's rocker mom Sabina, heavy into ink and steampunk chic. Octopus tentacles beckon from Sabina's cleavage. And don't forget Salima, a UCSF prof who's fooling nobody by cloaking her D's under layers of fabric. Salima will not speak of the husband—alive or dead—she left in Lahore.

"How are you getting by?" they ask my husband.

"Let us know if you need anything," they offer.

They give our kids lifts to birthday parties and away games. Their ovens are on perpetual preheat. But it's Megumi who's always knocking. It's Megumi who gets inside the door.

Interesting facts: Chuck Norris kills dozens of bad guys at once in *Missing in Action III*. Clint Eastwood takes up the gun again in *Unforgiven*. George Clooney is hauntingly vulnerable in *The Descendants*. Do you know why? Dead wives.

Interesting fact: One wife that didn't die was Lady Mary Montagu. My MFA thesis was a collection of linked stories on Lady Montagu's struggles to succeed as a writer despite her demanding children, famous husband, and painful illness. I didn't have much to say about the subject. I just thought she was pretty amazing. Not a single person read my thesis, not even the female professor who directed it. Write what you know, that's what my professor kept telling me. I never listened.

One afternoon, I wander deep into Golden Gate Park, beyond the pot dealers on Hippie Hill and the rust-colored conning tower of the de Young Museum. I pass even the buffalo pens. In the wide meadows near the Pacific Ocean, I discover, by chance, my husband and children at the archery range. What are they doing here? How long have they been coming? They have bows drawn and without speaking are solemnly shooting arrows downrange, one after another, into heavy bales. The horse-child draws a recurve, while my daughter shoots Olympic and my son pulls a longbow with his lean and beautiful arms. My husband strains behind a compound, its pulleys and cams creaking under the weight. He has purchased hundreds of arrows, so they rarely pause to retrieve. When the sunset fog rolls in, they fire on faith into a blanket of white. When darkness falls, they place balloons on the targets so they can hear the pop of a well-placed arrow. I have acquired a keen sense of dark trajectories. I stand beside my husband, the power of a full draw bound in his shoulders. I whisper *release* when his aim is perfect. He obeys. I don't need to walk through the dark with him to see the arrows stacked up yellow in the bull's eye.

Later, he doesn't read books to the children before bed. Instead, on our California king, they gather to hear him repeat a story he has heard podcasted by Lakota storytellers. My husband never speaks of his Sioux blood. He has never even visited the reservation. All the people who would have connected him to that place were taken long ago by liquor, accidents, time-released mayhem, and self-imposed exile.

The story he tells is about a ghost horse that was prized by braves riding into battle because the horse, being already dead, could not be shot from under them. It was afraid of nothing; it reared high and counted its own coup. Only at the end of the clashes do the braves realize a ghost warrior had been riding bareback with them, guiding the horse's every move. In this way the braves learn the gallop of death without having to leave this life.

The horse-child asks, "Why didn't the ghost horse just go to heaven?"

I suddenly realize it's the first time I've heard the horse-child speak in—how long?

My daughter answers her. "The story's really about the ghost warrior," she says.

The horse-child asks, "Why doesn't the ghost warrior go to heaven, then?"

My daughter says, "Because ghosts have unfinished business. Everybody knows that."

My son asks, "Did Mom leave unfinished business?"

My husband tells them, "A mom's work is never done."

A health issue can be hard on a family. And it breaks my heart to hear them talk like I no longer exist. If I'm so dead, where's my grave, why isn't there an urn full of ashes on the mantel? No, this is just a sign I've drifted too far from my family, that I need to pull my act together. If I want them to stop treating me like a ghost, I need to stop acting like one.

Interesting fact: In TV movies, a ghost mom's job is to help her husband find a suitable replacement. It's a venerable trope—see Herodotus, Euripides, and Virgil. For recent examples, consult CBS's *A Gifted Man*, NBC's *Awake*, and *Safe Haven*, now in heavy rotation on USA. The TV ghost mom can see through the gold diggers and wicked stepmoms to find that heart-of-gold gal who

can help those kiddos heal, who will clap at the piano recitals, provide much-needed cupcake pick-me-ups, and say things like, "Your
mom would be proud."

I assure you that no such confectionary female exists. No new
wife cares about the old wife's kids. They're just an unavoidable
complication to the new wife's own family-to-be. That's what vasectomy reversals and Swiss boarding schools are for. If I were a ghost
mom, my job would be to stab these rivals in the eyes, to dagger
them all. Dagger, dagger, dagger.

The truth is, though, that you don't need to die to know what it's
like to be a ghost. On the day my doctor called and gave me the diagnosis, we were at a party in New York. Our mission was to meet a
young producer for *The Daily Show* who was considering a segment
on my husband. She was tall and willowy in a too-tight black dress,
and while her breasts may once have been perfect, she had dieted
them down to nothing. Right away she greeted my husband with
Euro kisses, laughed at nothing, then showed him her throat. I was
standing right there! Talk about invisible. Then my phone rang
—Kaiser Permanente with the biopsy results. I tried to talk, but
words didn't come out. I walked through things. I found myself
in a bathroom, washing my face. Then I was twenty floors below,
on 57th Street. I swear I didn't take the elevator. I just appeared.
Then I was on a bus in North Carolina, letting a hard-drinking
preacher massage my shoulders while my friend was dying in Florida. Then it was my turn. I saw my own memorial: my parents'
lawn is covered with cars. They must buy a freezer to store all the
HoneyBaked Hams that arrive. My family and friends gather next
to the river that slowly makes its way past my parents' home. Here,
people take turns telling stories.

My great-uncle tells a story about me as a little girl and my decision to wed the boy next door. My folks got a cake and flowers and
had the judge down the street preside in robes over the ceremony.
The whole neighborhood turned up, and everyone got a kick out
of it. The next day brought the sobering moment when my folks
had to tell me the marriage wasn't real.

My brother tells a story about my first Christmas home from college and how I brought a stack of canvases to show everyone the
nudes I'd been letting the art-major boys paint of me.

My mother tries to tell a story. I can tell it will be the one about the Christmas poodle. But she is overcome. It scares the children the way she folds up in slow motion, dropping to the ground like a garment bag. To distract them, my father decides on a canoe ride—that always was a treat for the kids. Tears run from their eyes as they don orange vests and shove off. Right away, the horse-child screams that she is afraid of the water. She strikes notes of terror we didn't know existed. My son, in the bow, tries to hide his clutched breathing, and then I see the shuddering shoulders of our daughter. She swivels her head, looking everywhere, desperately, and I know she is looking for me. My father, stunned and bereft, is too inconsolable to lift the paddle. My father, who performed more than fifteen hundred field surgeries near Da Nang, my father, who didn't flinch when the power went out at Charity Hospital in New Orleans, my father—he slowly closes his pearl-gray eyes. They float there, not twenty feet from us, the boat too unsteady for them to comfort one another, and we onshore can only wrench at the impossibility of reaching them.

Back inside the New York party, I realized time had ceased to flow: my husband and the producer were laughing the exact same laugh, the lime zest of their breath still acrid in the air, and I saw this was in the future, too, all these chilly women with their iron-filing eyes and rice-paper hearts. They wanted something genuine, something real. They wanted what I had: a man who was willing to go off the cliff with you. They would come after him when he was weak, I suddenly understood, when I was no longer there to fend them off. This wasn't hysteria. It wasn't imagination. I was in the room with them. Here they were, perfect teeth forming brittle smiles, hips hollow as sake boxes.

"That story is too funny," the producer said. "Stop it right there. Save it for the segment!"

In a shrug of false modesty, my husband accidentally sloshed his soda water.

"Well," he said. "Only if you think it would be good for the show."

I suddenly put my hand on the producer's arm. She turned, startled, discovering me.

I used my grip to assess her soul—I felt the want of it, I calculated its lack, in the same way Lady Montagu mapped the microscopic world of smallpox pustules and Voltaire learned to weigh vapor.

You tell me who the fucking ghost is.

There is a knock at the door. It's Megumi!

My husband answers, and the two of them regard each other, almost sadly, for a moment.

They are clearly acknowledging the wrongness of whatever it is they're up to.

They head upstairs together, where I suddenly realize there are Costco-size boxes of condoms everywhere—under the sink, in the medicine cabinet, taped under the bedside table, hidden in the battery flap of a full-size talking Tigger doll!

Megumi and my husband enter our bedroom. Right away, the worst possible thing happens—they move right past these birth-control depots. They do not collect any condoms at all.

My kind of ghost mom would make it her job to stop hussies like Megumi from fucking grieving men, and if I were too late, it would be my job to go to Megumi late at night, to approach her as she slept on her shabby single-mom futon, and with my eyedropper dribble one, two, three purple drops on her lips, just enough to abort the baby he put inside her. In her belly, the fetus would clutch and clench and double up dead.

Megumi and my husband do not approach the bed. They move instead toward the armoire, beside which is a rolling rack of all the vintage dresses I could no longer wear once I lost my bustline. I moved them to the rack, but couldn't bear to roll them out of the room.

Megumi runs her fingers along these dresses.

She pauses only to eye a stack of my training bras on the dresser.

Interesting fact: While you can get used to being titless, the naked feeling of not wearing a bra is harder to shake. You just become accustomed to the hug of one. I recommend the A-cup bras from Target's teen section. Mine are decorated with multicolor peace signs.

Megumi selects a dress from the rack and studies it—it's an earthy pink Hepburn, with a boat neck, white trim, and pleated petticoat. At the Florida university where I met my husband, I was in his presence three different times before he finally noticed me. I was wearing that dress when he did. I wonder if he remembers it.

Megumi holds the dress to her body, studying herself in the mirror. Then she turns to my husband, draping the dress against her figure for his approval.

Interesting fact: The kanji for "figure" is a combination of the elements "next" and "woman."

I study my own figure in the mirror.

Interesting fact: The loss of breasts doesn't flatten your chest —it leaves you concave and hollowed-looking. And something about the surgery pooches your tummy. My surgeon warned me about this. But who could picture it? Who would voluntarily conjure themselves that way?

Megumi waits, my dress held against her. Then my husband reaches out. He has a faraway look in his eyes. With his fingertips, he tugs here and tapers there, adjusting the fall of fabric to the shape of her body. Finally, he nods. She accepts the dress, folding it in her arms.

I do not dagger her. I stand there and do nothing.

Interesting fact: My first novel no one would publish was about Scottsdale trophy wives who form a vigilante group to patrol their gated community. It contains, among other things, a bobcat killing, a night-golfing tragedy, the illegal use of a golf-ball-collecting machine, and a sex scene involving a man and a woman wearing backpack-mounted soda pistols. It was called *The Beige Berets*.

Interesting fact: My second novel no one would publish concerns two young girls who have rare powers of perception. One can read auras while the other sees ghosts. To work the ghost angle, I had their father live in Charles Manson's old apartment. To make the girls more vulnerable, I decided to kill off their mother, so I gave her cancer. To ratchet up the tension, I had a sexual predator named Mister Roses live next door. My husband came up with the name. In fact, my husband became quite enamored with this character. He was really helpful in developing Mister Roses's backstory and generating his dialogue. Then my husband stole this character and wrote a story from Mister Roses's perspective called "Dark Meadow." I can't even say the name of this novel without getting angry.

My husband does not return to the novel he was working on before my cancer. After the kids are asleep, he instead calls up the

website Bigboobsalert. He regards this on slideshow mode, so ladies with monstrous chests appear and fade, one into the next.
My husband has his hand lotion ready, but he doesn't masturbate.
He stares at a place just past the computer screen. I contemplate
these women. I can only see in their saucerous nipples and pen-
dulous breasts the superpower of motherhood. Instead of offering
come-hither looks to lonely men, these women should be feeding
hungry babies, calling on foundling wards and nursing the legion
orphans of the world. We should air-drop these bra busters into
tsunami zones, earthquake epicenters, and the remote provinces
of North Korea!

I kneel beside my husband, slouched in his ergonomic office
chair. I align my vision with his, but I can't tell what he's looking
at. Our faces are almost touching, and though he is lost and sad,
I still feel his sweet energy. *Come to bed,* I whisper, and he sort of
wakes up. But he doesn't rise to face our bedroom. Instead, he
opens a blank Word document and stares at it. Eventually, he types
"Toucan cereal."

"No!" I shout at him, "I'm the one who got cancer, I'm the one
who was struck. That's my story. It belongs to me!"

Interesting fact: Cancer teaches you to see the insides of things.
Do you see the "can" in "uncanny" or the "cer" in "concern"?
When people want to make chitchat with you, even though, if they
took the time, they could see that under your bandanna you have
no hair, it's easier to just say to them, "Sorry, I have some uncanny
concerns right now." If you're feeling feisty, try, "I feel arcane and
acerbic." Who hasn't felt that?

But sometimes you've got chemo brain and your balance is all
woo-woo and your nails are itching like crazy and you don't want
to talk to anybody. Be prepared for that.

Person 1: "Gosh, I haven't seen you in forever. How's it going?"
You: "Toucan cereal."
Person 2: "Hey, what's new? I'm so behind. I probably owe you
like ten messages."
You: "Vulcan silencer." Smile blankly. Hold it.

Our daughter takes on my voice. I study her as she admonishes her
brother and the horse-child to take their asthma medicine and do
their silent reading before bed. When lice outbreaks arrive, she is

the one who meticulously combs through their hair after my husband succumbs to frustration and salty talk.

I keep a hairy eyeball wide for Megumi. She doesn't come around, which makes me all the more suspicious. I wonder if my husband took some of that Pulitzer money and bought a "studio" in the neighborhood. You know, a place to hide your book royalties from the IRS and "get some serious work done." I flip through his key chain, but there is nothing new, just keys to the house, his Stanford office, the Honda Odyssey, five Kryptonite bike locks.

I use my powers of perception to scan the neighborhood for signs of this so-called writer's studio. I try to detect the effervescence of my husband's ever-present sparkling water, the shimmer of his condom wrappers, or the snap of Megumi's bra strap. My feelers feel only the fog rolling in, extinguishing the waking world block by block, starting with the outer avenues.

Interesting fact: The Miwok believed the advancing fog could draw one into the next world.

Interesting fact: Accidentally slipping into the afterlife was a grave concern for them. To locate one another in the fog, they darkened their skin with pigment made from the ashes of poison-oak fires. They marked their chests with the scent of Brewer's angelica. They developed signature calls by which they alone would be known.

For some reason, my family skips archery tonight. And there is no Native American story when the kids are put to bed. Even Bigboobsalert has to wait. In his office, my husband calls up his document and continues stealing my story. I don't shout at him this time. He is a slow and expressive writer. He works most of the night.

Interesting fact: My third, unfinished novel is about Buffalo Calf Road Woman, the Cheyenne warrior who struck the felling blow to Custer at Little Bighorn. I wrote about her life only because it amazed me.

My husband has my research spread before him: atlases of Native American tribes and field guides for botanicals and customs and mythology. I think this is good for him.

I'm there when he hits one last Command-S for the night.

I follow him upstairs. The children are sleeping in the big bed. He climbs in among their flopped limbs, and I want to join, but there is no room. My husband's head comes to rest on the pillow.

Yet his eyes remain open, growing large, adjusting focus, like he is trying to follow something as it disappears into the dark.

Interesting fact: My husband doesn't believe that dreams carry higher meanings.

Interesting fact: I had a dream once. In the dream, I stood naked in the darkness. A woman approached me. When she neared, I could see she was me. She said to me, or I guess I said to myself, "It's happening." Then she reached out and touched my left breast. I woke to find my breast warm and buzzing. I felt a lump in a position I would later learn was the superior lateral quadrant. In the morning, I stood in front of the mirror, but the lump was nowhere to be found. I told my husband about the dream. He said, "Spooky." I told him I was going to the doctor right away. "I wouldn't worry," he said. "It's probably nothing."

Eventually, my husband sleeps. An arm passes over one child and secures another. All the pillows have been stolen, then half-stolen back. The children thrum to his deep, slow breathing. I have something to tell him.

Interesting fact: My husband has a secret name, a Sioux name.

He's embarrassed by it. He doesn't like anyone to say it as he feels he doesn't deserve it. But when I utter the Lakota words, he wakes from his sleep. He sees me, I can tell, his eyes slowly dial me in. He doesn't smile, but on his face is a kind of recognition.

Through the bay windows, troughs of fog surge down Frederick Street.

"I think it's happening," I say to him.

He nods, then he drifts off again. Later, this will have been only a dream.

I near the bed and regard my children. Here is my son, his back grown strong from pulling the bow. Still I see his little-boy cheeks and long eyelashes. Still I see the boy who nursed all night, who once loved to hug fire hydrants, who ran long-haired and shirtless along a slow-moving river in Florida. His hair is buzzed now, like his father's, and his pupils behind closed eyes track slowly, like he is dreaming of a life that unfolds at a less jolting pace.

My daughter's hair is the gravest shade of black. If anyone got the Native blood, it is she. Dark skin and fast afoot, she also has fierce, farseeing eyes. She is the one who would enter the battle to save her brother, as Buffalo Calf Road Woman famously did. Tonight she sleeps clutching my iPhone, the alarm set for dawn, and in the set of her jaw I can feel the list of things she'll have to accomplish to get her siblings up and fed and off to school.

And then there is the horse-child.

Interesting fact: My youngest's love of interesting facts was just a stage. When my illness turned her into a horse, she never said "interesting facts" again.

Interesting fact: Horses cannot utter human words or feel human emotions. They are resilient beasts, immune from the sadness of the human cargo they carry.

She is once again a little human, a member of a weak and vulnerable breed. Who will explain what she missed while she was a horse? Who will hold her and tell her who I was and what I went through? If only she had never been a horse, if only she could remain one a little longer. What I wouldn't give to hear her whinny and neigh her desires again, to see how delicately she tapped her hoof to receive a carrot or sugar cube. But it is over. She'll never again gallop on all fours or give herself a mane by drawing with markers down her back. It will just have been a stage she went through, preserved only in a story. And that, I suppose, is all I will have been, a story from when they were little.

CATHERYNNE M. VALENTE

Planet Lion

FROM *Uncanny Magazine*

Initial Survey Report: Planet 6MQ441 (Bakeneko), Alaraph System
   Logged by: Dr. Savine Abolafiya, Chief Xenoecology Officer, Y.S.S.
Duchess Anne
   Attention: Captain Agathe Ganizani, Commanding Officer, Y.S.S.
Duchess Anne
   Satellites: Four
   Mineral Interest: Iron, copper, diamond, cobalt, scandium, praseodymium, yttrium. Only diamond in desirable quantities. Nothing sufficient to offset cost of extraction.
   Sentient Life: None
   Strategic Significance: None
   A small, warm world orbiting the white subgiant Alaraph. Average gravity is more or less comfortable at .85 Earth normal, but highly variable depending on how near it passes to 6MQ440, 6MQ439, and 6MQ450. Twenty-hour day, 229-day year. Abundant organic life. Excepting the polar regions, the planet consists of one continuous jungle-type ecosystem broken only by vast salt- and freshwater rivers. See attached materials for information on unique flora if you're into that sort of thing. You won't find anything spectacular. It does not behoove a xenoecologist to sum up a planet as "trees big, water nice," but I know you prefer me to keep these reports informal, and I have become both tired and bored, just like everyone else. If you've seen one little Earthish world, you've seen them all. Day is mostly day; night is mostly night; dirt is dirt; water is water. Green is good; most any other color is bad. Lather, rinse, repeat. The fact is the Alaraph star has a whopping eleven other planets, all gas giants, and each one of them

will prove far more appetizing to the powers that be than this speck of green truck-a-long rock.

My team came back calling it Bakeneko due to a barely interesting species of feline megafauna they frequently encountered. The place, I'm told, is crawling with them. Dr. Tum found one sleeping in their cook pit. We've been calling them lions. As you'll see during the dissection this weekend, the species does somewhat resemble the Thylacoleo carnifex *of late Pliocene Australia.*

Except, of course, that they're the size of Clydesdales, sexually trimorphic, and bright green.

Imagine a giant, six-toed, enthusiastically carnivorous marsupial lion with the Devil's own camouflage and you'll have it just about right. The "male" can be differentiated by dark stripes in the fur as well as the mane. The "female" has no stripes, but a ridge of short, dark, dense fur extending from the crown of the head to the base of the tail. The third sex is not androgyne, but simply an entirely separate member of the reproductive circus. We have been calling it a "vixen" for lack of better terminology. No agreement as to pronoun has been reached. The vixen is larger than the male or female and quite a different shade of green — call it forest green instead of emerald green.

The lions represent the only real obstacle to settlement of 6MQ441. Though I have tried to keep my tone light, five attached casualty reports attest to the danger of these creatures. They are aggressive, crepuscular apex predators. There are a lot of them. They show some rudimentary, corvid-like tool use. (Dr. Gyll observed one wedging a stick between the skull plates of a goanna-corollary animal to get at the brain. Dr. Gyll does go on to note that he also enjoyed the flavor of the brain more than the meat.)

At present, I recommend a severe cull before any serious consideration of Bakeneko as a habitable world. See supplementary materials for (considerably) more on this topic.

Moving on to the far more pertinent analysis of the Alaraph gas giant archipelago . . .

A lion moves the world with her mouth. A lion tells the truth with her teeth showing.

One lion rips the name Yttrium from the watering hole. She chews it. She swallows and digests it. She understands her name by means of digestion. One lion's name signifies a lustrous crystalline superconductive transition metal. This separates one lion from lions not called Yttrium. One lion called Yttrium drinks from the watering hole and digests the smallgod MEDICALOFFICER. She understands the smallgod by means of digestion. She feels the concept of honor. Lions who digest other smallgods do not always know what their names signify. One lion gorges on the bones of the smallgod. The bones taste like anatomical expertise and scalpel craft. She slurps up the blood of the smallgod. The blood reeks of formulae and the formulae run down the throat of one lion to fill her belly with several comprehensions of anesthetics and stimulants and vaccines and antibiotics. She gnaws at the meat of the smallgod. The meat becomes her meat and the meat has the weight of good bedside manner.

One lion called Yttrium hunts in the steelveldt called Vergulde Draeck. As well she hunts in the watering hole. All lions hunt in the watering hole. The watering hole networks the heart of every lion to the heart of every other lion into a cooperative real-time engagement matrix. The smallgod inside one lion lays down the words *cooperative real-time engagement matrix* in the den of one lion's brain. One lion called Yttrium accepts the words though they have no more importance than the teeth and hooves left over after a kill. The words mean the watering hole.

One lion hunts through her steelveldt in the shadow of burnt blueblack rib bones and sleeps in their shadows. As well she sees the watering hole all around her. The watering hole lies over the jungle like fur over skin. One lion stands in the part of the steelveldt where the million dead black snakes sprawl but never rot. She sees her paws sunk deep in the corpses of snakes. As well she sees her paws sunk deep in the cool blue lagoon of the watering hole. Comforting scents hunt in her nostrils and on her tongue. Ripe redpaw fruit. The brains of sunspot lizards. The eggs of noonbirds. Fresh water with nothing sour in it. One lion hunts alone in the steelveldt Vergulde Draeck. As well she hunts with every other lion in the watering hole. She hunts with one lion called Thulium. She hunts with one lion called Bromide. She hunts with one lion called Manganese. She hunts with one lion called Nickel who sired her and one lion called Niobium who bore her and one lion called Uranium who carried one lion called Yttrium in her pouch until she could devour the smallgod and enlist with the pride. In the watering hole every lion swims with every other lion. Every lion swallows the heart of every other lion. Every lion hunts in the den of every other lion's brain. Two hundred thousand lions hunt in the steelveldt Vergulde Draeck with one lion called Yttrium. Ten million hunt in the watering hole. The watering hole has enough water for everyone.

Every evening one lion called Yttrium wakes in hunger. She washes her muzzle in the Longer Sweeter River, which flows beneath the steelveldt Vergulde Draeck. As well she washes her muzzle in the lagoon of the watering hole. She leaps and prowls through the part of the steelveldt where husks of giant redpaw fruit lie broken open. Other lions also leap and also prowl. She greets them in the watering hole. In the watering hole they use each other's eyes to find the answer to hunger. One lion called Yttrium finds the words *triangulation, reconnaissance, target acquisition* floating inside her. She thanks the smallgod inside her for this gift.

One lion stops. She becomes six lions. Six lions chase down a pair of sunspot lizards skittering through the burnt blueblack bones of the steelveldt. Six lions sight a horned shagfur. They forget the lizards. The shagfur lumbers across the part of the steelveldt where the hundred thousand dead silver scorpions lie barbed and gleaming. It does not hurt itself but six lions know the scent of carefulness. In the watering hole six lions turn their bellies to the rich sun. In the steelveldt six lions open their jaws. Their green muzzles wrinkle back over black teeth. Out of their mouths the water of the lagoon comes rippling. The water of the lagoon possesses blue heat and blue light. Six lions open their mouths and the water of the lagoon roars toward the shagfur. The shagfur flies upward. The shagfur's neck snaps. Six lions suck the water of the lagoon back into their throats and with it the shagfur. They tear into its body and its body becomes the body of six lions.

A lion moves the world with her mouth.

Six lions stop. One lion called Yttrium pads alone across the part of the steelveldt where the wings of the billion dead butterflies crunch under her paws. As well she plays with one lion called Tungsten and one lion called Tellurium in the shallows of the watering hole. She bites the green shoulder of one lion called Tungsten. She feels the teeth of one lion called Tellurium in the scruff of her neck. One lion called Tungsten ate the shagfur with her. One lion called Tellurium hunts far away in the steelveldt called Szent Istvan. They growl and pounce in the sun. The sun in the watering hole shines dusk forever. The sun shines bright morning and day on the steelveldts. The watering hole forgot every light but twilight.

One lion called Yttrium enters the part of the steelveldt where the thousand dead squaresloths lie. Hot wind dries the shagfur blood on her whiskers. She feels the concept of holiness. Her paws leave prints in the home of the smallgods. Lions not called Yttrium lie or squat on their green haunches or stand at attention with their tails in the air. They lock their eyes to the heart and the liver of the smallgods. The heart and the liver of the smallgods look like the trunks of eight blue trees. The heart and the liver of the smallgods do not smell like the trunks of trees. The heart and the liver of the smallgods smell like the corpses of the hundred thousand silver scorpions and the light of the watering hole. Each of the blue trees belongs to one smallgod and not to the others. Each lion belongs to one smallgod and not to the others. One lion called Yttrium swallowed the meat of the smallgod MEDICALOFFICER. As well a million lions not called Yttrium chewed this meat in the watering hole. Many also own the name of Yttrium. Yttrium numbers among the one hundred and twenty-one sublimities of the smallgods. With one hundred and twenty-one words, the smallgods move the world and so all lions call each other by these utterings of power.

The other smallgods own the names of ENGINEERINGOFFI-CER and DRIVERMECHANIC and GUNNERMAN and GRENA-DIER and SQUADLEADER and INFANTRYMAN and SLUDGE-WARETECH. One lion called Tungsten lapped the blood of the smallgod DRIVERMECHANIC in the watering hole. One lion called Tellurium sucked the marrow from the bones of the small-god SLUDGEWARETECH. One lion called Yttrium hopes their child will feast upon MEDICALOFFICER like her when one lion called Tellurium finishes gestating it.

One lion called Osmium roars in the watering hole and in the steelveldt. He snatches the scruff of one lion called Phosphorus in his teeth and throws her to the ground in the home of the small-gods. His roar owns anguish. Her claws rake his chest. The roar of one lion called Osmium ends. Blood sheens his black teeth. The emerald shoulders of one lion called Osmium droop miser-ably. He tosses his mane at the four moons of coming night and cries out:

"Christ, Susie, why did you leave me? Wasn't I good enough?"

*

Strategic Analysis: Planet 6MQ441 (Bakeneko), Alaraph System
 Logged by: Cmdr. Desmond Lukša, Executive Officer, Y.S.S. Bolingbroke
 Attention: Captain Agathe Ganizani, Commanding Officer, Y.S.S.
Duchess Anne

Aggie, it is the opinion of this particular unpleasant bastard that xeno-ecologists should not mouth off about the strategic significance of a planet just because they know a little damned Latin and can call an oak an oak at five hundred yards. I've read Dr. Abolafiya's report and promptly used it for toilet paper. It's so like her to miss the forest for weeping about the trees. I spent all last night sitting in my quarters reading page after page about some damn green kittens! Who cares? The plain truth was staring her right in the face.

The fact is the Alaraph System represents a unique opportunity to engage the enemy on our own terms. Its remote location removes any concern about collateral damage. Those eleven (eleven!) gorgeous gas giants provide some pretty lush gravitational channels and fuel resources so ample as to be functionally infinite. 6MQ450 (Savine's idiots are calling it Nemea now) has a dozen terrestrial moons where we might even set up mobile staging domes and get some honest fighting into this mess. But it's that dumb green ball Bakeneko that makes it work. It's our lever and our place to stand.

Alaraph sits smack in the middle of a disputed sector. Sure, it's hicksville, galactically speaking, and Alaraph is only barely inside the border, but the sector also includes most of the Virgo neighborhood, which is very much at the center of concern at the moment. Our bestest buddies drew a line around the big lady in the sky, and we drew a line around her, and then they drew a bigger line, and so on. The charts look like a hyperactive schoolkid's drawing.

My recommendation is this: ignore Savine and her pretty kitties. Start settlement protocols. Make sure it's all on known-code channels. We'll probably have to actually put people in a ship with their spinning wheels and what-shit to make it look real. Hopefully we won't actually have to land them, but if we do, well, it won't be the first time. Hell, why not make it real? Build a base down there on Bakeneko, start churning out whatever we can. Barrack platoons. Make it look like we've got something we want in the jungle. Maybe we'll even find something.

They will respond militarily to such a provocation. They've detonated stars over less. And we will finally get to choose the real estate on which to hold our horrible little auction of death. We'll be ready for once.

As for the lions, honestly, I will lose precisely zero sleep over it. Let our jacked-up boys and girls play Hemingway down there with the big cats —they won't be a problem for long.

One lion called Yttrium cannot move. She sprawls flat on her belly in the shallow of the steelveldt's blueblack hipbone. The sky has fallen and broken her back. She whimpers. Everything whimpers when the monsoons come. Rain falls. The world grows heavy and hot. Every lion hides from the sky.

The smallgod inside her offers the words: *Due to the orbital proximity of Nemea, Maahes, Lamassu, and Tybault, Bakeneko lies in the midst of a gravitational whitewater rapids and may experience profound shifts in constants depending on the time of year and local occultations.* The words taste cool and hard and crunchy in her mouth. They feel like ice chips. One lion named Yttrium has never tasted ice. But her smallgod says that worlds hunt in the dark where ice covers every lonely thing.

One lion called Yttrium bounds through the tall grass of the watering hole. The sky in the watering hole still loves lions and does not crush their backs to jelly. One lion called Yttrium runs to run and not to hunt. One hundred other lions who digested the smallgod MEDICALOFFICER run so close by her she can feel the electric bristly of their fur against hers. As well seventy lions who gorged on the smallgod GRENADIER run. They feel the idea of unity. They wade into the lagoon when they no longer wish to run. They paddle and splash. One lion called Cadmium stands on the shore yelling:

"Form up! Form up! Secure the perimeter! Incoming!"

Several striped moths dance just out of reach of his jaws. They do not form up.

One lion called Yttrium experiences the sensation of a door opening and closing in a wall of ice. The experience takes place in her chest and in her muzzle. She has never seen a wall of ice or used a door. These ideas come from the same place as the names *Nemea, Bakeneko, Lamassu, Tybault.* The wall of ice slips down over her green fur and the door opens to swallow her and closes on her bones. One lion called Yttrium stops. She becomes one hundred lions.

One hundred lions standing in the water of the lagoon turn to seventy lions and scream together in hopeless misery:

"You said you loved me!"

Seventy deep green lions bellow back:

"I did! I do! You never had time for me. You loved your ship. You loved your war. You loved the idea of war more than the reality of me. I only joined up in the first place because I knew you'd never choose me over your commission. And I hate it out here. I hate puzzling out new ways to make people explode. I am *alone*. I had no one, not even you. So I found comfort and you want to punish me for it?"

"You went looking!" weep the hundred lions. Water churns around their shaggy knees.

"Yes, Emma, I went looking. Does that make it feel better?" The seventy lions growl. Their ruffs rise. "I went looking and Lara wanted me. You haven't wanted me in years."

One hundred lions snarl in the watering hole. Their black tongues loll through black teeth. "She's twenty-two! She's a kid. She doesn't know what she wants."

"You're thirty-five and all you ever want is another hour in your fucking lab." Seventy lions called GRENADIER rumble in indignation. "And Simon. Or did you think I didn't know about him?"

"Don't leave me, Ben," whimper one hundred lions as though even the perfect watering hole sun has fallen on their spines. "Don't leave me. I'll quit. I'll come home. All the way home. It'll be good like it was a million years ago. When I had short hair and you had piercings, remember? I'll never speak to Simon again. Don't make these last ten years a waste of time."

"She's pregnant, Emma. It's too late. I don't even think I want it not to be too late."

One hundred lions called MEDICALOFFICER crouch in the shallows. Their eyes flash. Their tails warn. "This is such a goddamned cliché. You're a joke. I hate you."

One hundred lions hurtle into seventy lions. Claws and teeth close on skin and meat. The watering hole froths white water. One hundred lions stop as fast as they began. One lion called Yttrium licks her wounds. She does not judge them serious. She opens her jaws in the steelveldt. The water of the lagoon ripples out and lifts up a burnt blueblack bone with its blue heat and its blue light. The bone settles down on top of a hollow stone full of objects. Once one lion called Yttrium flung a hollow stone up and dashed it against the corpses of the billion dead butterflies that cover the floor of the steelveldt. Objects jangled out. She did not know them. She ate some and still did not understand them. The smallgod inside her said: *Those are dresses and shoes. Those are hairbrushes and aftershave bottles.* One lion called Yttrium did not break the hollow stones anymore after that.

One lion called Yttrium has built three walls in this way. Other lions have done more. Soon she will make a roof that will keep out the sky. The lions change the steelveldt Vergulde Draeck with their mouths. One lion called Tellurium tells the watering hole that lions have changed the steelveldt Szent Istvan. With their mouths they built several places called barracks and one called commandstationalpha. One lion called Tellurium wishes to build more places. The smallgod SLUDGEWARETECH inside her requires big places. One lion worries for her. As well she builds their young. As well their young require big places.

But on monsoon days no one can work much except in the watering hole.

One lion called Arsenic crawls on his green stomach toward one lion called Antimony. One lion called Yttrium watches. Skinny pink fish flash in the water. MEDICALOFFICER calls them *self-maintaining debug programs.* One lion likes the flavor of the words and the fish equally.

One lion called Arsenic gnaws at dried lizard blood on his paws. He mewls: "I abandoned my kids, Hannah."

One lion called Antimony licks his face. "I never had any children. I had a miscarriage when I was in graduate school. I was five months along; the father had already gotten his fellowship on the other side of the world and moved in with a girl in Milwaukee. I never said anything. Didn't seem important to say anything. If I said something, it would have been suddenly real and happening and stupid instead of distant and not something that a girl like me had to worry about. I woke up in the hospital with a pain in my body like shrapnel, like a bullet in my gut the size of the moon. And I looked at my post-op charts and I think part of me just thought: *Well, that makes sense. All I can make is death.*"

One lion called Arsenic arches the heavy muscles of his emerald back. He rolls over and shows his striped belly to the sky of the watering hole. The smallgod SLUDGEWARETECH inside him howls and as well he howls: "I abandoned my kids, Hannah.

They're grown now and when I call they're always in the middle of something or just running out the door. They don't want to look at me. Nobody looks at me anymore. My wife just sent divorce papers to my office. Who does that? I called her over and over, just holding those papers in my hand like an asshole, and she wouldn't pick up. I called one hundred and twenty-one times before I got her. I counted. I was going to tell her I loved her. I was gonna make my case. I thought if I could make a grand enough gesture, I could still have someone to come home to. But the minute I heard her voice I just laid into her, yelling until my vision went wobbly. *You knew what this life would be when you married me. I'm doing this for us. For everyone. For our girls. Christ, Susie, why'd you leave me? Wasn't I good enough?* And she just took it all like a beating. When I ran out of breath, she said: *Milo, of course you were good enough. You were the best. But every time I looked at you, all I could see was what you'd done. Your face was my slow poison. If I let our eyes meet one more time, it would have killed me.*"

One lion called Antimony touches her green forehead to the green forehead of one lion called Arsenic. This begins the behavior of mating. He accepts her. Violet barbs of arousal flick upward along his spine. Her heat smells like burning cinnamon. But their joining cannot satisfy. A lion mates in threes. The smallgods mate in twos and do not feel the lack of a vixen lying over those needful barbs. Two lions thrust ungracefully. They hurt each other with a mating not matched to their bodies. The smallgods do not care. The smallgod ENGINEERINGOFFICER inside one lion called Antimony whispers:

"Good thing we're all gonna die tomorrow, huh? Otherwise we'd have to live with ourselves."

Letter of Application (Personal Essay)
　　Filed by: Dr. Pietro S. Aguirre
　　Attention: Captain Franklin Oshiro, V.S.S. Anansi

I've wanted to work with sludge my whole life. I suppose, if you take a step back for a second, that sounds completely bizarre. But not to me. Sludge is life; life is sludge. Without it, we're a not-particularly-interesting mess of overbreeding primates all stuck on the same rock. To say I want to work with sludge is akin to saying I want to work with God, and for me it is a calling no less serious than the seminary. I grew up in the Yucatan megalopolis, scavenging leftover dregs from penthouse drains and police

*station bins, saving sludge up in jars like girls in old movies saved their
tears, just to get enough to try my little hands at a crude recombinatory
rinse or an organic amplification soak about as artful as a finger painting.
I succeeded in levitating my Jack Russell terrier and buckling just about
every meter of plumbing in our building.*

*But now I'm boring whatever poor personnel officer has to read through
this dreck. A thousand years ago, people used to tell stories about taking
apart the radio and putting it back together again. Now we puff out our
chests and tell tales of levitating dogs. Let me spare you.*

*I believe sludge can be so much more. We're used to sludge now. It's as
normal as salt. We're so used to it, we don't even bother doing anything
interesting with it. We use sludge as lipstick and blush for the brain. Cheap
neural builds to brighten and tighten, a flick of telekinesis to really bring
out the eyes, some spiffy mass shielding to contour the cheekbones. You can
buy a low-end vatic rinse at the chemist.*

To me, this is obscene. It's like using an archangel as a hat rack.

*There is no better place to continue my research than the fleet. My pro-
gram to develop synthetic sources for sludge rather than relying indefinitely
(and dangerously) on the natural deposits of chthonian planets in the Al-
magest Belt speaks for itself. My précis is attached, but in the interests of
you, long-suffering personnel officer, not having to ruin your dinner with
equations, I present a simple summary: I believe sludge can win this war
for us.*

One lion called Yttrium feels the concept of apprehension.
Change hunts in the steelveldt and the watering hole. The monsoons broke in the night and the bones of every lion stretch up in
the easy air. The day wants pouncing. The day wants hunting. The
day wants scratching the back of one lion against the burnt blueblack rib bones of the steelveldt.

The smallgods want building. The smallgods want to form up.

One lion called Yttrium bounds down the part of the steelveldt
Vergulde Draeck where the twenty thousand tin jellyfish lie dead
and cracked apart. More of them crunch and pop under her paws.
The smallgod MEDICALOFFICER sends the words *mess hall* into
her belly. She opens her mouth and the blue light and heat of
the watering hole flow out and strangle a sunspot lizard to death
before it can squeak. The blue light and the blue heat pries open
the lizard's skull plates so that one lion called Yttrium can get at
the brains. She laps at her meal.

A burst of dead jellyfish shattering. One lion called Yttrium leaps to protect her kill as one lion called Gadolinium and one lion called Zinc crash through the tin corpse-mounds. Their fur bristles. Their snarls drip saliva. They wrestle without play. Birds flee up to the tops of the tallest trees. Two lions land so heavy, the steelveldt shakes. One lion called Yttrium searches for them in the watering hole. She finds them standing on either side of a warm flat stone. They do not move. They do not bristle. They do not wrestle or play.

"I don't want you that way, Nikolai!" one lion called Gadolinium growls in the steelveldt. He has landed on top. He pants. His eyes shine.

"I'm sorry," whimpers one lion called Zinc. "Oliver, come on, I'm sorry. It was stupid, I'm stupid."

"I have a husband at home," roars one green lion and the smallgod DRIVERMECHANIC inside him. "I have a *home* at home."

"I know," answers the smallgod INFANTRYMAN inside one lion called Zinc.

One lion called Gadolinium digs his claws into the chest of one lion called Zinc. "You don't know *anything*. You've never stuck around with anyone longer than it took to fuck them. You swagger around like a cartoon and you think none of us can see what a scared little kitten you are. Well, I got news for you—we can *all* see. I left more life than you'll ever have."

One lion called Zinc twists and springs free. Two lions face each other on steady paws. "You're probably right. But it goes with the job. We never stay anywhere longer than it takes to drink a little and fuck a little and kill a little and pack it all up again, so from where I sit, you're the idiot, making poor Andrew pine away his whole life back in whatever suburb of Nothingtown spat the two of you out. As for the swagger, I *like* swaggering. So fuck off. I was offering a little human contact, that's all. It's called comfort, you prig."

Wracking dry sobs come coughing up out of the black mouth of one lion called Gadolinium. "I'm so fucking lonely, Niko. It sounds like the most obvious thing in the world to say. I'm surrounded by people all the time and I'm so fucking lonely. I do my job, I eat, I stand my watch, and all the time I'm just thinking, *I'm lonely I'm lonely I'm lonely,* over and over."

"Everybody's lonely," purrs one lion called Zinc. His stripes gleam dark in the sun of the steelveldt. "You don't volunteer for this job if you're not already a lonely bastard who was only happy like four days in his entire dumb life. So stop being dumb and kiss me. Tomorrow we'll probably get our faces burned off before breakfast."

One lion called Yttrium returns to the dish of the sunspot lizard's skull. She feels the sensation of worry. She remembers other days and nights when every lion hunted as a lion and she heard no sacred speech for evenings on top of evenings. Now her ears ache and the sacred speech fills her own mouth like soft meat. One lion called Yttrium thinks these things as she begins the journey to the steelveldt Szent Istvan for the birth of her young by one lion called Tellurium and one lion called Tungsten. She wonders if the lions in the steelveldt Szent Istvan speak so often as the lions of the steelveldt Vergulde Draeck.

The light of the watering hole washes one lion called Tantalum. She stands in the lagoon. Her fur ridge stands erect.

"Form up! Form up! Secure the perimeter!" the smallgod SQUADLEADER inside one lion cries.

This time one lion called Yttrium listens. She must listen. Her body knows how to listen. How to form up. How to understand the idea of *perimeter*. She turns away from the road to the steelveldt Szent Istvan. She never takes her eyes from one lion called Tantalum in the watering hole as she crosses back into the steelveldt Vergulde Draeck. She crosses the part of the steelveldt where the million black dead snakes sprawl but never rot. The smallgod MEDICALOFFICER sends the words *electro-plasmic wiring* into her skull like a twig into the brainpan of a lizard. In the watering hole one lion called Tantalum roars:

"Enemy will come in range at 0900!"

One lion called Yttrium crosses the part of the steelveldt where the wings of the billion dead butterflies lie shattered. The smallgod MEDICALOFFICER writes the words *navigational arrays* on the inside of her eyelids. In the watering hole, one lion called Radium approaches one lion called Tantalum. The smallgod GUNNERMAN inside one lion rumbles:

"Nathan, this is a shitty life and you know it. We should have majored in Literature."

One lion called Tantalum roars another *Form up!* before answering: "Yeah? You ever tried to write a poem, Izzie? You'd get two lines into a damn haiku and quit because it didn't shoot lasers of death and kickback into your teeth."

One lion called Yttrium crosses into the part of the steelveldt where the hundred thousand dead silver scorpions lie barbed and broken. The smallgod MEDICALOFFICER wraps the words *weapons hold* around her heart.

One lion called Radium laughs so that her black teeth catch the heavy gold light of the endless dusk of the watering hole. "True. Drink?"

"Drink," agrees the smallgod SQUADLEADER from inside one striped green male.

One lion called Yttrium crosses into the part of the steelveldt where the husks of giant redpaw fruit lie broken open. The smallgod MEDICALOFFICER pushes the words *radioactive sludgepack engine core* into her soft palate. Other lions stand in formation. All of them carry the smallgod MEDICALOFFICER. All of them crackle with the musk of aggression. Their mouths glow blue. One lion called Yttrium experiences the sensation of a door opening and closing in a wall of ice. The experience takes place in her chest and in her muzzle. One lion called Yttrium stops. She becomes six hundred lions.

Six hundred lions called Emma roar.

Progress Report: Project Myrmidion
   Logged by: Dr. Pietro S. Aguirre, Senior Research Fellow, V.S.S. Szent Istvan
   Attention: Captain Griet Hulle, V.S.S. Johannesburg; Captain Bernard Saikkonen, V.S.S. Vergulde Draeck

This is a classic good news/bad news situation. The good news is that the project has achieved an enormous measure of success and is ready to deploy in small trials. I foresee few to no field issues. We recommend Planetoid 94BR110 (Snegurechka) for initial mid-range testing. There is a small colony of about fifteen hundred on Snegurechka, enough that any transcription errors will quickly become apparent. I have great confidence. We should be able to disperse the sludgeware into the atmosphere and, within six to eight days, have a squadron of about fifteen hundred fully trained soldiers, networked into a cooperative and highly adaptive real-time engagement matrix, which will program itself to conform to the cultural expectations of the subject in order to create a seamless installation. The population should split, more or less equally, among the eight typoprints specified. No adverse medical effects are anticipated. The sludge works with the organic material at hand, enhancing and fortifying it. If anything, they should end up in better health than before.

Now, the bad news. It has not proved possible to separate the skill sets of the typoprints from the personalities of the personnel from whom we pulled the prints. In a way, this makes sense—the process of learning is a deeply personal and individualized one. We do not only retain facts or muscle memory, but private contextual sense-tags. The smell of the foxglove growing in the summer when we took fencing lessons for the first time. The smeared lipstick of our childhood algebra teacher. Arguing about the fall of Rome with a fellow student who later became a lover. We cannot separate the engineer's understanding of propulsion from the engineer's boyfriend leaving her in the middle of her course, the VR game she played incessantly to blow off steam that summer, the terrible coffee at the shop near her dormitory. We may yet find a way to isolate the knowledge without the person, but it won't happen soon, and I understand that time is of the essence. At the moment, the process of print transfer suppresses the original personality to varying degrees, and, as time passes, the domination of the print approaches total.

It doesn't have to be bad news. The original squad consisted of basically stable personalities. They grew very close over the series of brief but intense missions we devised in order to achieve and log a full typoprint. (Casualty reports attached. Unfortunately, the final mission proved to be poorly chosen for research purposes.) They functioned excellently as a unit—they screwed around a lot, but these kinds of small squads usually do. Besides, no one expects these sludgetroops to last all that long. They are the definition of fodder. What difference does it make if they miss some guy back in Aberdeen for a few minutes before taking a shot to the head?

Six hundred lions called Emma race across the steelveldt Vergulde Draeck. Eight hundred lions called Ben lope across the part of the steelveldt where the husks of giant redpaw fruit lie broken open and oozing.

"You said you loved me!" bellow six hundred green lions called Emma.

"You never had time for me!" comes the battle cry of eight hundred lions called Ben.

They collide. Black claws enter fur and flesh. Black teeth sink into meat. Many lions open their mouths. The blue heat and the blue light of the watering hole rips out of their great jaws. It twists through the static-roughened air. The sludgelight seizes one lion called Osmium and one lion called Nickel and one lion called Manganese and one lion called Niobium and one lion called Tungsten and dashes their brains against the floor of the steelveldt.

"I am *alone.*"

"She's twenty-two!"

The jungle shakes. The jungle buckles. The jungle burns. The watering hole cannot handle so much information at once. It shivers. It cuts in and out. This also occurs in the steelveldt Bolingbroke and the steelveldt Duchess Anne and the steelveldt Johannesburg and the steelveldt Anansi and the hundred groaning steelveldts of the world.

"Don't leave me," shriek a million gasping emerald lions. "I'll come home. All the way home. It'll be good like it was a million years ago."

"It's too late. I don't even think I want it not to be too late," answer a million striped and bleeding lions too exhausted to stand.

Situation Report: Planet 6MQ441 (Bakeneko), Alaraph System
Logged by: Captain Naamen Tripp, Y.S.S. Mariana Trench
Attention: Anna Tereshkova, Chief Prosecutor

Bakeneko has been profoundly impacted by the disastrous engagement in the system. The planet is covered in the toxic wreckage of some seventy-three ships lost in action, many the size of cities. Spills of every kind have contaminated the environment and several species are rapidly approaching extinction already.

Of perhaps more concern is the population of marsupial lions first documented by Dr. Abolafiya aboard the Duchess Anne. They seem unaffected by the increase in ambient radioactivity or chemical pollution. Their aggression, if anything, has increased and gained complexity. However, they show signs of contact with a new strain of sludgeware of which we had been previously unaware. The planet is swarming with lions forming into standard military units, building barricades via kinetic sludge, retreating and attacking one another utilizing textbook ground strategies. They communicate in subvocal patterns that strongly imply the presence of a rudimentary neural link matrix. No implications are necessary to conclude that they have come in contact with telekinetic sludgestrands. Orbital observations show the lions have begun to deliberately alter the architecture of the crash sites according to an agreed-upon plan.

I have no explanation for how this could be, and yet it is. Nothing we have developed could affect a population of millions of animals in this way. I suggest you ask Dr. Aguirre what the hell is going on. I understand he is in custody.

I can only recommend a strict quarantine of Planet 6MQ441. There can be no further purpose to our presence anywhere near Bakeneko.

Four moons rise over the steelveldt. One lion called Yttrium opens her eyes. As well she opens her eyes in the watering hole. She finds only quiet. Some death. But every lion knows death. The smallgod inside her sleeps. It found the idea of satisfaction. One lion called Yttrium understands. Blood always brings satisfaction. Perhaps it will wake in hunger again. Perhaps not. One lion feels the concept of contentment. The watering hole gleams fresh and bright. It has many fewer personnel to maintain. Its resolution surrounds one lion in evening light. In the smell of sunspot lizards. In the profound togetherness of nine million lions breathing in unison. Reeds move in the breeze within the heads of every lion left.

One lion called Yttrium stretches her green paws in the moonlight and begins again the long walk toward the steelveldt Szent Istvan. She longs to hear the first roar of her young.

KIJ JOHNSON

The Apartment Dweller's Bestiary

FROM *Clarkesworld Magazine*

The Aincolo

YOU'RE SHOWING YOUR boyfriend what to put in a smoothie and you open a cupboard because he told you he had toasted coconut somewhere and you figure sure, coconut, why not; and that's where his aincolo is: squatting in the yellow serving bowl his mom gave him last year for Christmas. That's cool. You have lots of friends with aincolos. They get in everywhere. But he was so weird about it, picked up the bowl with the aincolo hunched down now, nothing visible but two eyes in a cloud of cream-colored fur, and took it out to the living room and hid it somewhere. Why? Why.

But this got you wondering what else there was: what porn on his hard drive, what numbers in his contacts lists, what texts, what friends, what memories; and you realized you really don't know anything about him and, more, that you don't really want to. You have your own secrets, one of them that you aren't over your last boyfriend yet, and that his is still the only name in your favorites list.

The Alafossi

The bathroom in your new apartment is problematic. Right after you moved, you noticed the fan made weird noises after you turned the shower off—rustling and little rippling squeaks, almost as though there were a bird up there. After a few days, you realized

there really *was* a bird up there, or maybe a couple. And after a
couple of weeks spent contemplating the matter while hot water
poured on your head during your hangover showers, you decided
that they were probably alafossi. You've seen them in the neighborhood, pulling on bits of trash they find or just hanging out in the
trees out front.

You told your landlord, not caring except you thought one
might fall into the bathroom fan. He told you that there's a screen
over the fan so you just dropped it. Anyway, it was winter and you
were worried they might not find another place, and the noises
were nice, like having a pretty upstairs neighbor and you pretending that she's maybe putting on her makeup at the exact time
you're shaving, or maybe even sharing your bathroom and leaning
in to your mirror with that look they get while they're doing their
eyes.

So everyone's getting along fine, and now it's spring; and all
of a sudden there are new noises, and you're like: babies. And it
kind of pisses you off, because there's a thing you can't ever tell
your friends because they would give you endless shit: you want all
that. You're kind of tired of drinking at the Harbor on weeknights.
You want a girlfriend who turns into a wife, and then babies and
even the hard job and the rest of it. You've only told one person,
your dad, and he said, Don't rush it; but you're ready, you are
fucking *ready*. Anyway, in the meantime, you stop smoking in the
bathroom, because it's bad for real babies so probably alafossi babies, too.

The Begitte

Your grandmother told you, "It's good luck to have a begitte in the
house," and they are generally pretty great to have. It's written into
your lease, like renter's insurance and no waterbeds, that a begitte
is okay. Your begitte, which you got from a buddy when he moved
in with his girlfriend, is a spotted one with crazy long white whiskers. It sleeps on the couch most of the time, looking like a novelty
throw pillow. It grooms itself and it does not shed.

Your begitte eats the things that you do not want: dead pens,
wire hangers, empty Kleenex boxes, old running shoes, Coke bottles, toothpaste tubes, the dead AA batteries at the back of the

junk drawer, the needle you lost in the carpet, your neckties from when you had the shitty job at Clement & Neleman, the JPEGs from other people's weddings, the breakup playlists a girlfriend sent you, some porn that got downloaded back in December.

It also ate that one picture of your old girlfriend from, what is it, ten years ago now? The one at the beach where it was pouring rain and she was freezing her ass off but then she got hit by that huge wave and even though she was soaked to the skin she started laughing and couldn't stop, and that was pretty much the moment you fell in love with her. The begitte was right about that one, too.

The Bergdis

There's a black-and-white picture of your mom with a bergdis, back when she was a librarian in St. Paul, before she met your dad and they moved to Iowa. It's hard to tell what color it is, but you can tell from the photo that it's a beautiful one, its long tail wrapped down her arm and around her wrist for balance, and its diamond-shaped face half-buried in her dark hair. She's looking at whoever is taking the picture and laughing, so hard.

Bergdises live anything from thirty to fifty years, but you don't remember seeing it or her talking about it. You don't know who is taking the picture. You don't remember ever seeing your mom laughing like that. There's actually a lot you don't know about the sorts of people that own bergdises.

The Crestone

One of your friends got a crestone a few months back. It's cute, a small reddish male with a black tail that she braids with a little yellow ribbon on the end. It licks crumbs off the kitchen floor. It kills spiders. It helps with zippers up the backs of dresses. If she is hanging a picture, it stands on the couch and lets her know by tipping its head how to straighten it. When she choked on a piece of take-out tikka masala last week, it dialed 911, though she managed to clear her throat before the EMT people showed up.

"You could call *me*," you say. "For stuff like that. You didn't need to get a crestone."

"Not the nine-one-one call," she says. "And I can't keep getting you to come over and kill spiders. Look, it's always there when I get home. What's wrong with wanting that?"

You understand, and you're tempted. A crestone would have your back, too. But maybe you would get a terrible crestone. Maybe it wouldn't tell you when your hem was down or remember your birthday. Plus, your boyfriend left; why wouldn't your crestone?

The Deliper

You still remember that last night. You were both crying, so why was this even happening? If neither of you wanted it, then why could neither of you seem to stop it? And if one of you did, then why wasn't it already over? And then it was, and you drove to a hotel and that was that. But you hated it, even after you got this apartment, even after you got the new furniture, the unsprung mattress, the silverware with the fake patina. You smacked the console table against the wall a little, just so that it had some dents. You hung some family pictures.

Getting the deliper was supposed to help, but it hasn't worked that way. Now there are two of you alone together, and the deliper hates this life just as much as you do.

The Hapsod

You find the hapsod behind the bed when you move it to vacuum, a task you generally avoid; only, last night your girlfriend brought a little jar of powdered honey over, promising to brush it onto you with a feathery cat toy shaped like a bird (which she also brought) and then to lick it off: something she had found online, or maybe one of her girlfriends had. You have to admit that it felt pretty good until she inhaled some, went off in a coughing fit, and dropped the jar. The powder went everywhere. And so, not generally the sort of guy who vacuums but aware of the possibility of ants, you get out the Hoover, pull the bed away from the wall, and find the hapsod.

It is quite small for a hapsod—which you have seen in an occasional YouTube video, plus some of your friends have admitted to encountering one: clearly an adolescent, crouched over the pale scattering of powder on the carpet next to a golf ball that has rolled under the bed even though you don't play golf and don't know anyone who does.

You are pretty sure your girlfriend would swoon over the blunt little antlers, the rabbit-soft gray fur, the immense eyes. Your phone is in your pocket. You could call her. She would be here in no time. She would rush in and coo over your hapsod. She would puzzle over what to feed it, and the words *we* and *us* would turn up a lot in that conversation. She might stay for the night; but really, who needs that? You and your hapsod are fine together. It's probably easier just to break up now and get it over with.

The Hericy

You pretty much stopped using your kitchen once you started that huge project at work, but now you're going to a dinner party hosted by your ex-boyfriend and his new girlfriend. You don't want to look like you're not over him, which you actually are even though you're a little tired of people asking you about it. You figure that hand-baked cheese crackers should fulfill your host-gift responsibilities nicely.

The oven is set to warm, though you're pretty sure the last time you used it was the last time you made cheese crackers. You pull open the door and peer in. Six sets of shiny black eyes peer out. It's your hericy, which vanished three months ago and you never could find, and you must have cried for weeks about it—only now there's another hericy too, a largish good-looking gray one, also some babies rolling around in a pile of shredded parchment paper on one of the racks. They've got a crumpled aluminum-foil dish of dried apricots and a small cast-iron skillet you're pretty sure is not yours, filled with water. Really, you had no idea hericies were so resourceful.

You pick one of the cuter ones and tuck it into the red Chinese take-out box you were going to use for the crackers. You know what's going to happen now. The new girlfriend is going to squeal and cuddle it, hold it up to your ex-boyfriend for him to cuddle it, too. The ex-boyfriend is going to look a little nervous, as though the hericy-bearing ex-girlfriend might make a scene. You know this because it's how you ended up with your hericy. Still, a hericy is pretty cool, so at least she'll have that.

The Lopi

When you move into the apartment on Vermont Street, the lopi are already there, two or three of them fluttering in the corners of each room, just where the walls and ceilings meet. What exactly do they look like? Like bats, like insects, like tiny silent birds the color of smoke? They never seem to rest. And what do they eat? Do they chew on your soap, lick the shampoo residue from the bottles in the bathroom? Or late at night, when you are trying but unable to sleep, do they swoop down to eat whatever has fallen into the aluminum liners under the stove's burners? Wikipedia is of limited assistance here.

Before you moved in, your landlord promised to replace the old windows and repaint the dirty walls, and also to take care of the lopi problem. The windows are done, the walls now a tasteful eggshell color, but the lopi remain, and, really, it's not worth calling the landlord about them. They're not that bad. They replace the pictures you don't hang. The whirring of their wings is a white noise that conceals the silence.

And there are nights when you are alone in the full-size bed in the single bedroom in the new apartment, everything so much smaller than your old life, and just as you fall asleep, you feel their feet on your face, delicate as antennae or memories.

The Louet

No one wants a louet, and yet here you are with one. It has no great love of incense. It eats cantaloupe and germ of corn, which it painstakingly chews from the kernels with its tiny scooplike teeth. It likes being read to, especially Henry James's lesser works. It frowns intelligently at certain places in his travel writing, but you are pretty sure it is faking it; your own appreciation of Henry James is shaky; how can something the size of a kitten be more aesthetically enlightened than you?

And yet it is the louet that suggested you not get the retro haircut; the louet that suggested you stay away from Cheever's later work and your most recent boyfriend. The louet is always right, and you are always wrong, and it is the despair of the louet that you never seem to figure this out before it's too late.

The Mume

The great thing about your mume is how it never makes you feel bad about anything. It loves the food you eat, the movies you watch, the clothes you wear. Feathers ruffled in excitement, it sits on your shoulder when you play computer games. It never gets bored. It never has needs. You're never wrong. You get the feeling that if the mume could speak, everything would end with an exclamation point. How many things in life make you feel as though you just won a trophy for general awesomeness?

It also doesn't care in the least that you were kind of an asshole to your last girlfriend. She didn't care at first either, but by the end she would call you on your shit, which you didn't want to hear, which is maybe the reason why she is gone and you have a mume instead.

The Orco

Most nights, you fall asleep while reading, and your book and your glasses end up in bed beside you, along with your phone, just in case, and your orco. You were always someone who liked to sleep touching, so sometimes in the night you reach across and feel the wand of an earpiece, the book's hard spine, the ruffle of the orco's hair against your palm, its breath on your hand. As long as you don't wake up all the way, it's like all the pieces of someone.

The Hooded Quilliot

You bring your new hooded quilliot home in a cardboard carrier and let it out in the living room. At first you see only the top of its head and then its eyes glaring up, and then the quilliot leaps out of the carrier and onto your coffee table.

Your hooded quilliot has lived in better places than this, with nicer people who made more money and they all adored, *adored* it. It had its own room. It ate oysters flown in from the coast and bruschetta. A professional groomer came every two weeks to trim its nails. *This*—the cute teak coffee table you got for fifteen bucks at an *amazing* garage sale last year, and the rest of it, too: your friends bringing homemade salsa and crab dip for card parties that last till four, and the shoes piled by the back door because everyone here goes barefoot—*this* is not what your quilliot is used to and, to be frank, it is all very, very disappointing.

But then, you're not the one that was in a little steel cage back at the shelter, with a yellow sheet of paper clipped to the bars that said "Abandoned."

The Ravock

There's all sorts of information about it online, postmortem predation. First they eat your lips, your ears, the end of your nose. Your eyelids. The flare of your nostrils. Fingertips. All the places a girlfriend would kiss you first.

Their weak paws and small teeth cannot make a way into your body until you are already dissolving. When is that, like a week after death? Would someone find you before then, and why? Would your absence be noted? When your friend Jason got dumped by his boyfriend, it was almost a week before you realized you hadn't seen any texts from him lately. You assumed he was talking to other people and, anyway, you're always getting busy or distracted, and so is everyone else.

You imagine it: a stroke, maybe, since you're not the overdose type; you, slumped over your dead laptop. Would there be shit? You look down at your ravock, curled into a tight ball on the rug by your feet where it's sleeping off dinner. It's making that little dreaming growling noise it does sometimes. How long would it wait?

The Gray Regia

Your regia hated your old boyfriend, the one who came over after you had your surgery to read children's books to you when you couldn't sleep. He used funny voices for the different animals and you would start laughing and then it would start hurting and you would tell him to stop. And he *would* stop, that was the amazing part. Most guys would have kept on reading, just for a moment or two, teasing maybe or just that little streak of meanness that all men have. He was even really nice to your regia, though it was pretty obvious what it thought of him.

But it didn't work out. You talked about moving in together but then there was an amicable sort of breakup, neither of you quite sure what was happening but both pretty sure it was the right thing. Maybe one of you just lost interest? Anyway, you have the new boyfriend. *He* would have kept reading, but your regia likes him better and maybe your regia knows what you deserve.

The Sandnes Garn

You knew you had a Sandnes garn at your old place, but it didn't bug you or anything. It's a pest, sure, but you learned to make some noise as you walked into your bedroom to give it time to hide. Under the bed? In the closet? The occasional glimpses were kind of cute, little furry horns and beady eyes peeping from behind the dresser you got from IKEA.

When you decided to move in with your girlfriend, your friends offered to help with the lifting. "Does your apartment still have that Sandnes garn?" one said. You nodded. "You need to set some traps or fumigate or something, 'cause otherwise you'll spread them to her place and she'll be pretty pissed. I'll take that dresser if you're not going to want it," he added.

He did take the dresser but you didn't fumigate, and when you got settled in, you realize he was right. You see it sometimes, when she's fallen asleep, half spooned against you, her hair a grapefruit-scented tickle in your face. The Sandnes garn sits on the chest of drawers that came from her mother's house, next to the picture of all her brothers. Its eyes gleam in the hall light. Your Sandnes garn is patient. It can wait. You'll fuck this one up, too.

The Skacel

There are close to a hundred species of skacel. While some can be easily distinguished by the casual observer, others may only be differentiated behaviorally or through DNA analysis. People, it seems, make a hobby of identifying their skacels, and a surprising number get the test, which costs between sixty-nine and just under two hundred dollars.

You're not willing to go that far, but you have spent some Friday nights clicking through the Internet looking for your skacel, which is small, short-beaked, and rose-colored. The short-beaked skacel is a sandy-olive color with a burgundy head and green eye markings. The roseate skacel has a narrow beak with a slightly hooked tip. The lesser skacel eats roaches, spiders, and other vermin but is neither roseate nor short-beaked; plus, your skacel tends not to eat them so much as kill them and leave them in the bathtub.

The eastern skacel drinks cold coffee from a saucer on the floor, which your skacel does not. The Kansas skacel can eat and digest Styrofoam take-out containers. The blue-faced skacel nests most often in linen closets, especially among the guest towels. Given short walks outside and plenty of toys, the Norway skacel can live happily in even the smallest apartment. The king skacel can be trained to retrieve items but resents neglect. Burney's skacel would prefer it if you stopped bringing girls over. So would the noro (a variety of skacel), plus it has some feelings about postmodernism.

Your old girlfriend probably wishes you had spent this sort of time on her. She has a skacel too, with an unmemorable beak but vivid yellow markings along the wingtips. You haven't been able to find that one, either.

The Smerle

You could take your smerle outside and people were always very impressed—an actual smerle, with the long feet and the outrageous tail and everything. Where did you get it? Was it imported?

If you didn't mind telling, how much did it cost? It was like baking your own bagels or driving a 1960s car: a lot of work, but generally worth it.

But then things changed. It started to droop and its colors faded. "Get another smerle," one of your friends advised. "Smerles love company."

"*I'm* company," you said, but you got another one anyway, this one chestnut-colored. Your smerle perked up and now you had *two* to walk on matching leashes: two smerles that played together, twined about one another; a pair that pretty much ignored you.

The Tatamy

"One tatamy grows lonely," your grandmother always says, like, "Troubles come in threes," and you figure that's about right. You started with the one. You were getting dressed for work one morning and there it was, curled tight into a gladiator sandal you'd almost forgotten you had. A week later, there was one in the other sandal, and then a few days later, two more peeked from your Uggs from college, and then there were what seemed like dozens, tucked into all the pairs of out-of-date shoes and boots you'd meant to take to Goodwill. They leave your sensible shoes, the work pumps and trainers, alone. You're not sure whether this is a judgment.

You have no idea what they eat, and you're not sure what they do with themselves when they are not tucked into your shoes like hermit crabs. All night you hear them rustling in your closet, often making small rhythmic bumps, as if they're mating or dancing to house. You don't mind that you are the only one in the apartment who is going to bed early or sleeping alone. But there are times when you imagine turning on the light, stepping into your old shoes, and dancing.

The Wolle

It's hard to pull the trigger on an apartment. The one-bedroom on Massachusetts Street has a southern exposure and tall windows that look down onto cute shops and busy sidewalks, though you wonder whether that would get on your nerves. It's small. If someone came, they wouldn't have anywhere to stay. There's no pet deposit if you get a begitte. Maybe later; right now you can't see making a commitment like that.

On the other hand, the two-bedroom out on California is cool and shady. It's a beautiful neighborhood, right next to a park with a really good disc-golf course. There is nothing on the hardwood floors and no curtains in the windows, so the rooms echo. Guests could stay in the second bedroom, if you bought a bed—but the rest of the time? You think you'll have a hard time filling that space. There are probably lopi.

Or you could just keep sleeping on the couch in Cortney's living room in her place on Vermont Street, and then you don't have to choose anything at all. It's a comfortable couch. She says she doesn't mind, says you're a great houseguest, says you're not a pain in the ass the way some people are. You take out the trash. If you borrow her car, you fill the tank. The two of you order takeout and watch television shows a season at a time. Her wolle curls up between you, dozing.

It occurs to you that in another life, *you* might very well be the begitte, the lopi, the quilliot.

S. L. HUANG

By Degrees and Dilatory Time

FROM *Strange Horizons*

"ON THE BRIGHT side," said Zara, poking at his glasses a week before, "this means you get new eyes."

But I don't want new eyes, he thought.

The surgery isn't bad, as surgeries go. The one he had when he busted his knee ten years ago, as a teen, was much worse. Or maybe it was worse because of what it had meant: that he'd never go out on the ice again.

That had been his identity, and he'd had to forge a new one from the fractured shards of cold and steel and sharpness. It had taken years, and he still wasn't sure the new version of himself wasn't brittle in places—the fault lines barely below the surface, just waiting for one tiny tap by a ball-peen hammer to make the whole construct shatter.

His eyes, his eyes have never been his identity. It won't matter to lose them.

He tells himself that over and over. Through the days following his diagnosis. On the night before the procedure, as he stares at himself in the mirror one last time, and the image blurs. In the hospital just before, as his surgeon squeezes his hand with her gloved one, and the broad white lights of the OR fade out, the last visual he will ever truly see.

He's told everyone else the same thing. *It's not the worst thing in the world, Ma. It's not like I'm an artist. Dad, don't worry—at least we have all the options we do these days, right? It's not that big of a deal.*

He tells himself one more time as he lies in bed following the operation, his world swallowed in darkness behind the bandages, a dull ache prickling through his face like it doesn't know where it wants to hurt. This is just a bump in the road.

In a year it won't even matter.

Cancer.

His doctor said it gently. It was part of a full sentence, even. "We found cancer cells." Later he wondered if she sat there and practiced her delivery before she made calls like this, pronouncing the words with such gravity and care, like she knew how fast he was about to fall and wanted her voice alone to reassure him she could catch him.

Cancer.

The word stalled out in his brain, and his world went sharp and too-bright—the gold tiles of the kitchen, the bright blue ceramic of the fat penguin saltshaker, a drooping rose Zara had laughingly given him when they'd walked the gardens the week before. He wasn't sure what he said back into the phone, only that his doctor must have asked him to come down to the clinic and talk to her in person, because he had. She talked to him and talked some more and kept talking, and then gave him a lot of pamphlets. Diagnosis, treatment options, recommendations. Everything in that same comforting voice, that gentle-calm-grave-understanding one.

After the operation he's blind for three and a half weeks. His parents offered to fly in and take care of him, but the thought of being waited on was worse than the fear of being helpless, and he said no. He's stacked food and water by his bed and run a string to the bathroom. Zara's on speed dial, and she checks in on him twice a day on her way to and from work.

He's too tired to be much company, but she stays longer than she has to anyway, sitting on the floor against his bed and watching TV while crunching popcorn. She translates anything visual with the snark of someone who's turned media cynicism into an art form: "Now they're turning down the dark alleyway! Ooo, I wonder what's going to happen *now.*"

The shows she picks are the type of awfully written crime shows where they narrate almost everything they're doing anyway— "Look, boss." "What is this?" "It's the DNA results. It says the suspect is his father"—and he finds he doesn't mind, for once. The white noise of the television and Zara's voice wash over him and the smell of buttered popcorn fills his nostrils, and he drifts in and out of sleep without ever closing eyes that no longer exist.

Zara's response was the best one, when he told her his diagnosis. "I'm sorry," she said. "I'm sorry we as scientists haven't fixed this yet. That we haven't fucking solved it. We should have a cure."

She was so angry. At the world. At her scientific brethren. At human progress.

With anyone else he might have said, "It's not your fault," but he'd known her too many years not to know what she meant.

"See? This is why science is *amazing*," she'd effused to him through high school, as she helped tutor him through chemistry and physics. "Look what we understand, look what we can build! How freakin' cool is that? This is why I want to do this forever. It'll be like diving into the greatest unexplored frontier."

He always had to admit: when she said it, it did seem cool. He liked seeing the world through her eyes.

It's almost a month before he goes for his implants. The sockets went in with the surgery, twined delicately into the optic nerve. Now he has to have the eyes fitted to the interface, fitted and calibrated and a lot of other words his surgeon and ophthalmologist and the biotechnician used, and he's sure he won't fully understand until he experiences them.

He's feeling better, mostly; at least, he has the energy to sit up for more than an hour at a time, which he counts as a victory. He's spent the weeks listening to more audiobooks than he can count and wishing he could at least get on his computer and game. Once he had Zara sign on for him, and he just lay with the headphones on, letting his guild's banter wash over him, but not seeing what they were laughing and shouting at hurt too much for him to do it again.

He still has mild headaches that drift behind his eye sockets and wake him in the middle of the night; he can't tell if it's pain or discomfort or a psychosomatic phantom. His doctor assures him he has no symptoms of rejection or infection or any of a dozen other complications that are possible but not overly likely.

Zara drives him for the final procedure. "I can't wait to see them," she says. "Are you excited?"

"Eh," he says. "Excited" isn't the word he would use.

"We gotta go to the bar next week and give them a test drive." Her words have grown wicked, slick with innuendo. "Metallic eyes are so hot. I bet the guys will be all over you. Can they give you ones that literally smolder?"

"I don't think so," he says.

Zara's right, of course. There are people who do this electively. Get their eyes replaced, for aesthetics or enhancement or to do careers that require what only artificial eyes can give them. It costs a pretty penny, and he's seen them stalking around and cocking their eyebrows as if to show off the unearthly sheen. Some of them choose inhuman colors, artistic ones, heightening the alien illusion as if to better show off their improved orbs.

He can't for the life of him imagine why anyone would do this by choice.

His cancer was rare, they told him. Even rarer for it to be in both eyes, still rarer to be so aggressive. It felt like a great bitter joke at one point, that out of all the people in the world he had beaten every probability, but instead of a lottery jackpot he'd won cancer.

Despite all the pamphlets and flowcharts his doctor had given him, her recommendations had been very sure. *Caught early. We don't think it's metastasized. We can get it all with surgery. Your prognosis will be excellent.*

It hadn't been a choice, not really. Not when his eyes were replaceable. They'd give him new ones, better ones. Gone the dorky glasses and astigmatism. Gone the squinting and blurriness. Gone the eyestrain when he stared at a screen for too long. His gamer friends even told him enviously how the new eyes would make his skills take off. "You could level up," said Yoshi, breathless. "You could go pro. All the professional gamers are enhanced."

He thought back to his youth, to coming out of a double axel and the edge slicing the ice with his body in perfect equilibrium, and flying, the scenery whirling past in an exhilarating blur. Enhancements weren't allowed in competitive sports. Sports were about pushing the human body, training to your limit, exploring the edges of what humanity could do. Like Zara said about science, except physical.

There was no point in nailed timing and glorious extended lines if you hadn't sharpened every edge of that move a thousand times, yourself. The summer before he'd gone to college, he'd had a second, far easier surgery, when the technology had come out to give him a different kind of new knee. Strong. Flexible. A knee he could skate on, if he wanted, but not compete.

He'd never gone back on the ice.

He's awake when they put the eyes in. They offer him something to sedate him a little, if he wants it, but he says no.

The sensation is strange. Loud. Like they're snapping bones in his face, even though he knows it's just the instruments and the metal crunching against the socket. There's no pain, but he's still not sure he made the right decision turning down sedation.

The moment when he can see again is sudden and without fanfare. One instant it's darkness, the next his left eye is filled with doctors poking sharp metal things into his eyeball.

They warned him it would be "disconcerting"—he almost crawls out of his skin. He manages not to do more than twitch, though he does try to blink reflexively. It doesn't work; his eyelids are being held open. It's like a bizarre horror movie.

His ophthalmologist grins at him over her mask. "Hey, he's back. Can you see us, Marcus?" She waves in his face like an exaggerated cartoon.

"Yes," he says. "Yes, I can see you."

His eye muscles twitch—he can't help it. The focus moves, flicking from one object to the other. Doctor. Nurse. Ceiling. Is it just his imagination, or is there some lag time?

It has to be his imagination. These eyes are better than human ones.

Then why does everything look so flat? The colors seem duller than he remembers, the light harsher. Maybe it's just the room.

His right eye flares to life. It's less startling this time.

Everyone assumed he'd be able to choose whatever fancy new features he wanted. "Get those superfast superspy ones," Yoshi said, making slashing noises that came through the headphones as they joysticked through their screens together. He wasn't sure whether the slashing noises were about the game or his hypothetical eyes.

"Like that guy who does acrobatics with fighter jets. Whatshis-name. I saw a documentary."

"I don't think you do tricks with fighter jets," he answered. Or maybe you did. Suddenly he wasn't sure.

Zara sent him studies on all the new developments. Research hospitals, the cutting edge, the conference in Singapore where they were talking about eyes that could wirelessly link up to your computer and smartphone and give you some sort of integrated heads-up display.

Insurance didn't pay for that sort of thing, of course. And his doctor even explained to him that a lot of the elective enhance-ments people got needed to be combined with a fancier type of neurosurgery, with a lot of words about nerve and electrical inte-gration that he didn't care to ask her to explain. "For you we have to make sure to take everything," she'd said. "Removing the cancer has to be the first priority. Once we do that, we'll use the standard implantation type, which integrates with the optic nerve behind the eye."

He nodded. Not having choices made them easy.

They give him a pair of dark glasses to go home with, and warn him he'll be photosensitive for at least three days and to lie for as long as he wants or needs to with his eyes closed. The mus-cles will take time to adapt, they tell him; some discomfort is normal.

It's less discomfort and more pain—sharp little flecks of it inter-mittently throughout the day, stabbing with his eye movement and over before he can do anything about them, and backgrounded by a fuzzy ache like the precursor to a migraine. He takes the doctors' advice and lies with his eyes closed, but restlessly. This is supposed to be over. He's supposed to be able to open his eyes now and move on with his life.

He goes back to work the following week, but takes frequent breaks to sit in a dark closet. His supervisor is understanding.

He doesn't even try to game. The mere thought of the 3D visu-alizations makes his head ache.

He wonders if these feelings will ever pass completely, or if this is his new reality.

*

"What color are you going to get?" people kept asking him, as if that were the most important thing. Probably because it was the most obvious feature to others, the bright array of metallics that the enhancers and transhumanists showed off so proudly.

He wanted as close to his old color as possible. Dark brown, unremarkable except that it was his. His lovers had always told him he had nice eyes.

They couldn't do brown. Only brighter colors. Something about the way light reflected in the lenses inside—brown was too dark. The physics would have allowed for a light beige, but no one wanted light beige, so it wasn't even in the palette they gave him to choose from. To be fair, he wouldn't have wanted light beige, either.

He wanted to say something stupid about his ethnicity at that point. *But I'm Thai.* Like that would be news to them. Like that made him different from everyone else with tan skin and black hair and dark complexions who would want brown eyes if they could get them. Like stating his ethnicity would change what was technologically possible.

He chose the darkest color he could, a deep, vibrant blue. In any other context, it would have been beautiful.

"I still don't think I'm going to be up to going out this week," he tells Zara, when she prods him to resume their relationship as perpetual drinking buddies.

He hasn't tried a mirror yet. He doesn't know what he looks like. But it doesn't matter; he doesn't want the staring, the fascinated questions from people who assume they're making small talk. The silent judgments from people who assume he did it for enhancement.

He also doesn't want people to know this part of him before they know his name, to see it splashed across his face without him choosing to tell them. Doesn't want to try to meet new people when this will inevitably and painfully be a conversation starter, his new acquaintances stepping on a land mine they don't even know is there. "I like your eyes." "I had cancer." ". . . Oh."

He foresees some awkward silences coming up in his dating life.

He wonders if this would have been easier if he'd been in a relationship when it happened. If a boyfriend looking at him like he was just the same would have made him feel so. Or if that person looking at him ever so slightly differently would have magnified every feeling of alienation.

He's started wearing sunglasses outside all the time, now.

He began paying attention to the transhumanist movement after his diagnosis. Zara knew about it, of course, and had her typical libertarian stance. "Hey, as long as they're not hurting anybody."

He read up on some of the politics online. People wanting to modify themselves. People wanting to modify their children. Other people claiming the right to hate and condemn them for it. It struck him as just as senseless as most politics.

The idea that he'd be entering this world involuntarily—the enhancers' realm, the political imbroglio—disturbed him. That he'd have to claim a stance, take a side, defend the technological advances by virtue of their medical purpose. Be grouped with the believers by default.

He shut his laptop. He had enough to worry about—he didn't want to deal with this, too. Not yet.

He assumed, from the beginning, that the new eyes would be better. Of course he did; that's why people chose to get them sometimes.

But they're not. They're just different.

Sure, in every objective sense he can see better. No glasses, and once the photosensitivity dies down, the detail he perceives is startling, especially texture. His vision is better than perfect. But the impression of flatness has persisted. His doctors tell him that no testing has shown anything less than normal depth perception, so maybe it's all in his head—but doesn't all vision happen in your head anyway? If it's in his head, doesn't that make it real automatically?

Despite the perfect vision, he constantly feels like he's seeing everything through a slightly dull filter, like someone fiddled with the brightness and contrast settings on his monitor. Nothing he can pinpoint, but it drags at him. Sometimes, some three o'clocks in the morning, he wants to claw out his new eyes and scream.

Sleeplessness.

The bouts of insomnia and anxiety started before his surgery. It wasn't nerves; he trusted his doctors. Instead, he would wake from cluttered dreams and stare into the darkness.

He'd stretch his eyes wide, willing the pupils to dilate, to suck in as much as they could possibly see.

Then he'd turn on the light and let the flash burn his retinas, let the purple splotches appear and his eyes tear up, wanting to hang on to the feeling.

The first time he looks in the mirror, depression smothers him, like tentacles wrapping thickly around his heart.

He's been mentally preparing himself for the color, for the metallic sheen. But the *shape* of his eyes is different. He hadn't expected that. They look wider to him, perpetually surprised, slightly goofy. He hates it.

Maybe the effect will diminish. The skin around the implants is still red and a little puffy, as if irritated at the interlopers. He knows how it feels.

He's never thought of himself as vain. He's always been decent-looking, but was arrogant enough to believe it didn't matter. That he didn't care. That appearance isn't what's important.

Until now, when he looks at his face and sees a freak.

Now he realizes he is vain, has always been vain, and maybe there's not a damn thing wrong with that.

He feels a sudden stab of guilt and empathy. He's only been able to tell himself he's indifferent to his looks because he's been lucky enough to be satisfied with them. He closes his eyes, shutting away the image in the mirror.

He'd cry, but his tear ducts are gone.

"Look out!" Yoshi bellowed in his ear the week before his surgery, as a troll burst through the wall. On the screen, his avatar ran.

Life and death, he thought. Such a simple decision to make.

His had been simple, too. "You're so strong," his mother kept telling him. "Your father and I talk about it, how brave you are."

Brave? Why? The doctor had told him he had cancer, and this was what needed to be done. What would they have expected him to do instead? Say no?

Life and death. It made things easy.

His avatar ran around the corner and dropped its hands to its knees, panting.

My days are like yours now, he thought at the computer-generated character. *The troll swings its club, and so we duck and kick and run. But it's not the fighting that's the hard part, is it?*

The pain improves; the headaches lift. He's doing dishes one day when it strikes him he's forgotten about his eyes for the last few minutes. He hadn't realized that until now he's been constantly aware of them, a low-level hum of discomfort, of difference.

As the days go by, it happens more often, for longer stretches. He's surprised sometimes when he catches his face in the mirror — his self-image is still one in which he has human eyes, and when the reality reminds him, his mood twists into depression.

But even that changes. The first time he looks in the mirror and doesn't notice his eyes, he realizes it happened five minutes later, and it jars him.

The human mind is infinitely adaptable.

Cancer.

When other people said the word, it was this huge, ominous, grave thing. People died of cancer. People lost loved ones to it. People wrote sad books and movies about cancer, and somebody always died and it was always tragic and noble and had important messages about the meaning of life.

Having cancer was different. He didn't feel particularly tragic. Or noble. Or enlightened.

It was just shitty.

He was fortunate to have a good prognosis. He'd slog through it and out the other side, and life would go on.

Life goes on.

His friends and colleagues get used to his eyes far faster than he does. For a while he watches for them to be still looking, still gossiping, still curious, but eventually even his paranoia has to admit that he's yesterday's news. The realization is somehow both relieving and depressing. After all, he still has to deal with his new eyes, and now he has to deal with them alone.

He starts seeing a therapist once a week. She's a very pleasant person who listens to him ramble and asks him gentle questions that make him feel less stupid. He's always more at peace after his sessions with her.

He starts forgetting to wear the sunglasses. He finally signs back on to his gaming group, and his friends greet him with whooping cheers for about thirty seconds before they're all focused on the game again. Their lack of continued concern is somehow both liberating and slightly disappointing. He files that away to talk to the therapist about.

A good part of the time now, when someone does a double take at him on the street, he doesn't remember why until he thinks about it.

"This is just something I have to get through," he told his parents once.

He hadn't thought that statement would be so full of raw truth.

A year passes.

He remembers thinking last year that in a year none of this would matter. He was both wrong and right about that: it matters, and it doesn't. The cancer changed him, but he adjusted. Nothing is radical. Nothing is revelatory. But nothing is inconsequential, either.

It's just . . . life. Like everything else.

He's started dating again. There haven't been as many awkward silences as he feared. It turns out he can say, "I had cancer in my eyes, but I'm okay now," and then smile and change the subject. Zara turns out to be right that his eyes probably attract more people than not, and he's learned not to mind.

He thinks about going to a rink and trying skating. Just for fun. Who knows, after all these years it might be more pleasant than painful. Zara offers to go with him. "I'll fall on my ass so much, I'll make you feel great. Instant moral support." He smiles. He doesn't have to decide anything now.

He starts struggling to find new things to talk to his therapist about, and they drop to meeting once a month, then as-needed. He keeps her card taped to the fridge.

Sometimes he sees transhumanist rallies on television or chances across articles on the Internet. He's still not sure how he feels about them. He'd say he's indifferent, but as a man with a fake leg and fake eyes, he's one of the media-dubbed "cyborgs" already.

Well, screw it. He's indifferent. It feels satisfying, somehow, to claim his right to have no political feelings about the technology in his body.

At night he sleeps well. And in the morning, he opens his eyes and goes about his day.

LIZ ZIEMSKA

The Mushroom Queen

FROM *Tin House*

IT'S THE MIDDLE of the night and the woman can't sleep. Perhaps it's the full moon, or the *fool* moon, the kind of moon that keeps you awake thinking stupid thoughts. She puts on her glasses and sees that it's 2:55 a.m. The man lies beside her, generating too much heat. There's a small brown dog nestled into her armpit. A white dog sleeps at her feet. She's wedged in like a crooked tooth.

For about an hour now she's been thinking about the two races of man. One race is very, very slow; they crawl upon the earth like slugs, leaving silvery slime trails wherever they go. The other is very, very fast, about as fast as electrons, and when they pass by they leave a radiant residue, though you can never be sure if you've actually seen them, or if there's a smudge on your glasses picking up the light in a funny way. The two races live side by side, completely unaware of each other, sucking on the same earth.

But on the night of the *fool* moon, a special moon that occurs once per decade—or every 9.3 years, to be exact—when the moonrise lag is equal to the moonset lag, causing great upheavals of the deep, cold waters of the Pacific Ocean, the slow race can sometimes catch up to the fast race.

All of this is just nonsense, of course. It's the duration that's the important part here. Nine-point-three years is a long time to be married.

The woman sighs, digs her toes into the fur of the white dog. She looks out the sliding glass doors at the garden in moonlight —they still don't have curtains. It really is beautiful out there, like a scene from *Last Year at Marienbad*, her favorite film, but enacted with owls, rabbits, voles, and coyotes. A tiny, mournful cry reaches her through the partially opened door, some small furred thing losing its life out beyond the chicken-wire fence and the scrub grass, where the man keeps the pile of lumber that once was the trellis under which they were married.

A bit of white flashes by in her peripheral vision—a flap of cloth?—then disappears behind the farthest clump of jade plant.

Kicking off the blankets, the woman rolls carefully from the bed without disturbing the dogs and the man. She shakes a sweater from a pile of clothing the man has left on the floor, where the jeans and underwear he shucked off still retain his shape, as if his body had dematerialized. She walks to the door and looks out. It's the one thing they had agreed on, a luxury but well worth it: the lawn, the decorative clumps of shrubbery, the drooping leaves of the Mexican bamboo, the flax. And then she sees it again, a figure in white moving very quickly across the grass, diving behind the nearest jade plant. It is coming closer to the house, where the dogs and the man lie paralyzed in sleep.

The woman slides the glass door open wider and steps out onto the deck, closing the door behind her so the dogs won't get out. She stands there under the moonlight. It has a definite tone, like minute silver shavings striking glass, a tone that shifts as the silver bounces off her head, her shoulders, her upturned face. The moon is past its highest point; she can feel her energy weakening. She thinks again about the two races of man. What if the fast race can sometimes clean up the messes of the slow? Her toes grip the worn redwood boards.

She steps off the deck onto the lawn. What is wrong with her marriage anyway? Nothing that she can point to, no crimes, no infidelities. Some petty cruelty in times of stress, but who isn't guilty of that? Nevertheless, she feels restless, bored, *slow.* There's nothing wrong, but everything's wrong: she'd like that on a T-shirt, please. For months now she's been fantasizing about being more than she is, but it isn't coming true. What if she could step into the fast, fast world without being missed? What she wants now, more than anything, is a placeholder, someone to keep her life intact while she goes on a little reconnaissance trip.

The woman reaches the jade plant just as another woman steps out to face her. They are nearly identical, mirror images, though the doppelgänger, as befits a creature of the moonlight, is more glamorous-looking than her sun-fattened twin. Even so, to examine herself three-dimensionally is unnerving for the woman. Mirrors don't tell half the story. Is this really how her nose looks in profile? The skin of the other is beaded with tiny water droplets, her white cotton nightgown translucent with moisture. The woman reaches out to touch her, but just as she's about to make contact, the other one grabs her by the throat and tosses her into the jade plant. Our woman is gone. Her double crosses the lawn, steps onto the deck, slides open the door, dries her feet on the pile of discarded clothes, and climbs into bed.

The big white dog lifts his head and wags his tail. Then he stops, sits up, and looks again. He's confused. His eyes tell him one thing, but his nose, the more reliable source, tells him another: she may look like his beloved mistress, but she smells, definitively, like rabbits. There's nothing the white dog loves more than killing rabbits.

He wags his tail again. The woman sleeps. Maybe his nose is wrong. He's getting old, almost six, though not very old for his breed. He has another six years in him, he can feel it, but things are starting to break down. He can't bank the curves like he used to while chasing the neighbor's cat off the lawn. Thank God the mangy creature was taken out by coyotes (tracked, tricked, cornered, and devoured—he had heard it all one night). Thank God he didn't have to suffer the humiliation of another failed chase, the cat's mocking glance as it jumped onto the fence and disappeared into the street, where the dog could not go without a leash.

The woman digs her toes into his fur, like the other one had done. She turns onto her side, pulls the blanket up to her chin, tucks the brown dog, that small, furry shithead, into the curve of her body, like the other woman had always done. Everything checks out, except for the strange straw-and-dandelion smell of rabbits. Perhaps, like his hips, his nose is starting to go.

Our woman, the original, sinks into the soft, moist ground at the base of the jade plant, terrified. She tries to scream but soil fills her mouth. She opens her eyes, but there is nothing but darkness, no air, no sound; the world is extinguished. And yet she lives on, packed in with the weight of the earth; no longer merely slow, she is *immobile*.

*

The small brown dog knows of course that the creature in bed with him is not his beloved mistress, but he also realizes that it would be dangerous to let on that he knows. This "woman" is so much a copy of *his* woman that it obviously took a great deal of effort to pull off the stunt, and great effort usually comes with great desire. The small dog knows there's nothing more dangerous in the world than desire. He also knows that to raise an alarm about this fake would be to risk the life of his true mistress, who is obviously being held captive somewhere.

What he needs to do now is to convince this dimwitted white brute to stop sniffing her like she's some kind of rabbit he'd like to snatch up in his teeth and shake to death. That stupid white fluff likes to leave his rabbit carcasses all over the lawn, those pretty little brownish gray rabbits that come to feed on the garden and leave their delicious little pellets behind for the small dog to find and eat. That's what the dumb white leg-humper is missing: this fake woman doesn't smell like rabbits; she smells like rabbit poo.

Some fun facts about fungus, the most prevalent organism on the planet.

About 250 million years ago, a meteorite struck down around Siberia, creating tidal waves, lava flows, hot gases, and searing winds. The land grew dark under a cloud of debris, causing 90 percent of its species to die out. Fungus inherited the earth.

Animals are more closely related to fungi than to any other kingdom. Millions of years ago, we shared a common ancestor. Man is just a branch off the fungal evolutionary tree, the branch that evolved the ability to capture nutrients by surrounding its food with cellular sacs, or stomachs. As animals emerged from the water, they developed a dense layer of cells to prevent the loss of moisture. Fungi, on the other hand, solved the problem of moisture retention by going underground.

Mycelium, a web-like mass of tiny branching threads containing one or more fungal cells surrounded by a tubular wall, is the vegetative part of fungus. It's the stuff that grows, spreads out, running through every cubic centimeter of soil in the world. Every time you step on a soccer field, a forest, a suburban lawn, you walk upon thousands of sentient cells that are able to communicate with one another using chemical messengers. Mycelium helps to heal and steer the ecosystem, recycling waste into soil. Constantly moving, mycelium can travel several inches a day. There have been experiments conducted in Japan that show slime mold successfully navigating a food maze, choosing the shortest distance between two points, disregarding dead ends.

Mushrooms are the fruiting bodies, the reproductive organs, of mycelium. They feed on rotting things, like rabbit poo, and troubled relationships.

The Mushroom Queen was tired of living underground. She can assume any form. Her skin is nicer than human skin, firm and white, and it has no pores, only spores, because mushrooms are self-propagating, which can get pretty lonely. So she deposed herself and came to the woman's house from the east, traveling west along the shore of a wide green river, over the Appalachians, beneath the Great Lakes, flowing right across the vast midwestern plains. She was born over a century ago in the unkempt garden of a red-brick house that was once a home, then a nursery, then a nunnery, and is now again a home. That is where *our* woman arrives now, sucked across the country and extruded from the ground beneath a trellis of tangled vines that sprout purple flowers in the summer. They have switched places, the discontent of one calling to the desire of the other. Nature abhors a vacuum.

The man thinks this woman is an improvement over the other. He does not know there's been a switch, only a sudden unexplainable change in personality. He doesn't question it, as he is unaccustomed to questioning good fortune when it rains down on his head. This woman is more pliable than the other, more eager. The other one never wanted to make love in the morning. As he sinks his fingers into her flesh and buries his face into her dark curls, he falls in love with her all over again.

The Mushroom Queen has gills behind her ears, but the man doesn't seem to notice. He delights in her damp, earthy scent, her luminous whiteness, the way her body forms around his. She opens her mouth to laugh at his jokes but no sound comes out. Already the walls of the bedroom are covered in green slime.

At breakfast, the man makes "the usual": boiled eggs, toast, a wedge of Brie, apricot jam, and good strong oolong tea. The Mushroom Queen sniffs the Brie with its waxy casing of *Penicillium camemberti*.

It wouldn't do to eat a distant cousin, so she pushes it aside. "You love Brie," says the man. The Mushroom Queen shrugs. "Maybe you're pregnant." A grin spreads across his face. She laughs her soundless laugh. If the Mushroom Queen wanted to propagate, all she would have to do is point a finger and a mushroom would bud out of its tip. She pushes her egg away, too fresh. "What can I get you instead?" says the man.

The contents of the compost bin would be nice, thinks the Mushroom Queen. She would like to take the bin to the guest room, where it is dark and damp, spread it out on the duvet, and roll around in the coffee grounds, potato peels, and carrot tops, but that wouldn't be good for their relationship.

This is her first time imitating human form, and the Mushroom Queen is not very good at it. One breast has come out larger than the other, and she forgot to grow earlobes—what will she do with all the earrings the other woman owns? Her hair moves by itself, as if animated by a celestial wind, for, unlike human hair, which is just dead keratin, the hair of the Mushroom Queen is alive— mycelium embedded with loam to make it black. Speech is difficult, though not impossible. Moving air through a mushroom is no problem, just look at the spore dispersal of the *Calvatia gigantea*, the giant puffball. It is the tone modulation she can't get right. Much easier to nod and smile; the man does all the talking anyway.

The Mushroom Queen bathes in the normal way when the man wants to take a bath with her, but she doesn't feel fully clean in water. Later that afternoon, while he's napping, she goes out into the garden and tears open a bag of premium potting soil, rubs herself down beneath the shade of the tree ferns.

Our woman's body is pressed down through a root sieve, releasing the one hundred trillion cells of her symbiotic microbiome into the soil. They wriggle away in search of a new host. What's left of her—the approximately 37.2 trillion cells that had once been organized into brain, liver, eyeballs, bellybutton—are absorbed by the tube-like hyphae of the North American mycelium web and fanned out across the garden. In her newly dematerialized state, she is simultaneously nowhere and everywhere. But this is just an illusion, a temporary form of vertigo brought on by the sudden vastness of her being. In reality, she covers a little less than three square acres, one edge dangling in the cool green waters of the Hudson, the other pushed up against the crumbling blacktop of Route 9. A red-brick house squats on her chest like a poorly digested meal. There's a maple tree growing out of her forehead, its flame-colored leaves the color of her panic.

Days pass. At night the mist rises from the Pacific, rolls up the cliff, and settles around the house, muffling it from the street noise and the neighboring houses. One morning when the dogs step out, they find the lawn covered in mushrooms. The woman used to come out with a weed puller and scoop out each fungus by the root, afraid the dogs would eat them. Her people had been mushroom eaters in the old country, but she'd lost the knack of sorting edible from poisonous. The dogs sniff the ground beneath the nearest jade plant. There's something lingering among the watery stems of the succulent, a sad, familiar scent of laundry detergent and lemon verbena hand lotion.

What does the Mushroom Queen end up eating? Fermented things, like pickles, soy sauce drunk directly from the bottle, kimchi, forgotten packages of ham gone slippery with pink goo, old strawberries melting into their green plastic basket, glued together by a whitish fur. She hides eggs under the quilt in the unused guest room until they rot, sucks out the yolks, and eats the shells. She drinks beer, endless bottles of beer, though the man is surprised. The other woman never touched alcohol, "empty calories" she called it. But the Mushroom Queen never gains weight, only biomass.

How does the Mushroom Queen feel about the dogs? They're competitors for the rabbit pellets, and they don't give anything back, their own waste too rich in erythrocytes from the meat they eat to grow mushrooms. And the dogs are suspicious of her, particularly the little one. It's a good thing they can't speak. The man ignores them; he doesn't even feed them. Their leashes hang limply from the doorknob. The Mushroom Queen can't risk walking them, can't expose herself to the neighbors, not knowing their names. Besotted with the myth of personhood, humans have names. Mushrooms have no such cult of personality. All is mycelium; mycelium is all.

*

It takes a great deal of concentration to concentrate the self, but nothing banishes lethargy like a well-defined villain. At five cell layers instead of one, our woman has condensed herself from three acres down to the size of the lawn in her own backyard, but still flat and thin enough to move through the soil without having to worry about snagging parts of herself on telephone poles and sewage pipes. She's heading west against the earth's rotation, gliding through the rich dark loam of the Hudson River Valley as easily as a manta ray swimming through water. She's heading home, never mind that home is the place from which she had recently dreamed of escaping.

The small dog leads the white dog on a tour of the woman's closet to check the shoes, but not one pair is missing, not even the pale blue sneakers she wore when she walked them around the block —the only time she ever left the house. The man left the house almost every other morning, coming back hours later smelling of coffee, cigarettes, and something else; something younger.

The woman had taken them on endless loops around the neighborhood, making sure to pass by the little parking lot where the tourists stop to gawk at the cliffs above the ocean, and also to admire the dogs and, by extension, the woman. She needed it, that daily dose. The man used to admire her, a long time ago, back when the dogs were just pups, but then he began spending his days staring into a glowing screen. The small dog liked to snuffle under his chair, looking for crumbs—the man is such a messy eater. He'd get up on his hind legs and peer at the screen, trying to make sense of the sinuous writhing shapes, until the woman walked into the room and the image changed instantly to regiments of black ants marching on a plain white ground.

Born into darkness, the Mushroom Queen cannot sleep at night. She wanders the house picking up objects at random, trying to guess their purpose. There are wedding photographs on the piano, the man and the woman surrounded by smiling friends and children playing musical instruments. The man is ducking under colorful streamers as the wedding party braids them around a maypole. The bride looks young and happy in her butterfly-embroidered skirt. Will she try to find her way back? What will happen if she does? Which one would the man choose?

The Mushroom Queen wants to experience love, that's why she came here in the first place, but she also wants to be *known*. She has learned about the distinction from the books in the basement of the red-brick house. Seeping into soggy cardboard boxes, she consumed page after page of *Romeo and Juliet, Pride and Prejudice, Wuthering Heights,* even *Gone with the Wind,* and realized that to be loved is not the same as to be known. For instance, Karenin loved his wife, Anna, in his own way, but he did not *know* her. How is the Mushroom Queen going to get the man to see her clearly, to fall in love with her without the use of deception?

There are so many things she can do: *Pleurotus ostreatus,* the oyster mushroom, to unclog his arteries; *Lentinula edodes,* the shiitake, with its powerful anti-cancer, anti-viral, and anti-herpes polysaccharides; *Ganoderma lucidum,* the reishi mushroom, for longevity and sexual prowess. On the other hand, there are the death caps and the *Amanita ocreata,* the destroying angel—so like the common button mushroom, except for the veil connecting its egg-shaped cap with its chubby stem like a fibrous foreskin. That and its ability to instantly dissolve the mammalian liver. The Mushroom Queen loves these mushrooms, but to win the man's affection, she'll do it the hard way, using nothing but the clumsy human heart, or a reasonable fungal facsimile.

The small dog is angry with the white dog. More than once he's come upon them in the hallway, the big white idiot lying on his back, paws in the air, tongue lolling out of his big stupid grin, writhing under the hands of the Mushroom Queen as she scratches the fur of his belly. Disgusting.

The small dog follows the imposter as the man leads her onto the lawn, to the hidden bower where he and the real woman used to make love in the afternoon. He watches from behind the acacia tree. He had seen before how the man leaned over the original, pumping the essence out of her, making her cranky and bloated, causing her to crave salt and sweet, spicy and sour. He had seen it but what could he do? The Mushroom Queen is not depleted by the man's attentions. Each day she grows stronger. Even now, as the man leans over her, she arches her neck, her eyes roll back until only the whites are visible, her mushroom-brown lips split apart in a silent yawl of pleasure.

*

Our woman trails the rains as they sweep across the continent. By early August she's made it all the way to the eastern slopes of the Rocky Mountains. She climbs the foothills, the land rising and falling, rising and falling, like a roller coaster. At five thousand feet she reaches a broad, high meadow sheltered from the winds by an aspen grove. She weaves in through the orange paintbrush and chamomile, primrose, fireweed, and horsemint. The air is cool and thin, the soil moist and rich. It would be lovely to settle down in this place, but vengeance keeps her moving. A jagged wall of granite rises above her, a hundred times more daunting than the Appalachians. Up ahead is the timberline, where there are no trees, no soil, and very little water. She can't go up but she can go *through*, releasing polysaccharides, glycoproteins, chelating enzymes and acids, creating micro cavities in the granite, but that would take too long, and time is running out—she can feel it in the very tips of her hyphae. She hunkers down among the lupines, pushing up mushrooms as she contemplates her next move.

The man would have liked the paradox of a mushroom attempting to scale a mountain. A paradigm shift is what you need, he would have said. They used to be good at playing games with words—it's what brought them together in the first place. But over time, they learned that there are only so many stories to tell, and only so many ways to tell them, and in the end, silence is better. At least now, if she made it home alive, they will have something new to talk about.

The Mushroom Queen's attention is beginning to wander. There's a hollow spot under the floor near the bookshelf where the termites have devoured an entire wooden slat. Rats gnaw all night long in the crawl space above the bed. The garage roof sinks in the middle like a swaybacked horse, pine roots have buckled the concrete driveway, silverfish scuttle among the cutlery—the house is calling to her and she has no choice but to respond. After all, she is a saprophyte, a primary decomposer of twigs, grass, stumps, logs, and other dead things. It's what she does; it's nothing personal. Besides, human love tasted so much better on the page. Already her hyphae are slipping in between the man's cells, prying them apart. Soon she will dissolve him. The dogs are next. For now their abundant fur has kept them safe, that and their reflexes. But how long can they dodge her sticky threads? The Mushroom Queen has stopped feeding them, hoping to slow them down. They are starving, growing weaker by the day. Even the rabbits have left the lawn.

Unloved, unbrushed, his belly empty, the small dog fills his days with happy memories. Like laundry day, when the woman used to dump the fresh load onto the bed and drop the small dog into the heap so he could root and dig and roll around in the warm fragrant cloth. No one does laundry now that the woman is gone. The dishes go unwashed, the floors unswept. Without the woman's constant ministrations, the walls themselves are caving in.

Back at the timberline, beetles arrive and land on the woman's mushroom caps, burrowing deeply into her soft pink flesh, piercing through into her spore-rich under layer. How good it feels to be cleaned out like this!

I cook, you clean, the man used to say, preferring the "deep eroticism" of a woman standing at the sink in purple rubber gloves.

Another rainstorm comes and the beetles are picked up by the wind, up and over the mountain they fly, spores clinging to their legs and wings. They settle down near Grand Junction, Colorado, depositing her spores onto the ground as they scuttle away into the fields. She sinks into the mulch and germinates a fresh new webbing of mycelium. Reborn, she waits a few more days to see how many more of her progeny will make the crossing. By early September she's half her size, but twice as determined.

Hugging the Colorado River all the way to the California border, our woman enters the Imperial Valley. Shimmying along irrigation canals, she runs her mycelium under fields of cabbages and cantaloupe, sucking up life-giving nitrogen as she fans up and out into San Bernardino County. From there she hops lawns all the way to Point Dume.

The Mushroom Queen has established a mycelial perimeter around the house extending from the Pacific Coast Highway to the very edge of the cliff above the Pacific Ocean. Through the septal pores of her naked hyphae tips, she is aware of her rival's imminent approach. The Mushroom Queen enters the kitchen in

black galoshes. She puts on a pair of purple rubber gloves, steps
into a couple of trash bags, making sure to tape the plastic se-
curely at the wrists and ankles, and wraps several yards of cling
wrap around her head and neck. Then she begins to whip up a
batch of poison. The house, the man, the dogs: they all belong to
her now. She's not willing to share them.

Giddy, triumphant, our woman breaks through the cracked terra-
cotta patio and surges under the grass, following the lawn mower
as the man, recklessly barefoot, paces out wide, even rows. The
Mushroom Queen walks behind him in her battle gear, a bottle of
viscous liquid attached to the garden hose, saturating the lawn in
the path created by the mower.

Our woman can taste the individual ingredients: olive oil, baking soda, apple cider vinegar. Such wholesome things, how often
had she used them herself, but now they are *dissolving* her. She
sinks down through the sod, then the three inches of trucked-
in dirt, the chicken-wire gopher barrier, and finally settles into
the sand and clay that are the true soils of this land. A fleeting
thought crosses her mind: without the artificial lawn, the fertilizer,
the monumental water bills—all things that she and her husband
fussed over together—the Mushroom Queen could never have
gained a foothold in their lives, because nothing grows in clay and
sand, not even fungus. Clinging to the underside of the mulch
layer, the woman crawls all the way to the back and takes shelter in
the shade of the disassembled trellis.

Our woman tries to will herself back into human shape, but it's
no good. She lacks the skill, and furthermore, she could no longer
remember what she looked like. The Mushroom Queen, as she
can see despite the many layers of Saran Wrap and Hefty Cinch
Saks, doesn't look very human anymore. Her forehead bulges in
the middle from the pressure of the cap, her body has grown cy-
lindrical, stem-like, but love is blind.

How can she fight the Mushroom Queen if she can't get by the
poisoned lawn? Perhaps she could enlist the aid of some parasitic
bacteria? But that might harm the dogs and the man and, really,
she's never been the kind of person to up the ante out of stub-
bornness until everything around her lies in ruins.

And then she remembers something she heard as she was

driven from the lawn, something whispered to her by the *Onycho-mycosis* fungus growing on the third toe of the man's left foot: the man knows there's been a switch.

He knows and he does not miss her at all.

The fight goes out of her completely. She shrinks a little bit further into herself, the sand and clay robbing her mycelium of precious fluids. If she stays here a moment longer, she'll have to wait until the spring rains to make her escape. Where will she go? Back to the meadow with the primrose and chamomile? Back to the garden behind the red-brick house with its ancient loamy soil? What had once been a prison now seems like Elysium.

And to be completely honest, she doesn't blame the man; he owes her nothing. Wishing to escape is the same as escaping. Her vanity is bruised, but maybe things are as they should be. What is a trellis after all but a perforated wooden barrier; a basket made of loose twigs through which the things you gather can fall out along the way.

She does not miss her human form. What a relief it is to escape that tired paradigm of head-torso-limbs, so much more trouble than it's worth. She likes her new spread-out state, her very own magic carpet; she can go anywhere.

She had longed to join the fast race, but now instead she's joined the eternal race: fungus will survive the destruction of the environment, the melting of the polar ice caps, the rising of the waters. Fungus will survive until the Earth falls into the sun, and maybe even after. She's gotten what she wanted. Well, almost.

She does not blame the white dog for betraying her with the Mushroom Queen. After all, he's just a dog, uncomplicated, happy-go-lucky, like the man, a love pig. But the small dog is different. She has always suspected that he isn't a dog at all, but a demoted human soul sent back to earth in a fur suit to atone for his sins. The small dog can be made to understand.

She has a plan, but it's risky, given her limited skills as a relatively new fungus. Her mycelium is plenipotent—it can create any type of mushroom—but she lacks control. Some of the beetles that came to her rescue in Colorado didn't make it to the other side of the mountain; they died writhing in the meadow. But what are her choices? The Mushroom Queen is distracted with the man, but eventually she'll turn the dogs into soil. At least if the woman can transform them, just as she had been transformed, digest their extracellular matrix, carefully separate their cells and braid them into her mycelium, they can be together.

The jade plant, a desert species, does not waste energy on growing an extensive root system. Its roots are shallow and wide and spread out from the stem horizontally mere inches below the surface in order to capture every drop of rain. These shallow roots act as a protective umbrella for the creatures that live below—an entire family of alligator lizards, a pair of carpenter bees. The male bee is black and shiny, about the size of a store-bought strawberry. When he takes to the air, his wings make the sound of a miniature chain-saw. The female looks even bigger than her mate because of the dusty saffron hairs covering her golden body. Wherever she flies, she leaves behind the scent of flowers—no wonder the male can't resist her. Under the jade plant where she first entered the soil, among the lizards and bees, our woman spins out fresh strands of mycelium and begins weaving a mat, a raft. A lure.

The small dog walks over to the nearest clump of jade plant. Shaky with hunger, he lifts his leg against the plump green leaves. That's when he sees them: three little mushrooms growing out of the lawn at the base of the plant. They're pink and tender with snug-fitting egg-shaped caps, arranged in an arc like the tips of a woman's fingers. Those familiar pink fingers that used to offer little bits of cheese, then reach for the tuft of hair that grows out of his head and scratch and scratch until he couldn't take it anymore. He can picture his mistress standing on tiptoe somewhere underground, reaching and reaching for the surface, only her fingertips break-ing through to the mist-dampened air.

   He starts digging frantically, trying to get her out before she suffocates, soil flying around him, clinging to his russet fur, but there are no fingers beneath the tips, no hand outstretched, no woman, just mushrooms. He sighs a deep, shuddering doggie sigh. She's never coming back, his beloved mistress; he'll never see her again. No one misses her but him. Despondent, he opens his small, sharp-fanged mouth and eats the mushrooms, one by one, until there's nothing left but a dug-out scar of earth at the base of the jade plant.

DEXTER PALMER

The Daydreamer by Proxy

FROM *The Bestiary*

DEAR GENEERTECH EMPLOYEE #_____:

Hello! We're glad that you're considering serving as the host of a Geneertech Corporation Daydreamer by Proxy. We know that this is not an easy decision to make. This document will provide answers to some of the questions asked frequently by prospective hosts. Over one hundred twenty Geneertech employees have chosen to host Daydreamers in the past three years, and all of them have gone on to have remarkably productive careers within the company. Seventy-three percent of hosts have received one or more promotions within two years of hosting, compared with a four percent promotion rate for the same period across the company as a whole. So we think you'll find hosting a Daydreamer to be an experience that's rewarding as well as fun. Some hosts wonder how they ever got along without them!

Why host a Daydreamer by Proxy?

Geneertech is a company that lives and dies by its employees —it is your loyalty, hard work, and creativity that have made us the world leader in the field of designer non-sentient life forms. But every day is a hard-fought battle with our competitors in the marketplace, and the Daydreamer by Proxy is a way for you to help ensure your continued loyalty to us in these perpetually difficult financial times.

Think: don't you feel more loyalty to Geneertech, more fealty, more *love*, in the morning? You arrive at your desk at sunrise, and your first cup of coffee helps you focus on your task: determining the proper shape of a creature's wing, or the best source genome for the *medulla oblongata* of a specially commissioned servant animal. All problems seem solvable. But in the afternoon, after you have received your cafeteria rations and worked for a few more hours, your mind begins to drift. Even though you love Geneertech as you love yourself, you cannot focus on the mission-critical tasks at hand—you would rather ponder a dead romance beyond recovery, or a chess position you abandoned last night in midgame. You are daydreaming to run out the clock until your shift ends. In short, you are stealing processor cycles from the company! But you are only human, you say. Nonetheless—tasks are not being completed; problems are not being solved; MoreauCorp is landing lucrative contracts and eating our lunch.

Hosting a Daydreamer by Proxy will allow you to concentrate on work-related tasks through the afternoon period until quitting time; you may also find that it yields significant quality-of-life benefits outside the workplace. Throughout your day it will serve as the better angel of your nature.

What does the Daydreamer by Proxy look like?

The Daydreamer by Proxy is the result of the combination of several proprietary genomes held by Geneertech, including variants of the silverfish and the Komodo dragon (but it is *not* part human, despite rumors you may have heard). It is about a yard long, an albino, somewhat reptilian, semi-conscious being. An array of two rows of twelve slender, translucent legs runs down either side of its body. You'll notice that its face shows evidence of the whimsical nature of its designers—beneath its snout, its long drooping whiskers hang down on either side of its squelching sucker of a mouth, while its large pink liquid eyes—not human eyes!—display a constant childlike cheer. The Daydreamer by Proxy is always happy! But it's happiest when it has a home, just as you are happy because you know that you have a home at Geneertech.

What is the installation process for a Daydreamer by Proxy?

The installation process will be an enjoyable, memorable experience for you! Upon arriving at the Geneertech campus, you'll go to the Installation Hall instead of your usual workspace. You'll be escorted to a room where you'll be shown excerpts from films you loved as a child, while an administered anesthesia starts to take hold. After an hour—clunk! You're gone.

While you're sleeping, a team of surgeons will drill an unobtrusive series of twenty-four holes along your spinal column and a twenty-fifth into the back of your neck, just at the base of the brain. Once that's done, the rest takes care of itself—we simply place and align the Daydreamer by Proxy on your back, and all on its own, it inserts its legs into the holes along your spine (and this sounds worse than it really is, but the legs have sharp claw-like appendages, and they'll burrow their way through your vertebrae to make direct contact with your spinal column). Meanwhile, what we call the Daydreamer's "information tube" slides out of the back of its neck into the twenty-fifth hole—the tube will then extrude a series of thin filaments that will interface with several of your brain centers, but you won't even feel it. (And don't be afraid of any mind-control stuff: the Daydreamer can intercept and receive signals from neurons, but it can't transmit. It's perfectly safe!)

The installation process takes about three hours; we'll also give you eight work-hours off with pay to become acclimated to your new friend. Then, the next day, you'll be ready to reap the benefits!

What are the benefits of a Daydreamer by Proxy?

We're glad you asked! The first, and most significant, is clarity of *mind,* clarity of *purpose.* Remember how your mind is in the afternoon, drifting toward that delusional, distorted memory of a love that escaped you, its playback suffused with false colors and delirium. Such is the duplicitous nature of daydreams; such is their insidious siren's call, luring employees toward the perilous shoals of decreased performance ratings. But once you have chosen to host the Daydreamer by Proxy, you will no longer be cursed with such afflictions. Your once-lazy brain will seek its usual refuge during the late hours of the second shift to find that your childhood sweetheart's once-soft skin has returned to the sandpaper that it truly was, that her once-poetic professions of love have returned to the stutters and lies they truly were. For your Daydreamer will have taken the burden of your daydreams upon itself. It will wear the false smile that would have crept upon your face; in your place it will experience the delusional happiness that would have distracted you from your duties. And you will experience the truer, better, more *authentic* happiness that comes from the accomplishment of a challenging endeavor. Believe us when we say this. Studies show.

That sounds great! What else can I expect?

Additional benefits include double rations from the cafeteria (you're eating for two now!) and an entire made-to-measure wardrobe provided by Geneertech, suitable for work, play, and formal occasions. (Since installation of the Daydreamer by Proxy is permanent, you'll find it difficult to shop for clothing off the rack. But no time is too early to step up to the elegance of bespoke fashion!)

Excellent! I can't wait to get started!

We don't blame you! But just so that you're completely informed in accordance with federal law, here are a few examples of the kinds of questions that come to us from hosts of Daydreamers by Proxy, before and after the installation procedure.

Q: My family doctor has advised me against installing the Daydreamer by Proxy, saying that there's a risk in "unnecessarily drilling holes along your spine, then permanently attaching a genetically engineered parasite to vertebrae C7-T12 that'll have access to both your spinal cord and your brain." He is being rather unreasonable about the whole thing. What can I say to him to convince him that this isn't nearly the problem he thinks it is?

A: Bwa-ha! The "parasite," as your self-interested family practitioner calls it, is perfectly safe. And if anything were to go wrong (which it won't: in the past forty installation procedures there has not been a single death), the extensive health coverage provided by Geneertech (health coverage that you would be hard-pressed to equal by moving to another company, that you'd have to do without if you were for some reason fired for non-performance) would ensure that in the event of an irreversible paralysis-induced paraplegia, you would be well taken care of. You can undertake the procedure without fear, whether that fear is of the non-negligible chance of the loss of motor control or the facility of speech, or of a job market that is notoriously unfriendly to people like yourself, who are no longer fresh out of college, easy to train, and ready to take on the world.

Q: As of late I have developed a certain rapport with a colleague who has also chosen to host a Daydreamer by Proxy. Though I would not call this love, or even lust—recent events seem to have inexplicably robbed me of the capability to feel such emotions—we do share a certain affinity for the tasks at hand, and during our prescribed off-task conversational periods, we have found that we both enjoy the films of Carl Theodor Dreyer. And our Daydreamers seem to get along as well—when they come within close proximity, they emit a certain keening chitter—*Chee-chee-cha? Chee-chee-chee-cha!*—and I can feel the legs of my Daydreamer clutching at my spine, producing shivers that are now the closest thing I can feel to erotic stimulation.

I am considering asking this woman to accompany me to a double feature of *The Passion of Joan of Arc* and *Vampyr* at the local drive-in. Now that I have a Daydreamer by Proxy, are the forms indicated in Standard Operational Procedure Three for managerial permission for interoffice liaisons sufficient, or must I fill out additional forms as well?

A: Good question! You don't need to fill out any additional forms besides those mentioned in SOP-3. However, you'll want to read the pamphlet entitled "Mating Procedures for Daydreamers by Proxy" before you hit the town with your new companion. And remember that Daydreamers by Proxy, whether living or dead, eggs produced by Daydreamers by Proxy, offspring that hatch from such eggs, and the genome sequence of the Daydreamer by Proxy are the property of Geneertech; theft of company property will be punished to the fullest extent of the law. Go get 'em, tiger!

Q: After six months hosting the Daydreamer by Proxy, I'm discovering some side effects other than the expected slight weight loss, constant hunger, and occasionally unreliable memory. For one thing, according to my wife, the Daydreamer's face is beginning to physically resemble mine: its eye color has changed from pink to brown, and its cute little Fu Manchu mustache has fallen off. "Now it does that little thing with its mouth that you do, when you're thinking hard," my wife says. "It's kind of cute."

In addition, it has begun to speak on occasion—its voice sounds like a poor imitation of mine, as if its throat is lined with gravel. No one would mistake its speech for my own, but it is somewhat embarrassing when I am deeply engaged in a task in my workspace and the

Daydreamer suddenly blurts out, "Taste this foie gras! Taste it!" or "Chicken: standing on sixteen," or "Aw, yeah, back that on up over here, baby."

Also, the Daydreamer by Proxy is seducing my wife. Though we have marital difficulties that are proving insurmountable, my wife and I still sleep in the same bed out of long habit. However, I sleep on my side with my back to her, which leaves the Daydreamer facing her. Recently I awoke in the middle of the night to hear the Daydreamer's raspy whisper. "Do you remember our first time?" it said. "We packed a picnic basket with decadent delicacies, broke into the abandoned opera house, and ascended to the darkened stage. Oh, at first we *tried* to practice restraint and decorum, but in the end we couldn't help ourselves: the feast ended with us smearing marmalade all over our faces and dousing each other's bodies with anisette. And then: the second, shameful feast that followed. Do you remember?" My wife stifled a giggle. "Yes, the shame, the *shame*," she whispered back. "Make me feel it again!" The Daydreamer's legs contracted tightly in my back, hard enough to make my feet kick. My wife has never giggled like that for me! And we have never even been inside an opera house: opera gives me hives! Our first kiss was in the linen aisle of a Wal-Mart! What on earth is going on here? What is to be done?

A: Relax: this is normal.

RACHEL SWIRSKY

Tea Time

FROM *Lightspeed Magazine*

BEGIN AT THE BEGINNING:

His many hats. Felt derbies in charcoal and camel and black. Sporting caps and straw boaters. Gibuses covered in corded silk for nights at the theatre. Domed bowlers with dashingly narrow brims. The ratty purple silk top hat, banded with russet brocade, that he keeps by his bedside.

The march hare, each foreleg as strong as an ox's, bucking and hopping and twitching his whiskers. Here, there, somewhere else, leading his hatter a merry dance between tables. Rogering by the mahogany slipper chair. Knocking by the marble bust of the Queen of Hearts. Upending rose-patterned porcelain so that it smashes on the grass, white and pink fragments scattering like brittle leaves.

Fur, soft and lush. Warmth like spring. That prey-quick heartbeat, thump-thump, thump-thump.

As he pushes into that plush passage, the hatter finds himself wondering what kind of hat might be made from the pelt of a hare. He imagines stretching out this glorious fur to be pulled until only the finest hare wool remains. He would brush it with long, liquid strokes of mercury nitrate, that crystalline solution which drove him mad long ago.

A pair they were:

The hatter, twitching and tottering. His muscles no longer obeying his mind.

The hare, biting and buckling. Wild as any animal in spring.

Intemperate, the both of them. Foolish, feral, barmy, off their heads. Imprudent. 'Round the bend. Daft.

Spent.

Twinkle, twinkle, little bat!
How I wonder where you're at!
Up above the world you fly,
like a tea tray in the sky.

Twinkle, twinkle, little Hare!
I have caught you in my snare!
Hop on down my bunny trail;
I could use a piece of tail!

Twinkle, twinkle, Hatter dear!
While some men may find you queer,
You are just my kind of chap!
Stick your feather in my cap!

The girl in the blue dress has been gone a measureless while. Her brief, uncivil interruption left its mark like a tea stain on the tablecloth. Abrasive as she was, the chit, she was the most interesting thing to happen in a while.

The caucus races are over. The white rabbit has been bustling about. The caterpillar has grown even more insufferable than usual. Of late, a strange pig has been spotted wandering the woods, in search of pepper.

The girl ought to cut her hair. Also, she's much too large, or much too small, or at any rate, definitely the wrong size. She demonstrates no aptitude for recital or croquet, and she never did show a proper appreciation for tea.

But interesting, briefly, yes. Though insufficiently mad.

It is never polite to go out-of-doors without a hat. One's hat should remain on one's head no matter the extremity. Even if the rest of one's clothing should happen to be removed by some improbable whim of the weather, such as a particularly dexterous gale with a penchant for buttons, one must be sure to hold one's hat fixedly on one's head.

The hatter is a poor man. He has no hats of his own. Those he keeps on his head or in his house are merely inventory, soon to be shuffled away when a purchaser is found.

The hatter sits by his hare, the animal's head lying in his lap so that he may stroke his long, satin ears. The dormouse has gone, seeking less tumultuous environs in which to nap. All is quiet but for the sound of cheshires hunting in the woods, all absent stalking and sudden teeth.

"Thank God for tea!" says the hatter by way of initial venture. "What would the world do without tea? I am glad I was not born before tea."

The words once belonged to Sydney Smith, but they're the hatter's now. He and the hare have taken to speaking entirely in quotations as one of the many diversions that occupy their endless tea time.

The hare seems unmoved by the hatter's adoring exclamation. He stares morosely into his teacup. "'Tis pity wine should be so deleterious," he says sadly, "for tea and coffee leave us much more serious."

The hatter takes affront. "There is a great deal of fine poetry and sentiment in a chest of tea!"

The hare gives a delicate, prudish sniff. "Love and scandal are the best sweeteners of tea."

"Tea tempers the spirit," answers the hatter, "and harmonizes the mind."

The hare, all conciliatory now, hops to his feet. He takes his lover's hand in his paw and tugs him toward the tea tables. "If you are cold," he says with lingering sweetness, "tea will warm you."

March hares make better lovers than white rabbits. Ask Mary Ann. She'll tell you the same.

Q: Why is a raven like a writing desk?
    A: Because they both have quills.
Q: Why is a vain woman like a hatter?
    A: Because they both love their hare.
Q: Why is tea time like eternity?
    A: One begins with tea and the other ends with it.

*

Let us be clear about this:

When the Queen of Hearts accused the hatter of murdering Time, she was telling the truth.

Did the hatter kill Time? Yes. Is that the reason why the hatter and the hare are forever caught in this interminable tea time hour? It is.

But is a soldier in the wrong when he dispatches an enemy of the empire? Is a father guilty when, in protecting his daughter from highwaymen, he resorts to his rifle?

No. A man should not be excoriated for self-defense.

Time provoked the hatter. No man can question it.

Tell the truth—have you not felt the indignities of Time? The way he rushes when you wish to linger with a lover, but dwells stagnantly on the endless sprawl of an agonizing wait? Have you no gray hairs? No twinges? No creaking joints?

Admit it. Time has provoked you, too.

A hatter should never be forced to construct hats at the behest of a deck of cards.

So many hats.

Hats for winning and hats for losing. Hats for playing Old Maid and Old Bachelor and Our Birds and Dr. Busby. Rain hats for days when shuffling threatens to leave anyone exposed. Debut hats for when the pack is first opened, and funeral hats for when everyone has become too wrinkled to go on.

Hats, always red and black, black and red. The hatter tried to give them vibrant yellows and restful blues, verdant greens and shimmering purples. When that failed to appeal, he offered hues only slightly off-true. Why not wear a scarlet bonnet or a crimson coronet with wired vermillion lace? A gray bowler, perhaps? A silver derby?

Certainly not, the cards replied, clutching their hearts and diamonds, brandishing their clubs and spades. *We want red and black and nothing more. Black, true black, as black as respectable ladies in mourning. Red, proper red, as red as the first summer roses (and we will not tolerate facetious remarks about roses that bloom in other colors).*

We like what we like and we want what we want, and if you will not provide it, then we will be forced to take our custom elsewhere, and then how will you earn your tea?

Who would not go mad from monotony as much as mercury?

Day after day, an endless scape of red and black, black and red, black, black, red, red, black, red, black, red, black. Pulling, carroting, mixing, carding, weighing, bowling, basoning, planking, blocking, dyeing, stiffing, steaming, lining. Dawn to dusk, only seeing the sun at tea time, that brief six o'clock break for Ceylon and cucumber sandwiches.

In nature, even rabbits do not have sex like proverbial rabbits, and so by extension, logic dictates that hares do not have sex like proverbial hares.

The tea party, however, is not nature. The march hare wears a pocket watch and a striped Arlington waistcoat and a cravat. His crimson wool frock coat is double-breasted with a pointed front. He sips Earl Grey from a rounded pot that faces his host, using a moustache cup to spare his fur.

Gentlemen do not importune ladies with unseemly urges, but neither the hatter nor the hare are gentlemen (or, for that matter, ladies). So once their verve is replenished by the restorative properties of Darjeeling, the two mad creatures return to their lustful adventures.

Now, you may find yourself overcome by distaste—or even disbelief—that a tea party, no matter how protracted, could eventually degrade into the kind of scene best left for a bawd house. But have you ever found yourself trapped in a single afternoon for a ceaseless, innumerable progression of what would be hours if Time were alive to account for them?

In truth, such scenes can occur even if Time is only sleepy. Try it for yourself. Host a tea and block the way out. See how long it takes your trapped guests to go to grass.

The normal amusements suffice awhile: small talk, singing, making personal remarks to young girls in blue dresses. But soon enough, if your gathering includes individuals of some sophistication—gentlemen who've traveled in foreign lands, ladies who double as cockish wenches, that old scoundrel everyone suspects as being the anonymous author of the blue editorials that turn up occasionally in the post—soon enough, someone will suggest a bit of knock and dock. First the knock. Then the knockers. By the time someone's about to answer the door, you'll have to pause to fan the dormouse with a napkin. Whoever knew the drowsy rat was such a prude?

The hatter and hare have always known theirs were restive souls
—Move along! One place on! New chair! New tea!—but before they
began this seeking of each other's flesh, they'd never realized that
the secret to dispelling their disquiet was exertion. Exorcise with
exercise. Move down! One more time! Switch sides! Switch ends!

In and out, up and down, across tables and under them. Sometimes sipping lapsang souchong. Sometimes lapping marmalade.

The hatter succumbs to cackling. The hare, overcome by de-
lectable sensations, chews mindlessly through his frock coat, the
hatter's derby, two embroidered tablecloths, and a linen napkin.

Parts previously known only by their anatomical designations
earn salty soubriquets. The hatter's whore pipe blows the grounsils
into the round mouth. The hare's snip of a plug tail prigs and
waps and tups away. Arbor vitae in blind cupid, gaying instrument
in the nancy, bawbles on the belly, fist around the lobcock, playing
the backgammon until it's a dog's ride, hatter and hare both worn
to nubs.

There is a secret to making tea time last forever.

One must not necessarily murder Time—although if one is
possessed of a distressing enough singing voice, this provides a
good start to the endeavor. One must simply prevent the moment
from ever reaching fruition.

Sit at the table. Fold your napkin. Tip your hat. Select a sand-
wich. Lay it on your plate. Pour milk. Decant your tea. Lift your
cup. Let its brim touch your lower lip. Tip the porcelain until a
hint of steam enters your mouth. Close your eyes. Inhale the scent
of warmth and Indian leaves. Press your tongue against your lip.
Imagine the rush of hot, dark, sweet liquid.

New tea! Change places! Start it all again!

> "The time has come," the Hatter said,
> "To talk of many things:
> Of white—and green—and flow'ring blends—
> Of spiced tisane that stings—
> And why the mad are hot to trot—
> And whether love has strings."
>
> "But wait a bit," the Hare replied,
> "Before you make a peep;

You've had fun chewing my bun,
But now I need some sleep!"
"No hurry," the Hatter agreed,
"I guess I went too deep."

But love has strings, the Hatter knew,
Though they remain unsaid.
They're tatters, tears, and arguments,
And cheeks left wet and red.
Perhaps he should have stayed alone
And buttered his own bread.

Many lovers have believed their trysts provide sanctuary from
Time. Their yesterdays forgotten and their tomorrows unimagi-
nable, they picture themselves frozen in the moment of mutual
embrace.

They are wrong.

Even the hatter and the hare, living in their chronological isolation, know that such things only last forever in the technical sense.

Time will eventually resurrect itself, as it always does, slicing the
world back into metered moments, ordering the sun across the
sky, pushing everything relentlessly onward, forward, skyward.

Outside the moment of tea time, the hatter must return to his
hats, the hare leap back to his hutch. Everything will change.

The return of Time will swiftly tear away the remnants of the
hatter's sanity. He thinks of this as he watches his hand, even now
shaking so that his teacup rattles in its saucer. When Time is reborn, his hands will flail without volition. Raucous, inappropri-
ate, he will bark and guffaw to keep the cards from guessing how
far gone he is. His ears will register sound but not meaning, his
tongue numb as he tries to form words. Another beaver pelt laid
out, the nitrate of mercury applied to it, and the hatter will tatter.
Eventually, mercury will kill him. It is an occupational hazard.

As for the hare, he does not know what to think of Time.
Long ago—or at any rate, before they understood that, as Time
was dead, he had forsaken them—the hare had pulled the
pocket watch from his vest and gazed at it appraisingly. Time
had never halted before in his experience, and he was inclined
to blame mechanical failure. The tea table was woefully under-
supplied with watch-making tools, but it was well stocked with

butter, so the hare decided to substitute the latter for the former. He crammed as much butter as he could into the gears, aiming to grease them along. Alas, its only effect was to kill the watch as thoroughly as Time himself. The hare slipped the watch back into his pocket and did not look at it again. Now he wonders if he might, in fact, have made the problem worse. Is Time trapped, unable to force its way through clogged gears to wind himself up again? What is the relationship between Time and timepiece?

At any rate, in retrospect, he is glad to have buttered Time. He does not wish to retreat into the woods, where his Arlington vest will become soiled and his pocket watch will be lost the first time he must bound away from a cheshire's leap. Even the white rabbit, traveling under the queen's protection, cannot hold on to his gloves and fan.

Worse than that, the day will end, and soon the week and then the month. He will become an April hare, a May hare, a June hare. Who knows what kind of personality he will have in July? What does an August hare feel? Are September hares kind? It seems a poor risk to regain his sanity at the cost of losing himself. Madness is a comfortable garment, though not so comfortable as his Arlington vest.

The hatter is a poor man. He has no resources to squander. Still, by dint of frugality, he has managed to scrounge a few extra swatches of felt from extravagant royal orders.

At night (when there was still Time to lead to night), after the hatter completed his work, he would delve into his meager stash of candle nubs and work for the minutes he could buy with scavenged wax. Velvet for his hare, the only material worthy of his plush pelt. He treated the hat with special care. He spent evenings over perfect stitches. He pricked his fingers to bleeding, and worked his eyes to tears, but scrupulously ensured neither could stain his work. He even cut two perfectly shaped holes in the brim, one for each of the hare's silken ears.

Not even a hare, he believes, should be without a hat.

You may think that it's fair to conclude that since the hatter loves his hare, it's clear that the hare loves his hatter.

You are mistaken. It's not the same thing a bit!

You might as well say that dressing a wound is the same as wounding a dress.

You might as well say that to like whom you tup is the same as to tup whom you like.

You might as well say that the heart knows what it wants so therefore it wants what it knows.

In the garden at the outskirts of the tea party, floral prudes gaze with dismay at the sight forced upon them by their regrettably placed beds.

The Daisy blushes red. The Rose curls her lower leaves to block her view. With a gasp, the Tiger Lily wilts into a faint.

When the hatter and hare are done with this round, all exhausted, the hare curls beside his beloved. The hatter sits with a cup of Assam. Light slants between branches, the lazy golden of a summer that can't decide whether six o'clock is afternoon or evening.

The hare stares restlessly up at the leaves. He has not been biding well; boredom has begun to rumple his fur.

Oh, he fears the return of Time as much as the hatter does; he has much to lose. However, he also feels a longing for what it was like to leap and hide, to smell fresh soil, to discover lettuces in unexpected places. He recalls the terror of a predator's chase, the thrill of elusion, the joy of new moments unfolding like the scandalized flowers.

"Old Time," mutters the hare, "his factory is a secret place, his work is noiseless, and his hands are mutes."

The hatter sits straight in apprehension. His hand withdraws from his partner's plug tail.

He recognizes this quotation as an expression of dissatisfaction, a rebellion against their idyll. He demands his lover's meaning. "Speech is the mirror of the soul," he says. "As a man speaks, so is he."

The hare recognizes an edge of bitterness in the hatter's voice. He does not want to argue. He knows the hatter will never admit that while there are benefits to timelessness, there are detriments, too. He holds his tongue and savors the tumbling light.

Acidly, the hatter says, "Silence is the wit of fools."

The hare ripostes. "Wit without discrimination is a sword in the hand of a fool."

"Wit is cultured insolence."

"Don't put too fine a point on your wit or it may be blunted."

"A paltry humbug! Those who have the least wit make them best."

"Words may show a man's wit, but actions his meaning."

"Bah!"

The hatter's hands are quivering now as much from rage as from mercury. The conversation has slipped its rails; it has become something else entirely. And still the hare will not reveal his meaning.

In anger, the hatter discards their prohibition against original speech. "Our wits," he sneers, "are worn too thin for witty exchanges."

Lulled by their return to familiar assay and counter, the hare has failed to notice that the hatter is blisteringly mad, and in more than his usual sense. Lazily, he replies, "Many that are wits in jest are fools in earnest."

The hatter whips to his feet. "Can't you hear?" he demands. "Is there a whit of use in those enormous ears? No more wit! Not a witty whit more! Our witless twittering is done!"

> The Hatter parted with his heart
> When tea time made him gay:
> The Hare (that tart!), he stole that heart,
> And took it quite away!
>
> Oh, Hare, my dear, though you appear
> Contented with our tryst:
> Boredom, I fear, has made you queer,
> And you've begun to list.

You might as well say that to lose what you love is the same as to love what you lose.

You might as well say that we meet then we part is the same as we part then we meet.

You might as well say that I'm undone by love is the same as my love is undone.

The tea has gone cold. Crumpets ossify on the platter. The pastries are more stone than scone.

The hatter has gone off to sulk at the far end of the tea table. He's pulled the tablecloth over his head. He makes a strange lump; the cloth, over his hat, looks as though it's covering some bizarre mushroom. The tea set is all askew, scattered by the yanking of the tablecloth. The teapot slumps on its side, spout jutting obscenely upward.

The hare lopes over to the flower bed. He nibbles restlessly on the violets until he becomes bored with their tiny screams.

He's almost drowsing when suddenly his prey senses twitch. He springs to his feet.

Whoosh! Thump. Sharpness. The hare's heart pounds as teeth close on his nape. He paws the ground, scrambling to get away, but it's got him fast.

"Murr hurr, ii aa oo?" comes a full-mouthed inquiry.

The hare sprawls on the ground, spat free.

Above him, the queen's pet cheshire stares down. "Sorry, March," he says casually, licking a paw. "Didn't recognize you."

The hare's heart beats the rapid tattoo of near escape. He stutters. "Wo-would you like some tea?"

"Kind of you to offer, but no," Cheshire says. "No time for tea." His grin beams. "Get it? No Time?"

The hare thinks it best to ignore Cheshire's attempt at humor; after all, the animal's teeth remain on gleaming display.

"What would you like, then?" asks the hare.

"Diversion," says Cheshire. "A chat. A nibble."

Fangs glisten. The hare trembles.

Cheshire curls his tail around his paws. "Have I ever told you what it's like to walk away from here?" Without waiting for a reply, he continues, "To leave here and go back into Time is like watching the sun rise and sink a thousand times in the blink of an eye."

Diffidently, Cheshire turns toward the tea table, surveying the scene with the aura of ownership that cats can cultivate when they wish. His ear twitches back toward the hare, signaling that he is still ready to leap.

"Except nothing like that, of course. The sun wouldn't stir herself on account of what beasties are up to. But *inside*. It's like that *inside*."

The cat turns back. He licks his chops.

"Not a bad arrangement. Staying here. Drinking tea. Never

getting older. Some might envy you." The feline leers. "But then, some envy the dead."

The hare shrinks. "The dead?" he asks, wondering if it's a threat.

But Cheshire does not advance, all claws and teeth. Instead he fades away, leaving his grin behind.

A raven is like a writing desk because the notes for which they are noted are not musical notes.

A raven is like a writing desk because Poe wrote on both.

A raven is like a writing desk because they both slope with a flap.

A raven is like a writing desk because there is a "B" in both and an "N" in neither.

It is strange to make a decision outside Time.

There is, first of all, the difficulty that it is impossible. A decision must have a cause; in turn, it must spur effects.

How is it possible for Time to die and yet for events to continue occurring in sequence? How many girls in blue dresses come and go? Tea be drunk and yet never run out? Love affairs ripen and spoil? Curiouser still, how can Time be dead in one locale, and yet continue to rule the affairs of those who are not stuck at interminable tea?

If you want rules, look elsewhere. This is Wonderland; we are all mad here.

The hare has made a decision. He stands at the table, beside a cup of tepid oolong, pocket watch in paw. Musingly, he looks between the tea and the watch, the tea and the watch.

The hatter perceives something has changed. It is a sense hatters have.

He pulls the tablecloth off of his head. Porcelain clatters about. The teapot falls and cracks.

The hare glances up at him. The hatter's face is drawn. The brim of his hat casts a long shadow across his features.

"The primary sign of a well-ordered mind is a man's ability to remain in one place," the hatter says.

The hare replies, "All changes, even the most longed for, have their melancholy." His tone is layered with both grief and expectation. "But growth is the only evidence of life."

The hatter's hands quake upon the table. He cannot control them.

"Friendship often ends in love," the hatter says, "but love in friendship—never."

The hare looks back down at the watch. Butter shines on motionless gears. "Love can do much," he murmurs, "but duty more."

The hatter gives a sigh like the wind that blows through a vanished cheshire. He stands, his hands still trembling at his sides. "Wait here," he says.

"Strings of tension—" the hare begins, but the hatter isn't listening.

He's walking toward the garden of talkative flowers, beyond which lies the small house he calls his own. The hatter has not entered there since tea began, but now he opens the door and disappears inside.

When he returns, he is all hunched and sad, his jacket pinched around his shoulders. His bow tie droops. He can't quite look at the hare; he looks away, mouth twitching with unsaid words.

In his hands, he holds a top hat that's a motley of the Queen's red and black, according to what he could scrounge. Each piece flawlessly felted, smooth and almost shining. Immaculate stitches circle the bicolored brocade band. Two round holes sit on either side of the brim, cut perfectly for long silken ears.

The hatter offers the hat, but the hare is afraid to take it. It is too beautiful, too clearly an artifact of affection. Besides, the hare's paws are full, the buttered pocket watch open in his palm.

With another sigh, the hatter sets the hat down carefully on the hare's head, mindful of his ears. The hat gives a formal, finished flair to the hare's gentlemanly attire. One could almost imagine him at a garden party, offering his arm to a lady before they go to play croquet. Even a hare should not be without a hat.

The hare's nose twitches. He can hardly think what to say. He stumbles a thank-you. "Gratitude is the memory of the heart—"

The hatter interrupts. "Look to your conscience, then," he says, folding his arms across his chest. He gives the pocket watch a dubious look. "Do it if you must."

What is Time anyway?

Time is a question. Time is the fire in which we burn. Time is

local. Time is limited. Time will not take a beating. Time is lend-
ing, borrowing, crashing—and recovering. Time is petty jealous-
ies and perverse grudges. Time is neither here nor there. Time is
an unfair dilemma.

Time is a dream . . . a destroying dream. It covers the face of
beauty and tumbles walls.

Time is but a phantom dagger that motion lifts to slay itself.

Time is a handful of sand.

The hare picks up his cup. His paw trembles as he tips the brim.
Dark, sweet liquid rushes into the gears. A swish, a rinse, a tilt. Tea
flows out again. Diluted butter runs onto the grass.

Time stirs.

You might as well say that timing a run is the same as to run out
of time.

A hatter should never be forced to construct hats at the behest
of a deck of cards.

Have I ever told you what it's like to walk away from here?

A raven is like a writing desk because love is like loneliness.

It is never polite to go out-of-doors without a hat.

The time has come, the tea set said, to talk of many brews.

You might as well say that falling silent is the same as silently
falling.

To tell the truth, a raven is not much like a writing desk at all.

What is Time anyway?

> Twinkle, twinkle. One, two, three:
> Swallow then set down your tea.
> Wipe your mouth. Return my heart.
> Time has come to make us part.

Time regains his unrelenting feet.

The girl in the blue dress, walking to the Queen's croquet grounds,
spending her time in conversation with men and women who fancy
themselves cards (in more than the literal sense). Going to meet
the griffin and the mock turtle and to sing the lobster quadrille
(no, she will not, won't not, will not, won't not, will not join the

dance). Becoming a towering presence at court. Waking beside her sister who is still reading from a book without pictures. Living her life in a land full of only ordinary wonders.

The hatter, returning to his felts and pelts, slipping, sliding, sluicing into mercurial madness.

The hare, off in the forest, risking the mutability of April.

Go on until you reach the end: then stop.

Headshot

FROM *Terraform*

@JMitcherCNN: Corporal, first of all, let me thank you for agreeing to this interview. By now all of America has seen the footage of your amazing headshot last week. Could you tell us the story, in your own words?

@CplPetersUSMC: Well sure, Jim. As you know, things went kinda crazy after I made that kill. I'm pushing 12k followers now. At the time the most I'd ever had online at once was . . . maybe a couple dozen? Fact is, there were only two people with me when it happened—@PatriotRiot2000 and @FrendliGhost. This was the night of the assault on Peshawar, remember? So half the nation was following the boys from First Airborne. No one wanted to miss a jump like that. I appreciate all the fans who've been with me since the beginning, but I want to give credit where it's due. It was just me, Riot, and Ghost that night.

@JMitcherCNN: Interesting. So you didn't even have quorum for engagement?

@CplPetersUSMC: No, sir. Not at first. But that night I wasn't even worrying about quorum. It was just a routine patrol and we weren't expecting any trouble. I was just chatting with Ghost and Riot. Both of those dudes have always had my back with nav and sit-reps and shit like that. But they were also just there when I needed someone to talk to, you know? That's even more important sometimes. When you're in the middle of a war zone, it's nice to hear the voice of some suburban kid from Detroit in your headset.

@JMitcherCNN: So how many other soldiers were taking part in this patrol?

@CplPetersUSMC: It was a six-man squad, but the tactical-scale guys had split us up to cover more ground. Ghost and Riot both thought that was dumb, but they'd been outvoted in the war room. When the numbers are small, bad ideas can get through more easily. That's the whole point of quorum. I admit, we were doing a bit of trash talking. They told me there were a lot of tac-scale folks online who had never even really followed a soldier. They just spend all their time zoomed-out, looking at satellite feeds, moving us around like chess pieces. I'm not saying that's wrong, but it can be dangerous. No one who's spent time with a soldier on patrol would have made that kind of call.

@JMitcherCNN: So it was just you, alone in an alley. No backup.

@CplPetersUSMC: That's right. So then Riot notices this big black car parked in the alley. It was dark as hell in there. All the streetlights were out, so I didn't notice it. But Riot, he's a real tech-head. He has my feed running in infrared, thermal, and laser-gated, each in a separate window. He don't miss much. And he's from Detroit, so he knows his cars. Anyway, it was a Lincoln. Most of the cars here are these shitty Soviet models from the '70s. Ain't that the ultimate irony? You can tell the guys on the Most Wanted list 'cause they all drive American cars.

@JMitcherCNN: So you knew someone important was nearby.

@CplPetersUSMC: Well, we suspected. Ghost is looking at the satellite heat maps, pulling up floor plans, checking the locations of windows. I knew I couldn't just storm in there by myself, but Ghost and Riot didn't trust the guys in the war room so they wanted to wait before calling in the cavalry. Those tac-scale yahoos would probably just send the squad in, guns blazing, just for the thrill of it. So Ghost guides me into this bombed-out office building across the street. I hoof it up five stories till I'm level with the building opposite. Sure enough, a light is on and I can see into the room. There are six or seven bearded dudes there with AKs slung over their shoulders. It looks like they're arguing and for a while I think they're going to shoot each other and save me the bother, but then another guy comes in. You can tell just by looking at him that he's some sort of head honcho—the owner of the car. I didn't recognize him myself. I ain't no racist, but with those beards they all look kinda the same. Riot, on the other hand, boots up some face recognition software and IDs him, lickety-split, as Jaques al-Adil.

@JMitcherCNN: The Jack of Clubs.

@CplPetersUSMC: Exactly. This guy's a face card. One of the top ten most wanted terrorists in the world, and I'm sitting in a window across the street from him, lined up for a perfect headshot.

@JMitcherCNN: But . . .

@CplPetersUSMC: But, as I mentioned, I didn't have quorum, so I couldn't take the shot. Legally. So, Ghost and Riot jump on their social networks and try to get the word out. Any patriotic American would upvote a shot like that, but we just didn't have enough bodies in the room. Of course all their friends are watching the assault in Peshawar, and not checking their messages. So you know what they do? Ghost goes and wakes up his parents, and Riot fetches his little sister and her boyfriend. Now, Riot's parents are real traditionalists who have never followed a soldier in their lives. Riot's always complaining about them, going on about how they're not upholding their responsibilities as citizens. They're old-timers, see? Got no interest in direct democracy.

@JMitcherCNN: Were they registered to vote?

@CplPetersUSMC: No! That's the thing. I think they were pre-screened through their driver's licenses or whatnot, but they certainly weren't registered for this theater. So I can hear Riot walking them through registration, trying to convince them how important this is, and they're trying to calm him down, and typing their email addresses wrong and having to start again, just like any other old folks. Have to laugh at it all, now.

@JMitcherCNN: I'm guessing it wasn't so funny at the time.

@CplPetersUSMC: It wasn't. But get this: the situation at Ghost's place is even worse. His sister is a hippie. A real peacenik, you know? She doesn't want anything to do with war. So I can hear him talking philosophy to her, trying to convince her to do the right thing for freedom and democracy just this once. And meanwhile I'm waiting with my rifle cocked and Jaques al-Adil's head in the middle of my sights. I've got to admit, Jim, I was sorely tempted to pull the trigger and just live with the consequences. But I thought to myself, if I shoot now I'm no better than he is. I'm here as a representative of my country. If I shoot without a quorum of consenting citizens, as the rules of engagement demand, then I'm no longer defending freedom and democracy, I'm just another terrorist.

@JMitcherCNN: Strong words, corporal.

@CplPetersUSMC: Well, if I didn't believe them, I never would have enlisted.

@JMitcherCNN: So what happened next?

@CplPetersUSMC: Well, then I hear gunfire coming from the next street over. I found out later that it was just Samuels and Gonzales showing off for some kids, but Ghost and Riot were too busy to keep me updated at this point, so it scared the hell out of me at the time. And it scared al-Adil and the rest of the folks around that table. They kill the lights and hit the floor. A minute later, I see the front door of the building open and four figures sprint to the Lincoln. One of them is al-Adil and he gets in the back seat. My HUD was still only showing Ghost and Riot online, but just as the car was pulling away, three more followers blipped into existence. I had quorum. Now they just needed to upvote engagement. The car was already turning the corner of the street when the votes came through. Five-out-of-five upvotes. Riot had persuaded his sister's boyfriend to log in and vote. I couldn't even see al-Adil by this point, all I could see was the car, but I had seen him climb into the back right-hand seat, so I aimed for where I thought his head would be.

@JMitcherCNN: And the rest is history.

@CplPetersUSMC: And the rest is history. Although it would never have gone so viral if Samuels hadn't been just around the corner. He was the one who saw all the gore. It's his POV feed that's trending. Over 10M now, I think.

@JMitcherCNN: But seeing yours makes the shot all the more astonishing. I encourage all our followers to watch Cpl. Peters's POV of the shot. If it had been a second later . . .

@CplPetersUSMC: Ghost and Riot have both made their screen-feeds public too. Be sure to check them out. Couldn't have done it without them.

@JMitcherCNN: So how do you think your job will change now that you have thousands of fans?

@CplPetersUSMC: Well, I certainly won't have trouble making quorum anymore . . . ROFL. On the one hand, it feels great to have the support of so many patriotic citizens behind me. But it'll be harder to have one-on-one chats with my followers. I'll do what I can to keep that personal connection. I've already set up a private channel for Ghost and Riot, so they'll always be able to talk to me directly, no matter how much chatter is going down. How will it change the job? I guess we'll just have to wait and see.

@JMitcherCNN: Just one more question, corporal, and then I'll let you go. Sergeant Pearson's recent court-martial has sparked a grassroots campaign to eliminate quorum altogether. Do you wish you had had more leeway? More freedom to act on your own initiative?

@CplPetersUSMC: Well, that's a great question, Jim. A lot of the older guys in the unit complain a lot about the whole direct democracy thing, but I think I like things the way they are. Maybe if I had missed the shot I would feel differently, but it seems to me that getting your folks out of bed to vote and debating philosophy with your sister before letting a soldier take a shot—that's how it should work. That's democracy.

@JMitcherCNN: Well said, corporal. And thank you for your service.

SALMAN RUSHDIE

The Duniazát

FROM *The New Yorker*

IN THE YEAR 1195, the great philosopher Ibn Rushd, once the *qadi*, or judge, of Seville and most recently the personal physician to the caliph Abu Yusuf Yaqub in his home town of Córdoba, was formally discredited and disgraced on account of his liberal ideas, which were unacceptable to the increasingly powerful Berber fanatics who were spreading like a pestilence across Arab Spain, and was sent to live in internal exile in the small village of Lucena, a village full of Jews who could no longer say they were Jews because they had been forced to convert to Islam. Ibn Rushd, a philosopher who was no longer permitted to expound his philosophy, all of whose writing had been banned and burned, felt instantly at home among the Jews who could not say they were Jews. He had been a favorite of the caliph of the present ruling dynasty, the Almohads, but favorites go out of fashion, and Abu Yusuf Yaqub had allowed the fanatics to push the great commentator on Aristotle out of town.

The philosopher who could not speak his philosophy lived on a narrow unpaved street in a humble house with small windows and was terribly oppressed by the absence of light. He set up a medical practice in Lucena, and his status as the ex-physician of the caliph himself brought him patients; in addition, he used what assets he had to enter modestly into the horse trade, and also financed the making of *tinajas*, the large earthenware vessels, in which the Jews who were no longer Jews stored and sold olive oil and wine. One day soon after the beginning of his exile, a girl of perhaps sixteen summers appeared outside his door, smiling gently, not knocking or intruding on his thoughts in any way, and simply stood there waiting patiently until he became aware of her presence and invited her in. She told him that she was newly orphaned, that she had no source of income, but preferred not to work in the whorehouse, and that her name was Dunia, which did not sound like a Jewish name because she was not allowed to speak her Jewish name, and because she was illiterate, she could not write it down. She told him that a traveler had suggested the name and said it was Greek and meant "the world," and she had liked that idea. Ibn Rushd, the translator of Aristotle, did not quibble with her, knowing that it meant "the world" in enough tongues to make pedantry unnecessary. "Why have you named yourself after the world?" he asked her, and she replied, looking him in the eye as she spoke, "Because a world will flow from me and those who flow from me will spread across the world."

Being a man of reason, Ibn Rushd did not guess that the girl was a supernatural creature, a jinnia, of the tribe of female jinn: a grand princess of that tribe, on an earthly adventure, pursuing her fascination with human men in general and brilliant ones in particular. He took her into his cottage as his housekeeper and lover, and in the muffled night she whispered her "true" — that is to say, false — Jewish name into his ear, and that was their secret. Dunia the jinnia was as spectacularly fertile as her prophecy had implied. In the two years, eight months, and twenty-eight days and nights that followed, she was pregnant three times and brought forth a multiplicity of children, at least seven on each occasion, it would appear, and on one occasion eleven, or possibly nineteen; the records are vague. All the children inherited her most distinctive feature: they had no earlobes.

If Ibn Rushd had been a scholar of the occult arcana, he would have realized then that his children were the offspring of a nonhuman mother, but he was too wrapped up in himself to work it out. The philosopher who could not philosophize feared that his children would inherit from him the sad gifts that were his treasure and his curse. "To be thin-skinned, farsighted, and loose-tongued," he said, "is to feel too sharply, see too clearly, speak too freely. It is to be vulnerable to the world when the world believes itself invulnerable, to understand its mutability when it thinks itself immutable, to sense what's coming before others sense it, to know that the barbarian future is tearing down the gates of the present while others cling to the decadent, hollow past. If our children are fortunate, they will inherit only your ears, but, regrettably, as they are undeniably mine, they will probably think too much too soon and hear too much too early, including things that are not permitted to be thought or heard."

"Tell me a story," Dunia often demanded in bed in the early days of their cohabitation. Ibn Rushd quickly discovered that in spite of her seeming youth she could be a demanding and opinionated individual, in bed and out of it. He was a big man, and she was like a little bird or a stick insect, but he often felt that she was the stronger of the two. She was the joy of his old age, but she demanded from him a level of energy that was hard to maintain. Sometimes all he wanted to do in bed was sleep, but Dunia saw his attempts to nod off as hostile acts. "If you stay up all night making love," she said, "you actually feel better-rested than if you snore for hours like an ox. This is well known." At his age, it wasn't always easy to enter into the required condition for the sexual act, especially on consecutive nights, but she saw his elderly difficulty with arousal as proof of his unloving nature. "If you find a woman attractive, there is never a problem," she told him. "Doesn't matter how many nights in a row. Me, I'm always horny. I can go on forever—I have no stopping point."

His discovery that her physical ardor could be quelled by narrative had provided some relief. "Tell me a story," she said, curling up under his arm so that his hand rested on her head, and he thought, Good, I'm off the hook tonight, and gave her, little by little, the story of his mind. He used words that many of his contemporaries found shocking, including "reason," "logic," and "science," which were the three pillars of his thought, the ideas that had led to his books' being burned. Dunia was afraid of these words, but her fear excited her and she snuggled in closer and said, "Hold my head while you're filling it with your lies."

There was a deep, sad wound in him, because he was a defeated man, had lost the great battle of his life to a dead Persian, Ghazali of Tus, an adversary who had been dead for eighty-five years. A hundred years earlier, Ghazali had written a book called *The Incoherence of the Philosophers,* in which he attacked Greeks like Aristotle, the Neo-Platonists, and their allies, Ibn Rushd's great precursors Ibn Sina and al-Farabi. Ghazali had suffered a crisis of belief at one point, but had recovered with such conviction that he became the greatest scourge of philosophy in the history of the world. Philosophy, he jeered, was incapable of proving the existence of God, or even of proving the impossibility of there being two gods. Philosophy believed in the inevitability of causes and effects, which was an insult to the power of God, who could easily intervene to make causes ineffectual and alter effects if He so chose.

"What happens," Ibn Rushd asked Dunia when the night wrapped them in silence and they could speak of forbidden things, "if a lighted stick is brought into contact with a ball of cotton?"

"The cotton catches fire, of course," she answered.

"And why does it catch fire?"

"Because that is the way of it," she said. "The fire licks the cotton and the cotton becomes part of the fire. It's how things are."

"The law of nature," he said. "Causes have their effects." And her head nodded beneath his caressing hand.

"He disagreed," Ibn Rushd said, and she knew that he meant the enemy, Ghazali. "He said that the cotton caught fire because God made it do so, because in God's universe the only law is what God wills."

"So if God had wanted the cotton to put out the fire, if He had wanted the fire to become part of the cotton, He could have done that?"

"Yes," Ibn Rushd said. "According to Ghazali's book, God could do that."

She thought for a moment. "That's stupid," she said finally. Even in the dark she could sense the resigned smile, the smile with cynicism in it as well as pain, spreading crookedly across his bearded face.

"He would say that this was the true faith," he answered her, "and that to disagree with it would be . . . incoherent."

"So anything can happen if God decides it's OK," she said. "A man's feet might no longer touch the ground, for example. He could start walking on air."

"A miracle," Ibn Rushd said, "is just God changing the rules by which He chooses to play, and if we don't comprehend it, it is because God is ultimately ineffable, which is to say, beyond our comprehension."

She was silent again. "Suppose I suppose," she said at length, "that God does not exist. Suppose you make me suppose that 'rea-

son,' 'logic,' and 'science' possess a magic that makes God unnecessary. Can one even suppose that it would be possible to suppose
such a thing?"

She felt his body stiffen. Now *he* was afraid of *her* words, she
thought, and it pleased her in an odd way. "No," he said, too
harshly. "That really would be a stupid supposition."

He had written his own book, *The Incoherence of the Incoherence*,
replying to Ghazali across a hundred years and thousands of miles,
but in spite of its snappy title it had not diminished the dead Persian's influence, and finally it was Ibn Rushd who had been disgraced, whose books had been cast into the fire, which had consumed the pages because that was what God had decided at that
moment that the fire should be permitted to do. In all his writing,
Ibn Rushd had tried to reconcile the words "reason," "logic," and
"science" with the words "God," "faith," and "Qur'an," but he had
not succeeded, even though he had used with great subtlety the argument from kindness, demonstrating by Qur'anic quotation that
God must exist because of the garden of earthly delights he had
provided for mankind: *And do we not send down from the clouds pressing forth rain, water pouring down in abundance, that you may thereby
produce corn and herbs and gardens planted thick with trees?* He was a
keen amateur gardener, and the argument from kindness seemed
to him to prove both God's existence and his essentially kindly,
liberal nature, but the proponents of a harsher God had beaten
him. Now he lay, or so he believed, with a converted Jew whom he
had saved from the whorehouse and who seemed capable of seeing into his dreams, where he argued with Ghazali in the language
of irreconcilables, the language of wholeheartedness, of going all
the way, which would have doomed him to the executioner if he
had used it in waking life.

As Dunia filled up with children and then emptied them into the
small house, there was less room for Ibn Rushd's excommunicated
"lies." The couple's moments of intimacy became less frequent,
and money was a problem. "A true man faces the consequences of
his actions," she told him, "especially a man who believes in causes
and effects." But making money had never been his forte. The
horse-trading business was treacherous and full of cutthroats, and
his profits were small. He had many competitors in the *tinaja* market, so prices were low. "Charge your patients more," Dunia ad-

vised him with some irritation. "You should cash in on your former prestige, tarnished as it is. What else have you got? It's not enough to be a baby-making monster. You make babies, the babies come, the babies must be fed. That is 'logic.' That is 'rational.'" She knew which words she could turn against him. "Not to do this," she cried triumphantly, "is 'incoherence.'"

The jinn are fond of glittering things, gold and jewels and so on, and often they conceal their hoards in subterranean caves. Why did the jinnia princess not cry "Open!" at the door of a treasure cave and solve their financial problems at a stroke? Because she had chosen a human life, as the "human" wife of a human being, and she was bound by her choice. To reveal her true nature to her lover at this late stage would have been to reveal a kind of betrayal, a lie, at the heart of their relationship. So she remained silent, fearing he might abandon her.

There was a Persian book called *Hazar Afsaneh,* or *One Thousand Stories,* which had been translated into Arabic. In the Arabic version, there were fewer than a thousand stories but the action was spread over a thousand nights, or, because round numbers were considered ugly, a thousand nights and one night more. Ibn Rushd had not seen the book, but several of its stories had been told to him at court. The story of the fisherman and the jinni appealed to him, not so much for its fantastic elements (the jinni from the lamp, the magic talking fishes, the bewitched prince who was half man and half marble) as for its technical beauty, the way its stories were folded within other stories and contained yet other stories, folded within themselves, so that the tale became a true mirror of life, Ibn Rushd thought, for in life all our stories contain the stories of others and are themselves contained within larger, grander narratives, the histories of our families, or our homelands, or our beliefs. More beautiful even than the stories within stories was the story of the storyteller, a queen called Shahrazad or Scheherazade, who told her tales to a murderous husband to keep him from executing her. Stories told to defeat death, to civilize a barbarian. And at the foot of the marital bed sat Scheherazade's sister, her perfect audience, asking for one more story, and then one more, and then yet another. From this sister Ibn Rushd got the name he bestowed on the hordes of babies issuing from his lover Dunia's loins, for the sister, as it happened, was called Dunyazad, "and what we have here filling up this dark house and forcing me to impose extortionate fees on my patients, the sick and infirm of Lucena, is the arrival of the Duniazát, that is, Dunia's tribe, the race of Dunians, the Dunia people, which is to say the people of the world."

Dunia was deeply offended. "You mean," she said, "that because we are not married our children cannot bear their father's name."

He smiled his sad, crooked smile. "It is better that they be the Duniazát," he said, "a name that contains the world and has not been judged by it. To call them the Rushdi would be to send them into history with a mark upon their brow."

Dunia began to speak of herself as Scheherazade's sister, always asking for stories, only her Scheherazade was a man—her lover, not her brother—and some of his stories could get them both killed if the words were accidentally to escape from the darkness of their bedroom. So Ibn Rushd was a sort of anti-Scheherazade, Dunia told him, the exact opposite of the storyteller of the *Thousand Nights and One Night:* her stories saved her life, while his put his life in danger. But then the caliph Abu Yusuf Yaqub was triumphant in war, winning his greatest military victory, against the Christian king of Castile, Alfonso VIII, at Alarcos on the Guadiana River. After the Battle of Alarcos, in which the caliph's forces killed a hundred and fifty thousand Castilian soldiers, fully half the Christian army, Abu Yusuf Yaqub gave himself the name al-Mansur, the Victorious, and with the confidence of a conquering hero he brought the ascendancy of the fanatical Berbers to an end and summoned Ibn Rushd back to court.

The mark of shame was wiped off the old philosopher's brow, his exile ended. He was rehabilitated, undisgraced, and returned with honor to his old position of court physician, two years, eight months, and twenty-eight days and nights after his exile began, which was to say, one thousand days and nights and one more day and night; and Dunia was pregnant again, of course, and he did not marry her, of course, he never gave her children his name, of course, and he did not bring her with him to the Almohad court, of course, so she slipped out of history—he took it with him when he left, along with his robes, his bubbling retorts, and his manuscripts, some bound, others in scrolls, manuscripts of other men's books, for his own had been burned, though many copies survived, he'd told her, in other cities, in the libraries of friends, and in places where he had concealed them against the day of his disfavor, for a wise man always prepares for adversity but, if he is properly modest, lets good fortune take him by surprise. He left without finishing his breakfast or saying goodbye, and she did not threaten him, did not reveal her true nature or the power that lay hidden within her, did not say, I know what you say aloud in your dreams, when you suppose the thing that would be stupid to suppose, when you stop trying to reconcile the irreconcilable and speak the terrible, fatal truth. She allowed history to leave her without trying to hold it back, the way children allow a grand parade to pass, holding it in their memory, making it their own; and she went on loving him, even though he had so casually abandoned her. You were my everything, she wanted to say to him. You were my sun and moon, and who will hold my head now, who will kiss my lips, who will be a father to our children? But he was a great man destined for the halls of the immortals, and these squalling brats were no more than the jetsam he left in his wake.

It is believed that Dunia remained among human beings for a while, perhaps hoping against hope for Ibn Rushd's return, and that he continued to send her money, that maybe he visited her from time to time, and that she gave up on the horse business but went on with the *tinajas*. But now that the sun and moon of history had set forever on her house, her story became a thing of shadows and mysteries, so maybe it's true, as people said, that after Ibn Rushd died his spirit returned to her and fathered even more children. People also said that Ibn Rushd brought her a lamp with a jinni in it, and the jinni was the father of the children born after he left her—so we see how easily rumor turns things upside down! They also said, less kindly, that the abandoned woman took in any man who would pay her rent, and every man she took in left her with another brood, so that the Duniazát, the brood of Dunia, were no longer bastard Rushdis, or some of them were not, or many of them were not; for in most people's eyes, the story of her life had become a stuttering line, its letters dissolving into meaningless forms, incapable of revealing how long she lived, or how, or where, or with whom, or when and how—or if—she died.

Nobody noticed or cared that one day she turned sideways and slipped through a slit in the world and returned to Peristan, the other reality, the world of dreams whence the jinn periodically emerge to trouble and bless mankind. To the villagers of Lucena, she seemed to have dissolved, perhaps into fireless smoke.

After Dunia left our world, the voyagers from the world of the jinn to ours became fewer in number, and then they stopped coming completely, and the slits in the world became overgrown with the unimaginative weeds of convention and the thornbushes of the dully material, until they finally closed up, and our ancestors were left to do the best they could without the benefits or curses of magic.

But Dunia's children thrived. That much can be said. And almost three hundred years later, when the Jews were expelled from Spain, even the Jews who could not say they were Jews, the great-grandchildren of Dunia's great-grandchildren climbed onto ships in Cádiz and Palos de Moguer, or walked across the Pyrenees, or flew on magic carpets or in giant urns like the jinni kin they were. They traversed continents and sailed the seven seas and climbed high mountains and swam mighty rivers and slid into deep valleys and found shelter and safety wherever they could, and they forgot one another quickly, or remembered as long as they could and then forgot, or never forgot, becoming a family that was no longer exactly a family, a tribe that was no longer exactly a tribe, adopting every religion and no religion, all of them, after the centuries of conversion, ignorant of their supernatural origins and of the story of the forcible conversion of the Jews, some of them becoming manically devout while others were contemptuously disbelieving. They were a family without a place but with family in every place, a village without a location but winding in and out of every spot on the globe, like rootless plants, mosses or lichens or creeping orchids, who must lean upon others, being unable to stand alone.

History is unkind to those it abandons and can be equally unkind to those who make it. Ibn Rushd died (of old age, or so we believe) while traveling in Marrakesh barely a year after his rehabilitation, and never saw his fame grow, never saw it spread beyond the borders of his own world and into the infidel world beyond, where his commentaries on Aristotle became the foundations of his mighty forebear's popularity, the cornerstones of the infidels' godless philosophy, *saecularis*, which meant the kind of idea that came only once in a *saeculum*, an age of the world, or maybe an idea for the ages, and which was the very image and echo of the ideas he had spoken only in dreams. Perhaps, as a godly man, Ibn Rushd would not have been delighted by the place history gave him, for it is a strange fate for a believer to become the inspiration of ideas that have no need of belief, and a stranger fate still for a man's philosophy to be victorious beyond the frontiers of his own world but vanquished within those borders, because in the world he knew it was the children of his dead adversary, Ghazali, who multiplied and inherited the kingdom, while his own bastard brood spread out, leaving his forbidden name behind them, to populate the earth.

A high proportion of the survivors ended up on the great North American continent, and many others on the great South Asian subcontinent, thanks to the phenomenon of "clumping," which is part of the mysterious illogic of random distribution; and many of those afterward spread out west and south across the Americas, and north and west from that great diamond at the foot of Asia, into all the countries of the world, for of the Duniazát it can fairly be said that, in addition to peculiar ears, they all have itchy feet. Ibn Rushd was dead, but he and his adversary continued their dispute beyond the grave, for to the arguments of great thinkers there is no end, argument itself being a tool to improve the mind, the sharpest of all tools, born of the love of knowledge, which is to say, philosophy.

NICK WOLVEN

No Placeholder for You, My Love

FROM *Asimov's Science Fiction*

I

CLAIRE MET HIM at a dinner party in New Orleans, and afterward she had to remind herself this was true. Yes, that had been it, his very first appearance. It seemed incredible there had been anything so finite as a first time.

He was seated across from her, two chairs down, a gorgeous woman on either side. As usual, the subject had turned to food.

"But I've been to this house a dozen times," one of the gorgeous women was saying. "I've been to dinner parties, dance parties, even family parties. And every time, they serve the wrong kind of cuisine."

She had red hair, the color of the candlelight reflected off the varnished chairs. The house was an old house, full of old things, handmade textiles and walnut chiffoniers, oil paintings of nameless Civil War colonels.

"Is that a problem?" said the young man on Claire's left. "Why should you care?"

"Because," said the redhead, pursing her lips. "Meringue pie, at an elegant soiree? Wine and steak tartare, at a child's birthday party? Lobster bisque at a dance? For God's sake, it was all over the floor. It seems, I don't know. Lazy. Thoughtless. Cobbled together."

She lifted her glass of wine to her mouth, and the liquid vanished the instant it touched her tongue.

The man who was to mean so much to Claire, to embody in his

person so much hope and loss, leaned over his soup, eyes dark with amusement. "It *is* cobbled together. Of course it is. But isn't that the best part?"

"And why is that, Byron?" someone said with a sigh.

Byron. A fake name, Claire assumed, distilled from the fog of some half-remembered youthful interest. But then, you never knew.

Whatever the source of his name, Byron's face had the handsome roughness earned through active living. Dots of stubble grayed his skin. A tiny scar divided one eyebrow. His smile made a charming pattern of wrinkles around his eyes. It was a candid face, a well-architected face, a fortysomething face.

"Because," said Byron, and caught Claire's eye, as if only she would understand. "Look at this furniture, the chandelier. Look at that music stand in the corner. American plantation style, rococo, Art Nouveau. Every piece a different movement. Some are complete anachronisms. That's why I love this house. You can see the spirit of the designers here. A kind of whimsy. It's so personal, so scattershot."

"You're such a talker, Byron," someone sighed.

"Look at all of you," Byron said, moving his spoon in a circle to encompass the ring of faces. "Some of you I've never seen before in my life. And here we are, brought together by chance, for one evening only. You know what? That delights me. That thrills me." His gesture halted at Claire's face. "That enchants me."

"And after tonight," said the redhead, "we'll go our separate ways, and forget each other, and maybe never see each other again. So is that part of the wonder for you, Byron, or does that spoil the wonder?"

"It does neither," Byron said, "because I don't believe it."

His eyes settled on Claire's. Again he smiled. She had always liked older men, their slightly chastened air, their solemn and good-humored strength.

"I don't believe we'll never see each other again," Byron said, looking at his spoon. "I don't believe that's necessarily our fate. And you know what? The truth is, I wouldn't mind living in this house forever. Even if they do serve alphabet soup at a dinner party."

He lifted his hand to his mouth and touched his spoon to his lips. And instantly the liquid disappeared.

*

When they had cleared the table, the entertainments began. There were board games in the living room, a live band on the lawn. Stairs led to a dozen shadowy bedrooms, with sad old beds, and rich old carpets, and orchids in baskets on the moonlit windowsills. In town, the music of riverbank revelry scraped and jittered out of ramshackle bars, and paddleboats rode on the slow Mississippi, jingling with the racket of riches won and lost.

Byron borrowed a set of car keys from the houseboy. Claire followed him onto the porch. The breath of the bayou was in the air, warm and buoyant, holding up the clustered leaves of the pecan trees and the high, star-scattered sky. Sweat held her shirt to the small of her back, as if a hand were there, pressing her forward.

"Shall we take a ride?" The car keys dangled, tinkling, from Byron's upraised hand.

"Wait," said Claire, "do that again."

"This?" He gave the keys another shake. The sound tinkled out, a sprinkling of noise, over the thick green nap of the lawn.

"It sounds just like it," Claire said. "Don't you hear it? It sounds just like the midnight chime."

"Oh, God, don't talk about that now. It's not for hours." Byron went halfway down the porch steps, held out a hand. "We still have plenty of time to fall in love."

The car waiting for them was an early roadster, dazzling with chrome, large and slow. Byron handled the old-fashioned shift with expert nonchalance. They slid past banquet halls downtown, where drunkenness and merriment and red, frantic faces sang and sweated along the laden tables. Often they pulled to the curb and idled, and the night with its load of romance rolled by.

At a corner café where zydeco livened the air, a young couple argued at a scrollwork table.

"But how can you define it? How can you even describe it?" The woman's arm swung as she spoke, agitating the streetlights with a quiver of silver bracelets.

"Well, it's easy enough to *define*, anyway." The man made professorial motions with his hands. "It was simply a matter of chemistry."

"But how would that be any different from, say, smell?"

"Oh, it wasn't, not really. Taste and smell. Love and desire. All variations on the same experience."

The couple lifted fried shrimp from a basket as they spoke, the small golden morsels vanishing like fireflies on their lips.

"It can't be so simple," the woman said. And the man leaned over the table, reaching for her face, and turned it toward his lips. "You're right. It's not."

"I used to have those kinds of conversations," Byron sighed. He grasped the old maple knob of the shift, and pulled away from the curb.

They drove out of town onto rural dirt roads, where moonlight splashed across the land. In a plank roadhouse, a dance party was underway, a fiddle keening over stamping feet. Parked in the dirt lot, soaked in yellow light, they conducted the usual conversation.

"Now, me?" Byron said. "Let me tell you about myself. I'm a middle-aged computer programmer who enjoys snuggling, whiskey, and the study of artificial environments. I have a deathly aversion to crowds, and I'm not afraid to admit it. I'm nowhere near as handsome as this in real life, and I can assure you, I've been at this game a very long time."

His face dimpled as he delivered his spiel, not quite smiling. Claire laughed at his directness. Byron thumped a short drumroll on the wheel.

"And you?"

"Oh, me?" Claire said. "Me? I'm no one."

"That's an interesting theory."

"What I mean is, I'm no one anyone should care about. *I* don't even care about me."

"That can't be true."

"I guess not. I guess what I mean is, I don't care who I used to be." Claire watched the figures dance in the building, the plank walls trembling as shadows moved like living drawings across the dirty windows. "I care what happens to me now, though. I care about nights like this."

Her lazy hand took in the dancers, the stars. Byron sat back, nodding.

Claire surrendered. "I don't know. There's an interesting woman back there, somewhere. A scholar, a geneticist. But it's hard to believe, nowadays, that she ever existed."

"Tell me about this geneticist," he said.

"Well." Claire afforded him a smile. "What do you want to know?

She looked like me. She talked like me. She loved all the things I love. She loved rainy windows and Scrabble and strong tea. She loved her body, because she had a nice one, and she loved to take long baths with organic soap, and she loved the idea that one day, far in her future, there might be someone to share those baths with her. Mostly, I think, she loved the idea that she could find a man who didn't care about any of those things. A man who would simply take her hand and say, 'Let's go.'"

The fiddle stopped. The dancers halted. The shadows on the windows settled into perfect sketches: honey-colored men and women with open, panting lips.

"She was young," Claire said. "And she was lonely."

Byron nodded. "I understand."

Someone threw open the roadhouse door. A carpet of gold rolled down the steps, all the way up the hood into the car, covering Claire in mellow light. Byron studied her. She knew what he was seeing. A beautiful blonde, a perfect face, a statue of a body with cartoon-sized eyes.

"But you're not," he said. And after a moment, he clarified: "Young. Not anymore. Are you?"

"No," said Claire. "Not anymore."

They drove to town along a different route, on dark, swampy roads where alligators slithered, grunting, from the wheels. On a wharf lined with couples and fishing shops, they stood at the wood rail, looking over the water, waiting together for the midnight chime. A gas-powered ferry struggled from shore, heading northeast toward a sprawl of dark land.

"I don't care," Byron said. "I don't care if you were a biologist. I don't care if you love Scrabble or tea. I don't care about any of that." He held out a hand. "Let's go."

The couples on the wharf had fallen silent, waiting. The very twinkling of the stars seemed to pause. Still, the ferry strained and chugged, heading for a shore it would never reach.

"Say it," Claire said. "You say it first, then I'll say it, too."

"I want to see you again," Byron said.

She took his hand. Before she could respond, the midnight chime sounded. It came three times, eerie and clear, like a jingle of celestial keys. And Byron and the river and the world all disappeared.

2

Claire didn't see him again for a thousand nights.

It felt like a thousand, anyway. It may have been more. Claire had stopped counting long, long ago.

There were always more nights, more parties, more diversions. And, miraculous as it seemed, more people. Where did they come from? How could there be so many pretty young men, with leonine confidence and smiling lips? How could there be so many women arising out of the million chance assortments of the clubs, swimming through parties as if it could still be a thrill to have a thousand eyes fish for them—as if, like the fish in the proverbial sea, they one day hoped to be hooked?

Claire considered them, contemplated them, and let them go their way. She dated, for a time, a very old, handsome man whose name, in some remote and esoteric way, commanded powerful sources of credit. His wealth opened up new possibilities: private beaches where no one save they two had ever stepped, mountain lodges where the seasons manifested with iconic perfection, pink and green and gold and white. But they weren't, as the language ran, "compatible"; they were old and tired in different ways.

She met a girl whose face flashed with the markings of youth: sharp earrings, studs, lipstick that blazed in toxic colors. But the girl's eyes moved slowly, with the irony of age. Theirs was a sexual connection. Night after night they bowed out of cocktail hours, feeling for each other's hands across the crush of dances. Every exit was an escape. They sought the nearest private rooms they could find: the neon-bright retreats of city hotels, secret brick basements in converted factories. The thrill was one of shared expertise. Both women knew the limits of sex: what moves were possible, what borders impermeable. They cultivated the matched rhythm, the long caress. Sometimes Claire's new lover—whose name, she learned after three anonymous encounters, was Isolde—fed delicacies to her, improbable foods, ice carvings and whole cakes, a hundred olives impaled on swizzle sticks, fruit rinds in paint-box colors, orange and lime, stolen from the bottomless bins of restaurants. It was musical sport. Isolde perfected her timing, spacing each treat. Claire eased into a languor of tension and release, her body shivering with an automatic thrill. As the foods touched her mouth, one by one, they flickered immediately into nothingness —gone the instant she felt them, like words on her tongue.

A happy time, this. But love? Every night they were careful to say that magic phrase, far in advance of the midnight chime.

"I want to see you again."

"I want to see you, too."

And so the nights went by, and the dates, and the parties, spiced with anticipation.

Soon, Claire knew, it was bound to happen.

The end came in Eastern Europe.

"We could have been compatible, don't you think?"

They were reposing, at that moment, in a grand hotel with mountain views, somewhere west of the Caucasus, naked in bed while snow flicked the window. Isolde lifted a rum ball from a chased steel tray, manipulating it with silver tongs. She touched it to the candle, collected a curl of flame, brought the morsel, still burning, to her mouth, and snuffed it out of existence, fire and all, against her tongue.

Claire clasped her hands around a pillow. "Do you think so?"

Isolde seemed nervous tonight, opening and closing the tongs, pretending to measure, as with calipers, Claire's thigh, her knee.

"Don't get me wrong. I'm not saying we *are* compatible. I'm only talking about, you know. What might have been."

Beyond the window, white flakes swarmed in the sky, a portrait of aimless, random motion.

"We're attracted to each other," Isolde said. "We have fun. We always have fun."

"That's true. We always have fun."

"Isn't that what matters?"

"Nothing matters," Claire said. "Not for us. Isn't that the common consensus?" She made sure to smile as she said it, lying back with her hands behind her head.

Isolde seemed pained. "I'm only saying. If things had been different. We might have worked. We might have . . ." She blushed before speaking the forbidden phrase. "We might have made a match."

Claire felt her smile congealing on her face. She marveled at that—watched, in the oak-framed mirror atop the dresser, as her expression became an expression of disgust. "But things *aren't* different. Wouldn't you say that's an important fact? Things are exactly, eternally what they are."

"Eternally. You can't know that."

"I can believe it." Claire sat up, looking out the window, where snowfall and evening had blanked out the sky. "If you want to know what might have been, just wait for the midnight chime. You'll get a thousand might-have-beens. A thousand Romeos and Juliets. A thousand once-upon-a-times."

Isolde was shaking, a subtle, repressed tremor that Claire only noticed by looking at the tongs in her hand.

"I know, I know. I'm only saying . . . I mean, how can you resist? How can you stop thinking about it? About us. About . . ." Her voice dropped. "About love."

Claire turned from the window, saying nothing, but the mood of the view filled her eyes, the gray mountains falling away into whiteness, the cold precipitation of a million aimless specks.

"I just like to imagine," Isolde whispered. "That's all. I like to imagine it could be different."

A clock stood on the bedside table, scuffed wood and spotted brass, a heavy relic of interwar craftsmanship. Isolde snatched it up with a gasp.

"What's the matter?" Claire said.

"I just realized."

"What? What did you just realize?" In Claire's tone was an implied criticism. *What can there possibly be,* she wanted to ask, *for us to realize? What can we discover that we don't already know?*

Isolde touched the clock face. "We're in a time-shifted universe. The midnight chime comes earlier here. At sunset."

They looked together at the window, where the sky had darkened to charcoal gray.

"We never said it," Isolde whispered. "We forgot to say it, this time." She lay beside Claire, a hand on her belly, saying in a shaking voice, "I want to see you again."

The clock ticked. Snow tapped the window.

"I want to see you again," Isolde repeated. "Claire? I want to see you again."

The clock hands had made a line, pointing in opposite directions. How precise, Claire wondered, would the time shift be? Sometimes these things could be surprisingly inexact. Sometimes, even the designers made mistakes.

"Claire, please say it. I'm sorry I said all those things. We're not really a match. I was only speculating. Anyway, it doesn't matter.

Does anything matter? We don't have to talk. We can go back to how it was. We can hang out, play games, have fun."

In only a moment, a new evening would begin: new faces, new men and women, new possibilities. A whole new universe of beautiful people, like angels falling out of the sky.

"Claire, *please* say it. I want to see you again."

"Maybe you will," Claire said.

And at that moment, the chime sounded, tinkling and omnipresent, shivering three times across the mountain sky. And Isolde and her voice and her tears disappeared.

3

A dry period, then.

Dry? No, that word couldn't begin to describe this life. It was desert, desolate, arid, barren, with a harsh wind that cut across the eyes, with sharp-edged stones that stung the feet.

Claire became one of *those people*. She was the woman who haunts the edges of dance floors, rebuffing with silence anyone who dares to approach. At house parties, she wandered out for impromptu walks, seeking the hyperbolic darkness between streetlights, the lonely shadows below leylandii. At dinner parties, she made jokes intended to kill conversation.

"Knock, knock," Claire said, when young men leaned toward her.

"Who's there?"

"Claire."

"Claire who?"

"Exactly."

"Here's a good one," Claire said, to a woman who approached one night on a balcony, the champagne sparkles of a European city bubbling under their feet. "A woman walks into a bar full of beautiful people."

When the silence became uncomfortable, the woman prompted: "And?"

"And," said Claire turning away, "who cares?"

She was bitter. But she didn't care about her bitterness. Like all things, Claire assumed, this too would pass.

On an Amazonian cruise, Claire hit her low point. It was, most surely, a romantic night. Big insects sizzled against the lamps that swung, dusky gold, from the cabin house. The river gathered white ruffles along the hull. A banquet was laid out on deck, river fish on clay platters borne by shirtless deckhands. The dinner guests lounged in a crowd of cane chairs. When Claire came up from below, she found the party talking, as always, about the food.

"I've been here a hundred times." The woman who spoke was white, brunette, beautiful. "I think I'm something of an expert on this universe. And what I always admire is the attention to local cuisine. Everything comes straight from the river. It's so authentic."

Claire, who'd entered unnoticed, startled them all with a loud, braying laugh.

"Excuse me?" said the woman. "What do you find so funny?"

The group stared, pushing back their chairs, eyes kindled with reflected lantern light.

"This," Claire said, and snatched a clay platter out of the hands of the serving men. "I find this funny." She dumped the fish on the floor, jammed the platter into her mouth. They all winced as her teeth clamped down, grinding on textured ceramic. "Mm, so authentic."

"What in the world," said the woman, "is the matter with you?"

"Nothing. I'm simply trying to eat this platter."

"But *why?*"

"Because why shouldn't I?" Claire smashed the platter on the deck. "Why shouldn't I be able to? What difference does it make? Why shouldn't anything—any of this—be food?" She stomped around the deck, offering to take bites of the rails, the lamps, the life preservers. "Why shouldn't I be able to perform the trick with anything I want? Why shouldn't I be able to pick *you* up and send you into the ether with just a touch of my tongue?"

She grabbed at the arm of a nearby man, who pushed his chair back, winking. "Please do."

Claire threw his hand down in disgust. "I should be able to pick up anything I see, and touch it to my lips, and make it disappear. And why can't I? It works with fish. It works with fruit. It works with soup and fried shrimp and wedding cakes."

Expecting protest, mockery, a violent reaction, she faced with dismay the rows of indifferent, idle faces.

"God, I'm so sick of this life," Claire finished weakly. "I'm sick of always talking about things I can never have."

"But are you sick of me?"

Claire turned and Byron was standing behind her, leaning on the rail beside the deckhouse, a beer bottle dangling from his hand.

"You?" Claire was stunned. She could hardly believe she recognized him, but she did.

Byron strolled forward and touched her hand. "You never said it."

"Sorry?"

"Eight hundred and ninety-two nights ago. New Orleans. I said I wanted to see you again. You never answered."

"I meant to." Claire struggled for breath, aware of the watching crowd. "I wanted to. I ran out of time."

He flung his beer bottle overboard. She waited without breathing for it to plunk in the distant water.

"We have time now," he said.

Dismissing the party with a wave, Byron guided Claire into a lifeboat. With a push of a lever, a creak of pulleys, he lowered them to the water and cut the rope. They drifted loose in darkness, a lantern at their feet. The big boat moved away on a thump of diesel, the strings of lamps and the hundred candles merging into one gold blur. Byron set the oars in the locks, rowing with a grace that seemed derived from real strength: strength of body, of muscle and sinew, strength that belonged to the kinds of people they had both once been.

"Do you know why we can't eat food?" Byron spoke at his ease, fitting sentences between the creak of the oarlocks. "Do you know why we have no taste, no smell, no digestion? Do you know why we can never eat, and only make food vanish by touching it to our lips?"

His voice sounded elemental, coming out of the darkness: the voice of the river, the jungle, the night.

"Appetite," Byron said. "We were made without appetite. We were made to want only one thing. True love."

He let the oars rest. They rocked on the water. The riverboat was gone now, its voices and music lost in buggy stridor.

"I don't believe that." Claire let her hand trail in the water, wondering if piranhas and snakes stocked the river, if the authenticity of the environment extended that far. "I don't believe any of this was planned. Not to that extent. I think it's all nothing more than a sick, elaborate accident."

He considered her words, the oars resting, crossed, in his lap. "You must believe that some of this was designed. You must remember designing it. Or designing yourself, I mean: what you look like, how you think. I've forgotten quite a bit, but I do remember that."

A fish nibbled Claire's finger. She lifted her hand, shook off the drops.

"I don't mean the world itself," Claire said. "I mean about what's happened to us. The way we live. Something's gone wrong. I don't think it was intentional."

Byron nodded. "Apocalypse."

"Plague. Asteroids. Nuclear holocaust."

"Economic collapse. Political unrest." He joined in her joking tone. "Or only a poorly managed bankruptcy. And somewhere out in the Nevada desert, sealed away in a solar-powered server farm, a rack of computers sits, grinding away at a futile simulation, on and on through the lonely centuries."

She waved away his glib improvisation, accidentally spraying his face with drops.

"I don't think that's what happened. Do you know what I think? I think we've simply been forgotten."

He smiled, nodding in time with the rocking boat.

"That's all," Claire said. "They made us, they used us for a while, they lost interest. They kept their accounts, or their subscriptions, or whatever, but they stopped paying attention. They don't care if we find love. They don't care about anything we do."

"And yet." Byron resumed rowing. "If they knew . . ."

"What?" Claire was irritated at the portentous way he trailed off. "If they knew what?"

He glanced behind him, checking their direction. "Oh, you know. If they knew how wonderfully independent we've become. How clever and shy. How suave in the art of romance. How proficient at avoiding any kind of commitment."

"In other words," said Claire, "just like them."

Byron rested a moment, the oars under his chin. "Meet with me again. Say the words."

Claire looked away from him, down into the water, the black oblivion sliding by. "This can't go anywhere. You know it can't. It can't become anything. *We* can't become anything."

"I don't care. Say the words."

"It can never be more than a casual thing."

"All well and good. Say the words."

"It can only make us unhappy. We can only go so far. We'll reach a certain point, and we'll realize we're done. Finished. Forever incomplete. It will be like picking up a delicious piece of food and seeing it vanish on our tongues."

"Brilliant analogy. Say the words."

"I want to see you," Claire said, tears in her eyes. "I want to see you, again and again."

(And wondering, even while she said this, and not for the first time, why the people who built this terrible world had left so much out, had omitted taste, had excised smell, had eliminated pleasure, drunkenness, pain, death, injury, age, and appetite, but had left in these two strange and unpleasant details, had endowed every person with sweat and tears.)

We're not like them, Claire thought, as Byron, letting the oars ride idle, leaned across the boat. *We look like them — we have their habits, their interests, their hopes, even some of their memories. We think and feel like them, whether they know it or not. We can even, in some ways, make love like them. But we're not like them, not really, and it all comes down to this: whatever we desire, whatever we do, we'll never know the difference between a drink and a kiss.*

When Byron's lips met hers, a precise and dry contact, it surprised Claire, momentarily, that neither of them disappeared.

4

How many times did they meet? Claire didn't bother to count. They saw each other in hunting lodges, English gardens, an undersea city, the surface of Mars, the gondola of a transatlantic blimp. To Claire, all locations were frames for Byron's figure. More than his body, more than the frankness of his smile, she began to love the touch of his hand, the way it overlaid hers on the rails of ocean liners, felt for hers, casually, in the press of theater lobbies. He was a man who coveted contact: half-conscious, constant. She loved his need to know she was there.

And still, he was something much stranger than a lover. In this world, there was one sure pleasure, and this was the pleasure Byron offered. Talk.

"What was it?" she asked him, one night as they mingled, duded out in rodeo getups, with the square-dancing clientele of a cowboy bar. "In New Orleans, that night, you sought me out. What was it that made you notice me?"

Byron didn't hesitate. "A question," he said.

"And what question was that?"

He pointed at their knee-slapping environs: the mechanical bull, the rawhide trimmings, the Stetsons and string ties and silver piping. "Our lives are a joke. Anyone can see that, I guess I wondered why you weren't laughing."

She laughed then, making herself sad with the sound.

Other evenings they shouted over a buzz of airplane propellers, under the bump of disco, across the chill seats of a climbing chairlift. But always they talked, endlessly, oblivious to their surroundings, one conversation encompassing a thousand fragmented days.

"And you?" Byron spoke between sips of drinks that vanished like snow under his breath. "What did you see in me?"

Claire smiled, silent. She knew he knew the answer.

In the private bedrooms of an endlessly itinerant courtship, they never stripped off their clothes, never attempted the clumsy gyrations that passed for sex. They lounged in lazy proximity, fully clothed. Claire felt no reserve. With Byron, there was no question of making a match. His worn, mature face, sadly humorous, told her he'd put all such questions behind him.

"Anyway, it doesn't matter." He often held her hand, rubbing her thumb with his. "You say we've been forgotten. Some people say we've been abandoned. But what would it change, if we knew the truth? Things would be the same whatever happened in— well, in what I suppose we have to call 'the real world.'"

"Would they?" Claire focused on the confidence with which he spoke, the weary conviction of his old, wise voice.

Byron narrowed his eyes. "That's what I believe. We were made to live this way. We were never meant to find a match." He lifted himself on an elbow, gazing across the folds and drapes of the bedroom, the swaddling silk abundance of an ancient four-poster bed. "Look, the idea is we're proxies, right? Our originals, they got tired of looking for love. The uncertainty, the effort. So they made us. Poured in their memories and hopes, built this playground, so we could do what they didn't want to do, keep mixing and mingling and trying and failing. And one day we would find a match, and that would be it, our work would be done, and we would be canceled, deleted, for them to take over."

Claire lay still, withholding comment. There was a real thrill, she thought, in hearing things put so plainly, the cynical logic of their lives.

"But what if," Byron said, "that wasn't ever their real goal? What if they never wanted love at all? What if they only *wanted* to want it —wanted, in some way, to be *able* to want it? You remember how things were. We all remember at least some of that world. Was it ever such a loving place? The overcrowding. The overwork. It was so much better to be alone. What if this place only exists . . . what if *we* only exist to . . . to stand in for something, represent something, some kind of half-remembered dream? A dream our originals had mostly given up, but still felt, in some way, they ought to be dreaming?"

"Oh, God," Claire sighed.

"I'm sorry." Byron touched the backs of the hands she held over her face. "I shouldn't be talking like this."

"It's not that." She dropped her hands. "It's that it's all so wrong. You make it sound even more hopeless than it is."

"I don't believe it's hopeless."

"But if we're only here to go on some futile, empty search . . . I mean, why?" She sat up, holding fistfuls of sheet. "We're a joke twice over. A fake of a fake. Even if they didn't know we would . . ." She was garbling her remonstrations, caught, as usual, between religion and philosophy. "I mean, why would anyone put us *through* this?"

He lay back, staring, pale as an empty screen. "Claire, what if I told you we could make a match?"

She held a pillow to her breast, suddenly cold, wondering if it was the kind of cold a real human being would feel. "Don't say that."

"I mean it."

"Don't say it. You know what will happen. I hate this world. I hate the people who made it. I hate myself, whatever I am, and I hate the woman I used to be. But I'm not ready to—"

"I'm not saying you have to."

She watched him with bared teeth, projecting all her fear onto his alarmingly calm face.

"I'm saying we can do it." Byron's eyes were like red wine, dark and flickering. "We can do it without giving anything up. We can commit to each other, forever, without being deleted or vanishing. We can declare our love, and no one will ever know, or interfere, or steal it away from us."

"That's impossible." She bit her tongue until she could almost remember what it felt like to feel pain.

"It's entirely possible."

"That's not how things work."

"You forget. I told you once, long ago, I have an interest in virtual environments. Or anyway, I used to. I know exactly how this world works."

She sat up, seeing excitement shining from him via those two bright giveaways, perspiration and tears.

"Do you remember, Claire? New Orleans?" He sat up, reaching for her hands. "There's a dock there that runs far out into the river. A ferry sets out from it, every night, toward the far shore. Each night, it leaves a second earlier; each time, it travels a second farther. One time out of a thousand, it reaches the far bank. If we're on that ferry when it touches land, we'll be on a border, a threshold, a place where the rules no longer apply. When the scenario resets, we'll be left behind. We can live there forever, or however long the world lasts.

"Claire." He insisted, at that moment, on holding both her hands, as if needing to be doubly sure she was there. "Nothing is entirely random. I know you don't keep count of the nights, but I do. I've been tracking the evenings, observing the patterns. And I've been looking for a person to take along with me, one person to share with me the rest of time. You are that person. Say the words. In five nights, we will meet again, at a dinner party in New Orleans. The ferry will set out at eleven-forty. Come with me, Claire. Be with me on that dock. Step with me, together, out of this world."

She saw her fists vanish inside his. The midnight chime would sound in a moment, and with it new crowds, new possibilities, new glories of music and excitement would be conjured out of the unending night. Could she leave all that behind, stand with this man forever on the shore of one permanent land? Together, they would walk, never changing, down unchanging streets, where dance music streamed out of immortal cafés, where orchids stood, never wilting, on the sills of bedroom windows, silvered by a moon that never set. But these would be their cafés, their moon, their orchids, and if there was no way to know how long it might last, still, they would own together that unmeasured quantity of time, laying claim to one house with its scattershot furniture, and never live in fear of the midnight chime.

Already, tonight, that chime was sounding, jangling a warning across the sky. But Claire had time to speak the charmed words.

"I want to see you again."

5

Around the long dining table in the house in New Orleans, Civil War colonels gazed out of their walnut frames. The candles were at work, scattering reflections, and the antique chairs creaked with conviviality. Claire sat next to Byron, intent on the French-style clock. Dinner was done, the plates cleared away, and two dozen puddings quivered in two dozen china bowls.

"Pudding," sighed a ravishing girl, dressed, like many, for the setting, in the rustling skirts of a southern belle. "You see what I mean? It's all so random. Radicchio salads, oxtail for dinner, and they serve us chocolate pudding for dessert."

Claire, seated across the table, reflected that this was the last time she'd ever have to have this conversation.

Twenty-four spoons dipped and rose. Twenty-four servings of pudding vanished, dispelled by the touch of twenty-four tongues.

When the party dispersed, Byron took Claire's hand. At the door, he bent to her ear, and she felt his warm whisper. "Three hours. Stay close."

They stepped out onto the porch. And Byron disappeared.

Claire spun in confusion. The porch, the house, the whole scene was gone. She stood on a dance floor, surrounded by feet that stamped and swung and kicked up a lamp-lit dust. The dim air shivered to the scratch of a fiddle. There was absolutely no sign of Byron.

Trying to get her bearings, Claire clutched at the jostling shoulders. She spotted a door and wriggled toward it. The energy of the dance, like a bustling machine, ejected her into humid air.

Claire stumbled down three wooden steps. Looking back, she recognized the roadside bar where she'd sat with Byron on their first meeting, several thousand nights ago.

What had happened? Claire staggered toward the road. The moon made iron of the land, steel of the river, and the lights of town were far away.

The ferry! It was only a few miles from here, no more than a two-hour walk. Claire thought she could make it, if she hurried.

She'd walked a quarter of an hour when a vintage roadster, roaring from behind, froze her like a criminal in a flood of light. Byron pushed open the door.

"Get in."

Claire hurried to the passenger side, jumped into the leather seat. Byron stomped on the gas, and the wheels of the car barked on gravel.

"It's glitching." Byron leaned forward as he drove. "The environment. The counters are resetting. Like I said, we're in a liminal place tonight. The rules are temporarily breaking down. Look."

He tapped his wrist, where a watch glimmered faintly.

"It's after ten," Byron said. "It's been over an hour since I saw you. We've lost a chunk of time, and I'm afraid—damn." He swerved, almost losing control, as he caught sight of something down the road.

Twisting in her seat, Claire saw the roadside shack, the one she'd just exited, sliding by.

Byron cursed and pushed down on the gas. They rattled up to the old roadster's maximum speed, forty, fifty. Swamps, river, and road flowed by. The shack passed again, again, again.

"All right, that does it." Byron braked so hard, Claire nearly whacked her head on the dashboard. He fussed with the gearshift and twisted in his seat, wrapping an arm around her headrest.

"What's happening?" she asked.

"Can't you tell? We're looping."

"But what are you doing?"

"Desperate problems call for desperate measures." Byron squinted through the tiny rear windshield. "The way I see it, if you can't hit fast-forward, hit rewind."

The car jerked backward.

And car and road and Byron all screeched out of being, and Claire found herself sitting at a café table, alone, deep in the tipsy commotion of town.

She jumped up, knocking over her chair.

Once again, Byron was nowhere to be seen.

Claire cursed, turned in a full circle, cursed again. A passing man in a bowler hat picked up her chair, righted it, and touched his hat.

"Crazy, eh? All these jumps?" He straightened his jacket with a roll of his shoulders, looking up at the sky, as if expecting heaven to crack.

"But what do we do?" Claire gasped. "How do we stop it?"

The man in the bowler hat smiled and shrugged. "Nothing *to* do, I guess. Except play along."

Pantomiming, he grabbed a nearby barber pole, swung himself through an open door, and promptly, like a magician's rabbit, blinked out of existence.

Partiers ran past, giggling and tripping, stretching their faces in merry alarm, like people caught in a thunderstorm. Firefly-like, they meandered through doorways, laughing as they winked in and out of existence. In a world of rules and repetition, Claire had long since observed, childlike chaos greeted any variation in routine.

But what do I do? Claire ducked into a drugstore entrance. *What can I do, what should I do?* She did her best to steady her mind, analyze the situation. The jumps, the cuts, the vanishings and re-appearances—they seemed to happen at moments of transition: entries and exits, sudden moves. If she found some way to game the system . . .

Turning, Claire jumped through the drugstore door. And again, and again, and again, jump after jump. On her fifteenth jump, the trick worked, the environment glitched. Claire tumbled into a banquet hall, crashing into a tray-bearing waiter, scattering scallops and champagne flutes. "Sorry, sorry . . ." Dashing toward the hall doors, Claire tried again. Another round of jumping propelled her into a rowboat, somewhere out in the stinking bayou. Gators splashed and rolled in the muck, grunting and hissing as they fled from her intrusion. Claire jumped into the water and ducked under, sinking her feet in the creamy ooze. She kicked, launching herself up into the air—

And found herself, sodden with mud, near the bank of the river, back in town.

How many times would she have to do this? Searching the bank,

Claire saw no promising doors. She threw herself into the river three more times. The third time, she emerged in a backyard swimming pool.

And so, through portals and windows, through falls and reversals, Claire skipped her way through the liminal evening, traversing a lottery of locations, careening in her soaked dress and dirty hair through car seats, lawn parties, gardens and gazebos, bedrooms where couples lay twined in dim beds. Sometimes she thought she saw Byron, hurrying through a downtown doorway or diving over the rail of a riverboat, moving in his own Lewis Carroll quest through the evening's hidden rabbit holes. Mostly, she saw hundreds of other adventurers, laughing people who leaped and jostled through doorways, running irreverent races in the night.

At last Claire stumbled out of a bait shop onto the dock, the ramshackle fishing shacks hung with buoys, the long span of planks laid out like a ruler to measure the expanse of her few remaining minutes—and there was the ferry, resting on the churn of its diesel engine, bearing Byron toward the far shore.

"Claire," he shouted over the water, and added something she couldn't hear.

Was it a freak of the fracturing environment, some cruel new distortion, that made the dock seem to lengthen as Claire ran? Was it a new break in that hopelessly broken world that made the planks passing under her feet seem infinite? By the time she came to the end of the dock, Byron and the ferry were in the middle of the river, and his call carried faintly down the boat's fading wake.

"Jump!"

Was he crazy? The distance was far too wide to swim.

"Claire, I'm serious, jump!"

And now, Claire understood: if it had worked before . . . a thousand-in-one chance, perhaps . . .

Far across the river, Byron was waving. Claire looked into the water. Briefly, she hesitated. And this was the moment she would think back to, a thousand times and a thousand again: this instant when she paused and held back, wondering how badly she wanted to spend eternity in one home, one world, with one man.

The next instant, she had flung herself headfirst into the water. And perhaps this world made more sense than Claire thought. Perhaps the designers had known what they were doing after all.

Because of all the cracks and rabbit holes in the environment, of all the possible locations in which she might emerge—

She was splashing, floundering, on the far side of the river, and the ferry was a few yards away.

Claire thrashed at the water, clawing her way forward, as the first of three chimes sounded over the water.

She'd forgotten to kick off her shoes. Her skirt wrapped her legs. She couldn't fall short, not after trying so hard, chasing potential romances down the bottomless vortex of an artificial night.

The second chime made silver shivers pass across the water.

So close. Claire tore at the waves, glimpsing, between the splashing of her arms, Byron calling from the ferry, leaning over the rail.

As she gave a last, desperate swipe, the third chime rang in the coming of midnight, the sound reminding Claire, as it always would, of the teasing jingle of a set of keys.

Around bright tables, under lamps and music, the partygoers had gathered, to mingle and murmur and comment on the food. So much beauty to be savored, so much variety: so many men and women with whom to flirt and quip and dance away the hours of an endlessly eventful evening. And after tonight, there would be more, and still more—men and women to be savored, sipped, dispelled.

If anyone noticed the woman who moved among them, searching the corners of crowded rooms; if anyone met her at the end of her dock, looking across the starlit water; if anyone heard her calling one name across the waves and throbbing music, they soon moved away. The party was just beginning, lively with romance, and the nights ahead were crowded with the smiles of unknown lovers.

MARIA DAHVANA HEADLEY

The Thirteen Mercies

FROM *The Magazine of Fantasy & Science Fiction*

After the Flood

BENEATH THE WATER, we good men perform our last Mercies, reversing and reversing.

The History of Everything

There's never been a world that isn't a world at war. That's the truest thing we know, and we've known it since we were boys, since before we got our orders and obeyed them.

We weren't equipped or expected to end that war. We were equipped to move over ground, kill those in our way, and begin again elsewhere, in another part of the world, in another part of the war. We were soldiers. We were born that way.

If ever asked to testify, we were to say only that we were soldiers and had always been soldiers and would always be soldiers.

We were to seek, and to destroy. We were to open mouths and pull out useful truths.

That was our mission. That was what we did.

That is why they sent us here.

Perhaps the war has ended and there's peace on Earth, but if there is, we don't want to know it.

The Punishment for Mercy

Out in the jungle where it rains in perpetuity, there's a woman who's lived for seven hundred years.

We were informed on the first day of our deployment that she'd looped a spell around us like a corral and that we'd suffer here for our sins. This was the arrangement the military court had come to.

General Steng ordered us not to disrespect the directive, though he laughed himself, in his tent. We all heard him, and we laughed, too.

We felt encouraged, held in the gentle hands of our government, given a false punishment that'd look real to the public, a pseudo-imprisonment on a verdant island. We expected that the sun would rise a hundred times and then we'd be returned to the world. This was only a joke. An old woman. What could an old woman do to us? What could an old woman do to anything?

That was during the early period, when we imagined we'd been sent to this island to perform a secret mission against the enemy rather than to die slowly of rot.

It's rained 2,478 of the past 2,490 days. In our leaking tents, in this, the seventh year of our deployment, we remain. Our sentence brought us directly from the trial to this jungle, blindfolded and gagged, wrists bound.

We're prisoners of our own government, not of any other enemy.

We look at the sky and try to plot our location, but the clouds cover the stars.

The First Coming of Nobody

"Nobody's coming for us," Lieutenant Matthias Granger says, looking up from his carving. "We'll die here."

He was from a small town before all this, a place where he'd thought to eventually own a pharmacy. He volunteered. His deeds at Kinotra are well documented. The photograph of his Eighth Mercy, the Reversed Mercy of Truth, was on the front page of the *Times*.

We keep our promise of pain, even if they are not deserving, those lines went. *Though a criminal be forgiven, he will still be punished.* The Eighth Reversed Mercy is the Punishment of the Innocent.

I don't turn my head when Lieutenant Granger speaks. He's beside the fire we've lit to keep mosquitoes at bay. General Steng hasn't emerged from his tent in fourteen days. We can hear him talking, to himself or to something else.

Our second-in-command, Major Mivak Priest, looks out into the trees and orders the men to sharpen their stakes. Humidity jams our rifles. Mold grows in our cartridges and fungi bloom in the barrels of our pistols. The sharpened stakes are—this is unspoken—also meant for falling upon should we reach the point of suicide, though there is no suicide protocol in our orders. We've been ordered to do the opposite of die.

"Nobody's coming!" Granger screams. "Do you hear me? Nobody!"

Then he stops making words and just utters sounds. I don't see the thing that takes Granger, but some of my men do. A tail, whipping and black. Claws.

My men begin to shout and shots are fired, but Nobody takes Granger into the dark, and there's not a man among us strong enough to follow. We stand in armed confusion for a minute. We can't go into the trees. They're outside our boundary.

"The old woman!" cries Lieutenant Lep Kvingsman, expert in the Seventh Mercy, Generosity shifted to Reverse Abundance, the expertise of famine provision. He's best friend to the deceased, and there are tears on his face. "It was the old woman! She came out of the trees and into the camp! I saw her!"

He's been in his hammock too long, scratching at his legs, humming a high spellsong that in better times would've summoned a naked girl to fall from the clouds and drape her long hair over his body. Here it only summons a bat, wings printed with slogans from the years when we thought we'd win this war.

I may be the only soldier who thinks about performing a Mercy for Lieutenant Kvingsman, but I suspect I'm not. We've not done it in seven years. It's an ecstasy. I have expertise in the Eleventh Mercy, the Reversed Mercy of Rebellion. My hands itch, and my teeth.

"It was the old woman," Kvingsman whispers. "She'll take us, one by one."

We refuse to listen to him.

Out in the trees, Nobody devours Lieutenant Matthias Granger, bone by bone, hair by hair, and we hear one scream, and then another. No one moves.

It's a Mercy, we decide. We'll take it as one.

The Brightest Colors, the Highest Resolution

There are worse Mercies than those we invoked at Kinotra, but ours were immortalized.

The photographs of my men performing the Thirteen Mercies are now as memorable to the viewing public as paintings by the Old Masters. They could be clicked into life-size, and then into sizes larger than life. A wound the size of a caterpillar becomes a jagged excision the size of a car. I am told, though I didn't see them, that for a time there were billboards on the roads leading to and from the capital, showing me with the prisoner in my arms, our faces the size of buildings and our expressions clearly visible, his agony, mine certainty.

We never learned who took the photographs. Whoever it was, he's among us now. We were all brought here together on the transport. Our betrayer is with us, living, eating, shitting. Our betrayer is our brother. Perhaps Granger was the photographer. We don't know.

Torture was nothing surprising to the public by the time the photos went viral, but the world's capacity for righteous horror was greater than we might have imagined. Before the photos of our company's mission at the Kinotra Prison were leaked, we would've been acquitted. We were elite soldiers, after all. We were decorated.

Images hit the Internet, and then the newspapers and televisions. There were protest marches, boycotts, assassination attempts. One of our mothers was murdered by a mob.

Does no one in the world realize what we did to save them? What we did, we did according to our orders. What we did, we did to save the world from worse Mercy.

The General and His Enemy

General Hyk Steng stands at his tent flap, tall and wiry, his head shaven with a knife made of slate. He's not a young man, thirty-five years into his career, but he spends nights lifting his own weight and his muscles are larger than they were when we arrived. There's nothing to do here but build mass in misery. We're living on lizards, coconuts, and Ready-Pac rations.

"I dreamed it would come," General Steng says, his eyes the eyes of someone damned a long time ago. His expertise is in the Thirteenth, the Mercy that would've ended all this.

"This begins our true campaign," he says. "The execution of our orders. We've been deployed to fight the enemy, and this is the enemy's incarnation."

Major Priest looks to the general for further instruction, but the general says nothing more. He just stares out into the green, smiling a little.

Things were bleak in the years after the war began, bleak enough that a man like Steng seemed like what we'd all been waiting for. The country wanted a man willing to shoot to kill, and he was put in charge of the military.

The general was a prisoner of war early in his career. There's video of him emerging from a cave in the mountains of Ghenari, a young man, hobbled and pale as bone, all his nails missing and his voice broken from screaming. This was in the days before the enemy began to take tongues. He went on to lead our country through several of the wars that didn't end. That was the way we spent the last years of that century.

In the mountains of Ghenari, the story went, the general ate his captors. He walked out of that cave carrying two men's roasted heads in his hands. He was nearly elected president after that.

We haven't seen our original orders, of course. This is a punishment, not a true deployment, or so we all thought until this moment, the general now informing us of our task. Some of us still believe that eventually our time here will end and a transport will come to reclaim us. The world will have forgotten our faces, and we'll be able to go home, wherever home is.

This punishment is, by all accounts, a Mercy unto itself. There was, in the months before the trial, talk of our execution by firing squad. The word *Mercy* doesn't mean what it once meant, not to us. Not to anyone.

We've been in the rain too long. Our skin is soft as felt, thin and tearing, and insects eat us from the inside out.

General Steng looks into the jungle. Out there, we hear them singing, whoever they are.

We're under constant invisible guard, but we aren't guarded from Nobody.

Justifications for Things Not Termed Torture

"Had we not torn out their fingernails," Commander Verald Wrenn said during the Vetroiso Offensive, "they'd have used them to tear out our eyes."

"Had we not silenced their soldiers," the other side's High Officer, Chemrai Lirez, said during the aftermath of that same negotiation, "they'd have screamed spells to call their gods. It was a service to the future of humanity to cut out their tongues. We could not allow the heavens to drop to Earth."

After Vetroiso, battalions of our tongueless soldiers were returned to us, and to the other side we returned soldiers with their nails peeled to the beds, along with a separate cargo of amputated fingertips and prints rendered in blood. It was all part of the business of war. The prisoners were exchanged, and everyone agreed to forget about them.

There've always been variations on Mercy. The enemy's children, for example, have always tied our children to trees and scalped them, and our children have always held the enemy's children underwater until they drowned.

General Steng went in person to the court in full uniform on the day of the verdict, not to plead but to show himself. He made no progress, never mind his fame.

By the time the events at Kinotra Prison happened, our spells had largely stopped working. Our gods no longer responded. Their gods were stronger. We were losing. The rest of the world had overtaken our reputation.

We were everyone's enemy.

The roads began to rise, rippling asphalt, and beneath them were tunnels filled with insurgents. A whole country crossed the borders into another. What else were we to do? We were angry, and we were in the right. We'd lost loved ones. We were defending our homeland.

We were trained in the Thirteen Mercies, all of us, in a silent camp in the desert. Each of us paid in his loved ones' blood. Each of us knew loss.

The Thirteen Mercies were a final attempt to blast our enemy into the dark.

I didn't say this when I was called to testify. I couldn't. There are still secrets. I was third-in-command when the Mercies at Kinotra occurred. I was off-shift, exhausted, and asleep on my cot when the rituals of the Twelfth were done, and no one called me to witness them, or to take part, yet here I am, along with my men and my commanders. Justice came down on us all, no matter our individual crimes. The government had been shamed, and the president himself accused by an international tribunal of 587 counts of war crimes against the Convention.

"My men were performing the Thirteen Mercies, and they were responding to direct orders," testified General Hyk Steng, but he refused to explain to the tribunal what that meant. He could not.

We'd all sworn, and the swearing was permanent. To speak the Mercies to the uninitiated would be to choke on blood. Those oaths couldn't be defied.

Those Who Love These Soldiers

Our orders say that we must stay alive at any cost, that we must take our instructions from no one but the president. We no longer know who the president is. For the first few years, planes flew over us. Once, they dropped a confetti of leaflets, but they were not in our language. One of my men claimed he could read them.

"They're love letters," he said. He had a fiancée at home, from whom he hadn't heard since our arrival on the island.

I have a son who's grown into a man since this deployment began. I've worked for this government my entire career, taken orders from my commanders, and to be abandoned here—

This jungle sings, but it doesn't sing for us. The mosquitoes here are as big as kites, and they come at night to drink us dry. Our uniforms are rotted. None of us can dress in a manner that shows respect. We're in shreds of camouflage, and our skin is smeared with mud.

There are no airplanes now, no messages dropped. There are no sounds coming from our radios. We don't know if there's still a world, and if there is, whether it remembers our faces.

We are loved by insects, by rain, and by Nobody.

The Qualities of Mercy

The Thirteen Mercies were a prayer, to begin with, a prayer for compassion, stating the many forms of god's goodness as revealed to a man named Moses, back in another world, back in another book.

The Thirteen Reversed Mercies were created by men as an insult to god, as the back edge of the original attributes. Everything good has something bad beside it. That's a thing we know by this point in the history of the world. To speak the Thirteen Reversed Mercies is to pray for unforgiveness. There are no gods to make things right. There are only men like us.

No one remembers, really, the Reversed Mercies' original purpose—we've forgotten the purpose of most old things—but the thing they are used for now is power. To speak them is to break oneself open and crack one's own heart. That's a portion of the training.

The Reversed Mercies become part of a soldier, and as he performs them, he entwines with them. The Thirteen Reversed belong to an ancient tradition of bad magic that once balanced the good, before the world went wrong. There's no good now. There hasn't been in some time. There's only bad, overwhelming the last little scraps of everything.

When our military took the Thirteen Reversed Mercies on, we did so with full knowledge of the dangers. We knew they were tainted, and that they'd wound us. We needed them. None of us would've made it intact out of Kinotra, not if the Mercies had been completed. We were prepared to die to save our country.

Instead our country sent us here to die condemned, not as saviors but as villains, as though our enemies were not the ones who'd forced us into this. Without provocation, we'd never have brought the Mercies into the war. It was the fault of the dead.

We performed the first Twelve. Only the Thirteenth remains, but we have no hope of completion.

Things Done by Women

The old woman keeps it raining. We can hear her singing, her voice more like a bird's than a woman's, and then more an insect's than a bird's.

We don't know what women's voices sound like anymore. It's been years since we last heard them. We haven't spent our lives among women, most of us, and though I must still have a son, I never knew his mother. We met in the dark, and left one another before the sun came up.

We're soldiers, and our lives are the war and the Mercies, not women, not children. We still don't know what the women did in the war, not with any certainty. Sometimes a woman in a position of authority gave an order and killed an entire company of men.

Enemies realigned and commands shifted. We weren't always warned. We were too occupied, there in our desert camps, mapping territories over ancient lines, tunneling, slingshotting into the sky in search of crows to augur over.

Sometimes women loved us, and sometimes they sent guns to kill us and told us we were not living up to their standards. Some of us hate women and some of us imagine lives in women's arms, but most of us know that none of it matters. The jungle sings in a woman's voice, and we listen, uneasy.

The Second and Third Comings of Nobody

Nobody kills three more of our company, tearing them from their hammocks and from their campfires: the expert in the Sixth Mercy, Slowness to Anger, Reversed to Swift and Killing Rage. The expert in the Second Mercy, Mercy After Repentance, Reversed to Deeper Rage After Confession. The expert in the Fourth Mercy, Mercy Without Confession, Reversed to Invented Crimes.

"This is the mission," says the general. "These are the measurements. Cut the wood to size."

He sends men to the jungle's edge to chop and strip trees, and in the mud he draws a structure, an arc of branches and boughs. Others of us weave rope from vines.

When Nobody comes to us for the third time, she's neither man nor woman, but crocodile. She's made of scales and coils, and she takes three more men, our experts in the First (the Mercy Before the Sin, reversed to Punishment Before the Sin Is Committed) and the Fifth (Unearned Kindness, Reversed to Unearned Violence), pulling them into the river and dragging them down. She takes Kvingsman as well this time and he screams for help, but we cannot help him. We are ourselves at the mercy of the general.

We watch Kvingsman's fingertips shudder above the waterline, and then they're gone, only a ripple marking the place Nobody has passed. And so we lose the Seventh Mercy, Kvingsman's expertise in the Mercy of Abundance, reversed to Famine and Loss.

In Kinotra, Kvingsman was photographed with his foot in the mouth of the enemy, forcing the man to swallow not only his boot but also the magic the sole contained, a magic that would keep the enemy, those who survived the Thirteenth, beneath our feet and starving for another two thousand years.

This crocodile isn't the incarnation of an enemy. She's our punishment. I know it, even if the general does not. We're meant to die of her. Something's changed in the outer world and she's been assigned to haunt us.

We missed a crucial order. We forgot how to pray.

The general says, "Cut the wood to size. Spin the rope."

Things Said by Good Men

In the tribunal, I was named personally. I stood beside General Steng in my dress uniform as the slide show of photos passed before us.

Though I was sleeping during the culmination of our cycle, though the working of the Eleventh had taken years from my life, though I'd now live to be no older than forty, I was proud.

I opened my mouth before that panel of deciders and told them I had no regrets about what I'd done. I told them my men had courage, and that we were acting on faith. I told them that we were good men seeking the truth.

The Feeding of the Animals

In the moments after Nobody takes Kvingsman, Major Mivak Priest has two stakes in his hands, and then he's running into the dark, outside the safety of our circle, the jungle live and hissing as he passes, and out there, the last screams of someone, the voices of the dead or of our invisible guards. No one yells anything we recognize.

We stand in shock in the clearing, waiting for the general to give orders to pursue him, but they don't come.

This is the first time one of us willingly leaves the circle of our prison. He's out there with the old woman, in the rain.

"He performs his Mercy now," says General Steng, and we hear an abrupt shriek, the voice of Major Priest, and a whoosh as the trees bend to the Twelfth Mercy, the Mercy of Errors Transformed to Merits, Reversed to Generosity Transformed to Cruelty.

Every animal in the jungle eats, and Mivak Priest is eaten. There's a great splashing, a struggle, but no more screams. Major Priest is gone.

The general looks impassively into the trees.

The left arm of Mivak Priest lands in the clearing, torn from his shoulder by too many teeth. The song of the old woman grows louder and the rain comes harder. We're wet through. Some of us are crying.

"Raise it," General Steng barks, and we look at each other, uncertain, but we do, finally, lifting the trees we've cut and hewn into their new configuration, a rectangle, and at the top an intricate structure of knots.

"Today we hang the crocodile," the general says. "We will bear no more loss. We will bear no more."

A Recipe for Mercy

I think yearningly of my Eleventh Mercy, the Mercy of Rebellion. The Reversed Mercy is the Crushing of the Rebellious. It says that the sins of rebellion shall not be lifted up. The spell is simple enough, though it requires wire and a razor blade, a grinding of coarse salt, a dish made of fine glass, and an envelope of something stronger than cocaine.

I have none of those ingredients here in the jungle.

There will be no more Eleventh, nor the feelings it evokes, the way the spell is crafted to fill its victim with hope of revolution, the way the room seems to disappear as my hands and the wire move closer. It's a Mercy, and it is a magic, and in the cycle of magics, I've had nearly as much power as the general does.

I will never see my son again, nor know what sort of soldier he may become.

I feel something rise inside me, a rebellion against the Mercies, a knowledge that there will be no forgiveness.

I decide to think about the desert and how we trained there until our skin was one with the sand. This was nothing regular, our training. We were elite. We were the good men, the best men, the only ones trained in the Thirteen Mercies, and all our training went to hell when the country turned against us. None of us knows why we've been condemned to a crocodile. Nothing like this punishment exists in our manuals.

I remember the way we learned the Mercies. I remember the blood I took from my son, how I poured it out into a circle and lit it on fire. I knew what he would feel, thousands of miles away, and I did it anyway. My baby in his crib. His mother leaning over him, puzzled, then frantic.

The skin of the sky peeled back like a wound full of gravel.

Our training was more important than love.

We would win the war with these weapons, we thought then. We'd take the land and pour our burned burdens out upon it. We'd be merciful, all of us, Reversing the Mercies of god until the sand turned to salt and then to fire.

There were no gods who could ignore it. There was no love that could satisfy it. We were the men, and we were winning.

I don't know anything like that now. The magic's worn off and all I am is a man in the dark, surrounded by men in the dark.

The Fourth Coming of Nobody

The general stands straight, his arms crossed. "Now we wait," he says.

We sit in the mud. We wait night and day, in the dark, in the gray downpour. All around us, the jungle crackles and things move within it. Our guards whisper but we can't understand them.

We're on an island surrounded by sharks, and the sharks are like Mercies. Any one of them could kill us, or they might all do it at the same time. We feel fed upon.

Eight of us are dead, and we have only five men left. Perhaps we're the last five men in the world.

"*There was an old woman,*" sings Major Rivel Harmer, practitioner of the Ninth Mercy—Keeping Kindness for Thousands of Generations, Reversed to the Keeping of Hatred, the grudge against grandchildren and great-grandchildren. "*Who lived in a shoe—*"

General Steng puts up a hand to silence him. None of us will take Harmer's tongue, but the general can do as he pleases. There will be no babble here in the jungle, no matter how frightened we are, no matter how the seventh year ebbs into a winter that isn't.

"There," the general hisses, staring into the trees where something orange glows. "She's there."

I crouch on legs that've lost muscle. An old man now, all at once, and us in possession of only five of the Mercies, not enough to break anything strong.

She comes out of the trees, body like a tree trunk, tail long and narrow, face pointed. We have our stakes, but our stakes are only twigs. She's older than we will ever be.

She looks us each in the eyes and smiles.

"Who are you?" the general shouts at her. "Who sent you?"

The crocodile writhes and her skin splits, blood dripping from hide. Her mouth opens wider.

"Who are you?" I shout in echo. "What kind of Mercy are you?"

The crocodile's no longer a crocodile. She ripples up out of the skin, her face through the teeth, her fingers through the claws.

"I am," the old woman says, "the Thirteenth Mercy."

The Mercy of the Uncleaning

The Thirteenth Mercy was originally the Mercy of the Cleansing of Sins. In Reverse, the Thirteenth is the Mercy of Filth, the bestowal of all of our sins into the souls of the enemy, the crushing beneath sins of everything living. Everyone is evil in the Reversed Mercy. It's constructed around the knowledge of hopelessness.

It is performed with bleach and wool.

Had we completed it at Kinotra, a cloud would've risen over the prison, and in it, the enemy would have drifted, driven forward across the sky by our hatred, sleepless and hungry forever.

The sacrifice stands for everything we've lost, everything we've given over to fighting, soldiers' lives spent placing bombs in public squares and buses, centuries of soldiers' time spent poisoning and lynching, all the labors of war both just and unjust, all the orders followed, all the sins accrued by souls that did not ask for them. The pursuit of the truth is complicated. Sometimes the truth hides in the organs of the enemy, and sometimes it does not.

There is no way to know unless one looks deep.

The Execution of Nobody

The general signals and the ropes spin up from the mud, wet and twisting, lassoing her legs and tail, knotting around her throat.

Major Harmer hauls Nobody up, grunting, hissing the phrases of his half-broken Mercy, cursing her children and her children's children, cursing her past and future.

Nobody opens her jaws and shows us teeth, and then opens claws and shows us fingers, the delicate hands of a woman pressed beneath the claws of a crocodile.

She has silver hair and orange eyes. Her scales are black enough to make her disappear. Our camouflage doesn't hide us. She's the kind of thing that can see in the dark.

At last we see her in full.

This crocodile hangs from our gallows now, we five remaining Merciful around her. We're winning. She's our enemy. When we kill her, we'll be free of everything.

We'll complete our Mercies and end this torment. Then home. We're all thinking it.

She's our mission, revealed to us at last. She's what we came here to destroy.

I can see her moving, her tail lashing. The rain doesn't cease. It's harder, hard enough to bend the trees surrounding us, and a wind gasps into life, breaking branches around the clearing.

Our gallows hang heavy with the monster and she swings, jerking, strangling, the bodies of our company already in her belly. She gags and chokes and becomes an old woman again. She's thin enough to break, but she doesn't. She hangs by her neck at the end of the rope, but gravity doesn't hold her. Not her, this old woman not old woman, her claws and her black-scaled tail, the crocodile parts that surround her body.

The Photographer

There's a click, a sound from the world, and I turn my head to see the general holding a camera like someone from a hundred years ago, a hood over his head to make a portrait of Nobody's execution.

Major Harmer makes a noise of betrayal.

The photos from Kinotra.

I think of a pale young man walking out of a cave with two charred heads in his hands, our punishment part of his Mercy.

"I will be Merciful," Nobody says, and smiles at us from the gallows. Her mouth is full of teeth. She isn't seven hundred years old, I think, but seven thousand, and she's been hired by someone to destroy everything.

That was supposed to have been our mission, not hers.

"You're mistaken," the general says, his eyes brighter than they were before, his face clenched. "This is the last round of Mercies. My Reversed Mercy will complete it."

She laughs, and her skin shudders off entirely from her female body and becomes a crocodile, smaller now, and then another woman, still smaller. The noose doesn't tighten, though we lean backward, gunless, ropes slipping through our hands.

We've failed in our Mercies, and now the general stands and shouts, and the woman in the noose doesn't. She does not hang. She doesn't die.

The crocodile skins she's left behind are jerking in the mud, and they rise up to tilt the gallows while she hovers there, arms extended, smiling.

The mud of the world begins to dissolve. The dirt of my garments, the filth of my skin, the matted hair and snarled beard, the quiet horrors I've fed on to fatten myself, all the dark things I've kept inside my heart.

The general screams, and I watch his body rise to her hands. She touches his face, and he hangs high in the air, the noose leaving her neck and looping around his.

"The Thirteenth Mercy," she whispers, "is the Mercy of Cleansing of Sins."

The Flood

Waters rise then. I remember, as we stand in river to our knees, as the jungle roars and sings, as our guards disappear beneath the surface, that the Mercy of the Flood is another Mercy, not one of the Thirteen, but an older measure. A Mercy that cannot be performed by humans, neither itself nor its Reverse.

Below the waters the old woman brings, battalions march tongueless and fingerless in the deep, and crocodiles swim through black silt, their eyes above the water, and cradles full of babies rock, and the land we fought over for so long is obliterated.

I see, as the waters rise up to my eyes, an image of a Mercy, the general's body bent back and hanging in midair as Nobody's jaws open his flesh, tearing his skin away from his bones and peeling him like something overripe and finished.

Beneath the water, we feel our enemies drowning as we drown, and we all begin again together, in a world without any of us.

DALE BAILEY

Lightning Jack's Last Ride

FROM *The Magazine of Fantasy & Science Fiction*

THEY SAY LIGHTNING JACK died in a fiery crash just outside of Atlanta, racing west toward freedom into the teeth of a setting sun. I remember the scene in digital video, the way I saw it then, on the ancient flat-panel affixed to the wall of a dingy apartment in Biloxi. He'd rolled coming out of a curve on I-20, and even then that struck me as laughable: three lanes of abandoned highway, all that room for error and him the finest driver that had ever lived.

Yet there it was on the screen. The networks looped the tape over and over in the days that followed, snippets of Lightning Jack's blistering death interspersed with archival footage of the moments that had made him a legend: hoisting his trophy in triumphant youth at his first Talladega, squiring Julie Marina down the red carpet to collect her Oscar, slamming into the wall as he roared out of the third curve at the last legal Daytona.

But they always came back to that final cataclysmic sequence. Captured by antiquated cameras installed in an era when I-20 still saw civilian traffic, it had, even then, the look of video you'll be seeing for the rest of your life, the flat, inarguable reality, the banal composition of history in the making: Hitler at the Reichstag, Kennedy in the motorcade. The opening images have the archetypal familiarity of a scene apprehended in a dream. The leaden vault of sky looms over a sweeping plane of empty asphalt. But for the heat rippling above the pavement, it might be a still photo. It's that static, that timeless. And then, suddenly, like an apparition, the car appears, a low-slung black blur, tires smoking as it clears the curve. The rear end slews to the right, threatening to send the vehicle into a spin, and then—impossibly, inconceivably—the driver overcorrects. It's over almost as soon as it begins, an anticlimax; only our knowledge of the man inside the car—only our knowledge of Lightning Jack's myth—redeems the paucity of drama. One moment the car is skidding. The next, it's airborne, skipping across the pavement like a stone. Then it smashes into the concrete crash barrier and jolts to a rest atop its shredded tires.

A moment of stillness follows, a moment in which I always expect the door to fly open and Lightning Jack to step out, cradling the Heckler & Koch G40 he cosseted like a baby, his lean face creased in a roguish grin as he prepares to go down in a hail of New Federal lead. He always vowed they'd never take him alive. But the door does not open. The car merely sits there, frozen beneath an armor-plated sky for a heartbeat longer. Then suddenly it bursts into flame.

New Fed officials turned the tape over to the newsnets not thirty minutes later. The story of Lightning Jack's final caper unfolded in the hours that followed. Soon enough the network faces had that footage as well, cobbled together from vehicle-mounted military cameras. It showed Jack's standard operating procedure for cutting a gasoline tanker out of a military convoy, a task as audacious as it was dangerous, requiring six people in the kind of rolling iron that would stiffen a gearhead's pecker: a Midori Spyder, a Mitsubishi Gilead, and, God help us all, Lightning Jack's sweet sugar itself, a modified black Chevy Dragon straight out of the heart of old Detroit. Three vehicles, two to take out the gunners in their crow's nests atop the tank, and one more—Jack's Dragon—to match the trucker wheel to wheel. Then, hurtling along at seventy, eighty, ninety miles an hour, the swingman would lever himself out the passenger-side window of the Dragon, fling himself across the void of racing gray pavement to the running board of the tanker, and take out the driver with a single pistol shot to the temple, bang through the window glass. The most perilous moments of all followed. The truck veered out of control as the swingman wrenched open the door, shoved the dead man aside, and took the wheel. If things went as planned, they'd coax the tanker with its three-car escort down the nearest exit and disappear into the tangle of surface streets below.

Fifty years previously, the maneuver wouldn't have been possible. A law-enforcement satellite would have lit them up the minute they cut that tanker loose. But in these days of peak oil and global warming, a satellite is lucky if it can punch a signal through the atmospheric murk once in a million pings. Still, it was a daring crime. In a U.S. of A. coming apart at the seams, with D.C. irradiated, Manhattan blown clear off the map, and insurgencies booming from sea to shining sea, a single thermos of petroleum was a hell of a thing to lose. There must have been half a dozen gangs working the black market in gasoline in those days, from Gallant Jim's up around the lakes to Victor Albertini's out on the left coast. But famous as some of them were, none of them could match Lightning Jack's crew or his legend. None of them could match his style. He'd sign in on Channel 19 to mock the truckers on their CB radios as the shit rained down, and he'd send thank-you notes—he had the prettiest script—when he was done.

But this time things had gone wrong. They'd taken out the driver and cut the tanker free of the convoy all right, but as the eighteen-wheeler swerved across the lanes, it clipped Lola Bridger's Spyder. She went spinning back into traffic where a tanker crushed her like a bug and jackknifed in the middle of the highway. The next fish in line slammed it side-on, igniting an explosion so big that it must have singed God's beard. A heartbeat later, the swingman rolled his own rig, reducing Joe Hauser's Gilead to a greasy stain on the pavement. Lightning Jack dropped the hammer, and that Dragon leapt forward like a rabid Doberman fixing to break its chain. Four and a half minutes later, it struck the crash barrier on I-20. That fire burned hot and clean. By the time it was done, there was barely enough left to put in a pine box. The networks reported it all the same and DNA confirmed it: the Feds had gotten their man.

But there are those who'll tell you that the charred carcass they pulled out of that car was a ringer and that Lightning Jack lives to this day. Some say he'd finally made his nut and retired to some clement place like the Upper Peninsula of Michigan or maybe Edmonton, others that he took his thieving ways out west, where he gave Victor Albertini a run for his money. That's the way with famous outlaws. Some men will attest to this day that Jesse James died of old age, and that John Dillinger wasn't the man the FBI pumped full of holes in front of the Biograph Theater.

I'm here to tell you that they're wrong. Lightning Jack died almost forty years ago. Don't bother telling me otherwise, because I'm the only man who knows the truth. After all, I was there. I knew Jack, you see. I knew him from the time he was a bean.

He'd already acquired the nickname—some say he gave it to himself—by the time I met him, and he was barely out of diapers then. The man—if you can call a seventeen-year-old boy a man —was flat great behind the wheel from the start, and I'll swear to that until my dying day. I knew it the first time I ever spoke to him. I'd been knocking around the Truck Series for a year by then, trying to catch on somewhere, when I saw him blow a sticker at the Charlotte Motor Speedway. I'd had my eye on him for weeks. He'd been in the lead until the tire betrayed him. This was maybe a flaw in his driving—he hadn't pitted as often as he should've—or maybe a flaw in the tire, but as he coasted into pit row, flapping leather, the field sped past him. I figured the wheel was too bent to mount a new scuff, but we'll never know for sure: the front tire carrier fumbled the exchange. Lightning Jack came out of that truck like a piston firing. His helmet went one way and Jack went the other, straight up into the tire carrier's face. Jack probably would have hit him—he *did* fire him—if Joe Hauser, the rear tire man in those days, hadn't simmered him down.

I'd known Joe since we'd been boys racing go-karts together. It was by his invitation that I was in the pit in the first place. I had an inkling that Joe might be able to broker me a job, and I had planned to show Jack that I knew my way around an engine, nobody better. But sometimes it's better to be lucky than good. Even so, I might have slipped the opportunity like I've slipped so many others if it wasn't for my own big mouth. I always was a talker, and an opinionated bastard to boot, and those traits have gotten me into more trouble than they have gotten me out of, but just then they worked in my favor, for as Jack vaulted the wall and strode into his pit stall, I couldn't help myself. I said, "You left money out there on the track."

Jack turned to face me and I saw then what a handsome devil he already was and would become. He aged well, Jack, and even when a New Fed bullet creased his forehead during the Tallahassee job a decade later, the scar it left behind only gave him a rakish look that seemed to make him more popular with the ladies. Some men you just can't beat.

"What did you say?" he asked, and the whole time Joe is standing behind him, slashing the edge of his hand across his throat. *Shut up, shut up.*

But I never could. So there we stood in the maintenance stall, me and Lightning Jack, everything stinking of spent oil and smoking rubber and sweat, and what I do is, I turn up the volume. "I said, you left money out there on the track."

"How do you figure?"

"Two ways. One, you were too aggressive. It ain't all about driving, son"—this though I didn't have but five years or so on him —"it's also about timing. You got to judge your tires and your fuel, and pit at the right time."

"I reckon driving has got me this far."

"Well, it's not likely to get you much farther. NASCAR is bigtime racing, son."

"Don't call me that again," he said, and I never did. Some men you have to learn not to push, and others you just know. Jack was one of the latter. I never met a man who had a more charming disposition, but you didn't cross him but once, not Jack. The front tire carrier could attest to that.

"What's the second way?" he asked.

"Hell, you know that. Prize money. Who knows whether you could have loaded a tire on that front wheel, but if you'd let the guy try, you might have placed. You don't have to win every time."

"The hell with placing. I want to win."

"Of course you do. But you have to take the long view. Rack up enough points, you win the series and advance to the next division. From there it's only a short hop to the show, Jack."

"You go on and get out of my garage," he said. "I don't know how you got in here anyway."

And he put his back to me.

I should have let him go. But no one ever missed a turn in hindsight, did they? Instead I said, "You need me, Jack. There's not a thing about cars that I don't know," and I think that's what did it. I wasn't asking, I was telling. And if Lightning Jack liked anything in a man, he liked confidence. He had it himself in spades. He wasn't a bragging man, but he knew there wasn't much he couldn't do with a car and he didn't get in his own way when it came to doing it. I think that's why he spun on his heel to look me over, a long, appraising look, like a man who's getting ready to drop a fair chunk of change on a brand-new piece of iron and wants to make sure he doesn't get taken.

"What's your name?" he said.

"Gus March."

"Well, Gus March, I reckon you can lug a tire as well as any man. I seem to have an opening in that department."

"It's a start, I guess. But I'll be running your crew inside a year," I said.

"That so?" He smiled as if he'd let go of some internal tension, the strain maybe of the race and losing it, and he looked simultaneously like the boy he was and the man he would become. There was something golden in that smile, a kind of glamour that would charm the knickers off just about every woman that swung into his orbit and make the men give up everything and follow him to the ends of the earth. I know because I felt it then, and before it was over I *did* follow him. He made a kind of chuffing noise, something between a snort and a laugh. Then he turned away again. "Don't let me down, Gus," he said, and his glamour hadn't rubbed off on me so much that I promised I wouldn't — not aloud, anyway. But I felt the promise in my heart. In the end, I did let him down, though. We always do, I guess. It's what makes us human. Still, that was a long time coming. In the meantime, I had other promises to keep, among them my pledge to be his crew chief before the year was out. I did it, too. It's true: there's not a thing about cars I don't know, and there's less that I can't fix. I'm not a bragging man myself. It's not bragging if you can do it.

Those were the twilight years of motor sports, of course, and if I grieved to see them go, I was glad I'd gotten in soon enough to see them at all. Sponsorship was way down and so were ratings. Things had gotten a lot like it was in the beginning, when a man with a car didn't have to have a twenty-million-dollar team to buy his place on pit row. He could earn it, the way Jack did, with his smile and his talent. He breathed new life into a dying sport, same as Ali had done for boxing. You couldn't tap a newsfeed back then without Lightning Jack smiling out at you. I can see him now, the way he was before a race, that unearthly calm he had about him. "Let's ride, Gus," he always said as he strapped himself into the cockpit, and for a while the ride was a wild one, like an out-of-control elevator hurtling to the top. You'd have thought the other drivers would have hated him, but Jack was funny like that, incandescent as the lightning bolt he'd painted down the hood of his midnight-black Dragon. He lit a room up, and people loved him for it. But even that wasn't enough to save us.

By then the soup we all took in with each breath was so thick that in some of the bigger cities—Tokyo and L.A., for instance —people wore surgical masks every time they stepped out the door. Electric vehicles had never caught on—they'd never solved the battery thing—and though public transportation had skyrocketed, plenty of people still gassed up to go. There's just something about a gasoline motor, the sense of contained deviltry in it, pistons hammering as gas explodes—actually *explodes*—in the cylinder and drives the crankshaft like a dervish in his finest hour. Meanwhile, the Feds down in Washington steadily whittled away at drivers' rights. It wasn't much more than window-dressing really. Peak oil had taken hold and the flow dried to a trickle. By the time Jack crashed coming out of the third turn in the last Daytona, there just about wasn't anyplace left where a man could wind a motor out anymore.

When NASCAR disbanded, Jack's team broke up, too. Me and Joe Hauser and Lola—the finest jack man I ever saw—stuck around for a while. Jack was glad to have us. We wanted to drive, even if it meant running thousand-dollar drags in the middle of the Birmingham night. Amateurs all around us, and Jack ate them up like candy hearts, so charismatic that they didn't mind watching him fold away their money. Jack was all about winning even then. But a time came when even Joe and Lola and I began to drift. The last of the street gas began to run out, for one thing. First it was a night or two between races; then it was a week or a month or more. Plus, there was the competition. A man can only go so long stealing lunch money before his conscience begins to nag him.

Jack fell into a funk. He took to drink, thickened up around the middle. I got to where I had to get away from it all. Before you knew it, I had a straight job, working on hydraulic lifters in Montgomery. Joe Hauser drifted out west and started pushing paper for an insurance company. Lola—the only one of us with a college degree—landed a position as an executive at a fiber-optic plant, and before you know it she was running the place.

Then the NRA's dirty bomb put the quietus to D.C. The New

Feds relocated to Buffalo, but by the time they got themselves organized, it was too late. Insurgencies had begun to break out like a bad case of the clap. States' rights and all that. I'm talking secession, the seizure of all military assets by right of eminent domain, and vigorous defense of self-declared borders. A dozen other special-interest groups followed the NRA into terrorism.

Jack, with his usual prescience, had seen the way things were headed. He showed up at the hydraulic plant one afternoon and took me to lunch. It was the kind of Alabama day where just breathing you sweat through your shirt. When we got into the air-conditioned diner, I heaved a sigh of relief. "Goddamn, but you're a sight for sore eyes, Jack," I said, and for a moment I couldn't do much more than stare at him. He was his old self, sinewy and lean behind a pair of aviator glasses, his unruly mop of hair close cropped.

"It's good to see you, too, Gus," he said. "Hell, not a minute goes by I don't think about you and the old days."

"Good times," I said, and for a moment we were silent in contemplation.

An icy-cold Coca-Cola appeared—you could see the glass sweating it was so cold—and then a couple of menus. I ordered a burger and fries without hardly noticing the lady serving us. Jack and I chatted in a desultory way about past times as we ate.

"You and Lola ever have anything together?" I asked at one point. I'd often thought about trying my hand with her myself —she'd have probably shot me down like a clay pigeon—only I feared horning in on Jack's territory, and I would never do a thing like that.

"Lola?" he said. "She was too important to the organization."

After that, the conversation turned in other directions. We were both melancholy by then, anyway. We missed the track, the stink of exhaust and the sizzle of anticipation as we took the pavement, the burst of activity whenever Jack slipped in to the pit. I ran the fastest crew on the circuit—I can't tell you how many times other drivers tried to poach my guys—but every time we rolled out onto the asphalt, we strove to shave a tenth of a second off our time. In a close race, a tenth of a second can make the difference between winning and losing.

So we chewed over what we'd been doing in the year or two since we'd last seen each other. I didn't have much to share. I worked at the hydraulics plant eight hours a day and saw a lady named Mary occasionally, but neither one of us really had our hearts in it. Jack didn't have much to say either. He'd spent a long time in that funk and then he'd pulled himself together, stopped drinking, hit the gym. I thought the conversation had hit that lull that old friends who've grown apart so often do, when they find themselves staring at each other across the gulf time has opened up between them. It saddened me. I didn't have many close friends in those days, and I hadn't realized how much I missed the easy camaraderie that grows up between men bound together in a common enterprise.

"How come you got yourself together like that?" I asked just to break the silence, and Jack got quiet all over again. He looked me over, and I recalled the first time we met, the way he'd studied me, like he was getting ready to surrender some serious change for a hunk of rolling iron, and he wanted to make sure he liked what he was seeing. I realize now that he was wondering whether he could trust me, and I'm glad he decided he could. Things would have gone differently if he'd chosen otherwise, and I might have been a happier man now, but it would have hurt something awful to know that Lightning Jack hadn't trusted in our friendship.

He didn't answer me. Not directly, anyway. What he said was, "Real tragedy what happened in Washington, wasn't it?"

I allowed it was, though I hadn't been especially fond of the party that was in power at the time. Nor the one that wasn't, either, if it came to that.

"This is only beginning," he said. He leaned forward, lowering his voice. "The whole thing's going to come apart, Gus. Wait and see. Nothing but spit and baling wire ever held this country together anyway. If it were a car, it would be a jalopy, sure."

I allowed that this was true, as well—with the caveat that, all due respect, it didn't take any genius to see it. "Hell, Jack, Georgia's already gone and you hear the same rumbling right here in Montgomery."

"Sure," he said, and now he leaned back, flung one arm across the back of the booth, and grinned. I thought our waitress, who was just then delivering the check, might go into heat. When she was gone, he ticked the rest of the secession risks off on his fingers. He finished up with California and the Midwestern Alliance and said, "You know what that means."

"War."

"That's right. And a hell of a big one, too."

"Best thing you can do is keep your head down when the shooting starts."

"I got a different perspective," Jack said. "The way I figure it, the New Feds are going to win this thing. I reckon at least half the military are going to stay loyal. You're going to see pockets of resistance to just about every insurgency that springs up, and soon enough Buffalo will be coordinating them. And the New Feds have the codes to the nukes. It's going to be a hair-raising ten years, but I think we have a window of opportunity here."

"Opportunity for what? To get our heads blown off?"

"We run that risk no matter what. There's no keeping out of the fray."

"So what do you have in mind?"

"Tell me, come war, what's the most valuable commodity on earth?"

"I don't know. Those nukes, I guess."

"Weapon of last resort, unless a terrorist gets ahold of one. The New Feds are going to try to keep it conventional—and you can't fight a conventional war without—"

"Oil," I said.

"You got it." He aimed a finger at me and dropped the hammer. Bang. "Just try firing up an Abrams tank on a Sears DieHard," he said, grinning that cocky grin of his, "and you'll see what I mean. The New Feds are already moving convoys of tankers down the old interstates. It's only a matter of time before someone picks one off."

"You're a crazy man. Let's say—just for the sake of argument —you can manage it. Who are you going to sell it to?"

"Anyone who wants it. Insurgents. Gearheads hungry to fire up their old iron. Hell, I'll ransom it back to the Feds. I don't care. I'm an amoral son of a bitch, Gus. I just want to drive."

"How do you plan to pull it off?"

He leaned forward and sketched it out for me, and I saw then that he *was* a madman. But something in his voice made me keep listening—the lure of the open road maybe or the hunger to feel a car come to life under my hands one more time. Maybe it was money and maybe it was love for Jack himself. A crew chief lives in the shadow of his wheelman, after all. Comforts him and cossets him and makes sure his car is purring like a kitten every time he takes the pavement. So yeah, I listened. Most of us never can say why we do the things we do. Oh, we can count out reasons like we count out change, but those are just rationalizations. We're mysteries to ourselves. That's the one true thing I know, so in the end I can't say why I did it. I can say only that I started off by telling him no. I thanked him for lunch and sent him packing, to pitch his crazy scheme to someone else — Joe maybe, or Lola. Anybody but me, brother. Hydraulics were the thing for me, and when the war came I'd follow my own advice — keep my head down and hope the draft board needed a gearhead more than another grunt.

Three months later, Alabama seceded from the union. I got my draft notice from the Citizens' Militia two months after that. I didn't make the appointment, though. I called Jack up and skipped town instead. He met me at the gate to tell me he'd pulled the crew back together. "Welcome home, brother," he said, clapping me on the back. "Let's ride."

Our first job was a disaster. The gunners in the crow's nests took one of our chase cars straight out of the game, spinning it off to the shoulder, where it slammed into a guardrail. A minute later it was moving again, but by then it was too late. The action had moved on. It limped to the rendezvous point, where we learned that the man in the turret — Vance Tyler, my gas man for a good half-dozen years — had caught a faceful of lead. Worse yet was the swingman, Paul Harrison. He'd worked behind the pit wall, wrangling air hose, and I think it was that more than anything else that caused him to volunteer to make the leap. He'd always longed to work the dangerous side of the wall. He miscalculated his jump and rolled up under the truck. The tires thundered over him, unwinding him like a ball of twine as Jack peeled away toward the exit.

Jack and I both took it hard. When we sheltered up at an abandoned garage, Jack told me he'd never matched speeds with the tanker. Paul hadn't had a clean shot at the running board. "Bullshit," Lola said later.

"Sure," I said. "Doesn't help *me* any, though."

"What do you mean?"

"Vance," I said.

"Well, don't cry about it," she told me. "Armor up."

We disassembled the gun turrets and rolled home under cover

of darkness, just another band of gearheads testing the night air. We weren't hot, not yet.

While Jack calmed our client, my crew and I went to work on the cars. The biggest challenge was balancing speed and weight. Jack was used to hitting 200 on the straightaways of a fast track like Daytona, and that was with restrictor plates. The question was how to maintain that kind of velocity on a vehicle that weighed considerably more than 3,300 pounds.

"That's the wrong question," Lola insisted.

"Then, what's the right one?" I demanded one day in the garage. I'd been complaining about the weight and drag of the aluminum armor we'd begun bolting to the Dragon's exterior.

"How to achieve your objective," she said. "Speed is not your objective."

"Then what is it?"

"You want to snatch a forty-ton vehicle off the highway. What do you think it is?"

Me, I thought about Vance Tyler and did just as she'd told me to: I armored up. I reckoned that top speed for a loaded tanker couldn't be more than a 100, 110 miles per hour on a long straightaway, and that without a convoy to slow it down. We had plenty of weight to give. We upgraded to rolled-steel armor and we were still hitting 150. Like I said, there's not anything I can't do with an engine if you give me enough time.

Which is enough car talk. I could talk about cars all day long if you let me, but this story is about Lightning Jack, and how he finally went under the running boards himself. The next job—and don't worry, I'm not going to belabor every one of *them,* either—went down outside of Baltimore. We scooped the tanker off 70 West and dropped it into Ellicott City. You have to understand, we never held on to the rigs for long. It was all very bang bang. Our job was to acquire and deliver. After that it was the customer's problem, and what they usually did was put it undercover somewhere quick and drain the tank into an idling fleet of smaller vehicles. But as I said, they could blow the thing sky-high on the spot if they wanted. We didn't care what they did with it. We were in it for the cash and—this was true especially of Lightning Jack, I think—the thrill of the thing.

And there were plenty of thrills. I took the gunner's position in Lola's Spyder after Vance died, so when Jack said, "Let's ride, Gus," it had a personal immediacy I'd never felt before. A night job, this was, and in the dark you couldn't see much more of that car than its taillights. There's tape of the raid, but the video has the cheap, washed-out quality of CCTV, and in the dark it has no resolution at all. You can see muzzle flash as the team breaks cover, swings in behind the convoy, and takes out the crow's nests on the last truck in line. There's some return fire from the truck's escort vehicles, but most of them are farther up in the convoy, already out of play. There are maybe two bringing up the rear, it's hard to tell. But none of that can communicate the sheer adrenaline rush of being there. I took out one of the escorts from the gun turret on Lola's Spyder. The other one rolled and skated down the highway on its roof, throwing up a rooster tail of sparks.

Up ahead, Jack's car veered in beside the tanker and locked speed. The dark swallowed the swingman—Dean Ford, the front tire changer who'd volunteered after Paul kissed the deck—but I knew he'd made the exchange because the truck began to drift out of true. For ten seconds, twelve at the most, everything hung in the balance. The trailer swung to the left, and the right front wheels of the tractor started to come off the ground. I thought the thing was going to ditch and go skidding across the pavement on its side. Then it righted itself and hit the exit to Ellicott City, the chase cars on its tail. It nailed the street going maybe sixty miles per hour, and that quick it was over. Ten minutes later, Jack makes the exchange with the client, and ten minutes after that, we're undercover in a bankrupt Toyota dealership on Baltimore Pike.

This is pit work, as exciting in its way as any tanker raid. The objective is to break the cars down as swiftly as possible—you can't cruise the streets in armored vehicles with gun turrets—and get the hell out of Dodge. My crew is fast. We've simulated this a thousand times, just like we did in the old days. The turrets come down and roof panels slide into place. Street tires replace sticky ones. Off comes the armor. Everything goes into a chaser van. Fifteen minutes later, we hit the street and branch off onto different routes, running by night to a second rendezvous point, two hundred, maybe three hundred miles away, wherever Jack has us sheltered up until we do it all over again. And there you have it. The anatomy of a job.

If we'd only run the one, everything would have been okay.

But there was no chance of that, not now. Jack loved to drive too much. As for me and Lola and the others, we loved the feel of an engine beneath our hands. There were just six of us by then. We doubled up on the road team and in the pits, doing half a dozen jobs each. We were all junkies and road dogs, hardwired for gears and adrenaline. I think that's what sustained us over the next nine months. I want to emphasize that. Months. You're reading this, you probably carry around a truckload of myths and misconceptions: that we had a ten- or twelve-year run, maybe, that we pulled off dozens of jobs before Lightning Jack's last ride. The truth is, we pulled seven tankers off the street in all, four in quick succession before we garaged the cars and laid up in Memphis, safe from the Feds in the heart of the New Confederacy.

After Baltimore, Jack sent out thank-you notes, leaking them to the newshounds. And sometime along the way—I think it was before number three, down in Charleston—he painted that incandescent lightning bolt from his NASCAR career down the rolled-steel armor on his hood. It was just like the old days: an express elevator to the top. His footage was playing every time you tapped a newsfeed. Like many race drivers, he was a little guy, Jack— 5'10" and 160 pounds or so. That weight-to-speed ratio again. But he seemed like a much bigger man. He was as handsome as Old Scratch himself, and he inspired loyalty like no man I've ever seen. For a while, he kept a suite in the Adler Hotel, wearing his brand-new scar from the Tallahassee job, entertaining women and dining out on his notoriety.

But the New Feds had taken notice. We were plenty hot by then. Word on the street was that Buffalo was aiming to scalp us. After a month or so of jumping at shadows, Jack picked up the Heckler & Koch, a lethal-looking bastard if I ever saw one. Soon we were all sporting ordnance, pretending to be gangsters, or maybe not pretending, though in my heart I was never anything more than an old pit boss. But Jack still had a case of the nerves, so we moved shop to a farm outside of Little Rock. It belonged to Eileen Sheldon, one of Jack's girls from the NASCAR circuit, and if she'd put a few miles on the odometer since then, well, who hadn't? She was still a fine-looking woman—big-boned and kind of rangy—and she took Jack into her bedroom that very night. More important, she had a big barn where we got to work upgrading the vehicles.

By then Lola and I had started sleeping together. As I've said,

I'd had a hankering for her all along—she was a petite kid, with dark hair and eyes so black you could catch reflections of yourself if the light hit them right—but like Jack, I'd known she had too much value as a jack man to even think about it. A crew is a finely oiled operation. The last thing you need is personal tension to gum up the works. But thinking wasn't part of the equation. A driver and his shotgun man have to trust one another completely, and a close brush with the grave—and every job counted on that score—left you with a yen for a little human warmth. When we reached the safe house after the job in Baltimore, we just kind of fell into the sack together. Nobody said a word about it, but after that it was understood: Lola Bridger was my girl. I count this as the biggest mistake of my life, but I couldn't know that then. And God, I loved that girl. In my heart I love her still.

A gentleman doesn't speak of such things—and I don't intend to in any detail—but late one night we found ourselves futzing around alone in Eileen Sheldon's barn. The radio was playing some old dance tune, slow and easy, and we'd both had a beer or three too many. Me, I was poking under Jack's hood, when Lola says something I don't hear. I straightened up to listen and, bonk, knocked myself dizzy on that rolled-steel armor. Next thing I know, Lola's saying, "You okay?" and we both got to giggling and one thing led to another and we ended up having it off right there in the hay. What I'm trying to say is, there was some heat in that relationship, if you take my meaning, and if neither one of us ever professed our love aloud, we didn't need to. It was understood.

We lingered three months on Eileen's farm, and it was a kind of idyll. Joe Hauser was a mean hand with a spatula. We ate like kings, and afterward Joe would sit back like a sultan and watch us wash up. Everybody but Jack took a hand in the suds. Nobody caviled, either. Jack was a different order of being. It would be unseemly for the wheelman to dirty his hands scraping leftovers into the disposal. But Jack and Eileen had it sweet and steady, and so did Lola and I. In retrospect, I think that was the best time of my life. If I could have stretched it out forever, I would have. But all good things, right?

Jack wanted to drive, and he'd gotten some intel on a convoy coming out of Buffalo and heading toward Nashville. Everything Jack had predicted had pretty much panned out the way he said it would. The United States had splintered along lines geographic

and sectarian—and these weren't always in agreement. The New
Feds were trying to put down insurgencies on half a dozen fronts.
The insurgents themselves were engaged with pockets of New Fed
loyalists in their midst who needed reinforcement and resupply:
guns, grub, and gasoline. The convoys would have been impossible
in another era, but the satellites were useless and the fighter jets
had been grounded by particulates in the atmosphere. The air war
was a joke, leaving the convoys to defend themselves against occasional skirmishes—and us. I was against the whole thing. I worried
about Lola behind the wheel of the Spyder, and I was none too
enthusiastic about taking more fire myself. But you didn't cross
Lightning Jack, and besides, part of me wanted to see what the
rebuilt vehicles could really do. I was a gearhead at heart.

The answer was, they did fine. We cut a truck free of the convoy
on 65 South, just north of Bowling Green, broke down the cars,
and hit the road again by nightfall, three hundred thousand New
Confederate dollars richer. I think Jack sold the gas back to the
New Fed loyalists who'd been scheduled to receive it in the first
place, which was good for a laugh, especially when the update hit
the newsfeeds. We pulled off two more jobs in the next two weeks:
Raleigh and Frankfort. We were really hot by then, and we scooted
for home under cover of darkness. A Fed patrol—maybe twelve
guys armed with popguns and rocks—stumbled across us at the
second rally point, but between Jack's G40 and five other buzzsaws,
we cut through them like a good wheelman cutting through the
pack. By this time we were back in New Confederate territory, and
we didn't face any more resistance on our way to Eileen Sheldon's
farm. When we rolled up, Eileen was waiting at the door to meet
us. We'd escaped pretty much unscathed—Lightning Jack was
nothing if not lucky—though the iron plating on our vehicles had
been dinged dozens of times and Dean Ford had taken a round
clean through the shoulder. Eileen disinfected and packed the
wound—Lord, I've never heard such a racket—but Dean pulled
through. His arm was never quite the same, though, and his days
as swingman were over.

Me, I hoped our days as outlaws were over, too. And they were,
though we didn't know it at the time.

For a while, the idyll resumed. We spent the stifling Arkansas days
working on the vehicles. We ate Joe's cooking. Evenings it cooled

down into the 90s. We sat on the porch drinking beer while Lightning Jack lounged on the hammock strung between two big oaks out front. Everything seemed free and easy, but the truth was the Feds had turned up the heat on Lightning Jack. He'd heisted three tankers in three weeks, and they needed to stop the bleeding. Plus, he was more famous now than he'd ever been in his NASCAR days. Taking him out would be a coup for Buffalo, and it might curtail the ravages of Gallant Jim and Albertini and the half-dozen other gangs that had sprung up in our wake. Worse yet, the rumors of undercover Federal agents that had forced us out of Memphis had started floating around in Little Rock. It was enough to make a man nervous.

Despite all that, Jack was anxious to get on the road again.

"I want to drive, Gus," he told me one afternoon out in the barn. He leaned against the hood of the Dragon and crossed his legs at the ankle. A shaft of sunlight pierced the roof—the barn had seen better days—limning him in a golden nimbus. The scar from the Tallahassee job was a vivid white streak across his forehead. A millimeter to the right—less, even—and it would have splattered his brains across the rear window of his black Dragon. Sometimes I think it would have been better that way.

"Remember when we met? You blew that race on the truck circuit because you were too aggressive."

"I remember."

"Sometimes you got to know when to pit, Jack."

"I want to win," he said.

"Well, the stakes are a lot higher than they were in Daytona."

I didn't say it—I didn't have to—but the stakes were life and death. I didn't know how many crow's nest gunners I'd killed, but I figured in all that shooting I must have taken my fair share. And that didn't include the seven tanker drivers who had gone down, or the boy I'd shot in that New Federal patrol that had stumbled across us after the Frankfort job. I still remembered him. I favored an older daisy cutter, the G39-X, a predecessor to Jack's Heckler & Koch, but it was still lethal. It had cut that boy nearly in half, and I couldn't stop seeing that image in my mind—the shocked look on his face as the bullets tore into his midsection and his mortality dawned on him for the second or two it took him to bleed out. He probably hadn't thought about it before, not in any real serious way, and he didn't have long to think about it then. But you could tell it made an impression. He was the one who stuck with me most, but none of them were very far from my mind in those days. I couldn't lie to myself that I was merely a crew chief anymore. The knowledge of what I had become and what I had done sometimes woke me up in the night to gaze out the window into the dark, rolling hills of the farm. When I'd showed up at Jack's gate after the Citizens' Militia had drafted me, I hadn't realized I was signing on for this.

Lola, too, seemed to be having some trouble coping—or that's what I thought, anyway. She grew distant and quiet, and while she still shared my bed, there were no more good-natured tussles in the hay. Sex became perfunctory, a grim duty. It's not that I didn't love her anymore. But a river of blood flowed between us now, and we couldn't find a way to bridge it. We didn't spend much time in the barn together, and when we did we kept our conversation to the point: "Reach me that spanner, will you?" or "Can you give me a hand with the lift?"

I guess the rest of the crew must have known before I did—love can blind you that way—but no one said a word. You didn't cross Jack, for one thing, but I think the true reason is that none of them wanted to break the glue that bound us all together. We'd divorced ourselves too much from the rest of the world for us to risk it. With those rumors of Federal agents in the air, even Little Rock was off-limits. So we lived for one another, and we lived for the cars, and we lived for Lightning Jack. He was the most solitary of us all, I suppose. As the wheelman, he stood a step above his crew, isolated by his skill and by his fame and by the scar that forever marked his identity. The easy days of living in the Adler Hotel and making the social rounds were over. He was a marked man, and I think he knew that he was living on borrowed time. I believe that's why he was so anxious to hit the road and boost another tanker—it was the only time he really felt alive anymore. And I think that's why he started sleeping with Lola, as well. For the thrill of it, nothing more. To this day I don't believe he meant anything personal.

It was Eileen who finally broke the whole thing open for me, like lancing an angry boil. We were in the kitchen alone, chopping up vegetables, when she said, matter-of-fact-like, "He's sleeping with her, you know."

In my heart I think I'd known it all along. When Lola came to me that night, I turned on my side and lay awake a long time, staring into the dark. I'd trusted Lola, sure. But I'd trusted Jack even more. I'd trusted our friendship, though he'd as much announced the truth himself, hadn't he? "I'm an amoral son of a bitch, Gus. I just want to drive."

But Lightning Jack's driving days were over.

Which brings us full circle, I guess.

Jack didn't wind up puttering around his garden in the Upper Peninsula, and he never gave Victor Albertini any competition out in the Golden State, either. But the conspiracy nuts are right about one thing.

The I-20 tape is a put-up job. You can argue that the video was manipulated, or even created from whole cloth, and don't think I haven't heard plenty of speculation along those lines. I've known people who could talk themselves blue in the face when it came to crash trajectories and video grain—and would, too, if you'd let them. But when it comes down to brass tacks, I agree with them. I've been around cars my whole life, and back in my NASCAR days I must have seen half a hundred crashes or more. Simply put, the overcorrection on the video isn't sufficient to cause the Dragon to roll. I know. I built the damn thing. The air dam was low and wide, never mind the weight of the rolled-steel armor. The downforce on that car was tremendous. Even in the skid, those tires would have stuck to that pavement like glue.

But let's assume for a moment that I'm wrong. Let's assume the video *is* real.

The question then is the matter of provenance. It can't be confirmed that the tape came in only half an hour after the crash. We have only New Fed assurances on that score, and the official files remain closed. And what about the cleanup? Where are the investigators and where are the glib network newsfaces doing stand-ups in front of the wreckage, their flawless features sculpted by the strobing blue and red beacons of the emergency lights? The most notorious outlaw of his era had just been killed. Where are the boots on the ground?

As for Lightning Jack, I did for him myself.

I suppose you've figured that out on your own by now, but I don't think any of us—even me—knew that I was capable of such a thing. Tension weighed heavily upon the farm by then. The sense that New Fed agents might any moment sweep down out of the hills was palpable, and we kept our weapons close to hand. After Eileen's revelation, Lola and I continued to share a bed. As long as she didn't leave, we could both—we could all—pretend it hadn't happened. But Eileen put Jack out of her room. Without explanation—he was the wheelman, after all, and he owed no explanations—he took to sleeping in the hammock, in the warm summer air. It was there that I did the thing.

It was nothing I had planned. I was drinking whiskey in the darkened kitchen one sleepless night, that's all, and I caught a glimpse of him through the window, dozing there. The knife lay in the drainer, close to hand. Without thinking about it, I took it and stepped outside. My foot fell upon the squeaky riser of the porch steps, but he didn't wake up. If he had, everything would have been different. We might have talked the thing through. I might have let his charm seduce me yet again. But he merely stirred, murmured something unintelligible, and lapsed back into slumber. He never knew a thing until I slipped the knife between his ribs—I can still remember just how easy it went in—and even then I don't think he believed it. He gazed up at me with a question in his eyes—a kind of wonder, I think, that I could betray him. He opened his mouth to speak, and I laid my hand across his lips. I leaned in close to his ear and began to slowly twist the blade, like a man tightening a lug nut.

"Shhh," I said. "Be still now, Jack. It's time to sleep."

A heartbeat passed, and then another, and then he did.

It's the rest of the thing I've never been able to figure to my satisfaction. We're entering the realms of pure speculation here, but I believe New Fed agents really *had* infiltrated Little Rock, and they must have been watching the farm for days, maybe longer. I slipped the noose, that's all. I hoofed it past dawn. Somewhere around eight a.m., I flagged down a bus out of Conway. I changed at the East Washington station in Little Rock, surrendering up a handful of cash for the first stagecoach out of town. It dropped me in Jackson, Mississippi, where I holed up in a cheap motel for weeks, living on vodka and takeout. As best I can figure, sometime during that period New Fed agents must have taken the farm. I can imagine it all too clearly: the stark white flare of muzzle flash

in the darkness, the hiccup of automatic weapons, the crew falling one by one, their bodies riddled by New Federal slugs—Joe
Hauser, Dean Ford, and the rest, Lola most of all. I can see her
lying in the doorway to the farmhouse, her arm flung out toward
the still-smoking SAR bullpup she cherished, her body cooling as
the sun rises over the Arkansas hills. I can see the blood. Imagination, I know, but sometimes imagination is enough. Sometimes
it's too much, and I wonder that a man as practical as I am—an
engine man to the core—should be cursed with so much of it.

The New Feds must have been furious at being deprived of
their prize. Three months after I landed in Biloxi and nailed down
a straight job—hydraulics, again—Buffalo released the tape and
Lightning Jack's saga came to an end. But the oil raids weren't
over, not yet. Lightning Jack had shown how the thing was done,
and the Midwestern Alliance and the New Confederacy both had
borrowed the technique, upped the firepower, and started knocking off entire convoys. The Feds—as Lola had put it to me in
Birmingham all those months ago—armored up. Military escorts
tripled in size, heavy ordnance came into play, and the tankers
themselves became rolling dreadnoughts. Cutting one out of the
pack was a suicide mission—as Gallant Jim found out in the Oak
Park Massacre. Not two months later, Federal agents killed Victor
Albertini in the lobby of a San Francisco hotel. Mason, Cholewin-
ski, and Smilin' Susie Samowitz all went down in the months that
followed. The Age of the Gasoline Outlaw was officially over.

Me? I kept my head down and waited for the New Feds to come
for me. They never did. It's been a lonesome kind of life these
last forty years. There've been women now and again, but no one
steady. I had too much road behind me to really settle down, and
I don't think I ever did get over Lola. Now that I'm an old man,
with eighty looming just beyond the horizon, I find myself thinking of her more often—and the truth is, not an hour has passed in
all those years past that I didn't think of her already. You probably
reckon that I dwell on her betrayal at the end, but the truth is I
think mostly of the good days that came before. There were a lot
of those good days, more than our fair share, considering the circumstances. We loved each other with a ferocity and desperation
that only the hunted can know. And more important still, we had
the things we loved in common to bind us together—love of the
pavement and the rolling iron that ran across it and the mighty

engines that made them go. As for the betrayal, I don't blame her much. As I've said, there wasn't a woman on the planet that Lightning Jack couldn't charm out of her knickers in ten minutes flat. She never had a chance, and neither did I.

If I'm going to be honest about it—and I don't see why I shouldn't be—I don't think Jack did, either. I guess I miss him most of all. I forgave him. I believe he was a prisoner: to his charisma and to his ego, to his skills and to his hunger for victory, and to the fame all those things together bought him. And despite all the harm we did—and we did great harm, I'll be the first to admit it; every night I am borne to sleep on a tide of blood—for all that harm, I believe to this day that Jack didn't have a bone of true malice in him. He just wanted to drive, and like a thousand other gearheads who cruised the night streets on black-market gasoline in those days, he was going to find a way to do it. The only difference is that he was Lightning Jack, had been all his life, and couldn't find a way to stop being Lightning Jack. He was a competitor; he had to have a stage. He never could pit before it was too late, and in the end he got everyone he loved—and he did love us in his way, I'm sure of that—killed. I have many regrets about those days, but I guess what I regret most of all is that I wasn't there to take my final stand with Lola and the rest of them. I betrayed them all. I should have stood by my wheelman to the end. There is something sacred about the work that binds a crew together, and I profaned that bond, and I have lived too long with my regret. I'm glad the finish line is in sight at last. I don't think I could stand another lap.

WILL KAUFMAN

Things You Can Buy for a Penny

FROM *Lightspeed Magazine*

"DON'T GO DOWN to the well," said Theo to his son. So of course
Tim went to the well. He was thirteen, and his father told him not
to. There was no magic to it.

To get to the well—and not the well in the center of the village,
because everyone knows where that well is, and no one has any stories about it except for whose grandfather dug it and how soon it's
going to go dry—you've got to go around behind the butcher's,
to the bottom of the muddy slope at the edge of the wood that the
butcher says he doesn't throw his offal down. Everybody knows the
butcher throws offal down the slope so the wet gentleman will eat
that instead of crawling up to eat the butcher's daughter.

At the bottom of the slope, look for the bones of the burnt cottage in among the willows, then look for the moon. You know this
only works at night, don't you? The wet gentleman won't come out
during the day. Walk toward the point halfway between the moon
and the cottage, and eventually you'll come to the well.

Tim sneaked from his father's house with a penny in his hand
and his dog at his side, a dog that he loved because it would never
lie to him or trick him, that he would play with even when the
other children invited him to join their games, because when he
told the other children to follow him, or wait for him, they would
laugh and run away, but not his dog. When his father tucked him
into bed, it was his dog he asked for a last kiss good night, its cold
nose snuffling at his cheek, because his dog never told him what to
do or sent him to bed without his dinner for not minding, because

what do dogs know? Maybe if Tim had been a king or a god, he could have loved the other children, or his father.

What happened to Tim when he went to the well? You must know how the story ends—or rather, that it never ends. Surely you've heard about the others who went to the well, like Ma Tathers.

When Ma Tathers went to the well, she got just what she paid for. She heard about the well because of what happened to Miser Horton, so she knew the wet gentleman lived there and would grant wishes if he was paid a penny. Miser Horton went because he knew the story of Little Susanne, and both of them got just what they paid for, too.

The story says Ma Tathers was so old when she walked the path between the moon and the burned-up cottage that her dugs dragged in the dirt. That's not a kind way to describe a poor old woman, but stories are seldom kind, especially to a poor old woman in a tattered housecoat, which was her only coat, which she wore thinner and thinner as she sat day after day patching up other people's clothes for pennies. Her eyes were milky, and she had to bring the cloth and the needle right up to her mottled nose to see what she was doing. Her grandsons, whom she was raising because their parents had died, would say to her, "Don't stick that needle so close to your eye, Grandma. You'll poke it one day, and it'll fall right out."

"That's no trouble," Ma Tathers would say. "I always got the other one." What she meant was "If my eye were worth a few pennies, I'd sell it right from my head."

Even though Ma Tathers had heard the stories, the same stories you've heard, and knew better than to think she could trust the wet gentleman, she did not know what else she could do. She would never take charity, even when it was offered, as though some bone in her body, maybe her fourth rib or her left shin, was so stubborn or proud it made her shift her ponderous breast, lift her swollen leg, and turn away from any helping hand. Without charity, and with her eyes going, and her grandsons getting bigger and needing more to eat every day, Ma Tathers didn't see where she could afford to buy what she needed but from the wet gentleman.

The day she decided she would go to the well, Ma Tathers worked as fast as she could, the needle fleet in her crooked fingers.

She stitched up every shirt and every pair of pants she could coax from the villagers, but that night she had fewer pennies than she'd earned the day before, just four dull coins sitting on the rough wood of her bare table. Spending one that night would mean three pennies for the next day's meals, and while the boys might not complain, their stomachs would grumble mightily. Of course, their stomachs would never grumble again once Ma Tathers got what she paid for at the well.

So she walked the moonlit path, and she dropped her penny down the dark stone mouth of the crumbling well. Instead of the ringing of a coin hitting stone, or the plop of metal falling into swampy muck, Ma Tathers heard the squelch of wet silk and the pattering of dripping water. The wet gentleman emerged from the well, top hat first, eyes hidden, shadowed from the moonlight by the flat brim. His face was long, home to a wide mouth that turned down at the corners. His suit was fine silk, his shoes shined even in the night, and he leaned on an ivory cane. All his raiment was soaked through, and water ran from all the creases, and a puddle formed at his feet. He was very tall, very thin, and Ma Tathers had not really expected him to exist.

The wet gentleman spoke with a voice deep and cold as his well. He said, "How does this night find you, madam?"

"I am tired," said Ma Tathers, who always answered plainly.

The wet gentleman said, "*You* are tired? I have been down this well since the first brick of your village was laid, soaking in cold water, waiting for the nights someone drops a penny on my head so I can crawl out and grant them a wish. But I forget myself, a gentleman never complains. Do tell me more about your troubles, miss."

"Is it true?" asked Ma Tathers. "What they say about Miser Horton and about Little Susanne?"

The top hat bowed as the wet gentleman looked Ma Tathers up and down. "Surely you didn't spend what must be one of your few pennies to hear a story?"

"No," said Ma Tathers. "I came because my grandsons are hungry, and I will not be able to feed them for much longer."

"So you wish to be young again," said the wet gentleman, and he took her hand. Music came out of the well, pipes and strings.

"No," said Ma Tathers, but the wet gentleman spun her, and ice-cold water ran down her arm, and her feet felt light, and her joints did not ache, and her back was straight, and she knew the steps to the dance he led her on.

"For selfless reasons," he said. "So you might live long enough to care for them until they can care for themselves."

"No," said Ma Tathers, but her hips swayed and did not pop or creak.

"How much easier would it be to raise two young men if you no longer hurt just from standing? If you could wash a pan and not feel like lying down and sleeping for a week, after?"

"No," said Ma Tathers, and she broke his grip. Her body sagged as the weight of years fell upon it again and pain settled back in her bones. "I know your tricks and I know your bargains, so whatever the price for my wish, it must be laid on me and not on my boys."

Even though he had been out of the well for some minutes, and even though he had spun with Ma Tathers, the water dripping from the gentleman's clothes had not slowed. The wet gentleman said, "Tell me, Joanna Susanne Tathers. Tell me your wish."

"Make sure my grandsons are fed. They can figure out the rest. I've taught Theo to sew, and the house is mine, and theirs when I am dead, the sole property of my family. Make sure they have enough to eat until they are able to earn food for themselves."

"And what price do you think I will ask? Have you not paid me my penny?"

"You will weave spells full of deceit. You will make something good into something evil by your trickery. Instead, I say you can take anything of my body. A meal for a meal. I have heard of your appetites, how the butcher leaves you offal so you will not eat his daughter."

"Some stories are just stories," said the wet gentleman. "But very well, I will feed your grandchildren, and I will not ask any payment of them for those meals." He held out his hand. "Do we have a deal?"

She took his hand and shook it firmly, and then she quailed and began to shiver. "What," she said, "what will you do to me?"

The corners of the wet gentleman's mouth twitched upward.

When Ma Tathers wandered back out of the woods in the morning, she could not recall the village, or her house, or her grandsons, or even her own name. The wet gentleman ate all those memories.

Her grandchildren brought her home and asked her if she felt ill, but when she opened her mouth, all that came out were stories about the wet gentleman who lived in the well. The boys fretted and cried, uncertain and afraid, and hungry from only having three pennies' worth of food that day. But then a knock came at the door, and when they opened it, they found a basket full of brown bread and hard cheese and cured sausage and even two apples. With a meal in them, and with a few morsels coaxed down their grandmother's throat, the future seemed ever so slightly less frightening.

The boys went on, as people do, and ate their meals, and cared for their grandmother, who did nothing but tell stories about the wet gentleman until she died.

One of the stories she told was the story of Miser Horton, a man so mean with his pocketbook that when he went down to the well, he stole the penny to pay the wet gentleman from the shoe of a boy who had left it behind to climb trees with his friends. Miser Horton strode through the woods holding up the hem of his cape so it would not get dirty and need to be cleaned, or snag and tear and need to be mended. The cape was velvet and very old, taken as partial payment for goods Miser Horton had sold decades earlier. He would proudly tell you the story of that deal if you asked, and maybe even let you touch the cape in question.

Miser Horton knew Little Susanne's story, but he, like all the rest who have heard stories and have followed the moonlight path with pennies in their hands, did not expect the wet gentleman to climb out of the well. Miser Horton recovered quickly from his shock, thanks in part to his immediate disdain for the wet gentleman's lack of care with his clothes. Did the man not know what water did to silk?

"How does this night find you, sir?" asked the wet gentleman.

"Jealous," said Miser Horton, getting directly to his business.

"*You* are jealous?" said the wet gentleman. "I have been down this well since the oldest tree in these woods was just a sapling, in the cold and wet and dark while above me people live in warmth and dry comfort, and I only get to visit when someone drops a penny on my head. But I forget myself, a gentleman never complains. Tell me more about your troubles."

"My wife has made me a cuckold," said Miser Horton. "Me. Even though I gave her a house and an allowance and children, she has been sneaking out of my bed when she thinks I am asleep."

"So you would like to be handsome," said the wet gentleman, and he reached out to place a hand on Miser Horton's shoulder. Horton stood taller, his stomach receding while his chest and arms strained the seams of his shirt. His scalp itched, and thick locks of hair drooped down over his brow. From the well came the voices of women, calling to him, sighing his name.

"No," said Miser Horton.

"To win back your wife," said the wet gentleman, "or make her jealous when all the other girls throw themselves at your feet and beg to take her place in your bed."

Miser Horton said, "No," and knocked the wet gentleman's hand from his shoulder. He sagged, his chest and arms draining into his belly, which expanded until his belt cut into it, and his scalp crawled as the hair slid back under the shiny skin. Miser Horton brushed at his cape, hoping the water would not stain the velvet. He said, "What good is being handsome? No one pays to look upon a pretty face."

"Yet you have paid to look upon mine," said the wet gentleman. "Let me earn your penny. Tell me your wish."

"Punish whoever stole my wife from my bed," said Miser Horton. "Make him poor, make his family poor. Make any children he may have poor for the rest of their lives, and their children, too, with nothing to their family's name but the meanest sort of shanty for a home until the end of his bloodline or the day of reckoning, whichever comes first."

"Very well," said the wet gentleman, and he offered his hand.

Miser Horton regarded it suspiciously. "This is no small service you offer me. What price must I pay?"

"You have paid me my penny," said the wet gentleman. "If I cannot deliver, you will have only lost the penny you already threw down a well, and you may find some other way to punish the man responsible for your wife's infidelity."

Miser Horton took the wet gentleman's hand, and then felt a chill on his shoulders. He reached up to pull his cape close, only to discover it was gone, and his shirt had turned from fine cotton to rough wool.

"What have you done?" he asked, and looked into the wet gentleman's face, where he saw the corners of that wide mouth flick upward.

"Do you not see, Horton Tathers?" said the wet gentleman. "*You* are responsible for your wife's infidelity, you with your petty jealousy and greedy character. Now go home to your shanty and tell your children the cost of doing business with the wet gentleman in the well."

Horton did just that, and one of the stories he told his children about the price you must pay the wet gentleman for a wish was the story of Little Susanne. Little Susanne lived in a cottage in the woods near the village with her mommy and daddy and her cat, Tugs. She loved Tugs very much. When Mommy and Daddy filled the cottage in the woods with terrible shouting, Little Susanne would pick up Tugs and take him outside and lean against a willow and hold him and pet him until he purred, then press her ear against his chest so all she heard was his warm, soft rattle and not the terrible shouting.

One day her daddy threw a chair at her mommy and it missed and hit Tugs instead, and Tugs yowled, and scrambled about with his front legs, his hindquarters dragging on the floor. Daddy grabbed Tugs by the neck and took him outside, and when he came back he didn't have Tugs with him. Little Susanne asked where Tugs had gone, and Daddy said he'd tried to help Tugs but Tugs had run off into the woods.

After crying for a week, Little Susanne decided to go to the wishing well. Maybe she knew about the well from even older stories, or maybe from exploring the woods, from taking children's paths over the ground and through imagination. Maybe you would know about the well too, even if you had never been told.

Little Susanne took a penny from her daddy's coin purse while he was snoring, and tiptoed through the door, careful not to let it creak or slam, and walked down to the well. She threw the coin in, and almost screamed when the wet gentleman's top hat poked out over the edge, followed by his shadowed eyes and wide, downturned mouth.

The wet gentleman bowed to her and said, "How does this night find you, miss?"

"Scared," said Little Susanne, being truthful. "And lonely. And sad."

"I understand," said the wet gentleman. "I have been down this well since your holy books were only dreams and firelight tales. That is a long time to be lonely, and sad, and scared."

"You're very wet," said Little Susanne. "Would you like me to bring you some clothes? My daddy has three shirts, and he might not miss one."

"That is very kind of you," said the wet gentleman, "but it would only get wet again, because I must go back down the well once I grant your wish."

"Oh," said Little Susanne. "If I don't make a wish, can you stay up here?"

"That is not the way the story goes, Susanne Joanna Smyth," said the wet gentleman. "I must tell you that a gentleman never complains, and you must tell me your wish."

Little Susanne tucked a toe into the dirt and mumbled something under her breath.

"You are scared, I understand that," said the wet gentleman. "Would you like to be grownup, so you can be brave and sure like your mommy and daddy?" He knelt down in front of her and took her hand in his and she grew, and her hips and breasts swelled, and she stood looking down at the wet gentleman, kneeling and holding her hand.

"No," she said.

"You can leave your parents' home and find a man to marry and live with him and never be lonely or scared again."

Little Susanne felt something else. She felt a stirring inside of her that was hot and safe and terrifying and awesome and hopeful and fearful all at the same time. From the well came the sound of a babe, crying for its mother. "No," she said, and she pulled her hand free. She shrank back into childhood until her eyes were level with the kneeling gentleman, water dripping from his hat and from his jacket, and the corners of his mouth twitched downward even further.

"I want Tugs back," she said. "I want him to purr to me and keep me company until I die. And . . ."

"Yes?" said the wet gentleman.

"And I want Mommy and Daddy to stop fighting."

"Two wishes?" said the wet gentleman, standing so that he towered over Little Susanne. "Have you brought two pennies?"

"No," said Little Susanne. "Do I have to choose?"

The wet gentleman tilted his head back and considered the stars through the leaves of the trees. "You do not have to choose," he said at last. "One wish will be yours, and one will be mine. You shall have your cat, and your parents will fight no more."

"Thank you," said Little Susanne, and she hugged the wet gentleman round his legs, which were stick thin and hard as rocks inside his suit, and she got all wet up the front of her nightclothes.

"Thank *you*," said the wet gentleman, "for the penny. Now go home."

As she walked home, Little Susanne saw a flickering orange glow through the trees. She heard a roaring, a snapping and popping. She smelled wood smoke, and something else, something oily and black, like when Mommy burned the bacon. Her house was on fire, and the heat singed her hair and dried her nightclothes. As she watched the house burn, Tugs stalked out from the woods and twined himself around her legs. She picked him up and held him to her ear, but even though she could feel the shudder of his purring, all she could hear was the fire.

That's how the villagers found Little Susanne when they ventured into the woods to investigate the fire. A family took her in, and she grew up in the village, always with her ageless cat at her feet or in her arms, and she married a good man with kind hands and a sharp mind, and one day she felt the stirring inside her, and remembered looking down at the wet gentleman on his knee at her feet, and knew she was pregnant.

She had many children, and told them about the wet gentleman in the well, that he was very powerful, and very dangerous, and not to be trusted, except maybe sometimes, because after all, Tugs stayed with her and purred for her until she died, whereupon he climbed onto her still chest, turned around three times and curled up and died as well, and was buried with her.

Her family's fortunes rose over time, until Horton Tathers inherited the estate. Then the family was poor. But the family never stopped telling stories about the wet gentleman. Horton told them, and Joanna told them, and Theo listened to his grandmother but did not believe her, at least, not until the day Theo and his wife could no longer pretend she was anything but barren, and Theo went into the woods.

He took the path between the moon and the burned-up cottage, and he threw a penny down the well, and the wet gentleman climbed out of the well and said, "How does this night find you, sir?"

The wet gentleman said, "*You* are troubled? I have been down this well since before you people learned to bake bricks."

He listened to Theo's troubles and said, "So you would like a new wife, one who is young and fertile."

When Theo finally refused him, the wet gentleman said, "No? Very well, tell me your wish."

And the wet gentleman said, "I see you've paid attention to the stories. But you mustn't worry, all I really want is a penny now and then, and I know I'll have another soon enough, when your son comes to visit me."

Theo went home, frightened, doubtful, half convinced it had been a dream, and in a few months his wife woke up ill and felt the stirring inside her. When their son was born, they named him Timothy, and Theo told Tim the story of Little Susanne, and of Miser Horton, and Ma Tathers. Theo told his son these stories to warn him, so the boy would know better than to ever go down to the well.

Tim said, "Why did none of them simply wish for the wet gentleman's power? You could do whatever you want, and you'd only ever owe yourself, and you wouldn't ever do anything bad to yourself or trick yourself."

And Theo took hold of his son's hands and said, "Don't go down to the well."

You already know what will happen next, and you can leave this story while Tim sneaks down past the butcher's, his loyal dog at his side and a penny in his hand. You can leave while the wet gentleman waits in the place that exists beneath the mouth of the well, his face split by a grin. You can leave this story while the wet gentleman thinks about the many pennies he has gathered, pennies that are copper, pennies that are bronze, and some that are small shells or glittering stones, and how long, how long it has been since he went down to the well, a boy clutching something that once upon a time stood for a penny. He has grown so much since then, and worn the finery of so many different ages, and through all that time he has remained a gentleman. Soon, soon he will be a boy again; a boy who will very much hate taking baths.

And you, you who get exactly what you pay for, there may always be some wet gentleman waiting for you to throw your penny into the well, but you can leave any time you want. There is no magic to that.

CHARLIE JANE ANDERS

Rat Catcher's Yellows

FROM *Press Start to Play*

1.

THE PLASTIC CAT head is wearing an elaborate puffy crown covered with bling. The cat's mouth opens to reveal a touch screen,
but there's also a jack to plug in an elaborate mask that gives you a
visor, along with nose plugs and earbuds for added sensory input.
Holding this self-contained game system in my palms, I hate it and
want to throw it out the open window of our beautiful faux-Colo-
nial row house to be buried under the autumn mulch. But I also
feel a surge of hope: that maybe this really will make a difference.
The cat is winking up at me.

Shary crouches in her favorite chair, the straight-backed Re-
gency made of red-stained wood and lumpy blue upholstery. She's
wearing jeans and a stained sweatshirt, one leg tucked under the
other, and there's a kinetic promise in her taut leg that I know
to be a lie. She looks as if she's about to spring out of that chair
and ask me about the device in my hands, talking a mile a minute
the way she used to. But she doesn't even notice my brand-new
purchase, and it's a crapshoot whether she even knows who I am
today.

I poke the royal cat's tongue, and it gives a yawp through its
tiny speakers, then the screen lights up and asks for our Wi-Fi password. I give the cat what it wants, then it starts updating and load-
ing various firmware things. A picture of a fairy-tale castle appears
with the game's title in a stylized wordmark above it: THE DIVINE

RIGHT OF CATS. And then begins the hard work of customizing absolutely everything, which I want to do myself before I hand the thing off to Shary.

The whole time I'm inputting Shary's name and other info, I feel like a backstabbing bitch. Giving this childish game to my life partner, it's like I'm declaring that she's lost the right to be considered an adult. No matter that all the hip teens and twentysomethings are playing *Divine Right of Cats* right now. Or that everybody agrees this game is the absolute best thing for helping dementia patients hold on to some level of cognition, and that it's especially good for people suffering from leptospirosis X, in particular. I'm doing this for Shary's good, because I believe she's still in there somewhere.

I make Shary's character as close to Shary as I can possibly make a cat wizard, who is the main adviser to the throne of the cat kingdom. (I decide that if Shary was a cat, she'd be an Abyssinian, because she's got that sandy-brown-haired sleekness, pointy face, and wiry energy.) Shary's monarch is a queen, not a king—a proud tortoiseshell cat named Arabella IV. I get some input into the realm's makeup, including what the nobles on the Queen's Council are like, but some stuff is decided at random—like, Arabella's realm of Greater Felinia has a huge stretch of vineyards and some copper mines, neither of which I would have come up with.

Every detail I enter into the game, I pack with relationship shout-outs and little details that only Shary would recognize, so the whole thing turns into a kind of bizarre love letter. For example, the tavern near the royal stables is the Puzzler's Retreat, which was the gray-walled dyke bar where Shary and I used to go dancing when we were both in grad school. The royal guards are Grace's Army of Stompification. And so on.

"Shary?" I say. She doesn't respond.

Before it mutated and started eating people's brain stems, before it became antibiotic-resistant, the disease afflicting Shary used to be known as Rat Catcher's Yellows. It mostly affected animals, and in rare cases humans. It's a close cousin of syphilis and Lyme, one that few people had even heard of ten years ago. In some people, it causes liver failure and agonizing joint pain, but Shary is one of the "lucky" ones who only have severe neurological problems, plus intermittent fatigue. She's only thirty-five years old.

"Shary?" I hold the cat head out to her, because it's ready to start accepting her commands now that all the tricky setup is over with. Queen Arabella has a lot of issues that require her Royal Wizard's input. Already some of the other noble cats are plotting against the throne—especially those treacherous tuxedo cats!—and the vintners are threatening to go on strike. I put the cat head right in front of Shary's face and she shrugs.

Then she looks up, all at once lucid. "Grace? What the fuck is this shit? This looks like it's for a five-year-old."

"It's a game," I stammer. "It's supposed to be good for people with your . . . It's fun. You'll like it."

"What the fucking fuck?"

She throws it across the room. Lucidity is often accompanied by hostility, which is the kind of trade-off you start to accept at a certain point. I go and fetch it without a word. Luckily, the cat head was designed to be very durable.

"I thought we could do it together." I play the guilt card back at her. "I thought maybe this could be something we could actually share. You and me. Together. You know? Like a real couple."

"Okay, fine." She takes the cat head from me and squints at Queen Arabella's questions about the trade crisis with the neighboring duchy of meerkats. Queen Arabella asks what she should do, and Shary painstakingly types out "Why don't you go fuck yourself." But she erases it without hitting send, and then instead picks SEND AN EMISSARY from among the options already on the screen. Soon Shary is sending trade representatives and labor negotiators to the four corners of Greater Felinia, and beyond.

2.

After a few days, Shary stops complaining about how stupid *Divine Right of Cats* is and starts spending every moment poking at the plastic cat's face in her lap. I get her the optional add-on mask, which is (not surprisingly) the upper three-quarters of a cat face, and plug it in for her, then show her how to insert the nose plugs and earbuds.

Within a week after she first starts playing, Shary's realm is already starting to crawl up the list of the 1,000 most successful kingdoms—that is, she's already doing a better job of helping to run the realm of Felinia than the vast majority of people who are playing this game anywhere, according to god knows what metrics.

But more than that, Shary is forming *relationships* with these cats in their puffy-sleeve court outfits and lacy ruffs. In the real world, she can't remember where she lives, what year it is, who the president is, or how long she and I have been married. But she sits in her blue chair and mutters at the screen, "No, you don't, Lord Hairballington. You try that shit, I will cut your fucking tail off."

She probably doesn't remember from day to day what's happened in the game, but that's why she's the adviser rather than the monarch—she just has to react, and the game remembers everything for her. Yet she fixates on weird details, and I've started hearing her talking in her sleep, in the middle of the night, about those fucking copper miners and how they better not try any shit because *anybody* can be replaced.

One morning I wake up and cold is leaking into the bed from where Shary pulled the covers back without bothering to tuck me back in. I walk out into the front room and don't see her at first, and worry she's just wandered off into the street by herself, which has been my nightmare for months now and the reason I got her RFID'd. But no, she's in the kitchen, shoving a toaster waffle in her mouth in between poking the cat face and cursing at Count Meesh, whom I named after the friend who introduced Shary and me in the first place. Apparently Count Meesh—a big fluffy Siberian cat—is hatching some schemes and needs to be taught a lesson.

After that I start getting used to waking up alone. And going to bed alone. As long as Shary sleeps at least six hours a night —which she does—I figure it's probably okay. Her neurologist, Dr. Takamori, was the one who recommended the game in the first place, and she tells me it's healthy for Shary to be focused on something.

I should be happy this has *worked* as well as it has. Shary has that look on her face—what I can see of her face, under the cat mask —that I used to love watching when she was writing her diss. The lip-chewing half smile, when she was outsmarting the best minds in Melville studies. So what if Shary's main relationship is with these digital cats instead of me? She's relating to *something;* she's not just staring into space all day anymore.

I always thought she and I would take care of each other forever. I feel like a selfish idiot for even feeling jealous of a stupid plastic cat face, with quivering antennae for whiskers.

One day, after Shary has already been playing *Divine Right of Cats* for four or five hours, she looks up and points at me. "You," she says. "You there. Bring me tea."

"My name is Grace," I say. "I'm your wife."

"Whatever. Just bring me tea." Her face is unreadable, half terrifying cat smile, half frowning human mouth. "I'm busy. There's a crisis. We built a railroad, they broke it. Everything's going to shit." Then Shary looks down again at the cat screen, poking and cursing.

I bring her tea, with a little honey, the way she used to like it. She actually thanks me, but doesn't look up.

3.

Shary gets an email. She gave me her email password around the same time I got power of attorney, and I promised to field any questions and consult her as much as I could. For a while, the emails were coming every day, from her former students and colleagues, and I would answer them to the best of my ability. Now it's been weeks since the last email that wasn't spam.

This one is from the Divine Righters, a group of *Divine Right of Cats* enthusiasts. They've noticed that Shary's realm is one of the most successful, and they want to invite Shary to some kind of tournament or convention . . . or something. It's really not clear. Some kind of event where people will bring their kingdoms and queendoms together and form alliances or go to war. The little plastic cat heads will interface somehow, in proximity to each other, instead of being more or less self-contained.

The plastic cat head already came with some kind of multiplayer mode, where you could connect via the Internet, but I disabled it because the whole reason we were doing this was Shary's inability to communicate with other humans.

I delete the email without bothering to respond to it, but another email appears the next day. And they start coming every few hours, with subject lines like "Shary Please Join Us" and "Shary, we can't do it without you." I don't know whether to be pissed off or freaked out that someone is cyber-stalking my wife.

Then my phone rings. Mine, not hers. "Is this Grace?" a man asks.

"Who is this?" I say, without answering his question first.

"My name is George Henderson. I'm from the Divine Righters. I'm really sorry to take up your time today, but we have been trying to reach your partner, Shary, on email and she hasn't answered, and we really want to get her to come to our convention."

"I'm afraid that won't be possible. Please leave us alone."

"This tournament has sponsorship from"—he names a bunch of companies I've never heard of—"and there are prizes. Plus, this is a chance to interface with other people who love the game as much as she obviously does."

I take a deep breath. Time to just come clean and end this pointless fucking conversation. I'm standing in the kitchen, within earshot of where Shary is sitting on a duct-taped beanbag with her cat mask and her cat-face device, but she shows no sign of hearing me. I realize Shary is naked from the waist down and the windows are uncovered and the neighbors could easily see, and this is my fault.

"My wife can't go to your event," I say. "She is in no condition to 'interface' with anybody."

"We have facilities," says George. "And trained staff. We can handle—" Like he was expecting this to be the case. His voice is intended to sound reassuring, but it squicks me instead.

"Where the fuck do you get off, harassing a sick woman?" I blurt into the phone, loudly enough that Shary looks up for a moment and regards me with her impassive cat eyes.

"Your wife isn't sick," George Henderson says. "She's . . . she's amazing. Could a sick person create one of the top one hundred kingdoms in the entire world? Could a sick woman get past the Great Temptation without breaking a sweat? Grace, your wife is just . . . just amazing."

The Great Temptation is what they call it when the nobles come to you, the Royal Wizard, and offer to support you in overthrowing the monarch. Because you've done such a good job of advising the monarch on running Greater Felinia, you might as well sit on the throne yourself instead of that weak figurehead. This moment comes at different times for different players, and there's no right or wrong answer—you can continue to ace the game whether you sit on the throne or not, depending on other circumstances. But how you handle this moment is a huge test of your steadiness. Shary chose not to take the throne, but managed to make those scheming nobles feel good about her decision.

Neither George nor I have said anything for a minute or so. I'm staring at my wife, whom nobody has called "amazing" in a long time. She's sitting there wearing a tank top and absolutely nothing else, and her legs twitch in a way that makes the whole thing even more obscene. Her tank top has a panoply of stains on it. I realize it's been a week since Shary has gotten my name right.

"Your wife is an intuitive genius," George says in my ear after the pause gets too agonizing on his end. "She makes connections that nobody else could make. She's utterly focused, and processing the game at a much deeper level than a normal brain ever could. It's not like Shary will be the only sufferer from Rat Catcher's Yellows at this convention, you know. There will be lots of others."

I cannot take this. I blurt something, whatever, and hang up on George Henderson. I brace myself for him to call back, but he doesn't. So I go find my wife some pants.

4.

Shary hasn't spoken aloud in a couple of weeks now, not even anything about her game. She has less control over her bodily functions and is having "accidents" more often. I'm making her wear diapers. But her realm is massive, thriving; it's annexed the neighboring duchies.

When I look over her shoulder, the little cats in their Renaissance Europe outfits are no longer asking her simple questions about how to tax the copper mine—instead, they're saying things like "But if the fundamental basis of governance is derived from external symbols of legitimacy, what gives those symbols their power in the first place?"

She doesn't tap on the screen at all, but still her answer appears somehow, as if through the power of her eye blinks: "This is why we go on quests."

According to one of the readouts I see whisk by, Shary has forty-seven knights and assorted nobles out on quests right now, searching for various magical and religious objects as well as for rare minerals—and also for a possible passage to the West that would allow her trading vessels to avoid sailing past the Isle of Dogs.

She just hunches in her chair, frowning with her mouth, while the big cat eyes and tiny nose look playful or fierce, depending on how the light hits them. I've started thinking of this as her face.

I drag her away from her chair and make her take a bath, because it's been a few days, and while she's in there (she can still bathe herself, thank goodness), I examine the cat mask. I realize that I have no idea what is coming out of these nose plugs, even though I've had to refill the little reservoirs on the sides a couple times from the bottles they sent. Neurotransmitters? Pheromones? Stimulants that keep her concentrating? I really have no clue. The chemicals don't smell of anything much.

I open my tablet and search for "divine right of cats," plus words like "sentience," "becoming self-aware," or "artificial intelligence." Soon I'm reading message boards in which people geek out about the idea that these cats are just too frickin' smart for their own good and that they seem to be drawing something from the people they're interfacing with. The digital cats are learning a lot, in particular, about politics and about how human societies function.

On top of which, I find a slew of economics papers—because the cats have been solving problems, inside the various iterations of Greater Felinia, that economists have struggled with in the real world. Issues of scarcity and resource allocation, questions of how to make markets more frictionless. Things I barely grasp the intricacies of, with my doctorate in art history.

And all of the really mind-blowing breakthroughs in economics have come from cat kingdoms that were being managed by people who were afflicted with Rat Catcher's Yellows.

I guess I shouldn't be surprised that Shary is a prodigy; she was always the brilliant one of the two of us. Her nervous energy, her ability to get angry at dead scholars at three in the morning, the random scattering of note cards and papers all over the floor of our tiny grad-student apartment—as if the floor were an extension of her overcharged brain.

It's been more than a week since she's spoken my name, and

meanwhile my emergency sabbatical is running out. And I can't really afford to blow off teaching, since I'm not tenure-track or anything. I'll have to hire someone to look after Shary, or get her into day care or a group home. She won't know the difference between me or someone else looking after her at this point, anyway.

A couple days after my conversation with George Henderson, I look over Shary's shoulder, and things jump out at me. All the relationship touchstones that I embedded in the game when I customized it for her are still in there, but they've gotten weirdly emphasized by her gameplay, like her cats spend an inordinate amount of time at the Puzzler's Retreat. But also, she's added new stuff. Moments I had forgotten are coming up as geological features of her Greater Felinia, hillocks and cliffs.

Shary is reliving all of the time we spent together, through the prism of these cats and their stupid politics. The time we rode bikes across Europe. The time we took up Lindy-hopping and I broke my ankle. The time I cheated on Shary and thought I got away with it, until now. The necklace she never told me she wanted that I tracked down for her. It's all in there, woven throughout this game.

I call back George Henderson. "Okay, fine," I say, without saying hello first. "We'll go to your convention, tournament, whatever. Just tell us where and when."

5.

I sort of expected that a lot of people at the "convention" would have RCY after the way George Henderson talked about the disease. But in fact it seems as though *every* player here has it. Either because you can't become a power player of *Divine Right* without the unique mind state of people with Rat Catcher's, or because that's whom they were able to strong-arm into signing up.

"Here" is a tiny convention hotel in Orlando, Florida, with fuzzy bulletin boards that mention recent meetings of insurance adjusters and auto parts distributors. We're a few miles from Disney World, but near us is nothing but strip malls and strip clubs, and one sad-looking Arby's. We get served continental breakfast, clammy individually wrapped sandwiches, and steamer trays full of stroganoff every day.

The first day, we all mill around for an hour, with me trying to stick close to Shary on her first trip out of New Hampshire in ages. But then George Henderson (a chunky white guy with graying curly hair and an 8 Bit T-shirt) stands up at the front of the ballroom and announces that all the players are going into the adjoining ballroom, and the "friends and loved ones" will stay in here. We can see our partners and friends through an opening in the temporary wall bisecting the hotel ballroom, but they're in their own world, sitting at long rows of tables with their cat faces on.

Those of us left in the "friends and family" room are all sorts of people, but the one thing uniting us is a pall of weariness. At least half the spouses or friends immediately announce they're going out shopping or to Disney World. The other half mostly just sit there, watching their loved ones play, as if they're worried someone's going to get kidnapped.

This half of the ballroom has a sickly sweet milk smell clinging to the ornate cheap carpet and the vinyl walls. I get used to it, and then it hits me again whenever I've just stepped outside or gone to the bathroom.

After an hour, I risk wandering over to the "players" room and look over Shary's shoulder. Queen Arabella is furiously negotiating trade agreements and sending threats of force to the other cat kingdoms that have become her neighbors.

Because all of the realms in this game are called "Greater Felinia" by default, Shary needed to come up with a new name for Arabella's country. She's renamed it "Graceland." I stare at the name, then at Shary, who shows no sign of being aware of my presence.

"I will defend the territorial integrity of Graceland to the last cat," Shary writes.

Judy is a young graphic designer from Toronto, with a long black braid and an eager narrow face. She's sitting alone in the "friends and loved ones" room, until I ask if I can sit at her little table. Turns out Judy is here with her boyfriend of two years, Stefan, who got infected with Rat Catcher's Yellows when they'd only been together a year. Stefan is a superstar in the Divine Right community.

"I have this theory that it's all one compound organism," says

Judy. "The leptospirosis X, the people, the digital cats. Or at least, it's one system. Sort of like real-life cats that infect their owners with *Toxoplasma gondii,* which turns the owners into bigger cat-lovers."

"Huh." I stare out through the gap in the ballroom wall, at the rows of people in cat masks all tapping away on their separate devices, like a soft rain. All genders, all ages, all sizes, wearing tracksuits or business-casual white-collar outfits. The masks bob up and down, almost in unison. Unblinking and wide-eyed, governing machines.

At first Judy and I just bond over our stories of taking care of someone who barely recognizes us but keeps obsessively nation building at all hours. But we turn out to have a lot else in common, including an interest in Pre-Raphaelite art, and a lot of the same books.

The third day rolls around, and our flight back up to New Hampshire is that afternoon. I watch Shary hunched over her cat head, with Judy's boyfriend sitting a few seats away, and my heart begins to sink. I imagine bundling Shary out of here, getting her to the airport and onto the plane, and then unpacking her stuff back at the house while she goes right back to her game. Days and days of cat-faced blankness ahead, forever. This trip has been some kind of turning point for Shary and the others, but for me nothing will have changed.

I'm starting to feel sorry for myself with a whole new intensity when Judy pokes me. "Hey." I look up. "We need to stay in touch, you know," Judy says.

I make a big show of adding her number to my phone, and then without even thinking, say: "Do you want to come stay with us? We have a whole spare bedroom with its own bathroom and stuff."

Judy doesn't say anything for a few minutes. She stares at her boyfriend, who's sitting a few seats away from Shary. She's taking slow, controlled breaths through closed teeth. Then she slumps a little, in an abortive shrug. "Yes. Yes, please. That would be great. Thank you."

I sit with Judy and watch dozens of people in cat masks, sitting shoulder to shoulder without looking at each other. I have a pang of wishing I could just go live in Graceland, a place of which I am already a vassal in every way that matters. But also I feel weirdly proud, and terrified out of my mind. I have no choice but to believe this game matters, the cat politics is important, keeping Lord Hairballington in his place is a vital concern to everyone—or else I will just go straight-up insane.

For a moment, I think Shary looks up from the cat head in her hands and gives me a wicked smile of recognition behind her opaque plastic gaze. I feel so much love in that moment, it's almost unbearable.

SAM J. MILLER

The Heat of Us:
Notes Toward an Oral History

FROM *Uncanny Magazine*

Craig Perry, university administration employee

JUDY GARLAND, DEAD. That's where it started. Dead five days before, in London, "an incautious overdosage" of barbiturates, according to the coroner, and her body had just come back to New York for burial. Twenty thousand people lined up to pay their respects. Every gay man in Manhattan must have gone, but I couldn't do it. I couldn't go see her in that coffin and disturb the delicate Dorothy Gale I had in my head. I don't know, I needed to move, to walk, to run. To do *something.* So I headed for the Hudson River Piers.

My sadness buoyed me up, made me feel like I was looking down on the entire city. I watched the sky go blue and orange and red and purple and indigo as the sun set, then watched the lights come on across the river in Jersey City. June 1969: The wet Manhattan air was like sick breath coming out of our collective throat.

I felt it in me, then. A spark. I didn't see it for what it really was, but I felt it.

That's why I went to the Stonewall.

Sadness is a better spark than rage. I remember thinking, *Revolutions are born on nights like this.* So many people would be mourning Judy. We'd all be miserable together. What couldn't we do, if we were all on the same page like that? Now it sounds like I'm trying to be portentous, given what ultimately went down that night, but I really did have that feeling.

Ben Lazzarra, NYPD beat cop

I checked with the sarge that afternoon. I always did, when I was off-duty and felt the urge and knew I couldn't fight it, knew I'd have to find a place to dance it out of me. I was lucky I was a cop and could check to make sure I wouldn't get swept up in a raid. Nothing was on the list for the Stonewall that night. That's how I know for a fact that what went down that night was not your standard gay club raid. Someone upstairs was pulling strings.

I spent the whole week agonizing over whether or not to go. That's how it always went. I'd wrestle with my fear and shame, and win, and go, and then feel so miserable and ashamed afterward that I leapt back into the closet for another few weeks. I needed some action, some booze, and some sweat and some sex with a stranger. Quentin and I had gone to the gym together, that afternoon, and I knew he had to work that night. He didn't ask where I was going when I went out. Even twins are allowed to have little secrets. But he was the reason I stayed in the closet, and was always so careful to not get dragnetted. Seeing my name in the paper in a story on a gay bar raid—that would kill Quentin quicker and deader than any bullet.

The world changed in two huge ways that night.

In the first place, the world changed because the gays fought back. The police and the press were equally dumbfounded by the idea that a bar full of fairies would refuse to submit to one of the raids that were standard—if monstrously unjust—operating procedure. The Stonewall itself had been raided less than a week before. The night of June 28, 1969, should have been no different.

Secondly, the Stonewall Uprising was the first public demonstration of the supernatural phenomenon that would later be called by names as diverse as collective pyrokinesis, group magic, communal energy, polykinesis, multipsionics, liberation flame, and hellfire.

None of the eleven different city, state, and federal government agencies that investigated the events of that night have ever confirmed or even ac-

knowledged the overwhelming number of witness testimonies describing the events that caused the police to so catastrophically lose control of a routine operation. The facts, however, do not seem to be in doubt. Ten police officers were vaporized that night, vanishing so utterly that the NYPD still considers them missing persons. Three more were cooked alive, charred to the point where dental records were needed to identify the bodies. No incendiary or flammable substances were found at the scene. Five paddy wagons full of arrestees were stopped when their engines spontaneously overheated, and the metal doors of the wagons were melted away to free the people inside —yet no blowtorches or welding equipment were found at the scene.

Since testimonials are all that's left to those of us frustrated with the Official Version, the oral history format seems to be our best bet. I know that many of the most outspoken voices of the Stonewall Uprising have reacted with anger and hostility at the news that I, of all journalists, was planning to compile such a history, and are urging their comrades not to speak with me. I understand their objections, and have precious little to show by way of proof that I've changed. I simply cannot not tell this story.

—Jenny Trent, Editor (formerly of the New York Times)

Craig Perry, university administration employee

I know it's dumb, but I felt like I had failed. Rage hadn't gotten me anywhere. Being black, being gay, I'd been raising hell my whole life. Screaming nonstop, at the top of my lungs, at the bullies and the cops and the priests and the rest of the hateful sons of bitches, trying to get my brothers and sisters to stand up together, and for what? The world was still so rotten that beautiful creatures like Judy Garland couldn't wait to get out of it. Sadness felt like the only rational response to a world like that.

Walking wasn't enough, so I went to the gym to get my mind off things. It didn't work. The twins were there, but not even the sight of *them* could cheer me up. One bearded and one mustachioed, both of their bodies the same impossible lumberjack/rugby player shape, wide-necked and wide-thighed, who did not seem to have aged a day in the seven years I'd been going to that gym. Sadness kept swallowing me back up, distracting me from the spectacle of them, happy and secure in their bubble of hetero-bro confidence. By the time I walked out of there, I was feeling incurably alone.

All I kept thinking was, *Tonight, more than any other night, I need to dance. I need to be among my people.*

Ben Lazzarra, NYPD beat cop

Stonewall was fucking depressing. People paint it as this great place where you could be who you really were. If that's who you really were, you were really fucked. Run by the mob, painted all black inside, stinking of mold and charred wood because it had been boarded shut for twenty years after a big fire. I mean, every gay bar was a piece of shit—what did you expect when you couldn't operate legally? The State Liquor Authority wouldn't issue licenses to gay bars, and nobody runs illegal businesses but the mob. They didn't even have running water, just a big plastic trough behind the bar, where they'd dunk the used glasses and then use them again. Not even any soap. The summer it opened there was a hepatitis outbreak.

But you went, because where else were you going to go? How else could you escape from the crushing weight of your waking life, and be among your own sick, twisted, beautiful kind?

Sergeant Abraham Asher, NYPD 6th Precinct police chief

We knew it was a full moon. Basic rule of policing: Don't do crowd-control-type stuff on full moon nights. I don't know why—people just lose their minds a little easier. This one had some pressure from upstairs, though, and was kind of a last-minute decision. But I can tell you this for goddamn sure: If I'da known Judy Garland had just died, we'd never have gone anywhere near the damn place.

That night essentially ruined my life. I got demoted. Every article painted me as a colossal idiot, and that's taken a huge toll on my family. But I got no cause to complain, because a lot of my men didn't come back from that night.

I used to think that faggots were poor creatures who couldn't help their perversion. I've changed my mind about that. Now I know for a fact they're born of hellfire and bent on burning us all up. And that we ought to put them all on a big boat, put it out to sea, and torpedo the son of a bitch.

Shelly Bronsky, bookstore owner

I was a waitress then, at the Stonewall, although "waitress" is a stretch. We picked up glasses and gave them to the bartenders, and we kept the cigar boxes full of money—no cash register, ever, or the cops would take it away during a raid as evidence that we were selling liquor without a license, as opposed to holding a private party, which is what the mob lawyers would argue to get the case against the building owner thrown out. We mopped up the toilets when they overflowed, which was always. At the end of every night, we'd go through the garbage of the neighboring bars and steal empty bottles of top-shelf liquor, so the next night when the mob guys came through, they could fill them up with their own shitty diluted bootleg stuff.

Sergeant Abraham Asher, NYPD 6th Precinct police chief

I hated the raids. We had to do them, because you can't just let filth and sickness fester in your city, but going into those places made my officers really lose their shit.

By midnight we were in position around the corner, thirty cops, waiting for the signal from the undercovers we'd sent inside. That was standard for a raid—undercovers went in early, always women, to finger the people who worked there, because those were more serious charges. The Stonewall had a big heavy door with wooden reinforcements, so every time we raided the place, it would take us six or seven minutes to break it down and get inside, and in that time the workers would drop everything and blend in with the crowd. Once we were in, it'd be like no one worked there.

But that night, it was weird. We kept waiting and our girls inside did not come out, and I tried to radio headquarters and couldn't get through. So we got pretty antsy pretty fast.

Tricksie Barron, unemployed

You got to talk to somebody else for that. I was there, but I was so drunk that night that we might have called up a bunch of flying monkeys to burn it down. All I remember is, I met the man of my dreams that night. I meet him most nights, but this one was extra special. Complimented my dress and everything. While we were dancing, he grabbed me by the ass, pulled me close, and said, "I like a girl who's packing more heat than me."

Craig Perry, university administration employee

It was a rough night for the older queens. Men wept like babies for Judy. I stood in their midst, baffled. What was wrong with them, these fools, these people, my people, dancing like all was well in the world? I wanted to grab them, shake them, fill them up with the rage that choked me.

A lot of them were men I'd been seeing there for the longest. Many had lost everything over the years, for being who they were, for living in the world they lived in. But they were too beaten down to ever fight back. Less than a month before, when I tried to organize a campaign against the *New York Times* for its policy of publishing the names of men arrested in vice raids—lists that invariably got everyone on them fired or divorced or sometimes institutionalized and lobotomized against their will—not a one of them wanted to do a damn thing.

Judy Garland got played again and again, sparking fresh tears and howls each time a song started. A bunch of women I had never seen before, who looked like they wandered into the wrong bar by mistake, joined in on a sing-along to the fifth straight time someone played "Somewhere Over the Rainbow." Now I know they must have been the undercovers, but then I just thought they were confused tourists.

I watched them dance, the poorest of our poor, the kids who got beaten and thrown out and sometimes way worse. Smokey Robinson said, *Take a gooood look at my face,* and they all sang along, even the boy with the scar across his face shaped like the iron his mother burned him with.

Again I thought about the twins at the gym, men of steel or stone, their bodies as perfect as the bond between them. I had never known any bond remotely like that. I was forty that summer, and I had come to believe that loneliness was an essential and ineluctable aspect of gay identity, or at least my own.

Diana Ross came on the radio. We danced, and we sang, *I hear a symphony*, and we *were* the symphony, for as long as the song lasted.

Annabelle Kowalski, stenographer

Judy who? Child, please. Don't you let the gay boys hoodwink you. Sure, some old queens were crying in their beer to "Over the Rainbow" that night, but divas die every day and nobody bursts into flames. That shit happened because we *made* it happen.

The raid itself came at one in the morning. I was in bed already. I lived a block and a half away. I heard the screams and shouts. I went to the window and saw two young black men, laughing, running. I hollered down, asked what was happening.

"Riot at the Stonewall!" they shouted. "Us faggots is fighting back!"

And I don't know how, but I knew this was my story. My chance. I pulled a jacket on over my bedclothes and ran.

—*Jenny Trent, Editor (formerly of the* New York Times*)*

Ben Lazzarra, NYPD beat cop

What you need to know is that I was *always* scared when I did stuff like that. Meeting men in darkness under the West Side Highway, accepting hurried blowjobs on late-night subway platforms, entering the Stonewall, I always expected the worst. It's ridiculous, but I wished Quentin could have been there. I never felt whole or safe without him. But of course he couldn't be.

We were dancing, all of us, packed together in that shitty room, hot and sweaty and happy. And for once, I wasn't scared. For once, I felt good and happy about who and where I was. We were safe there, from the cops and the mob and all the other bad men, safe in the heat our bodies made together.

I don't know what was different. I never liked dancing before.

For me, like for a lot of the Stonewall boys, dancing was what you did to figure out who you were going home with. But what I felt that night was a lot like what I had always felt at the gym, the same sense of power and energy, except without the constant shame and terror that I always felt around Quentin. The fear that he'd see me staring at some boy's backside, or spot some infinitesimal fraction of an erection, and Know Everything.

What I felt that night was joy. There is no other word for it.

This, I kept thinking. *This is sacred. This is joy.*

My twin brother and I added up to something, together. Quentin made me feel love, power, and safety, but never joy. We were locked into each other, a closed loop that gave us much but took away more.

People have told me that maybe if I had been honest with him, things would have gone down differently. I'd still have him. They're right, of course, every time. And every time, I want to punch them in the face until my fist comes out the other side.

Craig Perry, university administration employee

The frenzy was on me by then, and I was dancing like I might die when I stopped.

I danced up on a short built sparkplug of a man with his back to me. The shape of his ass assured me he'd be a prime catch.

That's when the house lights came up, blindingly bright and white, flickering like a theater warning us intermission was ending. I'd been caught up in a raid before. Taken to the precinct along with twenty other guys, and one of them got so scared because his name would be in the paper and his parents would find out and disown him, he jumped out the second-story window—and got impaled on the points of a wrought-iron fence. Took them six hours to get him off of there, with blowtorches and everything, and when they brought him to St. Vincent's, he still had spikes of iron in him. He survived, but he wished he hadn't.

So a lot of us knew what to expect when the Stonewall gave the signal. A lot of us screamed, high theatrical exaggerated wails, and laughed, and faked swooning, and to be honest I heard myself laugh. Kind of a crazy laugh, though, because I could finally feel the sadness start to ebb out of my rage. I didn't want to run. I wanted to fucking kill somebody.

The sparkplug, on the other hand, wasn't laughing.

"Fuck," he said, looking around in a panic, looking for another way out. Of course there wasn't one, because the fucking Stonewall was a death trap with no fire exit. He turned around. I saw his face.

"Hi," I said, absurdly, cheerfully, finding room in my rage for more laughter, because it was the bearded one of the twins from the gym.

Ben Lazzarra, NYPD beat cop

Nobody told me that the flashing white lights meant a raid. I thought there was a fire, or somebody won a raffle I didn't know about. It took me a while to pick up what was happening from what people were saying around me.

"What do we do?" I said, to Craig, except he wasn't Craig then, he was just the weirdly friendly black dude standing behind me.

"We wait, and keep our fingers crossed they don't take anybody in."

But I knew they'd be taking us in. An unscheduled raid, less than a week after the last one, meant this was more than just the shake-up each precinct was obliged to give from time to time. And for a minute I was fine. Relieved, even. When the worst thing you can possibly imagine happens, you're free from the fear of it for the rest of your life.

But sometimes the worst thing you can imagine isn't the worst thing that can happen.

"Everybody up against the walls," said a loud scary cop voice, and then repeated it, and the second time I knew who was speaking.

Quentin led the brigade into the back room, two rows of cops, each with a dozen sets of handcuffs at the ready. The dance floor emptied out, but I couldn't move. He stopped, five feet from me, snarling with rage at having to repeat himself, because someone had not immediately obeyed. And then he saw who it was.

"Benjy?" he said. His face, that perfect cop blank slate, cracked under the weight of what he was seeing. His twin brother, the man whose side he'd hardly ever left, the man with whom he'd joined the police force and struggled valiantly to fight the forces of evil, who now stood before him in a sweaty tight T-shirt in a den of iniquity, had been keeping from him a secret so terrifying that it threatened to strip the flesh from both our bones. The man who he knew better than anyone, he had not known at all.

Some lady with a gruff voice beside me hissed, "Oh, *hell* no."

Quentin said my name again, no question mark now, and that was the last word he ever said.

Shelly Bronsky, bookstore owner

Those gay boys parted like the Red Sea for the boys in blue. The cops marched in and men fell over themselves, running for the walls. One guy didn't, and that's what gave me the courage to pry myself free from the crowd and step forward. The scary-mustache cop who led the brigade stopped short, not five feet from me, and I saw something like fear come over his face.

"Oh, *hell* no," I hissed.

Someone behind me yelled, "Yeah!"

Some black gay protest queen, who I'd been seeing around since forever, stepped forward to join the two of us. "Hell no!"

The shouts spread. *Oh no, honey, no, you won't,* and *Ain't you got no real criminals to arrest.* I thought of the beautiful boy I knew from school, whose father pressed his face to the burner on the stove to make the men leave him alone, and the cigarette burns on my own upper arm where my mother tried to burn the lez out of me. We'd been swallowing fire for so long, fire and violence and hate, and in that moment of panic and fear and anger everything fell into place to feed the fire back.

And that's what we did.

Sergeant Abraham Asher, NYPD 6th Precinct police chief

I was born and bred in the Bronx, but I went to fight in Europe during World War Two. As a Jew, I felt I had to play my part in ridding the world of the fascist menace. Later on I'd join the police force for the same reason, because I felt it was my duty to make my city safe.

In the war I saw some rough things, went on some scary missions. And I've never in my life been more frightened than I was in that fag bar.

I'll tell you what I've told everyone else: It was too dark and too full of screaming and the smell of cooked flesh for me to say one way or another whether a wave of devil fire really shot out of nowhere to murder my men. If some of our boys who survived said that's what happened, I'm not going to call them liars.

Accounts of the uprising have been unsurprisingly whitewashed. All the major news outlets have blocked any mention of multipsionics — or whatever you want to call it. My own articles have been rejected by dozens of papers and magazines because I've refused to take out what they call "supernatural elements." Time, for example, is the least biased of the bunch, and their most enlightened pronouncement on the subject of sexual difference is that "homosexuality is a serious and sometimes crippling maladjustment."

Responsible parties have conducted exhaustive experiments. They won't talk about them publicly, but through my connections to the Stonewall veterans, I know that almost everyone who has gone on record about that night has subsequently been approached to participate in studies by the U.S. government, foreign governments, defense contractors, pharmaceutical companies, and leading organized crime families.

While the phenomenon has since been observed in hundreds of minor and major incidents, it simply refuses to submit to science. Studying individuals or groups, with or without duress, in labs or on the street or in the still-smoldering remains of the Stonewall itself, no one has been able to replicate those events, not so much as the lighting of a lone candle on a birthday cake.

—Jenny Trent, Editor (formerly of the New York Times*)*

Ben Lazzarra, NYPD beat cop

Fire sparked in the air all around us. It hung there like the burning of invisible torches, and then it spread, like fire does. It moved, writhed, twisted into a ring, surrounded the three cops that had led the battalion into the back room. Three that included my brother Quentin. The flames rushed in, fast as floodwater when a levee breaks, and incinerated them.

The rest of those cops ran. Fifteen of them, but the door from the back to the front rooms only let them out one at a time, and the anger of my fellow queers was quicker and smarter. Somehow, so swiftly, they had learned to control the flames. Without saying a word, the crowd turned its full rage on them—and the fire lashed out with such white-hot hunger that ten men simply vanished from this planet. Flame broke them down into the atoms they were made from, and carved a huge hole in the stone wall between the front and back rooms, too.

Everyone was screaming and yelling by then, rushing out into the street after the rest of the cops. Streaks of fire zinged and whooshed through the air around them. They left me alone with the charred heap of my brother.

Tyrell James, security specialist

I was there. I felt it. I know what we did. And I've been going all over the world, training people who've been pushed too far for too long, telling them how to fight back when the moment comes when their backs are up against the wall. And one day very soon, the people who like to push other people around are going to wake up and find out everything's changed.

Sergeant Abraham Asher, NYPD 6th Precinct police chief

I find it offensive, what those people are saying. They expect you to believe all you've got to do is get a bunch of people together who are mad and scared and then fire will rain down on the evil-doers? So, the Jews who went to the gas chambers weren't scared enough? The slaves weren't mad? It's a bunch of manure, if you ask me.

I'll tell you this much. Cops are a pretty cynical bunch, and we don't buy ghost stories. But there isn't a man or woman of the 20,000 on the force that doesn't know in our guts that something really real and really scary happened that night. Finding a couple fairies in a park and ticketing them for disorderly conduct used to be an easy count toward your quota, but to this day most officers will think twice before they do it. And we don't ever raid gay bars.

Craig Perry, *university administration employee*

It's not that no one in the whole history of human oppression was as pissed off and fucked over as we were that night—I think it's happened lots of times, except we're reading history the wrong way. We read it the way The Man wrote it, and when he was writing it, I bet he didn't know what to do with multipsionics. But I've studied this shit. The Warsaw Ghetto Uprising happened on Passover, after all, and the Haitian Revolution began with a spontaneous uprising at a *vodoun* religious ceremony. When people come together to celebrate, that's when they're unstoppable.

Ben Lazzarra, *NYPD beat cop*

People say the world changed for us that night, but I'm not sure I buy it. The world is the same, only more so. People still hate and fear us, they just hate and fear us *more*. People still bash and kill and lobotomize us, they just do it more. And we still know in our hearts, under the shame and self-loathing and all the other shit society has heaped on us, that we were born blessed by God with an incredible gift.

I've steered clear of all the scientists and scholars and reporters trying to turn that night into a research paper, but there's one thing I do know. It was *us*. The heat of us, of all those bodies full of joy and sadness and anger and lust, and the combination of the three of us: Me and Craig and that dyke. I can't explain it, that's just what I felt in that moment. We were the match and the sandpaper, coming together. All I know is it was *us*.

Craig Perry, *university administration employee*

We all went a little mad that night. Nobody knew what the hell had happened, but we knew nothing would be the same again. People danced and whooped and hollered and laughed. Three men skipped into the distance with their arms locked, singing, *We're off to see the wizard.*

I don't know why I didn't want to be with my people, then. I felt empty. Like I'd put my whole self into wanting something, and now I had it. I'd licked envelopes and organized protests and screamed at the top of my lungs for a decade or several, and the revolution had finally come . . . but answered prayers are always terrifying. What are you, when you get the thing you've built your life around trying to get?

My rage had burnt itself out. So instead of joining the jubilant crowds, I went to the Day-O Diner, where the Meatpacking District meets the Hudson River, where the coffee is strong and cheap and nobody goes there but bloody meat men ending their shifts, or clean meat men beginning theirs.

The twin sat by himself. His back was to the door, but after what had just gone down, I would have known that rugby-wide neck anywhere. I strolled past, pretending to be selecting a barstool, to confirm that he wasn't sobbing. His face was blank, staring into scalding black coffee for answers we both knew were not there.

"I'm sorry about your brother," I said, cautiously.

He looked up. "I know you from the gym," he said.

"He didn't know," I said, "did he? About . . ."

He shook his head.

"I'm sorry. I can't imagine. I just wanted to say—but you must want to be alone—"

"Don't go," he said. "Being alone is what I'm worst at."

He began to weep then, with his whole body. I sat and ordered refill after refill of black coffee, for both of us, until the sun came up.

I've interviewed Craig Perry a dozen times since Stonewall, and I don't think he's ever recognized me, ever made the connection. But he had come to see me, two weeks before the fire. He visited me at the office of the New York Times. He came to demand we stop printing the names of gay people caught up in vice raids and decency arrests. I think he thought I was merely the secretary, which is why my face didn't stay in his mind, but I was not. I was the one who wrote those articles. I had been writing them for eight years by then. Later on I went through all my old clippings and did the math: Thirteen hundred names, thirteen hundred people whose deepest darkest secret I spilled. If I put in the time, I could probably track down how many of them killed themselves, how many got fired or dishonorably discharged or institutionalized, but that wouldn't help anything but my own guilty need to suffer. Telling the story, the real story, is a much better way to pay off the crippling karma-debt I built up in the years before I knew better.

Craig before Stonewall was a different person. His rage was enormous, overwhelming, cutting him off from the rest of the human race. He wanted the revolution, right away, wanted it to come with fire and brimstone and the blood of every heterosexist son/daughter of a bitch to be spilled in the streets. I don't want to speculate on what changed, what he had after that he didn't have before, what aspect of what went down inside the Stonewall broke down his old anger. I don't know him like that. Journalists tend to write about people like they know what makes them tick, why they do the things they do, and at the end of the day it's the stories people tell about themselves that matter.

—*Jenny Trent, Editor (formerly of the* New York Times*)*

Ben Lazzarra, NYPD beat cop

No matter how many hours I spent at the gym after that, it was never the same. My muscle tone was never as sharp, my stamina never the same, and two months after Quentin died, I noticed wrinkles in my forehead for the first time. Whatever we were, together, the weird magic of us against the world was broken.

Craig and I slept together for a while, but that wasn't meant to be. We wanted different things in bed—plus what we both needed then was not a boyfriend. I had never had a best friend before. I loved Quentin with my whole heart, more than I loved myself, but until he was taken away I never had to think about how much happiness I had sacrificed by living my whole adult life with the paralyzing fear that he'd find out what I was.

Every year, on my birthday, Craig brings over two cakes and we blow out the candles with our minds. And every year he wonders why stopping fires is so much easier than starting them. For us, anyway. I don't tell him my theory, because he'd just laugh at it, but I believe joy is the only thing stronger than sadness.

Three Bodies at Mitanni

FROM *Analog Science Fiction and Fact*

WE WERE PREPARED to end the worlds we found. We were prepared to hurt each other to do it.

I thought Jotunheim would be the nadir, the worst of all possible worlds, the closest we ever came to giving the kill order. I thought that Anyahera's plea, and her silent solitary pain when we voted against her, two to one, would be the closest we ever came to losing her—a zero-sum choice between her conviction and the rules of our mission:

Locate the seedship colonies, the frozen progeny scattered by a younger and more desperate Earth. Study these new humanities. And in the most extreme situations: *remove existential threats to mankind.*

Jotunheim was a horror written in silicon and plasmid, a doomed atrocity. But it would never survive to be an existential threat to humanity. *I'm sorry,* I told Anyahera. *It would be a mercy. I know. I want to end it too. But it is not our place—*

She turned away from me, and I remember thinking: It will never be worse than this. We will never come closer.

And then we found Mitanni.

Lachesis woke us from stable storage as we fell toward periapsis. The ship had a mind of her own, architecturally human but synthetic in derivation, wise and compassionate and beautiful but, in the end, limited to merely operational thoughts.

She had not come so far (five worlds, five separate stars) so very fast (four hundred years of flight) by wasting mass on the organic.

We left our flesh at home and rode *Lachesis*'s doped metallic hydrogen mainframe starward. She dreamed the three of us, Anyahera and Thienne and I, nested in the ranges of her mind. And
in containing us, I think she knew us, as much as her architecture
permitted.

When she pulled me up from storage, I thought she was Anyahera, a wraith of motion and appetite, flame and butter, and I
reached for her, thinking she had asked to rouse me, as concili-
ation.

"We're here, Shinobu," *Lachesis* said, taking my hand. "The last
seedship colony. Mitanni."

The pang of hurt and disappointment I felt was not an omen.
"The ship?" I asked, by ritual. If we had a captain, it was me. "Any
trouble during the flight?"

"I'm fine," *Lachesis* said. She filled the empty metaphor around
me with bamboo panels and rice paper, the whispered suggestion
of warm spring rain. Reached down to help me out of my hammock. "But something's wrong with this one."

I found my slippers. "Wrong how?"

"Not like Jotunheim. Not like anything we've seen on the previous colonies." She offered me a robe, bowing fractionally. "The
other two are waiting."

We gathered in a common space to review what we knew. Thienne
smiled up from her couch, her skin and face and build all dark
and precise as I remembered them from Lagos and the flesh. No
volatility to Thienne; no care for the wild or theatrical. Just careful,
purposeful action, like the machines and technologies she specialized in.

And a glint of something in her smile, in the speed with which
she looked back to her work. She'd found some new gristle to
work at, some enigma that rewarded obsession.

She'd voted against Anyahera's kill request back at Jotunheim,
but of course Anyahera had forgiven her. They had always been
opposites, always known and loved the certainty of the space between them. It kept them safe from each other, gave room to retreat and advance.

In the vote at Jotunheim, I'd been the contested ground between them. I'd voted with Thienne: *no kill.*

"Welcome back, Shinobu," Anyahera said. She wore a severely

cut suit, double-breasted, fit for cold and business. It might have
been something from her mother's Moscow wardrobe. Her mother
had hated me.

Subjectively, I'd seen her less than an hour ago, but the power
of her presence struck me with the charge of decades. I lifted a
hand, suddenly unsure what to say. I'd known and loved her for
years. At Jotunheim I had seen parts of her I had never loved or
known at all.

She considered me, eyes distant, icy. Her father was Maori, her
mother Russian. She was only herself, but she had her mother's
eyes and her mother's way of using them in anger. "You look . . .
indecisive."

I wondered if she meant my robe or my body, as severe and
androgynous as the cut of her suit. It was an angry thing to say, an
ugly thing, beneath her. It carried the suggestion that I was unfinished. She knew how much that hurt.

I'd wounded her at Jotunheim. Now she reached for the weapons she had left.

"I've decided on this," I said, meaning my body, hoping to dis-
engage. But the pain of it made me offer something, conciliatory:
"Would you like me some other way?"

"Whatever you prefer. Take your time about it." She made a no-
tation on some invisible piece of work, a violent slash. "Wouldn't
want to do anything hasty."

I almost lashed out.

Thienne glanced at me, then back to her work: an instant of
apology, or warning, or reproach. "Let's start," she said. "We have
a lot to cover."

I took my couch, the third point of the triangle. Anyahera
looked up again. Her eyes didn't go to Thienne, and so I knew,
even before she spoke, that this was something they had already
argued over.

"The colony on Mitanni is a Duong-Watts malignant," she said.
"We have to destroy it."

I knew what a Duong-Watts malignant was because "Duong-
Watts malignant" was a punch line, a joke, a class of human civilization that we had all gamed out in training. An edge case so theo-
retically improbable it might as well be irrelevant. Duong Phireak's
predictions of a universe overrun by his namesake had not, so far,
panned out.

Jotunheim was not far enough behind us, and I was not strong enough a person, to do anything but push back. "I don't think you can know that yet," I said. "I don't think we have enough—"

"Ship," Anyahera said. "Show them."

Lachesis told me everything she knew, all she'd gleaned from her decades-long fall toward Mitanni, eavesdropping on the telemetry of the seedship that had brought humanity here, the radio buzz of the growing civilization, the reports of the probes she'd fired ahead.

I saw the seedship's arrival on what should have been a garden world, a nursery for the progeny of her vat wombs. I saw catastrophe: a barren, radioactive hell, climate erratic, oceans poisoned, atmosphere boiling into space. I watched the ship struggle and fail to make a safe place for its children, until, in the end, it gambled on an act of cruel, desperate hope: fertilizing its crew, raising them to adolescence, releasing them on the world to build something out of its own cannibalized body.

I saw them succeed.

Habitation domes blistering the weathered volcanic flats. Webs of tidal power stations. Thermal boreholes like suppurating wounds in the crust. Thousands of fission reactors, beating hearts of uranium and molten salt—

Too well. Too fast. In seven hundred years of struggle on a hostile, barren world, their womb-bred population exploded up toward the billions. Their civilization webbed the globe.

It was a boom unmatched in human history, unmatched on the other seedship colonies we had discovered. No Eden world had grown so fast.

"Interesting," I said, watching Mitanni's projected population, industrial output, estimated technological self-catalysis, all exploding toward some undreamt-of ceiling. "I agree that this could be suggestive of a Duong-Watts scenario."

It wasn't enough, of course. Duong-Watts malignancy was a disease of civilizations, but the statistics could offer only symptoms. That was the terror of it: the depth of the cause. The simplicity.

"Look at what *Lachesis* has found." Anyahera rose, took an insistent step forward. "Look at the way they live."

I spoke more wearily than I should have. "This is going to be another Jotunheim, isn't it?"

Her face hardened. "No. It isn't."

I didn't let her see that I understood, that the words *Duong-Watts malignancy* had already made me think of the relativistic weapons *Lachesis* carried, and the vote we would need to use them. I didn't want her to know how angry it made me that we had to go through this again.

One more time before we could go home. One more hard decision.

Thienne kept her personal space too cold for me: frosted glass and carbon composite, glazed constellations of data and analysis, a transparent wall opened onto false-color nebulae and barred galactic jets. At the low end of hearing, distant voices whispered in clipped aerospace phrasing. She had come from Haiti and from New Delhi, but no trace of that twin childhood, so rich with history, had survived her journey here.

It took me years to understand that she didn't mean it as insulation. The cold distances were the things that moved her, clenched her throat, pimpled her skin with awe. Anyahera teased her for it, because Anyahera was a historian and a master of the human, and what awed Thienne was to glimpse her own human insignificance.

"Is it a Duong-Watts malignant?" I asked her. "Do you think Anyahera's right?"

"Forget that," she said, shaking her head. "No prejudgment. Just look at what they've built."

She walked me through what had happened to humanity on Mitanni.

At Lagos U, before the launch, we'd gamed out scenarios for what we called *socially impoverished worlds*—places where a resource crisis had limited the physical and mental capital available for art and culture. Thienne had expected demand for culture to collapse along with supply as people focused on the necessities of existence. Anyahera had argued for an inelastic model, a fundamental need embedded in human consciousness.

There was no culture on Mitanni. No art. No social behavior beyond functional interaction in the service of industry or science.

It was an incredible divergence. Every seedship had carried Earth's cultural norms—the consensus ideology of a liberal democratic state. Mitanni's colonists should have inherited those norms.

Mitanni's colonists expressed no interest in those norms. There was no oppression. No sign of unrest or discontent. No government or judicial system at all, no corporations or markets. Just an array of specialized functions to which workers assigned themselves, their numbers fed by batteries of synthetic wombs.

There was no entertainment, no play, no sex. No social performance of gender. No family units. Biological sex had been flattened into a population of sterile females, slender and lightly muscled. "No sense wasting calories on physical strength with exoskeletons available," Thienne explained. "It's a resource conservation strategy."

"You can't build a society like this using ordinary humans," I said. "It wouldn't be stable. Free riders would play havoc."

Thienne nodded. "They've been rewired. I think it started with the first generation out of the seedship. They made themselves selfless so that they could survive."

It struck me that when the civilization on Mitanni built their own seedships, they would be able to do this again. If they could endure Mitanni, they could endure anything.

They could have the galaxy.

I was not someone who rushed to judgment. They'd told me that, during the final round of crew selection. *Deliberative. Centered. Disconnected from internal affect. High emotional latency. Suited for tie-breaker role. . . .*

I swept the imagery shut between my hands, compressing it into a point of light. Looked up at Thienne with a face that must have signaled loathing or revulsion, because she lifted her chin in warning. "Don't," she said. "Don't leap to conclusions."

"I'm not."

"You're thinking about ant hives. I can see it."

"Is that a bad analogy?"

"Yes!" Passion, surfacing and subsiding. "Ant hives only function because each individual derives a fitness benefit, even if they sacrifice themselves. It's kin selective eusociality. This is—"

"Total, selfless devotion to the state?"

"To survival." She lifted a mosaic of images from the air: a smiling woman driving a needle into her thigh. A gang of laborers running into a fire, heedless of their own safety, to rescue vital equipment. "They're born. They learn. They specialize, they work, sleep, eat, and eventually they volunteer to die. It's the *opposite* of an insect hive. They don't cooperate for their own individual benefit—they don't seem to care about themselves at all. It's pure altruism. Cognitive, not instinctive. They're brilliant, and they all come to the same conclusion: cooperation and sacrifice."

The image of the smiling woman with the needle did not leave me when the shifting mosaic carried her away. "Do you admire that?"

"It's a society that could never evolve on its own. It has to be designed." She stared into the passing images with an intensity I'd rarely seen outside of deep study or moments of love, a ferocious need to master some vexing, elusive truth. "I want to know how they did it. How do they disable social behavior without losing theory of mind? How can they remove all culture and sex and still motivate?"

"We saw plenty of ways to motivate on Jotunheim," I said.

Maybe I was thinking of Anyahera, taking her stance by some guilty reflex, because there was nothing about my tone *disconnected from internal affect.*

I expected anger. Thienne surprised me. She swept the air clear of her work, came to the couch, and sat beside me. Her eyes were gentle.

"I'm sorry we have to do this again," she said. "Anyahera will forgive you."

"Twice in a row? She thought Jotunheim was the greatest atrocity in human history. 'A crime beyond forgiveness or repair,' remember? And I let it stand. I walked away."

I took Thienne's shoulder, gripped the swell of her deltoid, the strength that had caught Anyahera's eye two decades ago. Two decades for us—on Earth, centuries now.

Thienne stroked my cheek. "You only had two options. Walk away, or burn it all. You knew you weren't qualified to judge an entire world."

"But that's why we're here. To judge. To find out whether the price of survival ever became too high—whether what survived wasn't human."

She leaned in and kissed me softly. "Mankind changes," she said. "This—what you are—" Her hands touched my face, my chest. "People used to think this was wrong. There were men, and women, and nothing else, nothing more or different."

I caught her wrists. "That's not the same, Thienne."

"I'm just saying: technology changes things. We change our-

selves. If everyone had judged what you are as harshly as Anyahera judged Jotunheim—"

I tightened my grip. She took a breath, perhaps reading my anger as play, and that made it worse. "Jotunheim's people are slaves," I said. "I can be what I want. It's not the same at all."

"No. Of course not." She lowered her eyes. "You're right. That was an awful example. I'm sorry."

"Why would you say that?" I pressed. Thienne closed herself, keeping her pains and fears within. Sometimes it took a knife to get them out. "Technology doesn't always enable the *right* things. If some people had their way, I would be impossible. They would have found everything but man and woman and wiped it out."

She looked past me, to the window and the virtual starscape beyond. "We've come so far out," she said. I felt her shoulders tense, bracing an invisible weight. "And there's nothing out here. Nobody to meet us except our own seedship children. We thought we'd find someone else—at least some machine or memorial, some sign of other life. But after all this time, the galaxy is still a desert. If we screw up, if we die out . . . what if there's no one else to try?

"If whatever happened on Mitanni is what it takes to survive in the long run, isn't that better than a dead cosmos?"

I didn't know what to say to that. It made me feel suddenly and terribly alone. The way Anyahera might have felt, when we voted against her.

I kissed her. She took the distraction, answered it, turned us both away from the window and down onto the couch. "Tell me what to be," I said, wanting to offer her something, to make a part of the Universe warm for her. This was my choice: to choose.

"Just you—" she began.

But I silenced her. "Tell me. I want to."

"A woman," she said, when she had breath. "A woman this time, please . . ."

Afterward, she spoke into the silence and the warmth, her voice absent, wondering: "They trusted the three of us to last. They thought we were the best crew for the job." She made absent knots with my hair. "Does that ever make you wonder?"

"The two-body problem has been completely solved," I said. "But for $n = 3$, solutions exist for special cases."

She laughed and pulled me closer. "You've got to go talk to Anyahera," she said. "She never stays mad at me. But you . . ."

She trailed off, into contentment, or back into contemplation of distant, massive things.

Duong-Watts malignant, I thought to myself. I couldn't help it: my mind went back to the world ahead of us, closing at relativistic speeds.

Mitanni's explosive growth matched the theory of a Duong-Watts malignant. But that was just correlation. The malignancy went deeper than social trends, down to the individual, into the mechanisms of the mind.

And that was Anyahera's domain.

"We can't destroy them," Thienne murmured. "We might need them."

Even in simulation we had to sleep. *Lachesis*'s topological braid computer could run the human being in full-body cellular resolution, clock us up to two subjective days a minute in an emergency, pause us for centuries—but not obviate the need for rest.

It didn't take more than an overclocked instant. But it was enough for me to dream.

Or maybe it wasn't my dream—just Duong Phireak's nightmare reappropriated. I'd seen him lecture at Lagos, an instance of his self transmitted over for the night. But this time he spoke in Anyahera's voice as she walked before me, down a blood-spattered street beneath a sky filled with alien stars.

"Cognition enables an arsenal of survival strategies inaccessible to simple evolutionary selection," she said, the words of Duong Phireak. "Foresight, planning, abstract reasoning, technological development—we can confidently say that these strategies are strictly superior, on a computational level, at maximizing individual fitness. Cognition enables the cognitive to pursue global, rather than local, goals. A population of flatworms can't cooperate to build a rocket unless the 'build a rocket' allele promotes individual fitness in each generation—an unlikely outcome, given the state of flatworm engineering."

Memory of laughter, compressed by the bandwidth of the hippocampus. I reached out for Anyahera, and she looked up and only then, following her gaze, did I recognize the sky, the aurora of Jotunheim.

"But with cognition came consciousness—an exaptative accident, the byproduct of circuits in the brain that powered social reasoning, sensory integration, simulation theaters, and a host of other global functions. So much of our civilization derived in turn from consciousness, from the ability not just to enjoy an experience but to *know* that we enjoy it. Consciousness fostered a suite of behaviors without clear adaptive function, but with subjective, experiential value."

I touched Anyahera's shoulder. She turned toward me. On the slope of her bald brow glittered the circuitry of a Jotunheim slave shunt, bridging her pleasure centers into her social program.

Of course she was smiling.

"Consciousness is expensive," she said. "This is a problem for totalitarian states. A human being with interest in leisure, art, agency —a human being who is *aware* of her own self-interest—cannot be worked to maximum potential. I speak of more than simple slave labor. I am sure that many of your professors wish you could devote yourselves more completely to your studies."

Overhead, the aurora laughed in the voices of Lagos undergraduates, and when I looked up, the sky split open along a dozen fiery fractures, relativistic warheads moving in ludicrous slow-motion, burning their skins away as they made their last descent. *Lachesis's* judgment. The end I'd withheld.

"Consciousness creates inefficient behavior," Anyahera said, her smile broad, her golden-brown skin aflame with the light of the falling apocalypse. "A techno-tyranny might take the crude step of creating slave castes who derive conscious pleasure from their functions, but this system is fundamentally inadequate, unstable. The slave still expends caloric and behavioral resources on *being conscious;* the slave seeks to maximize its own pleasure, not its social utility. A clever state will go one step further and eliminate the cause of these inefficiencies at the root. They will sever thought from awareness.

"This is what I call the Duong-Watts malignancy. The most efficient, survivable form of human civilization is a civilization of philosophical zombies. A nation of the unconscious, those who think without knowing they exist, who work with the brilliance of our finest without ever needing to ask *why.* Their cognitive abilities are unimpaired—enhanced, if anything—without constant interference. I see your skepticism; I ask you to consider the anosognosia literature, the disturbing information we have assembled on the architecture of the sociopathic mind, the vast body of evidence behind the deflationary position on the Hard Problem.

"We are already passengers on the ship of self. It is only a matter of time until some designer, pressed for time and resources, decides to jettison the hitchhiker. And the rewards will be enormous —in a strictly Darwinian sense."

When I reached for her, I think I wanted to shield her, somehow, to put myself between her and the weapons. It was reflex, and I knew it was meaningless, but still . . .

Usually in dreams you wake when you die. But I felt myself come apart.

Ten light-hours out from Mitanni's star, falling through empty realms of ice and hydrogen, we slammed into a wall of light—the strobe of a lighthouse beacon orbiting Mitanni. "Pulse-compressed burst maser," *Lachesis* told me, her voice clipped as she dissected the signal. "A fusion-pumped flashbulb."

Lachesis's forward shield reflected light like a wall of diamond —back toward the star, toward Mitanni. In ten hours they would see us.

We argued over what to do. Anyahera wanted to launch our relativistic kill vehicles now, so they'd strike Mitanni just minutes after the light of our approach, before the colonists could prepare any response. Thienne, of course, dissented. "Those weapons were meant to be used when we were certain! Only then!"

I voted with Thienne. I knew the capabilities of our doomsday payload with the surety of reflex. We had the safety of immense speed, and nothing the Mitanni could do, no matter how sophisticated, could stop our weapons—or us. We could afford to wait, and mull over our strategy.

After the vote, Anyahera brushed invisible lint from the arm of her couch. "Nervous?" I asked, probing where I probably shouldn't have. We still hadn't spoken in private.

She quirked her lips sardonically. "Procrastination," she said, "makes me anxious."

"You're leaping to conclusions," Thienne insisted, pacing the perimeter of the command commons. Her eyes were cast outward, into the blue-shifted stars off our bow. "We can't know it's a Du-

ong-Watts malignant. Statistical correlation isn't enough. We have
to be sure. We have to understand the exact mechanism."

It wasn't the same argument she'd made to me.

"We don't need to be sure." Anyahera had finished with the invisible lint. "If there's any reasonable chance this is a Duong-Watts,
we are morally and strategically obligated to wipe them out. This
is *why we are here*. It doesn't matter how they did it—if they did it,
they have to go."

"Maybe we need to talk to them," I said.

They both stared at me. I was the first one to laugh. We all felt
the absurdity there, in the idea that we could, in a single conversation, achieve what millennia of philosophy had never managed
—find some way to pin down the spark of consciousness by mere
dialogue. Qualia existed in the first person.

But twenty hours later—nearly three days at the pace of *Lachesis*'s racing simulation clock—that was suddenly no longer an abstract problem. Mitanni's light found us again: not a blind, quest-
ing pulse, but a microwave needle, a long clattering encryption of
something at once unimaginably intricate and completely familiar.

They didn't waste time with prime numbers or queries of intent
and origin. Mitanni sent us an uploaded mind, a digital ambassador.

Even Thienne agreed it would be hopelessly naïve to accept the
gift at face value, but after *Lachesis* dissected the upload, ran its
copies in a million solipsistic sandboxes, tested it for every conceiv-
able virulence—we voted unanimously to speak with it, and see
what it had to say.

Voting with Anyahera felt good. And after we voted, she started
from her chair, arms upraised, eyes alight. "They've given us the
proof," she said. "We can— Thienne, Shinobu, do you see?"

Thienne lifted a hand to spider her fingers against an invisible
pane. "You're right," she said, lips pursed. "We *can*."

With access to an uploaded personality, the digital fact of a Mitanni brain, we could compare their minds to ours. It would be far
from a simple arithmetic hunt for subtraction or addition, but it
would give us an empirical angle on the Duong-Watts problem.

Anyahera took me aside, in a space as old as our friendship,
the Khaya mahogany panels and airy glass of our undergraduate
dorm. "Shinobu," she said. She fidgeted as she spoke, I think to

jam her own desire to reach for me. "Have you seen what they're building in orbit?"

This memory she'd raised around us predated Thienne by a decade. That didn't escape me.

"I've seen them," I said. I'd gone through Mitanni's starflight capabilities datum by datum. "Orbital foundries. For their own seedships. They're getting ready to colonize other stars."

Neither of us had to unpack the implications there. It was the beginning of a boom cycle—exponential growth.

"Ten million years," she said. "I've run a hundred simulations out that far. If Mitanni is a Duong-Watts, in ten million years the galaxy is full of them. Now and forever. No conscious human variant can compete. Not even digitized baseline humans—you know what it took just to make *Lachesis*. Nothing human compares."

I nodded in silent acknowledgment. *Is that so terrible?* I wanted to ask—Thienne's question, in this memory so empty of her. *Is consciousness what we have to sacrifice to survive in the long run?*

She didn't even need me to ask the question. "I can envision nothing more monstrous," she said, "than mankind made clockwork. Nothing is worth that price."

And I wanted to nod, just to show her that we were not enemies. But I couldn't. It felt like giving in.

Sometimes I wondered at the hubris of our mission. Would Mitanni live and die not by the judgment of a jurisprudent mind but the troubled whims of a disintegrating family? We had left Earth as a harmonized unit, best-in-class product of a post-military, post-national edifice that understood the pressures of long-duration, high-stress starflight. No one and nothing could judge better. But was that enough? Was the human maximum adequate for this task?

Something in that thought chilled me more than the rest, and I wished I could know precisely what.

We met the Mitanni upload in a chameleon world: a sandboxed pocket of *Lachesis*'s mind, programmed to cycle from ocean to desert to crowd to solitary wasteland, so that we could watch the Mitanni's reactions, and, perhaps, come to know her.

She came among us without image or analogy, injected between one tick of simulation and the next. We stood around her on a pane of glass high above a gray-green sea.

"Hello," she said. She smiled, and it was not at all inhuman. She had Thienne's color and a round, guileless face that with her slight build made me think of Jizo statues from my childhood. "I'm the ambassador for Mitanni."

Whatever language she spoke, *Lachesis* had no trouble with it. Thienne and Anyahera looked to me, and I spoke as we'd agreed.

"Hello. My name is Shinobu. This is the starship *Lachesis,* scout element of the Second Fleet."

If she saw through the bluff of scouts and fleets, she gave no sign. "We expected you," she said, calm at the axis of our triplicate regard. "We detected the weapons you carry. Because you haven't fired yet, we know you're still debating whether to use them. I am here to plead for our survival."

She's rationally defensive, Thienne wrote in our collective awareness. *Attacking the scenario of maximal threat.*

At the edge of awareness, *Lachesis's* telemetry whispered telltales of cognition and feedback, a map of the Mitanni's thoughts. Profiling.

My eyes went to Anyahera. We'd agreed she would handle this contingency. "We believe your world may be a Duong-Watts malignant," she said. "If you've adapted yourselves to survive by eliminating consciousness, we're deeply concerned about the competitive edge you've gained over baseline humanity. We believe consciousness is an essential part of human existence."

In a negotiation between humans, I think we would have taken hours to reach this point, and hours more to work through the layers of bluff and counter-bluff required to hit the next point. The Mitanni ambassador leapt all that in an instant. "I'm an accurate map of the Mitanni mind," she said. "You have the information you need to judge the Duong-Watts case."

I see significant mental reprofiling, Lachesis printed. *Systemic alteration of networks in the thalamic intralaminar nuclei and the prefrontal-parietal associative loop. Hyperactivation in the neural correlates of rationalization—*

Anyahera snapped her fingers. The simulation froze, the Mitanni ambassador caught in the closing phoneme of her final word. "That's it," Anyahera said, looking between the two of us. "Duong-Watts. That's your smoking gun."

Even Thienne looked shocked. I saw her mouth the words: *hyperactivation in the neural—*

The Mitanni hadn't stripped their minds of consciousness. They'd just locked it away in a back room, where it could watch the rest of the brain make its decisions, and cheerfully, blithely, blindly consider itself responsible.

—*correlates of rationalization*—

Some part of the Mitanni mind knew of its own existence. And that tiny segment watched the programming that really ran the show iterate itself, feeling every stab of pain, suffering through every grueling shift, every solitary instant of a life absent joy or reward. Thinking: *This is all right. This is for a reason. This is what I want. Everything is fine.* When hurt, or sick, or halfway through unanesthetized field surgery, or when she drove the euthanasia needle into her thigh: *This is what I want.*

Because they'd tweaked some circuit to say: *You're in charge. You are choosing this.* They'd wired in the perfect lie. Convinced the last domino that it was the first.

And with consciousness out of the way, happy to comply with any sacrifice, any agony, the program of pure survival could optimize itself.

"It's parsimonious," Thienne said at last. "Easier than stripping out all the circuitry of consciousness, disentangling it from cognition . . ."

"This is Duong-Watts," Anyahera said. I flinched at her tone: familiar only from memories of real hurt and pain. "This is humanity enslaved at the most fundamental level."

I avoided Thienne's glance. I didn't want her to see my visceral agreement with Anyahera. Imagining that solitary bubble of consciousness, lashed, parasitic, to the bottom of the brain, powerless and babbling.

To think that you could change yourself. To be wrong, and never know it. That was a special horror.

Of course Thienne saw anyway, and leapt in, trying to preempt Anyahera, or my own thoughts. "This is not the place to wash your hands of Jotunheim. There's no suffering here. No crime to erase. All they want to do is survive—"

"Survival is the question," Anyahera said, turned half away, pretending disregard for me, for my choice, and in that disregard signaling more fear than she had begging on her knees at Jotunheim, because Anyahera would only ever disregard that which she thought she had no hope of persuading. "The survival of consciousness in the galaxy. The future of cognition. We decide it right here. We fire or we don't."

Between us the Mitanni stood frozen placidly, mid-gesture.

"Kill the Mitanni," Thienne said, "and you risk the survival of *anything at all.*"

It hurt so much to see both sides. It always had.

Three-player variants are the hardest to design.

Chess. Shogi. Nuclear detente. War. Love. Galactic survival. Three-player variants are unstable. It was written in my first game theory text: *Inevitably, two players gang up against a third, creating an irrecoverable tactical asymmetry.*

"You're right, Thienne," I said. "The Mitanni aren't an immediate threat to human survival. We're going home."

We fell home to Earth, to the empty teak house, and when I felt Anyahera's eyes upon me, I knew myself measured a monster, an accomplice to extinction. Anyahera left, and with her gone, Thienne whirled away into distant dry places far from me. The Mitanni bloomed down the Orion Arm and leapt the darkness between stars.

"Anyahera's right," I said. "The Mitanni will overrun the galaxy. We need to take a stand for—for what we are. Fire the weapons."

We fell home to Earth and peach tea under the Lagos sun, and Thienne looked up into that sun and saw an empty universe. Looked down and saw the two people who had, against her will, snuffed out the spark that could have kindled all that void, filled it with metal and diligent labor: life, and nothing less or more.

I took a breath and pushed the contingencies away. "This isn't a zero-sum game," I said. "I think that other solutions exist. Joint outcomes we can't ignore."

They looked at me, their pivot, their battleground. I presented my case.

This was the only way I knew how to make it work. I don't know what I would have done if they hadn't agreed.

They chose us for this mission, us three, because we could work past the simple solutions.

The Mitanni ambassador stood between us as we fell down the thread of our own orbit, toward the moment of weapons release, the point of no return.

"We know that Mitanni society is built on the Duong-Watts malignancy," Anyahera said.

The Mitanni woman lifted her chin. "The term *malignancy* implies a moral judgment," she said. "We're prepared to argue on moral grounds. As long as you subscribe to a system of liberal ethics, we believe that we can claim the right to exist."

"We have strategic concerns," Thienne said, from the other side of her. "If we grant you moral permit, we project you'll colonize most of the galaxy's habitable stars. Our own seedships or digitized human colonists can't compete. That outcome is strategically unacceptable."

We'd agreed on that.

"Insects outnumber humans in the terrestrial biosphere," the Mitanni said. I think she frowned, perhaps to signal displeasure at the entomological metaphor. I wondered how carefully she had been tuned to appeal to us. "An equilibrium exists. Coexistence that harms neither form of life."

"Insects don't occupy the same niche as humans," I said, giving voice to Anyahera's fears. "You do. And we both know that we're the largest threat to your survival. Sooner or later, your core imperative would force you to act."

The ambassador inclined her head. "If the survival payoff for war outstrips the survival payoff for peace, we will seek war. And we recognize that our strategic position becomes unassailable once we have launched our first colony ships. If it forestalls your attack, we are willing to disassemble our own colonization program and submit to a blockade—"

"No." Thienne again. I felt real pride. She'd argued for the blockade solution and now she'd coolly dissect it. "We don't have the strength to enforce a blockade before you can launch your ships. It won't work."

"We are at your mercy, then." The ambassador bowed her chin. "Consider the moral ramifications of this attack. Human history is full of attempted genocide, unilateral attempts to control change and confine diversity, or to remake the species in a narrow image. Full, in the end, of profound regret."

The barb struck home. I don't know by what pathways pain becomes empathy, but just then I wondered what her tiny slivered consciousness was thinking, while the rest of her mind thrashed away at the problem of survival: *The end of the world is coming, and it's all right; I won't worry, everything's under control—*

Anyahera took my shoulder in silence.

"Here are our terms," I said. "We will annihilate the Mitanni colony in order to prevent the explosive colonization of the Milky Way by post-conscious human variants. This point is non-negotiable."

The Mitanni ambassador waited in silence. Behind her, Thienne blinked, just once, an indecipherable punctuation. I felt Anyahera's grip tighten in gratitude or tension.

"You will remain in storage aboard the *Lachesis*," I said. "As a comprehensive upload of a Mitanni personality, you contain the neuroengineering necessary to re-create your species. We will return to Earth and submit the future of the Mitanni species to public review. You may be given a new seedship and a fresh start, perhaps under the supervision of a pre-established blockade. You may be consigned to archival study, or allowed to flourish in a simulated environment. But we can offer a near-guarantee that you will not be killed."

It was a solution that bought time, delaying the Duong-Watts explosion for centuries, perhaps forever. It would allow us to study the Duong-Watts individual, to game out their survivability with confidence and the backing of a comprehensive social dialogue. If she agreed.

It never occurred to me that she would hesitate for even one instant. The core Mitanni imperative had to be *survive*, and total annihilation weighed against setback and judgment and possible renaissance would be no choice at all.

"I accept," the Mitanni ambassador said. "On behalf of my world and my people, I am grateful for your jurisprudence."

We all bowed our heads in unrehearsed mimicry of her gesture. I wondered if we were aping a synthetic mannerism, something they had gamed out to be palatable.

"*Lachesis*," Anyahera said. "Execute RKV strike on Mitanni."

"I need a vote," the ship said.

I think that the Mitanni must have been the only one who did not feel a frisson: the judgment of history, cast back upon us.

We would commit genocide here. The largest in human history. The three of us, who we were, what we were, would be chained to this forever.

"Go," I said. "Execute RKV strike."

Thienne looked between the two of us. I don't know what she wanted to see, but I met her eyes and held them and hoped.

Anyahera took her shoulder. "I'm sorry," she said.

"Go," Thienne said. "Go."

We fell away from the ruin, into the void, the world that had been called Mitanni burning away the last tatters of its own atmosphere behind us. *Lachesis* clawed at the galaxy's magnetic field, turning for home.

"I wonder if they'll think we failed," Anyahera said drowsily. We sat together in a pavilion, the curtains drawn.

I considered the bottom of my glass. "Because we didn't choose? Because we compromised?"

She nodded, her hands cupped in her lap. "We couldn't go all the way. We brought our problems home." Her knuckles whitened. "We made accommodations with something that—"

She looked to her left, where Thienne had been, before she went to be alone. After a moment she shrugged. "Sometimes I think this is what they wanted all along, you know. That we played into their hands."

I poured myself another drink: cask strength, unwatered. "It's an old idea," I said.

She arched an eyebrow.

"That we can't all go home winners." I thought of the pierced bleeding crust of that doomed world and almost choked on the word *winners*—but I knew that for the Mitanni, who considered only outcomes, only pragmatism, this was victory. "That the only real solutions lie at the extremes. That we can't figure out something wise if we play the long game, think it out, work every angle."

For $n = 3$, solutions exist for special cases.

"Nobody won on Jotunheim," Anyahera said softly.

"No," I said. Remembered people drowning in acid, screaming their final ecstasy because they had been bred and built for pain. "But we did our jobs, when it was hardest. We did our jobs."

"I still can't sleep."

"I know." I drank.

"Do you? Really?"

"What?"

"I know the role they selected you for. I know *you.* Sometimes I think—" She pursed her lips. "I think you change yourself so well that there's nothing left to carry scars."

I swallowed. Waited a moment, to push away my anger, before I met her gaze. "Yeah," I said. "It hurt me too. We're all hurt."

A moment passed in silence. Anyahera stared down into her glass, turning it a little, so that her reflected face changed and bent.

"To new ideas," she said, a little toast that said with great economy everything I had hoped for, especially the apologies.

"To new ideas."

"Should we go and—?" She made a worried face and pointed to the ceiling, the sky, where Thienne would be racing the causality of her own hurt, exploring some distant angle of the microwave background, as far from home as she could make the simulation take her.

"Not just yet," I said. "In a little while. Not just yet."

VANDANA SINGH

Ambiguity Machines: An Examination

FROM *Tor.com*

INTREPID EXPLORERS VENTURING into Conceptual Machine-Space, which is the abstract space of all possible machines, will find in the terrain some gaps, holes, and tears. These represent the negative space where impossible machines reside, the ones that cannot exist because they violate known laws of reality. And yet such impossible machines are crucial to the topographical maps of Conceptual Machine-Space, and indeed to its topology. They therefore must be investigated and classified.

It is thus that the Ministry of Abstract Engineering has sent the topographers of Conceptual Machine-Space to various destinations so that they may collect reports, rumors, folktales, and intimations of machines that do not and cannot exist. Of these we excerpt below three accounts of the subcategory of Ambiguity Machines: those that blur or dissolve boundaries.

The candidate taking the exam for the position of Junior Navigator in the uncharted negative seas of Conceptual Machine-Space will read the three accounts below and follow the instructions thereafter.

The First Account

All machines grant wishes, but some grant more than we bargain for. One such device was conceived by a Mongolian engineer who spent the best years of his youth as a prisoner in a stone building

in the Altai Mountains. The purpose of this machine was to conjure up the face of his beloved.

His captors were weaponheads of some sort; he didn't know
whether they were affiliated with any known political group or
simply run by sociopath technophiles with an eye on the weapons
market. They would let him out of his cell into a makeshift laboratory every day. Their hope was that he would construct for them a
certain weapon, the plans for which had been found on his desk,
and had led to his arrest. The engineer had a poetic sensibility,
and the weapon described in his papers was metaphoric. But how
can you explain metaphors to a man with a gun?

When the engineer was a young boy, stillness had fascinated
him. He had been used to wandering with his family across the
Gobi, and so he had made a study of stillness. In those days everything moved—the family with the ger, the camels and sheep,
the milk sloshing in the pail as he helped his mother carry it, the
stars in the circle of open sky in the roof above his head, the dust
storms, dark shapes in shawls of wind, silhouetted against blue
sky. The camels would fold themselves up into shaggy mounds between the bushes, closing their eyes and nostrils, waiting for the
storm to pass. His grandfather would pull him into the ger, the
door creaking shut, the window in the roof lashed closed, and he
would think about the animals and the ger, their shared immobil-
ity in the face of the coming storm. Inside it would be dark, the
roar of the dust storm muffled, and in the glow of the lamp his
older sister's voice would rise in song. Her voice and the circle of
safety around him tethered him to this world. Sometimes he would
bury his face in a camel's shaggy flank as he combed its side with
his fingers, breathing in the rich animal smell, hearing with his
whole body the camel's deep rumble of pleasure.

In such moments he would think of his whole life played out
against the rugged canvas of the Gobi, an arc as serene as the motion of the stars across the night, and he would feel again that
deep contentment. In his childhood he had thought there were
only two worlds, the inside of the ger and the outside. But the first
time he rode with his father to a town, he saw to his utmost wonder that there was another kind of world, where houses were an-
chored to the earth and people rode machines instead of animals,
but they never went very far. They had gadgets and devices that

seemed far more sophisticated than his family's one TV, and they carried with them a subtle and unconscious air of privilege. He had no idea then that years later he would leave the Gobi and his family to live like this himself, an engineering student at a university in Ulaanbaatar, or that the streets of that once-unimaginable city would become as familiar to him as the pathways his family had traversed in the desert. The great coal and copper mines had, by then, transformed the land he thought would never change, and the familiarity was gone, as was his family, three generations scattered or dead.

Being tethered to one place, he discovered, was not the same as the stillness he had once sought and held through all the wanderings of his childhood. In the midst of all this turmoil, he had found *her*, daughter of a family his had once traded with, studying to be a teacher. She was as familiar with the old Mongolia as he had been, and was critical and picky about both old and new. She had a temper, liked to laugh, and wanted to run a village school and raise goats. With her, the feeling of having a center in the world came back to him.

So he thought of her in his incarceration, terrified that through this long separation he would forget her face, her voice. As the faces of his captors acquired more reality with each passing week or month or year, his life beforehand seemed to lose its solidity, and his memories of her seemed blurred, as though he was recollecting a dream. If he had been an artist, he would have drawn a picture of her, but being an engineer, he turned to the lab. The laboratory was a confusion of discarded electronics: pieces of machinery bought from online auctions, piles of antiquated vacuum tubes, tangles of wires and other variegated junk. With these limited resources, the engineer tried his best, always having to improvise and work around the absence of this part and that one. His intent was to make a pseudo-weapon that would fool his captors into releasing him, but he didn't know much about weapons, and he knew that the attempt was doomed to failure. But it would be worth it to re-create his beloved's face again, if only a machine-rendered copy of the real thing.

So into his design he put the smoothness of her cheek, and the light-flash of her intelligence, and the fiercely tender gaze of her eyes. He put in the swirl of her hair in the wind, and the way her anger would sometimes dissolve into laughter, and sometimes into tears. He worked at it, refining, improving, delaying as much as he dared.

And one day he could delay no more, for his captors gave him an ultimatum: The machine must be completed by the next day, and demonstrated to their leaders. Else he would pay with his life. He had become used to their threats and their roughness, and asked only that he be left alone to put the machine in its final form.

Alone in the laboratory, he began to assemble the machine. But soon he found that there was something essential missing. Rummaging about in the pile of debris that represented laboratory supplies, he found a piece of stone tile, one half of a square, broken along the diagonal. It was inlaid with a pattern of great beauty and delicacy, picked out in black and cream on the gray background. An idea for the complex circuit he had been struggling to configure suddenly came together in his mind. Setting aside the tile, he returned to work. At last the machine was done, and tomorrow he would die.

He turned on the machine.

Looking down into the central chamber, he saw her face. There was the light-flash of her intelligence, the swirl of her hair in the wind. *I had forgotten,* he whispered, *the smoothness of her cheek,* and he remembered that as a child, wandering the high desert with his family, he had once discovered a pond, its surface smooth as a mirror. He had thought it was a piece of the sky, fallen down. Now, as he spoke aloud in longing, he saw that the face was beginning to dissolve, and he could no longer distinguish her countenance from standing water, or her intelligence from a meteor shower, or her swirling hair from the vortex of a tornado. Then he looked up and around him in wonder, and it seemed to him that the stone walls were curtains of falling rain, and that he was no more than a wraithlike construct of atoms, mostly empty space—and as the thought crystallized in his mind, he found himself walking out with the machine in his arms, unnoticed by the double rows of armed guards. So he walked out of his prison, damp, but free.

How he found his way to the village near Dalanzadgad, where his beloved then lived, is a story we will not tell here. But he was at last restored to the woman he loved, who had been waiting for him all these years. Her cheek no longer had the smoothness of youth, but the familiar intelligence was in her eyes, and so was the love, the memory of which had kept him alive through his incarceration. They settled down together, growing vegetables in the summers and keeping some goats. The machine he kept hidden at the back of the goat shed.

But within the first year of his happiness, the engineer noticed something troubling. Watching his wife, he would sometimes see her cheek acquire the translucency of an oasis under a desert sky. Looking into her eyes, he would feel as though he was traveling through a cosmos bright with stars. These events would occur in bursts, and after a while she would be restored to herself, and she would pass a hand across her forehead and say, *I felt dizzy for a moment.* As time passed, her face seemed to resemble more and more the fuzzy, staccato images on an old-fashioned television set that is just slightly out of tune with the channel. It occurred to him that he had, despite his best intentions, created a weapon after all.

So one cold winter night, he crept out of the house to the shed and uncovered the machine. He tried to take it apart, to break it to pieces, but it had acquired a reality not of this world. At last he spoke to it: *You are a pile of dust! You are a column of stone! You are a floor tile! You are a heap of manure!* But nothing happened. The machine seemed to be immune to its own power.

He stood among the goats, looking out at the winter moon that hung like a circle of frost in the sky. Slowly it came to him that there was nothing he could do except to protect everyone he loved from what he had created. So he returned to the house and in the dim light of a candle beheld once more the face of the woman he loved. There were fine wrinkles around her eyes, and she was no longer slim, nor was her hair as black as it had once been. She lay in the sweetness of sleep and, in thrall to some pleasant dream, smiled in slumber. He was almost undone by this, but he swallowed, gritted his teeth, and kept his resolve. Leaving a letter on the table, and taking a few supplies, he wrapped up the machine and walked out of the sleeping village and into the Gobi, the only other place where he had known stillness.

The next morning his wife found the letter, and his footprints on the frosty ground. She followed them all the way to the edge of the village, where the desert lay white in the pale dawn. Among the ice-covered stones and the frozen tussocks of brush, his footsteps disappeared. At first she shook her fist in the direction he had gone, then she began to weep. Weeping, she went back to the village.

The villagers never saw him again. There are rumors that he came back a few months later, during a dust storm, because a year after his disappearance, his wife gave birth to a baby girl. But after that he never returned.

His wife lived a full life, and when she was ready to die, she said goodbye to her daughter and grandchildren and went into the desert. When all her food and water were finished, she found some shade by a clump of brush at the edge of a hollow, where she lay down. They say that she felt her bones dissolving, and her flesh becoming liquid, and her hair turning into wind. There is a small lake there now, and in its waters on a cold night, you can see meteors flashing in a sky rich with stars.

As for the engineer, there are rumors and folk legends about a shaman who rode storms as though they were horses. They say he ventured as far as Yakutsk in Siberia and Siena in Italy; there is gossip about him in the narrow streets of old Istanbul, and in a certain village outside Zhengzhou, among other places. Wherever he stopped, he sought village healers and madmen, philosophers and logicians, confounding them with his talk of a machine that could blur the boundary between the physical realm and the metaphoric. His question was always the same: *How do I destroy what I have created?* Wherever he went, he brought with him a sudden squall of sand and dust that defied the predictions of local meteorologists, and left behind only a thin veil of desert sand flung upon the ground.

Some people believe that the Mongolian engineer is still with us. The nomads speak of him as the kindest of shamans, who protects their gers and their animals by pushing storms away from their path. As he once wandered the great expanse of the Gobi in his boyhood, so he now roams a universe without boundaries, in some dimension orthogonal to the ones we know. When he finds what he is seeking, they say, he will return to that small lake in the desert. He will breathe his last wish to the machine before he destroys it. Then he will lay himself down by the water, brushing away the dust of the journey, letting go of all his burdens. With his head resting on a pillow of sand, still at last, he will await his own transformation.

The Second Account

At the edge of a certain Italian town, there is a small stone church, and beside it an overgrown tiled courtyard, surrounded entirely by an iron railing. The one gate is always kept locked. Tourists going by sometimes want to stop at the church and admire its timeworn façade, but rarely do they notice the fenced courtyard. Yet if anyone were to look carefully between the bars, they would see that the tiles, between the weeds and wildflowers, are of exceptional quality, pale gray stone inlaid with a fine intricacy of black marble and quartz. The patterns are delicate as circuit diagrams, celestial in their beauty. The careful observer will notice that one of the tiles in the far left quadrant is broken in half, and that grass and wildflowers fill the space.

The old priest who attends the church might, if plied with sufficient wine, rub his liver-spotted hands over his rheumy eyes and tell you how that tile came to be broken. When he was young, a bolt from a storm hit the precise center of the tile and killed a man sweeping the church floor not four yards away. Even before the good father's time, the courtyard was forbidden ground, but the lightning didn't know that. The strange thing is not so much that the tile broke almost perfectly across the diagonal, but that one half of it disappeared. When the funeral was over, the priest went cautiously to the part of the railing nearest the lightning strike and noted the absence of that half of the tile. Sighing, he nailed a freshly painted NO ENTRY sign on an old tree trunk at the edge of the courtyard and hoped that curious boys and thunderstorms would take note.

It wasn't a boy who ignored the sign and gained entry, however — it was a girl. She came skipping down the narrow street, watching the dappled sunlight play beneath the old trees, tossing a smooth, round pebble from hand to hand. She paused at the iron railing and stared between the bars, as she had done before. There was something mesmerizing about that afternoon, and the way the sunlight fell on the tiles. She hitched up her skirts and clambered over the fence. Inside, she stood on the perimeter and considered a game of hopscotch.

But now that she was there, in the forbidden place, she began to feel nervous and to look around fearfully. The church and the street were silent, drugged with the warm afternoon light, and many people were still at siesta. Then the church clock struck three, loudly and sonorously, and in that moment the girl made her decision. She gathered her courage and jumped onto the first tile, and the second and third, tossing her pebble.

Years later she would describe to her lover the two things she noticed immediately: that the pebble, which was her favorite thing, having a fine vein of rose-colored quartz running across it, had disappeared into thin air during its flight. The next thing she noticed was a disorientation, the kind you feel when transported to a different place very suddenly, as a sleeping child in a car leaving home awakes in a strange place, or, similarly, when one wakes up from an afternoon nap to find that the sun has set and the stars are out. Being a child in a world of adults, she was used to this sort of disorientation, but alone in this courtyard, with only the distant chirping of a bird to disturb the heat-drugged silence, she became frightened enough to step back to the perimeter. When she did so, all seemed to slip back to normality, but for the fact that there was the church clock, striking three again. She thought at the time that perhaps the ghosts in the graveyard behind the church were playing tricks on her, punishing her for having defied the sign on the tree.

But while lying with her lover in tangled white sheets on just such an afternoon many years later, she asked aloud: *What if there is some other explanation?* She traced a pattern on her lover's back with her finger, trying to remember the designs on the tiles. Her lover turned over, brown skin flushed with heat and spent passion, eyes alive with interest. The lover was a Turkish immigrant and a mathematician, a woman of singular appearance and intellect, with fine eyes and deep, disconcerting silences. She had only recently begun to emerge from grief after the death of her sole remaining relative, her father. Having decided that the world was bent on enforcing solitude upon her, she had embraced loneliness with an angry heart, only to have her plans foiled by the unexpected. She had been unprepared for love in the arms of an Italian woman —an artist, at that—grown up all her life in this provincial little town. But there it was. Now the mathematician brushed black ringlets from her face and kissed her lover. *Take me there*, she said.

So the two women went to the tree-shaded lane where the courtyard lay undisturbed. The tiles were bordered, as before, by grass and wildflowers, and a heaviness hung upon the place, as though of sleep. The church was silent; the only sounds were birdsong and distant traffic noises from the main road. The mathematician began to climb the railing.

Don't, her lover said, but she recognized that nothing could stop the mathematician, so she shrugged and followed suit. They stood on the perimeter, the Italian woman remembering, the Turkish one thinking furiously.

Thus began the mathematician's explorations of the mystery of the courtyard. Her lover would stand on the perimeter with a notebook while the mathematician moved from tile to tile, flickering in and out of focus, like a trout in a fast-moving stream when the sun is high. The trajectory of each path and the result of the experiment would be carefully noted, including discrepancies in time as experienced by the two of them. Which paths resulted in time-shifts, and by how much? Once a certain path led to the disappearance of the mathematician entirely, causing her lover to cry out, but she appeared about three minutes later on another tile. *The largest time-shift so far!* exulted the mathematician. Her lover shuddered and begged the mathematician to stop the experiment, or at least to consult with someone, perhaps from the nearest university. But, being an artist, she knew obsession when she saw it. Once she had discovered a windblown orchard with peaches fallen on the grass like hailstones, and had painted night and day for weeks, seeking to capture on the stillness of canvas the ever-changing vista. She sighed in resignation at the memory and went back to making notes.

The realization was dawning upon her slowly that the trajectories leading to the most interesting results had shapes similar to the very patterns on the tiles. Her artist's hands sketched those patterns—doing so, she felt as though she was on flowing water, or among sailing clouds. The patterns spoke of motion but through a country she did not recognize. Looking up at the mathematician's face, seeing the distracted look in the dark eyes, she thought: *There will be a day when she steps just so, and she won't come back.*

And that day did come. The mathematician was testing a trajectory possessed of a pleasing symmetry, with some complex elements added to it. Her lover, standing on the perimeter with the notebook, was thinking how the moves not only resembled the pattern located on tile $(3, 5)$, but also might be mistaken for a complicated version of hopscotch, and that any passerby would smile at the thought of two women reliving their girlhood—when it happened. She looked up, and the mathematician disappeared.

She must have stood there for hours, waiting, but finally she had to go home. She waited all day and all night, unable to sleep, tears and spilled wine mingling on the bedsheets. She waited for days and weeks and months. She went to confession for the first time in years, but the substitute priest, a stern and solemn young man, had nothing to offer, except to tell her that God was displeased with her for consorting with a woman. At last she gave up, embracing the solitude that her Turkish lover had shrugged off for her when they had first met. She painted furiously for months on end, making the canvas say what she couldn't articulate in words —wild-eyed women with black hair rose from tiled floors, while mathematical symbols and intricate designs hovered in the warm air above.

Two years later, when she was famous, she took another lover, and she and the new love eventually swore marriage oaths to each other in a ceremony among friends. The marriage was fraught from the start, fueled by stormy arguments and passionate declarations, slammed doors and teary reconciliations. The artist could only remember her Turkish lover's face when she looked at the paintings that had brought her such acclaim.

Then, one day, an old woman came to her door. Leaning on a stick, her face as wrinkled as crushed tissue paper, her mass of white ringlets half-falling across her face, the woman looked at her with tears in her black eyes. *Do you remember me?* she whispered.

Just then the artist's wife called from inside the house, inquiring as to who had come. *It's just my great-aunt, come to visit,* the artist said brightly, pulling the old woman in. Her wife was given to jealousy. The old woman played along, and was established in the spare room, where the artist looked after her with tender care. She knew that the mathematician had come here to die.

The story the mathematician told her was extraordinary. When she disappeared she had been transported to a vegetable market in what she later realized was China. Unable to speak the language, she had tried to mime telephones and airports, only to discover that nobody knew what she was talking about. Desperately she began to walk around, hoping to find someone who spoke one of the four languages she knew, noticing with horror the complete absence of the signs and symbols of the modern age—no cars, neon signs, plastic bags. At last her wanderings took her to an Arab merchant, who understood her Arabic, although his accent was strange to her. She was in Quinsai (present-day Hangzhou, as she later discovered), and the Song dynasty was in power. Through the kindness of the merchant's family, who took her in, she gradually pieced together the fact that she had jumped more than 800 years back in time. She made her life there, marrying and raising a family, traveling the sea routes back and forth to the Mediterranean. Her old life seemed like a dream, a mirage, but underneath her immersion in the new, there burned the desire to know the secret of the tiled courtyard.

It shouldn't exist, she told the artist. *I have yearned to find out how it could be. I have developed over lifetimes a mathematics that barely begins to describe it, let alone explain it.*

How did you get back here? the artist asked her former lover.

I realized that if there was one such device, there may be others, she said. *In my old life I was a traveler, a trade negotiator with Arabs. My journeys took me to many places that had strange reputations of unexplained disappearances. One of them was a shrine inside an enormous tree on the island of Borneo. Around the tree the roots created a pattern on the forest floor that reminded me of the patterns on the tiles. Several people had been known to disappear in the vicinity. So I waited until my children were grown, and my husband and lovers taken by war. Then I returned to the shrine. It took several tries and several lifetimes until I got the right sequence. And here I am.*

The only things that the Turkish mathematician had brought with her were her notebooks containing the mathematics of a new theory of space-time. As the artist turned the pages, she saw that the mathematical symbols gradually got more complex, the diagrams stranger and denser, until the thick ropes of equations in dark ink and the empty spaces on the pages began to resemble, more and more, the surfaces of the tiles in the courtyard. *That is my greatest work,* the mathematician whispered. *But what I've left out says as much as what I've written. Keep my notebooks until you find someone who will understand.*

Over the next few months, the artist wrote down the old woman's stories from her various lifetimes in different places. In the few days since the mathematician arrived, her wife had left her for someone else, but the artist's heart didn't break. She took tender care of the old woman, assisting her with her daily ablutions, making for her the most delicate of soups and broths. Sometimes, when they laughed together, it was as though not a minute had passed since that golden afternoon when they had lain in bed discussing, for the first time, the tiled courtyard.

Two weeks after the mathematician's return, there was a sudden dust storm, a sirocco that blew into the city with high winds. During the storm the old woman passed away peacefully in her sleep. The artist found her the next morning, cold and still, covered with a layer of fine sand as though kissed by the wind. The storm had passed, leaving clear skies and a profound emptiness. At first the artist wept, but she pulled herself together as she had always done, and thought of the many lives her lover had lived. It occurred to her in a flash of inspiration that she would spend the rest of her one life painting those lifetimes.

At last, the artist said to her lover's grave, where she came with flowers the day after the interment, *at last the solitude we had both sought is mine.*

The Third Account

Reports of a third impossible machine come from the Western Sahara, although there have been parallel, independent reports from the mountains of Peru and from Northern Ireland. A farmer from the outskirts of Lima, a truck driver in Belfast, and an academic from the University of Bamako in Mali all report devices that, while different in appearance, seem to have the same function. The academic from Mali has perhaps the clearest account.

She was an archaeologist who had obtained her PhD from an American university. In America she had experienced a nightmarish separateness, the like of which she had not known existed. Away from family, distanced by the ignorance and prejudices of fellow graduate students, a stranger in a culture made more incomprehensible by proximity, separated from the sparse expatriate community by the intensity of her intellect, she would stand on the beach, gazing at the waters of the Atlantic and imagining the same waters washing the shores of West Africa. In her teens she had spent a summer with a friend in Senegal, her first terrifying journey away from home, and she still remembered how the

fright of it had given way to thrill, and the heart-stopping delight
of her first sight of the sea. At the time her greatest wish was to go
to America for higher education, and it had occurred to her that
on the other side of this very ocean lay the still unimagined places
of her desire.

Years later, from that other side, she worked on her thesis, taking lonely walks on the beach between long periods of incarceration in the catacombs of the university library. Time slipped from
her hands without warning. Her mother passed away, leaving her
feeling orphaned, plagued with a horrific guilt because she had
not been able to organize funds in time to go home. Aunts and
uncles succumbed to death, or to war, or joined the flood of immigrants to other lands. Favorite cousins scattered, following the
lure of the good life in France and Germany. It seemed that with
her leaving for America, her history, her childhood, her very sense
of self had begun to erode. The letters she had exchanged with
her elder brother in Bamako had been her sole anchor to sanity.
Returning home after her PhD, she had two years to nurse him
through his final illness, which, despite the pain and trauma of his
suffering, she was to remember as the last truly joyful years of her
life. When he died she found herself bewildered by a feeling of utter isolation even though she was home, among her people. It was
as though she had brought with her the disease of loneliness that
had afflicted her in America.

Following her brother's death, she buried herself in work. Her
research eventually took her to the site of the medieval University of Sankoré in Timbuktu, where she marveled at its sand-castle
beauty as it rose, mirage-like, from the desert. Discovering a manuscript that spoke in passing of a fifteenth-century expedition to
a region not far from the desert town of Tessalit, she decided to
travel there despite the dangers of political conflict in the region.
The manuscript hinted of a fantastic device that had been commissioned by the king, and then removed for secret burial. She had
come across oblique references to such a device in the songs and
stories of griots, and in certain village tales; thus her discovery of
the manuscript had given her a shock of recognition rather than
revelation.

The archaeologist had, by now, somewhat to her own surprise, acquired two graduate students: a man whose brilliance was
matched only by his youthful impatience, and a woman of thirty-

five whose placid outlook masked a slow, deep, persistent intelligence. Using a few key contacts, bribes, promises, and pleas, the archaeologist succeeded in finding transportation to Tessalit. The route was roundabout and the vehicles changed hands three times, but the ever-varying topography of the desert under the vast canopy of the sky gave her a reassuring feeling of continuity in the presence of change. So different from the environs of her youth—the lush verdure of south Mali, the broad ribbon of the Niger that had spoken to her in watery whispers in sleep and dreams, moderating the constant, crackly static that was the background noise of modern urban life. The desert was sometimes arid scrubland, with fantastic rock formations rearing out of the ground, and groups of short trees clustered like friends sharing secrets. At other times it gave way to a sandy moodiness, miles and miles of rich, undulating gold broken only by the occasional oasis, or the dust cloud of a vehicle passing them by. Rocky, mountainous ridges rose on the horizon as though to reassure travelers that there was an end to all journeys.

In Tessalit the atmosphere was fraught, but a fragile peace prevailed. With the help of a Tuareg guide, an elderly man with sympathetic eyes, the travelers found the site indicated on the manuscript. Because it did not exist on any current map, the archaeologist was surprised to find that the site had a small settlement of some sixty-odd people. Her guide said that the settlement was in fact a kind of asylum as well as a shrine. The people there, he said, were blessed or cursed with an unknown malady. Perhaps fortunately for them, the inhabitants seemed unable to leave the boundary of the brick wall that encircled the settlement. This village of the insane had become a kind of oasis in the midst of the armed uprising, and men brought food and clothing to the people there irrespective of their political or ethnic loyalties, as though it was a site of pilgrimage. Townspeople coming with offerings would leave very quickly, as they would experience disorienting symptoms when they entered the enclosure, including confusion and a dizzying, temporary amnesia.

Thanks to her study of the medieval manuscript, the archaeologist had some idea of what to expect, although it strained credulity. She and her students donned metal caps and veils made from steel mesh before entering the settlement with gifts of fruit and bread. There were perhaps thirty people—men and women, young and

old—who poured out of the entrance of the largest building, a
rectangular structure the color of sand. They were dressed in ill-fit-
ting, secondhand clothing, loose robes and wraparound garments
in white and blue and ochre, T-shirts and tattered jeans—and at
first there was no reply to the archaeologist's greeting. There was
something odd about the way the villagers looked at their guests—
a gaze reveals, after all, something of the nature of the soul within,
but their gazes were abstracted, shifting, like the surface of a lake
ruffled by the wind. But after a while a group of people came forward and welcomed them, some speaking in chorus, others in
fragments, so that the welcome nevertheless sounded complete.

"What manner of beings are you?" they were asked after the
greetings were done. "We do not see you, although you are clearly
visible."

"We are visitors," the archaeologist said, puzzled. "We come
with gifts and the desire to share learning." And with this the new-
comers were admitted to the settlement.

Within the central chamber of the main building, as the visitors' eyes adjusted to the dimness, they beheld before them something fantastic. Woven in complex, changing patterns was a vast
tapestry so long that it must have wrapped around the inner wall
several times. Here, many-hued strips of cloth were woven between
white ones to form an abstract design the likes of which the new-
comers had never seen before. People in small groups worked at
various tasks—some tore long lengths of what must have been
old clothing, others worked a complex loom that creaked rhyth-
mically. Bright patterns of astonishing complexity emerged from
the loom, to be attached along the wall by other sets of hands.
Another group was huddled around a cauldron in which some
kind of rich stew bubbled. In the very center of the chamber was
a meter-high, six-faced column of black stone—or so it seemed
—inlaid with fine silver lacework. This must, then, be the device
whose use and function had been described in the medieval manuscript—a product of a golden period of Mali culture, marked by
great achievements in science and the arts. The fifteenth-century
expedition had been organized in order to bury the device in the
desert, to be guarded by men taking turns, part of a secret cadre
of soldiers. Yet here it was, in the center of a village of the insane.

Looking about her, the archaeologist noticed some odd things.
A hot drop of stew fell on the arm of a woman tending the caul-

dron—yet as she cried out, so did the four people surrounding her, all at about the same time. Similarly, as the loom workers manipulated the loom, they seemed to know almost before it happened that a drop of sweat would roll down the forehead of one man—each immediately raised an arm, or pulled down a headcloth to wipe off the drop, even if it wasn't there. She could not tell whether men and women had different roles, because of the way individuals would break off one group and join another, with apparent spontaneity. Just as in speech, their actions had a continuity to them across different individuals, so as one would finish stirring the soup, the other, without a pause, would bring the tasting cup close, as though they had choreographed these movements in advance. As for the working of the loom, it was poetry in motion. Each person seemed to be at the same time independent and yet tightly connected to the others. The archaeologist was already abandoning the hypothesis that this was a community of telepaths, because their interactions did not seem to be as simple as mind reading. They spoke to each other, for one thing, and had names for each individual, complicated by prefixes and suffixes that appeared to change with context. There were a few children running around as well: quick, shy, with eyes as liquid as a gazelle's. One of them showed the travelers a stone he unwrapped from a cloth, a rare, smooth pebble with a vein of rose quartz shot through it, but when the archaeologist asked how he had come by it, they all laughed, as though at an absurdity, and ran off.

It was after a few days of living with these people that the archaeologist decided to remove her metal cap and veil. She told her students that they must on no account ever do so—and that if she were to act strangely, they were to forcibly put her cap and veil back on. They were uncomfortable with this—the young man, in particular, longed to return home—but they agreed, with reluctance.

When she removed her protective gear, the villagers near her immediately turned to look at her, as though she had suddenly become visible to them. She was conscious of a feeling akin to drowning—a sudden disorientation. She must have cried out because a woman nearby put her arms around her and held her and crooned to her as though she was a child, and other people took up the crooning. Her two students, looking on with their mouths open, seemed to be delineated in her mind by a clear, sharp boundary, while all the others appeared to leak into each other, like figures in a child's watercolor painting. She could sense, vaguely, the itch on a man's arm from an insect bite, and the fact that the women were menstruating, and the dull ache of a healing bone in some other individual's ankle—but it seemed as though she was simultaneously inhabiting the man's arm, the women's bodies, the broken ankle. After the initial fright a kind of wonder came upon her, a feeling she knew originated from her, but which was shared as a secondhand awareness by the villagers.

"I'm all right," she started to say to her students, anxious to reassure them, although the word "I" felt inaccurate. But as she started to say it, the village woman who had been holding her spoke the next word, and someone else said the next, in their own dialect, so that the sentence was complete. She felt like the crest of a wave in the ocean. The crest might be considered a separate thing from the sequence of crests and troughs behind it, but what would be the point? The impact of such a crest hitting a boat, for example, would be felt by the entire chain. The great loneliness that had afflicted her for so long began, at last, to dissolve. It was frightening and thrilling all at once. She laughed out loud, and felt the people around her possess, lightly, that same complex of fear and joy. Gazing around at the enormous tapestry, she saw it as though for the first time. There was no concept, no language that could express what it was—it was irreducible, describable only by itself. She looked at it and heard her name, all their names, all names of all things that had ever been, spoken out loud without a sound, reverberating in the silence.

She found, over the next few days, that the conjugal groups among the people of the settlement had the same fluidity as other aspects of their lives. The huts in the rest of the compound were used by various groups as they formed and re-formed. It felt as natural as sand grains in a shallow stream that clump together and break apart, and regroup in some other way, and break apart again. The pattern that underlay these groupings seemed obvious in practice but impossible to express in ordinary language. Those related by blood did not cohabit amongst themselves, nor did children with adults—they were like the canvas upon which the pattern was made, becoming part of it and separate from it with as much ease as breathing. On fine nights the people would gather around a fire, and make poetry, and sing, and this was so extraordinary a thing that the archaeologist was moved to ask her students to remove their caps and veils and experience it for themselves. But by this time the young man was worn out by unfamiliarity and hard living—he was desperate to be back home in Bamako, and was seriously considering a career outside academia. The older female student was worried about the news from town that violence in the region would shortly escalate. So they would not be persuaded.

After a few days, when the archaeologist showed no sign of rejoining her students for the trip home—for enough time had passed by now, and their Tuareg guide was concerned about the impending conflict—the students decided to act according to their instructions. Without warning they set upon the archaeologist, binding her arms and forcing her to wear the cap and veil. They saw the change ripple across her face, and the people nearby turned around, as before. But this time their faces were grim and sad, and they moved as one toward the three visitors. The archaeologist set up a great wailing, like a child locked in an empty room. Terrified, the students pulled her out of the building, dragging her at a good pace, with the villagers following. If the Tuareg guide had not been waiting at the perimeter, the visitors would surely have been overtaken, because he came forward at a run and pulled them beyond the boundary.

Thus the archaeologist was forced to return to Bamako.

Some years later, having recovered from her experience, the archaeologist wrote up her notes, entrusted them to her former student, and disappeared from Bamako. She was traced as far as Tessalit. With the fighting having intensified, nobody was able to investigate for over a year. The woman to whom she had left her notes returned to try to find her, guessing that she had gone to the settlement, but where the settlement had been, there were only ruins. The people had vanished, she was told, in the middle of a sandstorm. There was no sign of their belongings, let alone the great tapestry. The only thing she could find in the empty, arid, rocky wasteland was a small, round pebble, shot with a vein of rose quartz.

In the notes she left behind, the archaeologist had written down her conclusions—that the machine generated a field of a certain range, and that this field had the power to dissolve, or at least blur, the boundary between self and other. She wrote in French, and in

Arabic, and in her mother tongue, Bambara, but after a while the
regularity of her script began to break up, as a sand castle loses
its sharp edges and recognizable boundaries when the tide comes
in. Thereafter her notes turned into intricate, indecipherable symbols reminiscent of the great tapestry that had hung in the main
chamber of the settlement. These continued for several pages and
finally, on the last page, she had written in French: *I cannot bear it.
I must return.*

Thus end the three accounts.

Candidates will observe the requisite moment of contemplation.

The candidate will now consult the Compendium of Machine
Anomalies, the Hephaestian Mysteries, and the Yantric Oracle,
which will help put these accounts in context. Having completed
its perusal, the candidate will make the requisite changes to its
own parts in order to generate hypotheses on these questions. Is
the negative space of ambiguity machines infinite? Is it continuous? Are the conceptual sub-spaces occupied by each machine
connected to each other—by geography, concept, or some other
as-yet-undiscovered attribute? What can we make of the relationship between human and machine? If an engineer can dream a
machine, can a machine dream an engineer? An artist? A mathematician? An archaeologist? A story? Is the space of ambiguity
machines set like a jewel or a braid within the greater expanse
of the space of impossible machines? Is it here, in the realm of
dream and imagination, that the intelligent machine might at last
transcend the ultimate boundary—between machine and non-
machine? To take inspiration from human longing, from the organic, syncretic fecundity of nature, the candidate must be willing
to consider and enable its own transformation.

Begin.

TED CHIANG

The Great Silence

FROM *e-flux journal*

THE HUMANS USE Arecibo to look for extraterrestrial intelligence. Their desire to make a connection is so strong that they've created an ear capable of hearing across the universe.

But I and my fellow parrots are right here. Why aren't they interested in listening to our voices?

We're a nonhuman species capable of communicating with them. Aren't we exactly what humans are looking for?

The universe is so vast that intelligent life must surely have arisen many times. The universe is also so old that even one technological species would have had time to expand and fill the galaxy. Yet there is no sign of life anywhere except on Earth. Humans call this the Fermi paradox.

One proposed solution to the Fermi paradox is that intelligent species actively try to conceal their presence, to avoid being targeted by hostile invaders.

Speaking as a member of a species that has been driven nearly to extinction by humans, I can attest that this is a wise strategy.

It makes sense to remain quiet and avoid attracting attention.

The Fermi paradox is sometimes known as the Great Silence. The universe ought to be a cacophony of voices, but instead it's disconcertingly quiet.

Some humans theorize that intelligent species go extinct before they can expand into outer space. If they're correct, then the hush of the night sky is the silence of a graveyard.

Hundreds of years ago, my kind was so plentiful that the Río Abajo Forest resounded with our voices. Now we're almost gone. Soon this rainforest may be as silent as the rest of the universe.

There was an African grey parrot named Alex. He was famous for his cognitive abilities. Famous among humans, that is.

A human researcher named Irene Pepperberg spent thirty years studying Alex. She found that not only did Alex know the words for shapes and colors, he actually understood the concepts of shape and color.

Many scientists were skeptical that a bird could grasp abstract concepts. Humans like to think they're unique. But eventually Pepperberg convinced them that Alex wasn't just repeating words, that he understood what he was saying.

Out of all my cousins, Alex was the one who came closest to being taken seriously as a communication partner by humans.

Alex died suddenly, when he was still relatively young. The evening before he died, Alex said to Pepperberg, "You be good. I love you."

If humans are looking for a connection with a nonhuman intelligence, what more can they ask for than that?

Every parrot has a unique call that it uses to identify itself; biologists refer to this as the parrot's "contact call."

In 1974, astronomers used Arecibo to broadcast a message into outer space intended to demonstrate human intelligence. That was humanity's contact call.

In the wild, parrots address each other by name. One bird imitates another's contact call to get the other bird's attention.

If humans ever detect the Arecibo message being sent back to Earth, they will know someone is trying to get their attention.

Parrots are vocal learners: we can learn to make new sounds after we've heard them. It's an ability that few animals possess. A dog may understand dozens of commands, but it will never do anything but bark.

Humans are vocal learners too. We have that in common. So humans and parrots share a special relationship with sound. We don't simply cry out. We pronounce. We enunciate.

Perhaps that's why humans built Arecibo the way they did. A

receiver doesn't have to be a transmitter, but Arecibo is both. It's an ear for listening, and a mouth for speaking.

Humans have lived alongside parrots for thousands of years, and only recently have they considered the possibility that we might be intelligent.

I suppose I can't blame them. We parrots used to think humans weren't very bright. It's hard to make sense of behavior that's so different from your own.

But parrots are more similar to humans than any extraterrestrial species will be, and humans can observe us up close; they can look us in the eye. How do they expect to recognize an alien intelligence if all they can do is eavesdrop from a hundred light-years away?

It's no coincidence that "aspiration" means both hope and the act of breathing.

When we speak, we use the breath in our lungs to give our thoughts a physical form. The sounds we make are simultaneously our intentions and our life force.

I speak, therefore I am. Vocal learners, like parrots and humans, are perhaps the only ones who fully comprehend the truth of this.

There's a pleasure that comes with shaping sounds with your mouth. It's so primal and visceral that throughout their history, humans have considered the activity a pathway to the divine.

Pythagorean mystics believed that vowels represented the music of the spheres, and chanted to draw power from them.

Pentecostal Christians believe that when they speak in tongues, they're speaking the language used by angels in Heaven.

Brahmin Hindus believe that by reciting mantras, they're strengthening the building blocks of reality.

Only a species of vocal learners would ascribe such importance to sound in their mythologies. We parrots can appreciate that.

According to Hindu mythology, the universe was created with a sound: "Om." It's a syllable that contains within it everything that ever was and everything that will be.

When the Arecibo telescope is pointed at the space between stars, it hears a faint hum.

Astronomers call that the "cosmic microwave background." It's the residual radiation of the Big Bang, the explosion that created the universe fourteen billion years ago.

But you can also think of it as a barely audible reverberation of that original "Om." That syllable was so resonant that the night sky will keep vibrating for as long as the universe exists.

When Arecibo is not listening to anything else, it hears the voice of creation.

We Puerto Rican parrots have our own myths. They're simpler than human mythology, but I think humans would take pleasure from them.

Alas, our myths are being lost as my species dies out. I doubt the humans will have deciphered our language before we're gone.

So the extinction of my species doesn't just mean the loss of a group of birds. It's also the disappearance of our language, our rituals, our traditions. It's the silencing of our voice.

Human activity has brought my kind to the brink of extinction, but I don't blame them for it. They didn't do it maliciously. They just weren't paying attention.

And humans create such beautiful myths; what imaginations they have. Perhaps that's why their aspirations are so immense. Look at Arecibo. Any species that can build such a thing must have greatness within it.

My species probably won't be here for much longer; it's likely that we'll die before our time and join the Great Silence. But before we go, we are sending a message to humanity. We just hope the telescope at Arecibo will enable them to hear it.

The message is this:

You be good. I love you.

X

Contributors' Notes

Notable Science Fiction and Fantasy Stories of 2015

Contributors' Notes

Charlie Jane Anders is the author of *All the Birds in the Sky* (2016). Her fiction and journalism have appeared in *Tor.com*, *The Magazine of Fantasy & Science Fiction*, *Asimov's Science Fiction*, *Lightspeed Magazine*, *Tin House*, *ZYZZYVA*, the *San Francisco Chronicle*, the *New York Times*, and dozens of anthologies. Her story "Six Months, Three Days" won a Hugo Award. She was a founding editor of the science fiction blog *io9* and organizes the Writers With Drinks reading series.

▪ I've always had a hard time balancing absurdism and personal, emotional storytelling. This is probably the biggest thing I struggle with as an author. And when I was first invited to contribute a story to an anthology of video game stories, *Press Start to Play*, I gravitated toward the absurd angle —games offer a chance to talk about our relationship with, and dependence on, technology, and they speak directly to the weirdness of our pop culture fantasies. So I spent months wrestling with a sprawling tale of social collapse, AI uprising, and bizarre games. The deeper I got into this weird post-cyberpunk scenario, the less of a center the story seemed to have. There were just too many threads to pull at, and no central skein to hold on to. It wasn't until I was shamefully late for my deadline that I finally had the courage to throw out that whole exercise in gratuitous strangeness and start over, with a much simpler story that drew on my own experience of having a loved one with dementia. The resulting story is still totally absurd —but, I hope, more in the way that the inescapable tragedies of real life are always absurd and logic-defying.

Dale Bailey is the author of *The End of the End of Everything: Stories*, *The Subterranean Season*, and five other books. He lives with his family in Hickory, North Carolina.

▪ "Lightning Jack's Last Ride" began as a title, nothing more. I spent a long time trying to sort out what it might belong to before I stumbled across Baby Face Nelson in some article or other, which got me thinking about the outlaw mystique Nelson shared with so many of his fellow Public Enemies—Pretty Boy Floyd, Machine Gun Kelly, Ma Barker, and John Dillinger, among others. Murderous villains every one, but to a Depression-era America starved for heroes, they had a certain glamorous appeal. And while I had fun inventing a new outlaw age and a rogues' gallery to inhabit it, it was the tension between the killer and his charisma that gave the story impetus. Gus might attest that Jack doesn't have a bone of true malice in his body—Gus might even believe it—but the truth is, Jack is a stone-cold killer. The question is why we might ever think otherwise.

Ted Chiang is a graduate of the Clarion Science Fiction and Fantasy Writers' Workshop. His fiction has won four Hugo, four Nebula, and four Locus Awards. His collection *Stories of Your Life and Others* has appeared in ten languages and was recently reissued by Vintage Books. He lives near Seattle, Washington.

  ▪ There are actually two pieces titled "The Great Silence," only one of which can fit in this anthology. This requires a little explanation.

  Back in 2011, I was a participant in a conference called Bridge the Gap, whose purpose was to promote dialogue between the arts and the sciences. One of the other participants was Jennifer Allora, half of the artist duo Allora & Calzadilla. I was completely unfamiliar with the kind of art they created—hybrids of performance art, sculpture, and sound—but I was fascinated by Jennifer's explanation of the ideas they were engaged with.

  In 2014 Jennifer got in touch with me about the possibility of collaborating with her and her partner, Guillermo. They wanted to create a multi-screen video installation about anthropomorphism, technology, and the connections between the human and nonhuman worlds. Their plan was to juxtapose footage of the radio telescope in Arecibo with footage of the endangered Puerto Rican parrots that live in a nearby forest, and they asked if I would write subtitle text that would appear on a third screen, a fable told from the point of view of one of the parrots, "a form of interspecies translation." I was hesitant, not only because I had no experience with video art, but also because fables aren't what I usually write. But after they showed me a little preliminary footage, I decided to give it a try, and in the following weeks we exchanged thoughts on topics like glossolalia and the extinction of languages.

  The resulting video installation, titled *The Great Silence*, was shown at Philadelphia's Fabric Workshop and Museum as part of an exhibition of Allora & Calzadilla's work. I have to admit that when I saw the finished work, I regretted a decision I had made earlier. Jennifer and Guillermo had previously invited me to visit the Arecibo Observatory myself, but I had declined because I didn't think it was necessary for me to write the text. Seeing footage of Arecibo on a wall-size screen, I wished I had said yes.

In 2015 Jennifer and Guillermo were asked to contribute to a special issue of the art journal *e-flux* as part of the 56th Venice Biennale, and they suggested publishing the text from our collaboration. I hadn't written the text to stand alone, but it turned out to work pretty well even when removed from its intended context. That was how "The Great Silence," the short story, came to be.

Seth Dickinson is the author of *The Traitor Baru Cormorant* and a lot of short stories. He studied racial bias in police shootings, wrote much of the lore for Bungie Studios' *Destiny,* and helped develop the open-source space opera *Blue Planet.* He teaches at the Alpha Workshop for Young Writers. If he were an animal, he would be a cockatoo.

▪ We all want to survive, but not at *any* cost, right? Some tactics are abominable—plunder, infanticide, torture. We'd rather die than resort to atrocity. But what if someone *else* makes an awful choice, survives, thrives, and inherits the universe? What if, in the long run, everyone and everything will tend to sacrifice their values in the name of competitive edge, because it's that or go extinct?

As we gain more technological control over our own bodies and minds, we also gain the ability to shave away more of ourselves in the pursuit of advantage.

This is a story about how much we might sacrifice to go on. Three lovers armed with a doomsday weapon must decide whether to exterminate an elegant mutilation of the human condition . . . and whether their own very human flaws make the choice impossible.

"Three Bodies at Mitanni" was deeply inspired by Peter Watts's *Blindsight.* Readers interested in the fears that drive the story might want to Google up a case of parallel evolution called "Meditations on Moloch."

Maria Dahvana Headley is the *New York Times*–bestselling author of the young adult novels *Aerie* and *Magonia,* the historical fantasy *Queen of Kings,* the memoir *The Year of Yes,* and the novella *The End of the Sentence* (with Kat Howard). With Neil Gaiman, she is the editor of the young adult monster anthology *Unnatural Creatures.* Her short fiction has been nominated for the Nebula and Shirley Jackson Awards and anthologized in many best-of-the-year collections. *The Mere Wife,* a novel-length adaptation of Beowulf, is forthcoming in 2017.

▪ I bought a crocodile in the Catskills. The crocodile dealer only took cash, and so I slipped her a wad of bills I'd earned making up stories. It was basically my last money on earth. I was a year out of a marriage, and in the sort of dark place everyone who's ever bought a deacquisitioned Victorian museum diorama element has ever been in. I tripped over this taxidermy under a tarp and knew my life would be healed if only I had a crocodile. My crocodile is nearly eight feet long. I live in New York City. This was the purchase of a batshit person. I called my journalist best friend to help me hang the crocodile. We blithely drilled almost entirely through the fuse box in my apartment and then praised heaven we had not been electrocuted. The drywall defied us. The crocodile was astonishingly heavy. I put in an emergency call to my friend the accordionist, who took one look at our wrongful methods (we were drilling blind, through crocodile feet) and diagrammed a new notion, that of hanging my crocodile with chains. We did that. It took three of us, swearing and spitting all the while. I told the Internet about the hanging of the crocodile. People, in particular the poet Matthew Zapruder, insisted this ought to be a Borgesian story. I wrote said story for two years. During those years, the world remained in ever-increasing war, my best friend the journalist died suddenly and randomly on assignment, and I walked the streets of New York weeping for weeks, attracting a mob of men who followed behind me insisting that I smile, as though my expression were their only magical hope for happiness. I went dark some more. I tried to fathom the world by analyzing all of its details. Somewhere in there, I read the torture memos. Somewhere else, I realized that all I ever wrote about was ferocious resurrection, underestimated women, vengeance and mercy. I decided I didn't care if that was all I ever wrote about. I sold "The Thirteen Mercies" to C. C. Finlay at *F&SF,* and for him I tore it up and reassembled it again. It's about bad magic, good magic, unfair mortality, dangerous old women, following wrong orders, and trying to figure out what mercy means. But underneath, it's all about crocodile hanging and those who help you do it.

S. L. Huang has a degree in mathematics from MIT, which she now uses to write an eccentric novel series about a superpowered mercenary mathematician. The series started with her debut novel, *Zero Sum Game,* and the fourth book was published this year with the fifth upcoming. Her short fiction can be found at *Strange Horizons, The Book Smugglers,* and *Daily Science Fiction,* among others. She currently lives in Tokyo, where she's on the lookout for a place to race motorcycles.

▪ I never intended to publish this story. I wrote it for catharsis during treatment for my second cancer, then later sent it to a friend and said, "Do you think this is submittable?" and she said yes. Every piece of this story is an aspect of my own health experience refracted through a science fiction lens, and in that way, it's the most personal story I've ever written.

But the most important part of it, to me, is that this story was also very much a reaction against every other story about cancer I saw growing up. My first cancer happened when I was twelve, and it has continually frustrated me how media represents cancer as some sort of noble, beautiful tragedy that exists to teach people important lessons about the meaning of life. It's not. It's real, it sucks, and it has an impact—but not a one-dimensional one. Above all else, I wanted this story to be honest about that. I wanted to write a cancer story in which nobody dies, in which nothing is noble or enlightening . . . and in which, afterward, the world moves on. Because in the end, that's all I'm striving for myself: moving on.

Adam Johnson is the author most recently of *Fortune Smiles*, winner of the 2015 National Book Award and the Story Prize. He is also the author of *The Orphan Master's Son*, winner of the 2013 Pulitzer Prize, the Dayton Literary Peace Prize, and the California Book Award and a finalist for the National Book Critics Circle Award. His other previous books are *Emporium*, a short story collection, and the novel *Parasites Like Us*. He is the Phil and Penny Knight Professor of Creative Writing at Stanford University and lives in San Francisco with his wife and children.

Kij Johnson has won three Nebulas and the Hugo, Sturgeon, and World Fantasy Awards. Her most recent books are *The Dream-Quest of Vellitt Boe* and the short story collection *At the Mouth of the River of Bees*. She received her MFA from North Carolina State University in 2012. In the past, she has worked in publishing, comics, trading-card and role-playing games, and tech. Currently she is an assistant professor of creative writing at the University of Kansas and the associate director for the Gunn Center for the Study of Science Fiction.

▪ I try never to do the same thing twice: always a new voice, a new mode. That said, there are some things I turn to again and again. I write consistently about animals, as creature, metaphor, stand-in, symbol. I write a lot about loneliness, the gaps between people and whether they can be bridged. I also seem to be incapable of playing with form; even conventional narrative is for me a game, to see what I can do with it. Finally, I love impossibilities that might (or might not) be possible. "The Apartment Dweller's Bestiary" started as a single entry, but I realized that there was a lot that could be said in the intersection of these recurring elements. Strangely distanced as it is, it's also very personal.

Will Kaufman received an MA in English from UC Davis and an MFA in creative writing from the University of Utah, and attended the Clarion Science Fiction and Fantasy Writers' Workshop. His stories have appeared in a number of journals, including *The Collagist, PANK, Unstuck, Lightspeed Magazine, 3:AM,* and *Unlikely Story*. He currently lives in Los Angeles with his wife and their hopes for the future. You can find him online at kaufmanwrites.com.

▪ This story is a direct result of the six weeks I spent at the Clarion Workshop in 2013. The form and style is definitely a response to the pressures and inspirations of Clarion.

For my little fairy tale, I started from the idea that the division between the community and the individual is naturally an elided thing, and with the notion that what we presume to be private is not. For me, the warning of this sort of story has never been "be careful what you wish for," but rather to never forget that your desires never affect you alone—and neither do your punishments.

"Things You Can Buy for a Penny" was a strangely easy story to tell myself. I wrote the opening first, starting from a simple joke and progressing to a simple setup: Timmy would go to the well, and the well is not a good place. Although, I confess, I'm not sure where the wet gentleman actually came from. Was "a gentleman" a convenient vessel for a creature of rules, or was he always waiting? Then I wrote (out of order) the interactions between my victims and the wet gentleman—between people struggling with rules both real and imagined and a creature required absolutely to abide by a set of rules. The rest only took a nudge to fill itself in around those vignettes.

This story appeared in a night, and the only real changes I made to that first draft were to the ending. I realized that the objects of desire had not yet had a chance to speak, to have their own desires recognized. And that's how the wet gentleman got his wish.

Kelly Link is the author of four collections, most recently *Get in Trouble* (2015). With Gavin J. Grant, she runs Small Beer Press. She lives in Northampton, Massachusetts. If you want to know anything else, you can ask her at twitter.com/haszombiesinit.

▪ I've been thinking about this story for over ten years now. For a long time, the first sentence was "The vampires were conjugating in the courtyard." But I never got any further than that, until deciding that what I really wanted was to write something in the same genre as Iain M. Banks's Culture novels. I owe thanks to Cassandra Clare, who supplied a swimming pool that I could swim in whenever I got stuck. (A swimming pool is about as close as I ever want to get to outer space.) I'd also like to thank Holly Black, Sarah Rees Brennan, and Joshua Lewis, and also Richard Butner and the Sycamore Hill workshop, which took a good, hard look at this. I didn't take all of the suggestions, but I liked every single one of them.

Sam J. Miller is a writer and a community organizer. His fiction has appeared in *Lightspeed, Asimov's Science Fiction, Clarkesworld, Apex, Strange Hori-*

zons, and the *Minnesota Review,* among others. His first book, a young adult science fiction novel called *The Art of Starving,* will be published in 2017. His stories have been nominated for the Nebula and Theodore Sturgeon Awards; he's also a winner of the Shirley Jackson Award, and *this* story was nominated for the World Fantasy Award. He lives in New York City and at www.samjmiller.com.

▪ The seed of "The Heat of Us" was planted on the night Donna Summer died. I was walking home from work, feeling pretty blue—I think "Bad Girls" is probably the second-best album of all time—looking across at the sad lonely lights of the city coming on, all those people by themselves, all the separate sadness that a certain group of people would be feeling. And I remembered that the Stonewall Uprising happened on the night that Judy Garland died. And I thought "revolutions are born on nights like this." But that seed didn't break into blossom until I attended the Clarion Science Fiction & Fantasy Writers' Workshop and I saw how exponentially my writing improved through being part of a community of writers and readers, how I could share their strengths and (hopefully) lend them mine. So this is a story about community—about how people are stronger together than separate, and how when we work together we can achieve things so incredible they're indistinguishable from magic.

Dexter Palmer is the author of two novels, *The Dream of Perpetual Motion* (2010) and *Version Control* (2016). He holds a PhD in English literature from Princeton University and lives in Princeton, New Jersey.

▪ Though I've published two novels, I rarely write short stories. "The Daydreamer by Proxy" was part of *The Bestiary,* an anthology of original material edited by Ann VanderMeer and published by Cheeky Frawg Books/Centipede Press. The premise of the anthology was that each of the invited writers was given a letter of the alphabet and asked to write a story that described a fictional creature whose name began with that letter. Thank goodness I was assigned the letter D: not too common; not too unusual; perfectly acceptable to work with.

The composition of the story was influenced by the fact that I knew the hardcover edition of the anthology would be illustrated. What sort of odd thing did I want to see someone try to draw? How much descriptive detail would be enough, without being so much that it would constrain the artist and bore the reader? The illustrator, Ivica Stevanovic, did a great job: his drawings are uniquely imaginative while being faithful to their source material and are just as unsettling as I'd hoped they'd be.

All of the anthology's contributors were also asked to provide short accompanying author's notes: the assignment was to "reimagine yourself as a fantastical beast." This was mine: *The Dexter Palmer lives in the darkened corners of libraries, dining on ink and wood pulp. Its gestation period is unpredictably long; its offspring are unnatural, no two of them alike.*

Salman Rushdie is the author of twelve novels—*Grimus, Midnight's Children* (for which he won the Booker Prize and the Best of the Booker), *Shame, The Satanic Verses, Haroun and the Sea of Stories, The Moor's Last Sigh, The Ground Beneath Her Feet, Fury, Shalimar the Clown, The Enchantress of Florence, Luka and the Fire of Life,* and *Two Years Eight Months and Twenty-Eight Nights*—and one collection of short stories: *East, West.* He has also published four works of nonfiction—*Joseph Anton, The Jaguar Smile, Imaginary Homelands,* and *Step Across the Line*—and coedited two anthologies, *Mirrorwork* and *The Best American Short Stories 2008.* He is a member of the American Academy of Arts and Letters and a Distinguished Writer in Residence at New York University. A former president of the PEN American Center, Rushdie was knighted in 2007 for services to literature.

• I've long been interested in the jinn, and also in the philosopher Ibn Rushd (Averroës), in honor of whom my father renamed our family. They come together in this story, forming a union of reason and fantasy, as Francisco Goya recommended. Eventually, this story grew into the novel *Two Years Eight Months and Twenty-Eight Nights,* which carries the love story of the jinnia princess Dunia and Ibn Rushd forward into the present day, or something like it.

Sofia Samatar is the author of the novels *A Stranger in Olondria* (2013) and *The Winged Histories* (2016). Her work has received the John W. Campbell Award, the William L. Crawford Award, the British Fantasy Award, and the World Fantasy Award.

• "Meet Me in Iram" grew out of my interest in the intersection of speculative fiction and autobiography. Every word of it is true.

Vandana Singh was born and raised in New Delhi, India, and has been a denizen of the Greater Boston area for over ten years, where she is also a physics professor at a small and lively state university. Her short stories have been published in numerous best-of-the-year volumes and most recently include a novella, *Of Wind and Fire,* in an anthology about women scientists (*To Shape the Dark,* ed. Athena Andreadis). She is a winner of the Parallax Award and a Tiptree Honor, was a participant in Arizona State University's Project Hieroglyph, and was a guest of honor at the Science Fiction Research Association annual conference in 2015. Her work includes a short story collection, *The Woman Who Thought She Was a Planet and Other Stories* (New Delhi), reprinted in 2013, as well as an ALA Notable children's book, *Younguncle Comes to Town.*

• When a young friend told me of a dream he had about a strange machine, it occurred to me to conjure up a lexicon of impossible devices. The first story in the triptych is embroidered around the possibility suggested by the machine in the dream—thank you, JLH! When the dust had settled after the first story, it suggested something, a pattern in the sand that took me to another place, another story, and a quite different machine. That in turn provoked the third story. But it wasn't a linear process because as I wrote one story, I necessarily had to change the others until they were braided together in a way that made literary topological sense. Yet they remained disparate until I found the context that knitted them into a canvas: a space—the greater space of impossible machines where perhaps we might bridge the gulf between human and machine. Yearnings, longings, separations, distances both literal and of the heart, the way that the physical and psychological subtexts of the world inform each other—these are the things that move me and move the story.

Julian Mortimer Smith has published more than a dozen short stories in some of the top speculative fiction magazines, including *Asimov's Science Fiction, Terraform, Daily Science Fiction, Crossed Genres, Andromeda Spaceways Inflight Magazine,* and *AE: The Canadian Science Fiction Review.* He's also written nonfiction articles about such topics as the North American Conker Championship and the Shag Harbour UFO Incident. He has worked as an editor for a romance publisher, as a copywriter for a Web design company, and as a clarinetist for an army. He currently resides in a small lobstering town in southwest Nova Scotia but has lived in various cities across Canada and the UK. He is working on a novel for young adults.

• When I was in university, I went to see a talk by Professor Barbie Zelizer on how photojournalists depict war. She pointed out that we rarely see photographs of dead bodies in newspapers. The images we see of war are often highly aestheticized, sanitized for consumption around the breakfast table. When images of death do appear in newspapers, they provoke strong reactions—outrage, letters to the editor, canceled subscriptions. They are sometimes even shocking enough to galvanize peace movements.

In "Headshot," I tried to imagine how our appetite for war might change if ordinary civilians had to give their consent and bear witness to each act of killing. I set out to write a hopeful story, to imagine a world in which we weren't allowed to look away. But I think it turned into something of a bitter satire. You be the judge.

Rachel Swirsky is a short story writer living in Bakersfield, California. Her short fiction has been nominated for the Hugo Award, the Locus Award, the World Fantasy Award, and the Sturgeon Award. She's twice won the Nebula Award, in 2010 for her novella *The Lady Who Plucked Red Flowers*

Beneath the Queen's Window and in 2014 for her short story "If You Were a Dinosaur, My Love." She graduated from the Iowa Writers' Workshop in 2008 and Clarion West in 2005. She once played the Mock Turtle in a children's production of *Alice in Wonderland.*

- *Alice in Wonderland* is one of my father's favorite books. It was always part of my life. When I started working on this story, my father gave me a worn, annotated copy that's about as old as he is. I love the derangement of *Alice in Wonderland.* The odd images and strange characters are disconcerting in the best possible way. Unlike a lot of other children's books, the novel holds up well to adult rereading. Clever prose and insight keeps it sharp.

Retellings fascinate me. I'm endlessly intrigued by the ways people can recombine characters, plots, and imagery. I wrote a scrap of the first hatter/hare scene on a whim and then set it aside, but found myself coming back to it over several years.

The story didn't develop in a linear way. I played with quotes; I shuffled passages; I didn't know what would happen next. A surprising amount of text came about almost by coincidence. I'd sit down to write a parody of one of the poems from the original, and how it came out shaped the way the story moved. Quotes steered conversations here and there of their own accord. I chased after tidbits and irony.

I don't know if I could set out to write another story like this one because the process was so idiosyncratic. But I really loved the way it turned out and am gratified that others have enjoyed it, too.

Catherynne M. Valente is the *New York Times*–bestselling author of over two dozen works of fiction and poetry, including *Palimpsest,* the Orphan's Tales series, *Deathless, Radiance,* and the crowdfunded phenomenon *The Girl Who Circumnavigated Fairyland in a Ship of Her Own Making.* She is the winner of the Andre Norton, Tiptree, Mythopoeic, Rhysling, Lambda, Locus, and Hugo Awards. She has been a finalist for the Nebula and World Fantasy Awards. She lives on an island off the coast of Maine with a small but growing menagerie of beasts, some of which are human.

- The seed of "Planet Lion" was an idle joke about "psychic lions" made one late night around the house. The idea sort of took hold, and I could not let go of the image of a planet of psychically networked large carnivores. I wanted to contrast the immediate, first-person experience of this alien animal consciousness wakening within a technology matrix that they couldn't fully understand and had to translate into a language meaningful to their experience, with a traditional military science fiction story of space warfare and its repercussions. It's a story, ultimately, of colonization, careless colonization, and how a technologically superior force can take much more than just territory. It can take the very minds and memories of its victims and replace these with something in its own image. This process is essentially the core goal of any imperial project—to copy and paste itself into every cell in the universe.

Nick Wolven's short stories have appeared in *Asimov's Science Fiction, F&SF, Analog, Clarkesworld,* and the *New England Review,* among other publications. His writing has been republished in *The Best Science Fiction of the Year,* edited by Neil Clarke, and *The Year's Best Science Fiction,* edited by Gardner Dozois. He lives in New York City.

▪ I can't for the life of me remember what made me think it would be a good idea to write a science fiction story based on Eudora Welty's classic meditation on middle-aged romance, "No Place for You, My Love." Why mess with perfection? Why trivialize the sublime? Why invite invidious and unflattering comparisons by juxtaposing one's own writing with a work that's already unquestionably amazing? I can only say that at some point I found myself with a half-finished draft of this piece on my hands, and it seemed only right to finish it. And then, at a later point, I found myself with a contract to publish this story on my hands, and it seemed only right to take the money.

There must have been an earlier point at which I thought to myself, "Hmm, you know what would be cool—a satire of the modern dating scene that's *also* a tribute to the great American genius of southern lyricism." But one trick to the act of writing (if not the art of writing) is that you learn not to probe too deeply into the sources of your own inspiration.

At any rate, the Welty story is well worth a read, for those who haven't heard of it. Of the contemporary dating scene, speaking as a New York denizen, I can only say: Beware!

After several years as a book agent in New York and then a film agent in Los Angeles, **Liz Ziemska** finally gathered together enough courage to try this writing thing herself, only to discover that it was much, much harder than it looked. Eventually, she completed an MFA at the Bennington Writing Seminars. It was David Gates, her first teacher at Bennington, who told her to quit imitating (insert famous author) and let her voice be as strange as it wanted to be. Her work has appeared in *Tin House, Interfictions:2,* and *Strange Horizons* and has been nominated for a Shirley Jackson Award and longlisted in the *Best American Nonrequired Reading.* "The Mushroom Queen" won a Pushcart Prize.

▪ I've always been interested in science and have an undergraduate degree in biology, though I decided in my senior year not to go to medical school. When I became a literary agent, I loved scouring scientific trade magazines in the hopes of finding scientists who were also beautiful writers. A friend of mine directed a documentary about global warming. In the goody bag given out after the premiere party I found a book called *Mycelium Running*, by Paul Stamets. I put it on my bookshelf, promising to read it one day. When I started writing fiction, someone told me that I should try dream journaling to fight writer's block. For years I would wake up, pull the journal from my nightstand, and scribble away until I got the dream down before it could evaporate. One night during a particularly bright moon, I woke up in the middle of the night and had a reverie of a woman, my putative twin, standing at the edge of the lawn next to the jade plant. I wrote that down and put it away. One day, while cleaning my bookshelf, I found the mushroom book and started reading. Then I knew exactly whom I had encountered on that moonlit night. A scientist I admire has a book out this year that asks the question "Are we smart enough to know how smart animals are?" My story asks the question "Are we smart enough to know how smart fungi are?"

Notable Science Fiction and Fantasy Stories of 2015

Selected by John Joseph Adams

THE BEST AMERICAN SERIES®

FIRST, BEST, AND BEST-SELLING

The Best American Comics

The Best American Essays

The Best American Infographics

The Best American Mystery Stories

The Best American Nonrequired Reading

The Best American Science and Nature Writing

The Best American Science Fiction and Fantasy

The Best American Short Stories

The Best American Sports Writing

The Best American Travel Writing

Available in print and e-book wherever books are sold.

Visit our website: *www.hmhco.com/bestamerican*